To the Butte Creek Canyon "Fans"
(and not just because they're family either!)
RACHEL WESTLUND, FERNE ASKIM, and
CAROLYN JONES
and
To HOWARD, who still makes my world go round
and after forty years of marriage still surprises me
with flowers for absolutely no reason at all
other than he thought of it.

Coming Home

Chapter 1

Standing on her small deck at the rear of the house and staring out at the hot, dry landscape below her, Roxanne Ballinger decided that she hated September in Oak Valley. And August and probably July, too. The valley was seared by the heat, the pastures were eaten down, and the hay fields shorn of their crops lay fallow and burnt amber and yellow by the sun, except, she reminded herself, those places in the valley where the water table was high and the land stayed green all year. She made a face. Too bad her newly acquired house didn't overlook that area—it'd be nice to stare out at green fields this time of year. Then she shrugged. But if she overlooked those fields, she wouldn't have such a majestic view of Mt. Sebastian in the distance and all the other smaller mountains and hills that tumbled down to the valley floor on its eastern side.

This was not, she admitted, the valley's most attractive time of the year . . . at least she didn't think so.

And she wondered, not for the first time, what the hell she was doing here. And with a house of her own. She glanced back at the small A-frame building and amended her thought: a cabin of her own. She should be in New York. Tucked comfortably away in her elegant air-conditioned Park Avenue penthouse apartment. Looking forward to all the fabulous entertainment the city had to offer, anticipating the pulsating excitement she'd find on the crowded streets, ready to be seduced by the glamour and vitality of the city. Everything she could humanly want would be at her fingertips. And if she didn't want to venture out, a telephone call would bring all that the city had to offer right to her doorstep: clothes, food, jewelry, handsome men . . .

Thinking of the last handsome man who had shared her life, she grimaced. Todd Spurling was an executive editor at one of the major New York publishing houses and their affair had lasted for a grand total of almost five weeks. They'd met this past June at one of the glittering pub parties being held for the launch of some celebrity biography and it had been, she admitted, lust at first sight. As one of the top models in the business, her face had often adorned the covers of such magazines as *Cosmo*, *Vogue*, and the like, and justly famous for her generous display of scantily clad limbs in the Victoria's Secret catalog, she was often seen at these sorts of parties. The life of a celebrity, she had discovered, was as much about seeing as being seen and since she was considered one of the "beautiful people" she was invited everywhere. She had nearly refused to attend the party. She'd been unsettled and restless, having just returned from Oak Valley and her brother Sloan's wedding. She almost stayed home that night— the idea of being just another body in another scintillating crowd didn't appeal to her—a feeling she had been experiencing more and more over the past couple of years. But in the end she decided that a night of rubbing shoulders with the famous and want-to-be-famous might be more enjoyable than staring at the walls of her apartment.

She had not gone to the party looking for romance. She snorted. Good God, no! In fact, she had been in a surly mood and rather off men in general. Not that she didn't like men—she did. It was just that lately she'd begun to think that men were really more trouble than they were worth. Maybe, she thought with a sigh, she'd just reached that point in life where she wanted to concentrate on what she wanted, without having to consider what someone else might like—or not. Making the decision to move back to Oak Valley had been a big one and quite frankly, she didn't want the distraction of a man in her life. Then she'd met Todd Spurling . . . Todd who was every woman's dream: urbane, considerate, polite, and utterly smitten with her. Todd had also been tall, handsome, blond, broad-shouldered, and had the bluest eyes she'd ever seen and the moment their eyes had met . . . Her lip curled. The moment their eyes met she started thinking with a another part of her anatomy than her brain. Apparently

Todd had, too, because in less than a month after meeting, they'd been living together in her apartment. And less than a week after that, she'd tossed him out on his gorgeous buns—his gorgeous *married* buns, disgusted as much with herself as with him.

Roxanne shook her head, her glorious blue-black mane of hair glistening like a raven's wing in the hot sunlight. You'd think at my age, I'd know better, she thought wryly. You'd think that after nearly twenty years of living in the fast lane that I'd learn not to be so impulsive, that at the wise old age of thirty-eight, I'd not be so willing to fling caution to the winds and just leap into the nearest brawny pair of arms. Finding out that Todd had been married, something he had conveniently forgotten to mention when they had been falling into bed together, had been a blow to her pride and her esteem. She had been horrified. For all of her wild reputation, and despite gossip and innuendo to the contrary, married men had been completely off her list. And while gossip and rumor had her sleeping with a new lover every week, the truth of the matter was that there hadn't been that many. She thought about it. Less than a handful. Maybe. She'd always been more cautious about sex than some of her contemporaries. Being raised in Oak Valley did that to a person. Even among the wealthy and powerful Ballinger clan, values considered these days to be old-fashioned had been the rule and though she had shaken the dust of the valley from her feet at nineteen, the mores of the valley had been a little harder to put behind her. Besides, with all the diseases out there, she'd never jumped into bed with just anyone. So why had she acted differently with Todd?

She bit her lip. She wasn't promiscuous. She'd never been promiscuous, not even in her rambunctious twenties when she'd been so greedy and eager to experience life and all it had to offer—so eager to gain polish and sophistication, determined to show the world that she wasn't just a beautiful bumpkin from some hokey place in the sticks. Sure, she'd made some mistakes. She wouldn't deny that. She'd been young, confident, OK, maybe arrogant, certainly convinced that the world was hers for the taking. She'd been like a kid given free rein in a candy store and face it, New York was *some* kind of candy store for a young woman raised in a place without a stoplight, let alone neon lights and nary a Burger King or mall in sight. She could justify some of those early mistakes, but the affair with Todd Spurling shook her. She'd simply taken one look into those mesmerizing blue eyes of his and . . . She snorted. And acted like a silly teenager in love for the first time. But it hadn't been love—she'd retained enough sense to realize that fact. It had been . . . Oh, what the hell—it had been stupid and reckless and totally unlike her. Maybe she'd still been all dreamy-eyed from watching Sloan and Shelly exchange their wedding vows and for one wild moment, when she'd looked up into Todd's face, she'd thought to find the same love shared by her brother and his bride. She shook her head. Which was really stupid and pathetic. And impulsive—something she'd always been. She took a deep breath. She was going to try very hard *not* to be impulsive anymore—especially when it came to men. She didn't need a man in her life, especially not right now when she was embarking on a whole new adventure. She smiled. An impulsive one at that.

Her gaze fell to the valley floor. So here she was. Back in Oak Valley. A place she couldn't get away from fast enough nearly twenty years ago, but now . . . It was odd, she thought, how after all those years of being happily swept along by the glamour and excitement found in all those famous cities across the world, London, Paris, Madrid, and Athens, she found herself drawn more and more to the tranquility and predictability of Oak Valley. Where once she'd forced herself to return home for short visits every other year or so, the past couple of years, those visits had been increasing in both frequency and duration, the longing for the valley reaching out across the distances and tugging at hidden places in her heart. She had discovered amusements that had once held her enthralled were now boring and mundane. She smiled crookedly. Words she had once used to describe Oak Valley. Funny how life turned around on you. Now it was everywhere *else* that was boring and mundane and Oak Valley that held an irresistible appeal.

At first, she'd put this longing for the valley down as a whim, but instead of the need to be here decreasing, she'd found that it had grown. She was, she realized, tired of being *Roxanne*—the face and body that sold millions of magazines, and no doubt an equal number of pairs of scanty underwear—she wanted to be plain old "Roxy," the oldest Ballinger daughter. Sloan's sister. And Ross and Ilka and Sam's sister. She wanted to wear worn blue jeans and scuffed boots and wander into Heather-Mary-Marie's, the local gift store, and be greeted by half a dozen people who had known her since she had been born and who were not the least impressed by her face, body, and reputation. She wanted a life that didn't involve always being "on," always photographed, always gossiped about . . . She grinned. Well, that was going too far. The valley gossip was legendary and she was quite certain that her purchase of a dead, reputed marijuana grower's property was currently the hot topic of conversation everywhere in the valley. Her grin widened. At least she'd taken some of the heat off of Sloan and Shelly and given the residents something new to speculate about.

The marriage of Sloan Ballinger to Shelly Granger in June had set the valley on its ear. Not only because of the swiftness with which the courtship had progressed but the very fact that a Ballinger was marrying a Granger. The Ballinger/Granger feud was the valley's favorite legend—though it had been a series of conflicts rather than one specific incident. Ballingers and Grangers just naturally took opposite positions . . . on *any* thing. While most of the ugliness had happened decades ago, every time a Ballinger and Granger came face-to-face, the valley collectively held its breath and with bright, eager eyes watched to see if sparks would explode out of thin air. Mostly they did, but sometimes, as in the case of Sloan and Shelly . . . Roxanne smiled wistfully. In the case of Sloan and Shelly magic happened.

She gave herself a shake and turned back to the house. Cabin, she amended, and again wondered what the devil she'd been thinking of when she'd bought it. It wasn't as if the Ballingers didn't own thousands of acres in the valley and foothills and mountains surrounding the valley that she could have chosen to settle on. Nor was it as if she wasn't more than welcome to stay as long as she pleased in the family mansion and childhood home on the valley floor—her parents would be thrilled. And if she had wanted, her father, Mark, would have built her a place of her own on one of the many parcels of land owned by the family. She hadn't *needed* to buy six hundred forty acres, an entire square mile, of mostly useless, mountainous terrain on the west side of the valley. It wasn't, even she would admit, a fabulous piece of land, altogether she probably had only about eighty acres that could be called flat—and that was stretching the word "flat." The rest of the land was sheer, forested hillside with small benches of gently rolling ground here and there—included in the eighty acres of "flat" ground. It wasn't even great timberland—too much underbrush, blackberry vines, buck brush, manzanita, with oaks and madrones intermixed with the pine and fir. But it was hers, she thought with pride. Hers. Bought with her own money. Not family money. She didn't have to share it with a damn person. It was *hers*. And as for the cabin that came with the place. . .

Roxanne was positive that no other self-respecting Ballinger, except herself, would have considered the rough wood-framed building a prospective home. She laughed to herself. Call her crazy—her sister, Ilka, already had and her parents, their expressions askance, had asked her at least a dozen times if she was sure that this was what she wanted. She had assured them that yes, she really did want the place. The land had its own beauty, but she loved the cabin. It had, she had pointed out to her stunned family, potential. It wasn't big, but it had everything she wanted—or soon would have once she added on and remodeled. Of course she could understand their reaction—the place had sat empty for months and local vandals had broken in several times and practically torn the place apart. Not content with wreaking destruction on the cabin, they'd also prowled around and punched out a few walls in the small pump house and the falling-down shack that served as a garage. Roxanne shook her head. They'd really done a number on the place—not one structure had escaped their mark. It had taken several days of hard, sweaty work to make the cabin *almost* livable— if you ignored the damage to the walls and floors— which Roxanne did—the remodeling would take care of that. As for the other buildings, she dismissed them. The garage would be torn down and a new one built and the same went for the pump house—the damage done to them she could live with for the time being.

Built at the very edge of one of those benches, the cabin was perched nearly three thousand feet above the valley floor. From the deck and from the east-facing floor-to-ceiling windows, she had stupendous views; the main level was one spacious room, except for the small kitchen area, a bedroom the size of a closet, and a tiny bathroom tucked into a corner. The upper floor had a larger bathroom and two rooms. The decor left something to be desired, but she had no doubt that with a lot of elbow grease and a full checkbook, she'd have it looking just the way she wanted in no time at all.

At the moment, with the exception of a chaste twin bed, a battery-run lamp, an oak end table, a portable CD player, and a new side-by-side almond-colored refrigerator/freezer, set up to run on propane, the place was empty. The original kitchen consisted of a battered stainless-steel sink, propane stove/oven, and a couple of metal cabinets. Her nose wrinkled. Marijuana growers apparently didn't do much cooking.

Of course, she reminded herself, it hadn't been *proven* that the former owner, Dirk Aston, had really been a marijuana grower—that'd merely been the conclusion of the valley residents. How else, they had asked, did someone unemployed and with no outside income earn enough money to live up there all by himself? And what about that brand-new truck he drove? Where did the money to buy it come from? And why did he have those two greenhouses and black plastic piping running all over the place? And remember all those rolls and rolls of chicken wire and bags and bags of manure? Don't tell me he wasn't growing dope! When she argued that if his profession was so obvious he would have been busted and the property confiscated, the sages had looked wise. Dirk was small-time, they'd said. Not big enough for CAMP (Californians Against Marijuana Production) and the DA's office to go after, they'd said. Lots of guys like Dirk around, they'd said. Sheriff's office knew who they were, but there were worse offenses than growing a little marijuana to keep them occupied. Sheriff's office might harass guys like Dirk now and then, but no one took them serious—bigger, more important fish to fry.

Roxanne didn't doubt that the valley had the correct reading of the situation but it hadn't deterred her. She *loved* this place. It was isolated, yet town was only about six miles down a twisting gravel road that took almost twenty minutes to traverse—in good weather. Her nearest and only neighbor, Nick Rios, who was staying in the Granger house, was a couple of heavily forested miles away, and after the packed, surging humanity of New York, it was a great feeling to know that she could walk stark-naked out her own door and yodel at the moon and no one would see or hear her. Not that she was going to do that. But she could. If she wanted.

Grinning to herself, Roxanne walked inside the cabin. Crossing to the new refrigerator, she took out a bottle of water and, after twisting off the cap, wandered out the other door of the cabin. There was a small deck here, too, this one covered, and she had a charming view of a small, meandering meadow before the ground rose and forested hillside met her gaze. Like many places in the country, the rear of the cabin was both the entrance and the back door. It had always struck her as strange to drive up to the back of a house, until she took in the fact that the front had the views and no one in their right mind would sacrifice view for a front yard or driveway. The much-speculated-about greenhouses were situated to the south of the cabin, and sipping her bottled water, she'd started to amble in that direction when the sound of an approaching vehicle caught her ear.

She wasn't expecting anyone, and puzzled, she turned back to walk over to the wide gravel area where her own jaunty, rag-topped Jeep was parked. A second later, a red truck, a one-ton dually, roared up the last incline and stopped in a cloud of dust.

Recognizing the truck and the very tall, very big man who stepped out of it, her spine stiffened and her fingers tightened around the bottle of water. Jeb Delaney. Absolutely the last person she wanted to see.

Like the lord of all he surveyed, he strolled over to where she stood. Roxanne once surmised that the commanding air about him came from his job—a detective with the sheriff's department. There was a sense of leashed power around him, like a big hunting tiger on a slim lead, but even she had concluded that it was nothing he did on purpose, it was just . . . Jeb.

Most people liked Jeb Delaney. Old ladies doted on him; young women swooned when he smiled at them; men admired him, and young boys wanted to grow up to be just like him. Just about everybody thought he was a great guy. Roxanne was not among them. He rubbed her the wrong way and he always had. She couldn't be in his presence for more than five minutes before she was thinking of ways to knock his block off. It wasn't a new emotion—she'd felt that way since she'd been seventeen years old and he'd busted her for possession of a joint of marijuana. She'd been embarrassed and humiliated as only a teenage girl can be and she'd never forgiven him. The stern first-time warning and confiscation of the joint wasn't for her, nope, he'd made an example of her—probably, she thought crabbily, because she'd been friends with his brother, Mingo, and he hadn't wanted Mingo to become corrupted. It had been the worst incident of her young life—the whole valley had known the story about how he'd handcuffed her in the high school parking lot and put her in the backseat of his patrol car. Fortunately, he hadn't taken her to jail, as all her bug-eyed friends had thought, Mingo among them; he'd driven her home, giving her a tongue-lashing along the way that still made her cringe. Tight-lipped, he'd turned her over to her parents. She'd spent the rest of the school year grounded and endured the disappointed look in her parents' eyes—she'd hated that most of all. Hated the knowledge, too, that she had flaunted the joint practically right under his nose, just daring him to do something about it. She scowled. Well, he'd done something all right. He'd ruined that year of school. She brightened. Of course, she *had* gained a bit of notoriety over the affair, which had made her a big deal among her friends.

That time was behind her now and over the years most of her cocky edges had been sheared off, but to this day, the sight of Jeb Delaney still had the power to scrape her nerves raw. It puzzled her when she thought about it. She made friends easily and had a reputation for being charming and easy to work with. She liked people—she couldn't have been the success she was if she hadn't. But Jeb Delaney . . . Jeb Delaney set her teeth on edge and made the hair on the back of her neck rise up . . . and, a small voice nagged, excites you more than any man you've ever met in your life.

A big man, he stood six feet five and had the shoulders and chest to match. His arms were muscled beneath his plain blue chambray shirt and the tight, faded blue jeans he was wearing fit his lean hips and powerful thighs like a second skin. Sunglasses, dusty black boots, and a wide-brimmed black Stetson completed his garb.

Watching him with all the enthusiasm she would have for an invasion of rattlesnakes, Roxanne demanded, "What are you doing here?"

Jeb stopped about two feet from her and removed his sunglasses. His handsome face was expressionless as his gaze roamed over her, taking in the long, long tanned legs revealed by her pink-striped shorts and the firm breasts only half hidden by the cut of her white halter top. There had been a few times in her career, not many, that she had posed nude, but she had never felt so very *naked* as she did at this very moment with Jeb Delaney's knowing black eyes moving over her.

Her lips tightened. "I repeat: what are you doing here?"

"Just being neighborly?" he offered with a quirk of his brow.

She snorted. "Jeb, I haven't a clue as to what rock you sleep under at night, but neighbors we're not."

He rubbed his jaw. "Yeah, I guess not." He looked around. "Seems an odd place for you to buy."

"And that's your business because . . . ?"

Jeb sighed and pushed back his black Stetson. "Are you always so prickly with everyone or is it just me?"

She smiled sweetly. "Just you—I like everybody else."

He grinned, white teeth flashing beneath his heavy black mustache. It made him look like a brigand, a very, very attractive brigand, and Roxanne didn't like the way her heart leaped at the sight of that grin. The jerk.

Her foot tapped. "Are you going to tell me what you're doing here or are we going to spend the morning exchanging insults?"

"Princess, I haven't insulted you . . . yet. You just keep tossing those smart remarks out of that pretty mouth of yours and I might just have to do something about it." His gaze fastened on her mouth and something dark and powerful leaped in the air between them. Then Jeb seemed to shake himself and took a breath. "Look," he said quietly, "I just wanted to see if the gossips were right about you buying this place." He glanced around. "After Dirk was killed, Danny and I came up here to double-check the place—it was a shambles—certainly not the sort of place I'd ever expect you to buy. Thought I'd take a drive up here and check it out. Since you're here, I guess this is one time that the valley gossip was right on the mark."

She was being rude. She knew it. She hated herself for doing it, but she just couldn't seem to stop. Looking down at her pink-painted toes in the flip-flops, she made the supreme effort and muttered, "The gossips are right. I did buy it."

"Why? Like I said, this sure isn't the kind of place one would expect the exalted *Roxanne* of fame and fortune to buy. Now, a mansion in San Francisco, where you could invite all your famous friends and hold wild bashes, yeah, I could see that. But here? A dead dope-grower's digs in the middle of nowhere? Don't tell me you're thinking of turning your hand to growing a little marijuana on the side?" Coolly, he added, "Not your style, Princess."

Who the hell was he, Roxanne thought furiously, to look down that oh-so-handsome nose of his at her? Most people, especially men, fell over themselves trying to attract her attention, but not Jeb. Oh, no. He

couldn't even be polite. And the contempt in his voice
when he called her "Princess". . . . She squirmed, feeling seventeen again and hating him with all that same
thwarted fury. Her jaw tightened. What right did he
have to condemn her lifestyle? She was a big girl now.
All grown-up. She'd like to bloody that handsome
nose of his and slap that cool expression on his face
into next week.

Knowing she was getting herself all in a snit over
nothing, she took a deep calming breath. She'd tried to
be polite. OK, not much, but she'd made the effort and
what did she get for it? Disparaging remarks and insults. "Is this an official inquiry?" she asked tightly.
"Otherwise, my reasons are my own and I don't have
to share them with you. In fact, get off my property."

A muscle clenched in his jaw. "You know, someday
someone is going to teach you some manners."

Her lip curled. "You volunteering?"

His gaze swept over her. "Yeah," he said slowly.
"Maybe."

He swung on his heels and climbed into the truck.
The engine snarled to life and with more force than
necessary, he spun the vehicle around and nosed it
down the hill.

For several minutes after he'd left, Roxanne stood
there staring at nothing. What the hell was the matter
with her? With anyone else, she would have offered a
smile, refreshments, and the hand of friendship. She
bit her lip. So why not with Jeb? Because I'm a bitch?

Nah. Because he's a jerk. Pleased with her conclusion, she headed for the greenhouses.

It was only ten o'clock in the morning, but already the heat was savage—by noon, every living thing, plant and animal alike, would be gasping for relief— relief that wouldn't come until the sun set. Despite her brief apparel, Roxanne still felt the heat and after walking a couple of hundred yards in the direction of greenhouses decided she'd put off investigating them until early tomorrow morning. Before it got hot. She grimaced. Yeah. Right.

She started back to the cabin when a rustling in the heavy brush to her right had her freezing in her steps. Visions of bears and cougars leaped to her mind—she knew the area abounded with them—and she cursed herself for not carrying some sort of weapon. Even a big stick would have been a comfort at the moment. Trying to remember everything she'd ever known about confronting a bear or a mountain lion, she faced the direction of the noise and edged backward toward the cabin.

The noise grew fearsome and just when she was certain she couldn't stand the suspense any longer, a horse and rider, followed by three dusty, panting cow dogs, burst into view.

Recognizing the wiry rider, a battered beige cow-boy hat on his head, Roxanne's heartbeat slowed to normal and a welcoming smile lit her face. "Acey Babbitt!" she exclaimed. "You nearly gave me a heart attack. I was certain that a bear had me in mind for breakfast."

Acey grinned, blue eyes bright in his sun-worn face. "And a tasty meal you would have made." Beneath an impressive pair of white handlebar mustaches, he smacked his lips. "Yes, ma'am, you do look good enough to eat—even to an old cowpoke like me."

She chuckled. "Why, Mr. Babbitt, are you putting the moves on little ole me?"

"Might . . . if I were twenty years younger and you were twenty years older," he said, wriggling his bushy white eyebrows. "Of course, if you don't mind a fellow who creaks when he walks, I'd sure be still willing to give it a try."

Roxanne laughed again, not at all fooled by his hopeful expression. Acey Babbitt was seventy-five years old if he was a day and one of the dearest men Roxanne had ever known—and one of the biggest teases. His prowess with cattle and horses alike was legendary and throughout his long career, at one time or another, he had worked for almost every ranch in the valley, including the Ballingers. Just about every kid in the valley, including herself and her siblings, had learned to ride under Acey's gentle but steely guidance. And while he may have worked for others, his first loyalty had always been to the Grangers. She knew he was living in the apartment over the barn at the Granger place and that he was working for Shelly, Sloan's wife.

"OK, enough lecherous talk—you've convinced

me that you're hell on wheels," she said with a smile. "What brings you out here?"

Acey made a face. "One of them fine expensive cows that Shelly brought out from Texas is due to calve and danged if she didn't find the only break in a fence for miles around. We discovered it last night about dark. Wasn't much we could do about it then, but Nick and I have been out since before daybreak trying to track her down."

Roxanne frowned. "Wouldn't she head for gentler ground? Toward the valley? My place is so rough, I'm certain goats would turn up their noses at it, let alone a cow ready to calve."

"Don't want to hurt your feelings none, but you're right about that—this has to be some of the roughest ground I've ridden in many a day and I didn't really have much hope of finding her. We figured right off that she'd head down to the valley, but we didn't find any tracks leading in that direction. For the last hour or two, we've been working up and down the ridge, hoping to see sign of her. No such luck so far."

"Well, I'll keep my eye open, but I don't think she'll come this way."

"If you do see her, just give the house a call. Nick's got an answering machine." He paused. "You got a phone out here?"

"Cell phone. The magic of modern technology."

He glanced around. "I heard you'd bought the Aston place. Couldn't hardly believe it." His sharp blue eyes came back to her. "What're you going to do with it?"

"Not grow marijuana," she snapped, her eyes glittering.

Acey held up a hand. "All right. All right. I just had to pry some." He bent his gaze on her. "You've been gone a long time, Roxy. Lived in New York and all them other fancy places. You were always too damned pretty for your own good, but you were always a good kid. I figure you still are, but there are some folks who are a bit more suspicious. Lots of talk in the valley about what you're gonna do up here." He smiled at her. "Glad I'll be able to put their minds at rest."

"Are you serious?" she asked, astounded. "People really think I came home from New York to grow marijuana?"

Acey pulled on his ear. "No one with any sense . . . but you know, we got a few poor souls in the valley that got shortchanged in life—they have more feathers in their heads than brains. Don't let it bother you none."

"Did you know Dirk Aston?"

"Not real well. And no, I don't know if he grew marijuana up here or not. I do know that he ran with some rough fellows with bad reputations—Milo Scott, for one, but it wasn't none of my business. If you're real curious, you might talk to Jeb. I know he's a detective these days and isn't doing patrol anymore, but he knows more about what goes on in these hills than just anyone else." Acey wiggled his brows. "Except for maybe me. All kidding aside, you should talk to Jeb. He's a good man. A good deputy."

"Could we please talk about something else besides Deputy Delaney—I just ate."

Acey shrugged, but there was a little gleam in his eyes. "Sure. Anything else you want to know before I slope off?"

"I heard that Dirk Aston was murdered, shot, in Oakland. That he was involved in some sort of turf war? Is that true? Or just more gossip?"

"Maybe he was. And maybe he wasn't. Like Jeb says, Aston could have been just a victim of circumstances. Nothing to prove it either way. The way I hear it, drive-by shootings happen all the time—especially in the area of Oakland where he was found. Could have been that Dirk was in the wrong place at the wrong time. That's my take on it and the take of just about anyone with any brains. Dirk was small-time. Liked to talk big and act tough, but no one paid any attention to him. And as for any gossip about you growing marijuana up here . . ." He shook his head. "That's just plain foolishness. And anyone who knows you knows it."

"Thanks, Acey. I needed to hear that." Especially, she thought to herself, after Jeb's visit. El Jerko himself.

He nodded, his eyes kind and shrewd beneath the wide brim of his hat. "Figured as much. Those fellows with feathers for brains talk too much and half the time don't even know what they're talking about. Don't pay 'em any mind."

He glanced around. "So what *are* you going to do up here?"

She grinned. "Haven't a clue. Ain't it grand?"

Chapter
2

Wearing an expression that would have frightened Dracula, Jeb punched the gas and roared away from Roxanne's place. Heedless of the curves and the clouds of dun and gray dust billowing up behind him, he rocketed down the winding road, sending gravel flying.

A half mile later when he hit the main road, not much wider or less winding than what he'd been driving on, common sense and a fondness for his own neck—and that of others—had him easing up on the gas and driving with some signs of sanity. His expression was still black, though, and his thoughts were equally so.

Why was it, he wondered grimly, that he had only to be thirty seconds in Roxanne Ballinger's presence before his temper snapped? All it took was one taunting glance from those huge golden eyes of hers and that belligerently lifted chin angled up at him and his brain turned to a seething mass of violent impulses.

Worse, his body betrayed him—anytime he came within ten feet of the woman he was instantly, achingly hard with a boner that would have done a stallion proud. More damning, out of nowhere would come the overwhelming urge to sling her over his shoulder, dump her on the nearest available space, and jump her bones. And he didn't even *like* her!

He scowled. Jesus! He was forty-five years old. He wasn't a hormone-driven teenager anymore. He'd been married. Twice, he thought with a wince. He was a respectable member of the community. Hell, he was a sheriff's deputy, a sergeant and a detective at that. He should know better. He should have better control. And yet, one sight of Roxanne Ballinger and he was in knots—infuriated and fascinated, aroused and angry at the same time.

The fascination he could understand. She was a gorgeous female. Even when his temper was fraying and he was certain he disliked her intensely, he was aware of that. Too aware. Maybe that was the problem. His lips thinned and his hands tightened on the steering wheel. He was not, *not,* he repeated, going to become one of a long line of pecker-brained fools who had fallen for those stunning looks of hers. You couldn't pick up a magazine or turn on a television when there wasn't something about Roxanne's love life mentioned. Of course, he realized that the numbers of lovers she'd had over the years had to be inflated—unless she spent every available minute on her back and he doubted that. He didn't doubt much else about the stories he'd read and heard about her, but common sense told him she couldn't have been *that* promiscuous and still have appeared on and in all the magazines that she had.

It annoyed the hell out of him that he wasted any time at all thinking about Roxanne. He wasn't a saint and he didn't expect other people, even females, to be either, but there was something about Roxanne . . .

Cursing under his breath, he wrenched his thoughts away from the vexing subject of Miss Roxanne Ballinger. There were far more important things in life to contemplate. Such as what he was going to eat for lunch. Yeah, that should occupy his mind for five seconds at least.

As the red truck nosed around the last curve before the road dropped to the valley floor, Jeb spotted a black and silver Suburban pulling a two-horse trailer just starting up the road. He recognized the rig. Sloan Ballinger's. Roxanne's oldest brother.

He'd known Sloan all of his life. He liked and respected Sloan and he supposed one could say that they were, after a fashion, friends. They shared some common ancestors a few generations back, just as he did with Shelly, but they weren't exactly what one would call family. He'd been tickled when Sloan and Shelly had married in June and had been observing their unfolding marriage with an avuncular eye. Sloan and Shelly deserved to have a happy and successful marriage—some youthful misunderstandings and, he suspected, some ugly plotting by Shelly's dead brother,

Josh, had caused them to waste nearly seventeen years. But that was behind them and he, for one, wished them the best of luck.

Josh's place, where Shelly had lived when she had returned to the valley in March, was about five miles up the road from here and he figured that Sloan was headed there. At the moment, Nick Rios, Shelly's partner in the cattle operation, was living in the house—along with Shelly's cousin from New Orleans, Roman Granger. Jeb had been, and was, a frequent visitor so he was familiar with the entire setup.

Pulling over onto one of the few wide spots on the road, he waited until Sloan came even with his vehicle.

Rolling down his window, Jeb called out, "Where're you headed? Up to Nick's place?"

Sloan nodded. "Yes. One of Shelly's cows found a break in the fence and Nick and Acey have been looking for her for hours, but no luck. She's due to calve any day and Shelly's pretty frantic about her. We're going to join the search. I've got our horses in the trailer and she drove on ahead of me in the Bronco. Didn't you pass her?"

Jeb cleared his throat. "Uh, I was just coming down from your sister's new place." Two spots of dark red color appeared in his tanned cheeks. "Shelly must have been past Roxanne's cutoff before I hit the road."

Sloan flicked up one black brow and his eyes, very like his sister's, were alight with amusement. "Is that so? And how did you find my sister? Well, I hope?"

"Just as damn snippy and full of herself as usual. Ordered me off her place." He sent Sloan a long-suffering look. "I know she's your sister, but damn-it-all, Sloan, I sometimes don't see how you can be related."

Sloan laughed. "I sometimes wonder myself." He studied Jeb a moment. The interplay between his sister and Jeb had always provided him with entertainment, ever since high school. They were like wildfire and combustible fuel. Put them together and poof! Explosive.

"So what did she do now that has you all in a temper?" Sloan asked.

"I am not," Jeb gritted out, "in a temper. I'm just baffled that she just goes right ahead and does exactly what anybody with any sense wouldn't even consider."

Sloan murmured, "Remember how my dad told her not to ride that big brute of a stallion of his?"

"Yeah . . . and the very first thing she did once his back was turned was climb on the back of one of the meanest horses I've ever laid eyes on. She was damned lucky she didn't get killed when he bucked her off. Scared your folks to death." Looking thoughtful, Jeb nodded. "Guess she doesn't take kindly to advice—I'll remember that the next time I have to deal with her."

"Good luck."

Sloan started to roll up his window when Jeb asked, "You want help looking for that cow? I could go get a horse and join up with you."

Sloan shook his head. "Appreciate the offer, but I think the four of us can handle it." He grimaced. "And if we can't—I'll call you."

They parted. Hitting the pavement Jeb increased his speed and shortly was turning onto the main drag of St. Galen's. The town of St. Galen's was small and consisted of a string of family-owned businesses and small houses that crowded along either side of the two-lane state highway that cut through the middle of the valley. Even its admirers would admit that St. Galen's wasn't a pretty or a quaint town, it was poor and it was practical. Some of the stores were empty, some needed paint, but Jeb viewed them all with affection. This was his town and he loved every inch of it, even the uneven and cracked sidewalks—where there were sidewalks. To his fond eye, St. Galen's had a charm all its own. Rough and contrary, but appealing in its own down-to-earth-take-me-as-I-am fashion.

He parked his truck in front of Heather-Mary-Marie's and not bothering to lock the door, slammed it behind him as he got out. Walking past the oak half barrel filled with pink cosmos and white petunias, he pushed open one of the double-glass doors that led inside the rectangular log building.

Heather-Mary-Marie's was as close to an old-fashioned dry-goods store as one was likely to find in this day and age. A little bit of everything could be found on the shelves, from clothes to plastic funeral wreaths. The store was owned and run these days by Cleo Hale, the granddaughter of the original founder who had named it for his three daughters. Not only did the store sell gifts, cards, Lotto, and clothing, but nearly half the population was in and out of its doors every day. Cleo was as good as any newspaper for being able to impart the latest news—and no censor ever put a lock on her tongue.

Cleo was busy wrapping up a package for a customer when Jeb stepped inside and the tinkle of the bell on the door brought her brilliant red head around. Seeing Jeb, she grinned at him and said, "Go on back to the storeroom. Those shirts I ordered for you are on the shelf to the right just as you enter. Be with you in a sec."

The customer, Sally Cosby, who worked as a waitress across the street from Heather-Mary-Marie's at The Blue Goose Inn, giggled. Her friendly brown eyes dancing, she said, "Better be careful, Jeb. If I were a good-looking guy like you, don't know if I'd go in the back with Cleo."

Jeb had known both Cleo and Sally all his life. At sixty-five Cleo was old enough to be his mother, but there was nothing motherly about Cleo, although she did have a daughter from the first of five marriages. Cleo stood six feet tall, and while slim, she had the shoulders of a football player. A pair of gold earrings dangled almost to the top of those broad shoulders and she was wearing her hair in an improbable shade of red and twisted up in a French roll that had gone out of style in the sixties. A purple silk shirt and tight black jeans completed the picture. On anyone else those earrings, those clothes, and that hair would have looked bizarre, but not on Cleo. She had never been a beauty, her features tending toward heavy and plain, but with her big blue eyes, wide smiling mouth, and that torch-light hair, it seemed a perfect fit. Jeb kinda liked the whole picture—even the earrings. And he adored Cleo. She'd been razzing and ragging him for as long as he could remember but she also had one of the kindest hearts he'd ever known. In any crisis in the community, Cleo Hale was one of the first people to react and send out the call for help.

As for Sally, he'd watched her grow up and had danced at her wedding fifteen years ago when she'd married Tim Cosby, a local logger. Sally came from a long-time valley family and was a noted local horse-woman—her thirteen-year-old twin daughters seemed to be following in their mother's footsteps. They already had a reputation for being hell on horseback, as their mother had been at that age, and had ridden half the boys in the valley into the ground. There wasn't much he didn't know about Sally and Cleo—or them about him. There were few secrets in the valley.

Cleo snorted at Sally's comment. "Oh, hell, honey, he's safe—he's too old for me."

Jeb chuckled, waved a hand in their direction, and ambled to the back of the store. In the storeroom he found the half-dozen shirts Cleo had mentioned. Picking out three of them, all plaids and cowboy fit, he headed back toward the front of the store.

For almost noon on a Thursday, with Sally gone,

the store seemed oddly deserted. Plopping the shirts down on the wooden counter, he said, "Things look kinda quiet."

Cleo nodded, her expression a little glum as she rang up the sale and bagged the three shirts. "It's September, Jeb—after the arrival of the welfare checks. Blackberry Harvest's only a memory. School's in session. Rodeo's over." She brightened. "Of course, once deer season opens, in a couple of days, the place will get lively again."

The bell over the door rang and both Cleo and Jeb turned to look. A wiry built man with sandy blond hair stepped inside, saying, "Hey, Cleo, I wanted to talk to you about those socks you . . ."

Spying Jeb, the newcomer froze. A tight expression crossed his features, and nodding curtly in Jeb's direction, he said, "Jeb. Didn't know you were in here." He glanced at Cleo. "I'll come back another time."

"No reason," Cleo said easily, aware of the tension between the two men. "Jeb was just on his way out." And to emphasize it, she handed Jeb his bag of shirts.

"Oh, I don't know," Jeb drawled, taking the bag. "Think I'll go look at those clocks you've got in that case against the wall. Maybe buy one for my kitchen. You go on and help Scott."

"That's OK," Scott muttered, "I'll come by later." And scooted out the door.

Cleo glared at Jeb. "I know Milo Scott's a pain in the butt—I'm not fond of him myself—if you'll remember he's the main suspect in the trashing of my place a while back. Personally I think he's a mean, sneaky, twisted, little weasel—and that's when I'm feeling kindly toward him, but I've got a business to run and he was a customer on a day that has seen few of those—and you, you wretched creature, drove him off."

"Oh, lighten up, Cleo, you didn't lose much—he was only going to buy a pair of socks."

Cleo snorted. "And how do you know that, Mr. Big Britches? He might have bought a whole dozen."

"A lowlife like Scott? Nah."

"You know, your prejudice is showing—not an attractive trait for an officer of the law. Aren't you supposed to be objective?"

Jeb grimaced. "You've got me there. I just can't stand the fellow, Cleo. I know he had something to do with Josh's suicide . . . or *supposed* suicide . . ." When Cleo would have interrupted, he raised a hand. "OK, forget about Josh. You know that Scott's connected some way with just about every drug deal that goes down in the county and that he's tight with every hippie-type, and some not so hippie-types, out there growing pot in the backyard—or the national forest."

"And if I turned my nose up at every marijuana grower in the area, I wouldn't have much of a business. Come on, Jeb. Most of those guys are harmless and they're only growing it for their own use." Jeb shot her a look and she shrugged. "All right, so maybe they sell some to him and so maybe he transports it down to the Bay Area. Big deal."

"Cleo," Jeb began patiently—and this was a discussion they'd had many a time—"marijuana is against the law."

"Like I said, big deal."

Jeb sighed. "That's the sort of attitude that makes enforcement that much harder." He didn't want to argue with Cleo—half the time he suspected that she was just jerking his chain. Turning away he muttered, "Never mind. And as for your erstwhile customer—don't worry, he'll be back. It's not as if you've lost the sale forever." Glancing out the double-glass doors, his eyes narrowed as he watched Milo Scott walk across the street to The Blue Goose. "See, he's just going to Hank's place."

Cleo followed Jeb's gaze. "And I suppose," she said dryly, "having driven him away from me, now you're going to go over to Hank's place and lose him a customer."

Jeb laughed. "No, I'm not going to The Blue Goose. Scott can enjoy his meal in peace. And when he's done, I'm sure he'll come back and buy the damned socks."

"Hmm, you know that's a funny thing. I know I ordered them for him, and if I recollect correctly they came in last week, at least I think they did, but damned if I can find them." She smiled slyly at Jeb. "That seems to happen a lot with Scott's orders. I just seem to misplace his stuff all the time. Can't figure it out."

Smiling, Jeb shook his head and left. Cleo did have her ways and he, for one, didn't want to be on her bad side. Climbing into the truck, he tossed his bag on the seat and turning on the ignition backed out of the parking slot. Ten minutes later he was pulling onto the gravel road on the east side of the valley that led to his place. He'd purchased this parcel of land, a hundred sixty acres, a quarter section, with a house and barn in the foothills about five years ago . . . and it hadn't escaped his attention that with her new purchase he and Roxanne were on opposite sides of the valley.

Figures, he thought, as he pushed open the door to the stone and wood house. Opposites in everything we do. Probably why she irritates me so.

The house was about thirty years old and built in the ubiquitous ranch style with a two-car attached garage. It wasn't big but it did have three bedrooms and two baths and though he had taken a lot of ribbing about a confirmed bachelor like him buying what was clearly a family home, it suited Jeb just fine. He'd turned one bedroom into a weight room, took the master bedroom for himself, and the third bedroom had become a catchall for everything he didn't quite know what to do with. The family room was small, actually just an extension of the kitchen in the rear of the house. The living room in the front was seldom used; in fact, beyond shoving a black leather couch, a couple of lamps, and an old red plaid recliner in it, Jeb hadn't done much with the living room. He spent most of his time, when he was even at the house, in the kitchen/family room and the deck that opened off of it. Walking through the house, he headed right for the re-

frigerator and pulled out a cold long-necked bottle of
Heineken's. Twisting off the cap and tossing it on the
dark blue and cream tiled counter, he took a deep, satisfying swallow and wandered outside to the deck.

Even in the speckled shade of the redwood lattice
roof, the deck was hot, the valley baking below him,
and after a second, he stepped back inside the house.
Standing at the glass sliding doors, he took another
drink of beer and stared across at the western foothills
that embraced the far side of the valley. Unerringly his
gaze settled on the faint outline of Roxanne's rooftop,
the sun glinting off the windows of the cabin. Probably only five or six miles as the crow flies separated
them, but to Jeb the distance was insurmountable. And
why in God's name did she have to buy that place,
where every time I look across the valley, the first
thing I'll see is her place? He scowled. The truth of the
matter was that he could look at miles of forested hill-
sides without his eyes ever once touching Roxanne's
place. But to his everlasting disgust, recently the first
place he looked at in the morning and the last thing at
night was the A-frame cabin he knew held the infuri-
ating person of Roxanne Ballinger. It was a habit, he
decided grimly, that he was going to have to break.

Turning away, he walked over to the refrigerator
and a few minutes later was sitting at the heavy oak
table in the family room with his feet on the chair opposite him, enjoying a ham, mustard, lettuce, and dill
pickle sandwich on whole wheat bread. He learned
long ago that he wasn't much of a cook, but he'd also

discovered that he didn't like starving. Hence, his cupboards held canned tuna, chili, soup, fruit, and an array of condiments that would have surprised some people. The refrigerator was always stocked with milk, beer, and sandwich makings; his freezer was full of bags of potato chips, pretzels, extra loaves of bread, frozen dinners, and a few steaks for special occasions. Some onions and potatoes were kept in one of the crispers of the refrigerator and he'd been known to feast on a potato nuked in the microwave with chili, cheese, and chopped onion and feel as if he'd slaved over a four-star dinner. Sandwiches were easier.

Taking another bite of his sandwich, he picked up the local paper that had been lying on the table and began to read. It was pretty boring and since he was with the sheriff's department, he already knew all the interesting pieces that hadn't been printed. Reduced to reading the classified ads, the banging on his front door followed by his brother's voice was a welcome diversion.

"I'm in the family room," he yelled. "Come on back."

Garbed in a khaki shirt and pants, a man who bore a strong resemblance to Jeb wandered into the room a moment later. Pushing forty, Mingo Delaney wasn't quite as tall as Jeb, or quite as big. They shared the same crop of unruly black hair, the same tawny complexion, and the same knowing black eyes. The ladies in the area were divided as to which one of the Delaney brothers was the handsomest. Mingo had his supporters and Jeb his. One thing was certain; the Delaney brothers were about two of the most attractive single men for miles around. The fact that they came from one of the leading families in the valley—their father was a retired judge—and were both unmarried caused all sorts of excited pleasure in the hearts of every unattached woman under the age of fifty in the county . . . and maybe beyond.

Walking over to the refrigerator, Mingo helped himself to a beer and dragged out the makings for a sandwich. It was clear he was very familiar with his brother's house and comfortable in it.

When his sandwich was fixed to his satisfaction, he popped open the freezer and grabbed a bag of potato chips. Taking the chair across from Jeb, he took a big bite of his sandwich.

Amusement glimmered in Jeb's eyes. "You're welcome."

Mingo looked confused. Then he grinned. "Hey, I just bypassed all unnecessary chatter. You know you'd have told me to get myself something to eat. I just anticipated you."

Jeb shook his head and took a bite of his own sandwich. "So what are you doing out here? Weren't you supposed to be doing something in the backcountry today? Checking culverts or something like that?"

Mingo worked for the Department of Forestry and was attached to the small substation just outside of St. Galen's. His range of territory was in the Mendocino

National Forest that lay to the east and about ten miles beyond the valley in the mountains.

"Yep. And I did that already. Was up and checking out the various sites by daybreak. Even though it's cooler in the mountains, I didn't want to be clambering all over in this heat. Besides, it's lunchtime."

They ate in silence a moment, then Mingo asked, "So? What are you doing on your vacation?"

The vacation was a sore spot. Jeb loved his job—so much so that he viewed taking time off more as punishment than a pleasure. Because of that, he rarely took time off and it just accumulated and accumulated on the books. It had reached the point where Bob Craddock, the sheriff himself, had ordered Jeb to use some of it up. Grumbling and cursing, Jeb had complied, wondering what in the hell he was going to do for a whole damned month.

Picking up a potato chip from the pile near Mingo's plate, he said, "Let's see, now. I've rebuilt all the fences—they weren't in bad shape so that didn't take long. I hung a couple of pictures in the living room that I had in the spare room. Changed the oil on the truck. Repainted my bathroom. Oh, and on Monday I finished that stall and rented an airless sprayer and painted the barn—Grecian blue if you're interested. Very exciting stuff. I don't know if my heart can stand much more of it."

Mingo winced. "You know, you're not really getting into the spirit of things. You should have gone away somewhere. Like San Francisco. Or LA. Gotten a taste of the big, bad cities." He winked. "And big, bad women."

"A woman is the last thing I need," Jeb muttered, his eyes instinctively going to the glass sliding doors and to the foothills on the opposite side of the valley.

Mingo caught the direction of his gaze and after taking a swallow of his beer, he asked innocently, "So, have you been up to see the lady?"

Jeb scowled. "What makes you think I'm going to waste my time checking on Roxanne Ballinger?"

Mingo grinned. "And how did you know I was referring to that particular lady? I don't remember mentioning her name."

Knowing Mingo had him, he grimaced and leaned back in his chair. "Yeah, I drove up and verified that she bought the damned place."

"What's it going to hurt? Personally, I'd rather have a beautiful bundle like Roxanne living up there than Dirk Aston. That guy was bad news. Think you'd be thrilled one more scumbag was off the streets—and out of the valley."

"That's not the point. The point is that Oak Valley is no place for the likes of Roxanne. She's nothing but trouble spelt with a capital T and I do mean capital."

Mingo opened his eyes very wide. "You'd rather have a fuzzy-faced pot grower living across the valley from you than a gorgeous chick like Roxanne? Jeez, have you been out in the woods too long. You know, this vacation might have been a very good thing for you, old man. You need to get a grip. Women, especially women like Roxanne, are to be revered and enjoyed, not tossed aside like last week's garbage."

"What do you expect from someone with my track record when it comes to women? You can't say someone with two, not one, but two failed marriages behind him really appreciates the finer nuances in dealing with the opposite sex," Jeb said, his expression bleak.

Mingo hesitated. Looking at the condensation on his bottle of beer, he said carefully, "Don't you think it's time that you quit beating yourself up about that? You made some mistakes, I'll grant you that, but I don't suppose it ever occurred to you that the failures of both your marriages might not have been entirely *your* fault. It does take two to tango, you know. And two to make a failed marriage."

Jeb shut his eyes. It was an old argument between them and he supposed that Mingo had a point. It was just . . . It was just that he never expected to end up at forty-five living alone, with two failed marriages behind him . . . and no kids. When he could look at it realistically, which was seldom, Mingo was right, it wasn't all his fault that both his wives had left him. Hell, even he would admit that his first marriage to Ingrid Gunther, the daughter of an Austrian baron who had bought up half the south end of the valley, hadn't been smart. He'd just turned twenty-two and Ingrid had been twenty-one and they'd taken one look at each other and fallen into cosmic heat. They married four months later and for three months they had been deliriously happy screwing each other blind. By spring, the edge had been off their appetite for each other and Ingrid had been bored and contemptuous of life in Oak Valley. Oak Valley was Jeb's life, it always had been and he figured it always would be. He'd tried to explain it to Ingrid, but she hadn't listened. In the end she gave him an ultimatum, either resign his job and follow her to Austria or. . . . By June, their marriage was over and she had returned to Daddy and her jet-setting ways. Sometimes when he was lonely and blue he wondered if he'd given in to Ingrid if the marriage might have survived. . . .

"You're thinking of Ingrid, aren't you?" Mingo demanded, cutting into his thoughts.

"Yeah, I was, how did you know?" Jeb asked, surprised.

"Because you always get that look on your face—as if you'd committed a crime against nature. I can't for the life of me figure out what you had to feel guilty about: she left you."

Jeb's gaze dropped to the table. "Yes, she did, and if you remember correctly, so did Sharon."

Mingo snorted. "You know you're the only one that didn't have a clue about Sharon. She married you because she wanted out of the valley and didn't have enough gumption to do it on her own. When you got your master's degree in criminology, she thought, like half the county, that you'd take off like a shot and get a position with some big city police department. Must have broken her calculating heart when she found out that you were perfectly happy to stay right where you were."

Jeb looked uncomfortable. His marriage to Ingrid he could, on a good day, put down to youthful indiscretion, but with Sharon Foley. . . . With Sharon, he'd been certain he'd found a soul mate. They were both valley born and raised. They had a shared history and seemed to like a lot of the same things.

He hadn't known that Sharon wanted out of Oak Valley. Oh, she might have loved him at first, but she'd had her eye on a future *away* from Oak Valley and that idea never occurred to Jeb. He came home one night to find a note on the kitchen table from his wife explaining that she was running away with the guy who owned a tree-trimming business in Santa Rosa. Jeb had been devastated. He hadn't had a clue and discovered that while Sharon was cute as a button, she was also as sly as a snake.

A wounded look in his eyes, his gaze dropped to the table. He had loved Sharon. He'd believed that she'd been happy, that they shared the same goals. If he'd known, he thought bitterly, that Sharon had had her eyes on a life somewhere else, he'd never have married her. He had been certain she felt about the valley the same way he did. He'd pictured them growing old together, their children gathered around them; his grandchildren romping on his lap. But Sharon had other dreams. Dreams he hadn't shared. Dreams he hadn't even known about. He smiled painfully. He hadn't known about a lot of things. Certainly he hadn't had any idea she'd been seeing another man, but he had known she was unhappy in the valley. Desperate to make her happy, during those last months together, he'd arranged weekends away in the wine country, the coast, even several nights in San Francisco. But it wasn't enough. When she'd begun to pressure him to apply for a job in San Francisco, he'd dug in his heels, telling her that this was home, this was where he wanted to be. He still remembered the look on her face. Hands on her hips she'd faced him. "You know," she'd said evenly, "not everyone wants to be buried alive in a dull place like this. Some of us would like memories of something more exciting than the FFA Field Day Parade or the Labor Day Rodeo." The next evening he'd found the note.

In his bleakest moments he wondered if there was something inherently wrong with him. Not one but two wives had left him. And each time, he realized now, the final straw had been his desire to remain in the valley. He'd tried to look at it from all different angles but it always came up the same: he'd wanted to stay, they'd wanted to leave. Had he been wrong? Had he been too stubborn? Had there been a compromise that he'd overlooked?

After Sharon's defection, he'd been full of self-doubts, wondering where he'd gone wrong, wondering what was wrong with *him* that two women hadn't wanted to remain married to him. He'd hurt for a long time, brooded and suffered in silence for a while and eventually came to the conclusion that marriage just wasn't for him. It appeared he wasn't very good at it and he wasn't about to try again. Nope. Not for him. Love 'em and leave 'em had been his motto for the past twelve years and he saw no reason to change it.

Jeb took a swallow of his beer and looked at his brother. "Leave it alone."

"I would if I thought you weren't still beating yourself up over something that wasn't your fault."

"I'm not. I'm fine."

Aware of the warning note in Jeb's voice, Mingo let the subject drop and after finishing his sandwich said good-bye and left. Jeb sat there at the kitchen table, staring off at nothing. Maybe he did still beat himself up about the two divorces. So what? He *had* failed. Two times.

Pushing aside his uncomfortable thoughts, Jeb got up and walked outside. There was work to do, but reminding himself that he was on vacation, he opted to spend a leisurely afternoon. He let his dogs, Dawg and Boss, a pair of mixed breeds, out of their kennel and after letting them run around some and hike their legs, or as in the case of Dawg squat and piddle on every bush within fifty yards, brought them into the house for company. Lying on the couch in the living room, the dogs flopped down on the floor beside him, he lost himself in a book in the Prey series by John Sanford.

Twilight was falling when he fed the dogs and let them out of the house for another run. While waiting for them to return, he popped another beer and sat out on his deck, enjoying the cooling night air. The dogs came bounding up eventually and after giving him slobbering kisses, took their usual positions lying on the deck beside him. Silence fell. The stars came out, twinkling silver against the black of the sky. Jeb sat letting the quiet and peacefulness seep into him. He was in a good mood. Content, even. Then, inevitably, his gaze was drawn to the light glowing across the valley in the window of Roxanne Ballinger's cabin. It was like a beacon in the night. One light shining out in a wall of blackness. His lips tightened. This used to be his favorite time of night, but now, now, he thought bitterly, it was the absolute pits.

Chapter
3

Wearing only an oversized white T-shirt and sipping a glass of iced tea, Roxanne sat outside for a long time as darkness had fallen, just soaking up the tranquility, reveling in the refreshing coolness that had come on the heels of the setting sun. The rustling of the wildlife in the forest nearby drifted to her, soothing and thrilling at the same time. What was that sound? A fox? A raccoon? Or, she shuddered deliciously, a mountain lion? Maybe a bear? And the night sky above her. Breathtaking. Endless black velvet littered with millions of glittering diamonds. Below her, the lights of town gleamed and winked up at her, making her feel like an eagle in an aerie, staring down at the world. Her gaze drifted across the foothills to the east and she was delighted to spy a light halfway up the shadowy hillside. It gave her a feeling of intimacy to see that other light glowing in the vast darkness. My neighbor, she thought with a giggle, across the way.

As the hour grew late, the coolness increased, and

almost shivering, she went inside her cozy cabin. There was still no electricity in the cabin, but between her battery-operated lamps and the propane-run appliances, she had managed just fine. And her cell phone. Of course, she wasn't going to be long without power: tomorrow her brand-new generator was to be delivered, along with a second tank to hold propane.

Snuggling down into the twin bed she'd set in the main part of the cabin, she went to sleep dreaming of all that she would accomplish the next day. And when the dawn broke, she bounded out of bed full of enthusiasm. A quick shower, a cup of coffee perked on the stove in an old aluminum coffeepot, a bowl of Total and a banana, and she was ready for anything. Today, she wore a pair of jean Capri pants and a white shirt sprinkled with blue forget-me-nots, her glorious hair neatly plaited in a French braid.

It was still early when she took her second cup of coffee out on the deck and stood, admiring her views. The morning air was soft, the sky brilliant blue, and the mountains and foothills that surrounded the valley endless green spheres reaching toward the heavens. Delight welled up inside of her. She was so lucky! Putting down her cup, she did a little dance around the deck. Lucky. Lucky. Lucky!

Humming to herself, she picked up her cup and walked inside. Finding the stack of CDs she brought with her, she rummaged through them until she found one by Cher. Putting it into the portable CD player, aware that there were no neighbors to consider, she turned it up as loud as it would go. The cabin vibrating with Cher belting out "Half Breed," "Gypsies, Tramps and Thieves," and a variety of other songs in that vein, she made her bed and cleaned the kitchen.

With those chores done, the outside began to call insistently to her. She ignored the siren call for a while, but knowing that in a couple of hours the heat would be blistering, she went outside, unable to resist the urge a moment longer.

Everywhere her eye fell, she could see labor—hard labor, and lots of money just pouring out of her checkbook, but it didn't deter her. She'd worked at the top of her game for years—with fees to match—and while she had lived well, she had also invested. If she spent wisely, she should be able to bring the place up to par—at least what *she* considered par—and with a bit of hoarding, still have a decent pad to keep the wolf from the door. She'd explained to her agent Marshall Klein that while she was more or less "retired," she would do some charity gigs and if a *really* special job came up, and the mood suited her, she might accept it.

Smiling, she wandered around the front of the cabin. Stepping back, she eyed it. She had plans for expansion, but she didn't want to lose the character of the A-frame. Sam Tindale, the architect Sloan had recommended back in early May when the offer she'd made on the place had been accepted, was coming up this afternoon with the final plans. She'd approached Sloan first, since he was an architect, too, but with an expression of horror on his handsome face, he had refused. "Absolutely not," he'd stated bluntly. When she'd looked hurt, he added, "Do you remember that tree house we built as kids?"

"Yes," she'd said slowly, the memory of their fierce fights on the way to go about it coming back. She'd even hit him with a board when he'd put a window where she hadn't wanted one. She'd grinned at him. "You're right. Our relationship will be much better if we don't work together."

He'd hugged her. "My thoughts exactly."

Escrow hadn't officially closed until last week—Aston had died in January and probate had taken time, but impatient as always, she'd set the paperwork in motion to start construction the instant her offer had been accepted. She had followed Tindale around as he had made the site inspections, sketching out the changes she wanted to make, and before she'd left for New York, he had magically transformed her ideas into reality—on paper. A contractor, Theo Draper, out of Ukiah had been chosen to do the work and he'd had the joy of dealing with the County Planning Department and getting all the permits. Roxanne didn't know how it had been accomplished, but to her delight, construction was to begin on Monday—and Sam and Theo had both warned her, that her *real* headaches would begin then.

Telling herself that they were just exaggerating, she left off her contemplation of the cabin and walked to the greenhouses that were situated around a bend, out of sight of the cabin. She knew the general layout and boundaries of the land, but beyond the cabin, she hadn't paid a lot of attention to the outbuildings or the property itself, so it was all an adventure for her. She peeked in the biggest greenhouse, noting the gravel floor, the slatted wooden shelving that ran the entire length of the building, and the black plastic piping draped overhead. Had Aston really grown marijuana in here? It seemed kinda bold to her. Wasn't growing marijuana a clandestine occupation?

Shrugging, she wandered over to the second building, discovering it was the same as the first, except smaller. Poking around outside, near the tree line, she found several half-used as well as new bags of chicken manure, peat moss, and some rolls of chicken wire. A dusty heap of tattered netting lay between the two greenhouses; closer inspection revealed that not only was it netting, but that it was camouflage netting. A *lot* of camouflage netting. It didn't take a genius to figure out that Aston had probably used it to make the greenhouses less noticeable from the air. Maybe he *had* been growing marijuana up here, Roxanne thought. Well, it had nothing to do with her. He was dead. She owned the property. And she wasn't, she muttered to herself, despite what a certain jerk in the sheriff's office might speculate, going to take up where Aston had left off.

Her almost twenty-acre bench was irregularly shaped and not exactly flat. It rose and fell in gentle swales; in some places it was as wide as seven hundred feet or more, in others it narrowed down to less than two hundred. Sections of it were wooded and choked with brush, some were open, a couple were swampy and damp, others thick with the ever-present yellow star thistle, blackberry vines, the occasional bull thistle, poison oak, and a variety of wild grasses and weeds. Mostly weeds, she admitted, as she brushed off several tiny burrs that clung to the legs of her pants. Some people called them "stick-tights" but in her family they were known as "beggar's lice." She hated them. And star thistle. And poison oak. Walking back toward the cabin, she tried to decide which one she hated the most. Hard choices—especially between star thistle and poison oak. She finally decided that star thistle had her vote as most hated. Poison oak at least provided habitat and food for the birds. Star thistle did nothing but ruin the grazing and choke out natural grasses.

She came around the bend, the greenhouses behind her and the cabin still several hundred yards away, when she heard a low, and to her, menacing bellow. She froze. The picture of a red-eyed rogue bull, snorting fire and brandishing a pair of horns six feet wide, flashed through her mind. Carefully she turned her head in the direction from which the sound had come. It was a matted thicket of pines and manzanita not fifteen feet to her left and as she stared at it, her heart thudding hard in her chest, there came another bellow, followed by the sound of a large animal crashing through the brush. A second later, less than ten feet from where she stood with her feet rooted to the ground, the biggest, blackest cow she had ever seen in her life stepped out into the open. A tiny gleaming black calf wobbled into view behind the enormous creature.

Shelly's cow, she thought with one part of her brain. And calf. She swallowed. She'd grown up around cattle, but it'd been a long time since she'd faced one on foot. Cattle weren't nearly as intimidating from the back of a horse—especially a horse that could outrun them—but it had been ages since she'd seen one from that view either. Uneasily she remembered that even the gentlest cow with a calf could be notoriously unpredictable; they'd been known to charge and maul anyone unlucky enough to get in their way. Angus had no horns, but at the moment that was small comfort to Roxanne. With that huge head, the cow could smack her into the next county or leave her just a grease spot on the ground, that is, if the creature didn't trample her beneath those enormous hooves. Roxanne eyed the cow. The cow eyed her. Standoff.

Slowly, very, *very* slowly, Roxanne edged toward the cabin never taking her eyes off the cow. It didn't help her mood when the cow snorted and lowered her head and pawed the ground.

"Hey," Roxanne said in a soft voice, "I'm leaving. Believe me, I don't want to tangle with you or your baby. You just stay right there and I'll just go into my nice, safe cabin, OK?"

Her voice seemed to soothe the animal and with every foot that increased the distance between them,

Roxanne's feeling that she just might survive this encounter grew. When she guessed there was enough distance between them, and the cow seemed more interested in the calf than pounding her into dust, she turned and streaked like a bullet to the cabin. Reaching the cabin, she leaped up the two steps and flew through the door, slamming and locking it behind her. And promptly wet her pants.

A cow, she thought with a half-hysterical laugh, a damn cow made me pee my pants. Maybe I have been away from the country too long—maybe I should stay in New York.

After a quick shower and a change of clothes, she was still shaking her head over the incident, chagrined and embarrassed that a cow, granted a very big cow, had sent her fleeing to safety as if menaced by a horde of New York thugs. Wearing a pair of low-rise black jeans and a burgundy and white cropped top that showed off a nice expanse of her trim abs, she walked into the main part of the cabin. Finding her cell phone, she punched in Nick's phone number.

When he answered, she said, "Guess what I've got in my backyard."

"I hope a big pregnant Angus cow," he replied, recognizing her voice.

"Not exactly—she's had her calf. They both look good."

"Great! What a relief. Keep an eye on them and we'll be over just as soon as we can get hooked up and the horses loaded in the trailer."

Biting her lip, Roxanne hung up. Keep an eye on them? Yeah, right. Like she was going to risk life and limb again. She made a face. Well, she was. Cowardice didn't suit her. She took a deep breath and went outside. Hell, she reminded herself, it was *only* a cow . . . with a calf.

Keeping a wary eye out for the cow, armed with a shovel she'd found around the side of the cabin, she traipsed off to face her black-hided nemesis. She figured, if the cow charged and she couldn't outrun her, a couple of solid whacks with the shovel might convince the cow to go bother someone else. She'd only walked about hundred fifty feet from the cabin when the cow, calf at her heels, ambled into view.

Prepared this time, Roxanne didn't find the cow frightening. In fact, having gotten over her initial fright, it was obvious that the cow was more interested in her newborn calf and grazing than wreaking mayhem on a puny human. Leaning against a tree a safe distance from cow and calf, she settled down to wait for the cow posse.

It wasn't more than a half hour later that she heard the sound of Nick's rig grinding up the road to her place. The cow had proven amiable, staying in view, and had been busy grazing, her calf, after nursing, napping on the ground beside her.

Nick, Acey, and Roman piled out of the pickup. With his white mustaches and smaller wiry frame, Acey looked like a little gnome as he stood between the two taller, younger men. Not for the first time

Roxanne was struck by the similarities between Nick and Roman. Both were tall and lean and moved with the same smooth pantherlike grace. Both had thick black hair and green eyes that gleamed like emeralds. She smiled. And both were too damned handsome for their own good. Watching them, she wondered, as she had often, about the gossip in the valley that had long ago tagged Josh Granger as Nick Rios's father—which would have made him Shelly's nephew and likewise, although distant, a cousin of Roman's.

In the spring the valley had been stunned and avid to learn that Shelly's father, dead more than twenty years, was, at her request, being disinterred from his grave at a local cemetery and a DNA sample being taken. Everyone knew that Josh had been cremated after committing suicide in March, which had eliminated *his* DNA, but between the DNA of Shelly, her father, and to a much lesser extent Roman's, the truth about Nick's parentage could finally be proven . . . or not. Maria Rios, Nick's mother, was as closemouthed as a clam about the whole situation. She had always refused to confirm or deny Josh's fatherhood so the valley waited with bated breath for the results. To everyone's frustration, Shelly, Nick, Roman, Sloan, Maria, and even Acey, who probably knew the results of the testing, had gone around with sealed lips. Roxanne had tried to wheedle the information out of Sloan and had gotten a long, cool stare for her efforts. Privately speculation was still running rampant and the fact that Nick and Shelly were in a partnership to-

gether to reestablish Granger Cattle Company and
Nick was living in Josh's house only added to the fuel.
If Nick *wasn't* Josh's son, why were he and Shelly
closer than two peas in a pod? And if he *was*, why
wasn't the family admitting it? Roxanne took another
look at the two men. If you asked her, she'd bet that
Josh was Nick's father. Trouble was, no one was asking her. Or telling her.

The men split up, Acey and Nick walking to the
rear of the stock trailer hitched to the truck, Roman
heading in her direction. Two of Acey's cow dogs,
Blue and Honey, leaped out of the back of the pickup
and with tails wagging danced around the truck and
trailer.

Leaving the others, Roman walked up to Roxanne.
"Pretty exciting stuff, huh?" he asked with a grin.
There was the faintest hint of the South in his words,
and coupled with a feline grace and a handsome face,
Roxanne, and half the female population, found him
utterly charming. "Cows in the backyard," he drawled,
"bet nothing like that happens in New York."

She laughed. "No, there we just worry about mug-
gers, rapists, and murderers—little things like that."

Nodding toward the cow and calf, he said, "Nick
called Shelly before we left. She was *very* relieved.
Don't be surprised if she and Sloan show up before
we're through."

Roxanne nodded. She knew all about Shelly's plans
for Granger Cattle Company. At one time Granger
Cattle Company had been a major player in the cattle

market, but with Josh Granger at the helm, the entire
operation had nearly gone belly-up. With Nick at her
side, Shelly was attempting to reestablish the Granger
Cattle Company. This spring Shelly had imported several cows that carried Granger blood from Texas and
Roxanne knew that Shelly, Nick, even Sloan, had been
anxious for the first of the calves to arrive.

"If I'm going to have company, guess I better go
put on another pot of coffee." She blinked up at the
sun, realizing that the day was heating up. "Maybe
iced tea would be better."

"I'll help you." Amusement glittering in his green
eyes, he said, "Now if we just had one of Maria's
apple pies, Acey would feel all this effort was
worth it."

Maria, Nick's mother, had been the housekeeper for
the Grangers nearly all of her life and her apple pies
were legendary. Recently, it had seemed whenever
there was a crisis one of Maria's pies appeared from
the freezer and once baked and devoured was a fitting
end to the episode. Acey, in particular, thought it was
a great way to celebrate . . . *any*thing.

Roxanne sent him a look. "I'm afraid you're going
to have to settle for coffee or iced tea and granola
bars—I wasn't planning on entertaining."

Roman grinned. "A bit touchy this morning, are
we?" Tongue in cheek, he added, "Not finding the
country the bucolic paradise you thought it would be?"

"Don't you start—I get enough of that from my
family." She scowled. "And that big jerk, Jeb."

Roman put a friendly hand on her shoulder. "Just teasing." A brow quirked. "Jeb's been giving you a bad time?"

"No, not exactly. It's just that everyone seems to think that I'm some hothouse flower and will wilt in the real world—they should try living in the modeling world. Believe me, hothouse flowers die in that competitive field. You have to be tough—and I'm a lot tougher than people give me credit for."

Roman didn't disagree. He and Roxanne had dated a couple times and had discovered they liked each other too much to ruin a beautiful friendship by falling in love, or lust, as Roxanne characterized it. They had happily settled on being friends and confidants. More than most people, Roman knew that there was a lot more going on behind the beautiful airhead facade she presented to the public. She was smart. She was funny. And she was tough.

Mounted on their horses, the blue heeler, Blue, and the black and white Border collie/Mcnab mix, Honey, trotting behind them, Nick and Acey rode up to where Roxanne and Roman were standing.

Both men tipped their cowboy hats in Roxanne's direction. "Morning," said Nick. "How're you liking it up here?" He grinned, his green eyes very like Roman's glinting with laughter. "Bet that cow gave you a start."

Roxanne made a face. Not for the life of her would she admit that she'd had the pee scared out of her. Airily, she replied, "Yeah, you could say that." She tipped her head in the direction of the cow. "So what's the plan?"

Acey scratched his chin. "First thing, we're gonna get the calf and get that navel dipped. Be tricky 'cause it's a fact that momma cows don't like you messing with their babies, but it ain't like we haven't done it before. Since you don't have any corrals, we thought about just herding her home through the woods, but with the calf, it'd probably be easier just to load them up in the trailer. Roman can drive it home and Nick and I can follow on horseback."

Nick looked at Roman. "We need you to turn the rig around and open the trailer doors wide. I've got a couple of panels tied on the side of the trailer and if you'll set them up like a pair of arms, we think we can just drive the cow and calf up into the trailer."

Roman nodded. "Sounds like a plan."

The first part of the plan went slick. Acey and the two dogs kept the cow distracted while Nick jumped down from his horse, flipped the calf over, and dipped the navel with a solution of Novalsan to prevent infection. He had just enough time to leap on his horse and trot away before the cow broke through Acey's line and raced to her calf. It was as they started herding the cow and calf toward the trailer that the plan fell apart.

Cow and calf moved right along until confronted by the yawning black hole of the opened trailer. The cow stopped dead in her tracks, examined the trailer and then with her calf scampering at her side did an about-face and hightailed it to the woods. Even with two men on horseback and a pair of dogs working her, she proved fearless, stubborn, elusive, and downright obdurate. The cow paid no more attention to the snapping dogs than she did the insects and just plain didn't give the men on horseback any respect at all. They'd get her going in the right direction and she'd veer off into the woods. Swearing, Acey and Nick urged their horses forward and plunged into the brush after her. Eventually, after crashing around in the underbrush, the cow would break cover, the terrified calf at her side. This was repeated several times, tempers fraying every time it happened. Once, they separated the cow from her calf, but before Acey could get it on his horse, the cow charged and Acey wisely forgot about catching the calf and got the hell out of her way. The dogs fared worse; Blue took a vicious kick that sent him yelping and limping off on three legs. Having vanquished one of the enemy, the cow disappeared into the brush once more, Nick riding hard behind her. Concern on his weathered face, the cow forgotten for the moment, Acey called to the dog. When Blue half slunk, half limped over to him from his hiding place under a manzanita bush, Acey swung off his horse.

Roxanne held her breath as Acey examined the dog.

"He's OK," Acey called out a few minutes later. "The leg isn't broke. He'll be fine, but he's in no condition to tackle that cow again today." Roxanne understood what was left unsaid: cows killed working dogs—even well-trained, smart dogs—and an injured dog was just a fatality waiting to happen. Ten minutes later Honey was slammed against a tree, propelled through the air by a powerful whack of the cow's head. After satisfying himself that Honey was not injured, just the breath knocked out of her, Acey ordered her to join Blue in the back of the truck. He wasn't getting his dogs killed by some rank range cow.

The day grew hotter; tempers flared and worry about the calf increased. All the running and crashing around in the underbrush wasn't good for a newborn. They'd given up on trying to load the cow and calf in the trailer and were now just concentrating on trying to herd the pair home. The cow wasn't having any of that either. She seemed dead set on remaining right where she was.

Hot, dusty, their faces sweat-stained, Nick and Acey took a break and walked their equally hot and sweaty horses over to where Roman and Roxanne had been watching. Wordlessly, Roxanne handed them tall glasses of iced tea. Roman had two buckets filled with water for the horses. The four humans turned and stared at the black cow. Now that the cow was no longer being harassed, she was contentedly cropping the yellow weedy grass not thirty feet away from them. The calf was lying flat out on the ground beside her.

"That is undoubtedly the meanest bag of T-bones I've ever come across," Acey admitted with a malevolent glance at the cow.

"Oh, come on, Acey. She's got a newborn at her side. All cows are cranky at a time like this," Nick said. "And look at the bright side—we know where she is."

"There ain't no bright side," Acey muttered. "It's downright humiliating. I can't believe that after all these years, I'm being outsmarted by hamburger on the hoof."

The sound of a vehicle approaching had them all turning to look in that direction. They'd half been expecting Shelly and Sloan to turn up and for a moment there was confusion when a big red truck pulled into view.

Roxanne recognized the truck immediately. Jeb Delaney. And who invited him? she wondered sourly.

A smile on his face, Jeb stepped out of the truck. Wearing jeans, boots, a black checkered shirt, and a black cowboy hat, Jeb walked to the quartet. By way of explanation, he said, "Shelly phoned me. Said she and Sloan were tied up." He nodded to the cow. "So you guys ready to start loading her?"

"Start?" Acey asked in bitter tones. "What the hell do you think we've been doing half the morning? That piece of beef is the crankiest, rankest critter this side of the Mississippi—and that's no bullshit. She put Blue and Honey on the ailing list—and I'm not likely to forgive her for that. If you've got your gun on you, I'd just as soon you shoot her between the eyes."

"Proving difficult, is she?" Jeb said lightly, his gaze skimming over Roxanne in her cropped top and jeans. "I've known a female or two like that." He looked back at Acey. "All it takes is a little finesse."

Nick snorted and gestured to the cow. "Well, be my guest and finesse all you want. We'll just sit here and watch."

Jeb studied the cow and calf for several minutes. He eyed the trailer and the distance from it to the cow. Then the two men and their horses.

"She won't load?" he asked.

"Not so far," Nick answered. "And believe me we've tried."

"And she won't herd?"

"Nope," Acey said. "We've tried that, too."

Jeb pushed his hat back. "Guess we'll just have to trick her then."

"And how do you intend to do that?" Roxanne asked, challenge in her voice and her eyes.

Jeb winked at her. "Watch and you might learn something, Princess."

"So what do you plan to do?" Roman asked hastily, aware that Roxanne was nearly vibrating with temper at Jeb's taunting words. They really did rub each other the wrong way, he thought, amused. It would be interesting, he admitted, to see who emerged alive if they were locked up together in the same room for fifteen minutes. His money was on Roxanne, but he imagined that Jeb could hold his own. Maybe that was the problem: neither of them was willing to give an inch.

Jeb grinned and glanced at Roman. "Gonna find out if I'm still as fast on my feet as I once was." He looked at Nick and Acey. "Get those panels down. Have those doors ready to swing shut. Oh, and make certain the safety door at the front of trailer is open—when I go out, I'll be in a bit of a hurry."

Nick and Acey grinned at him. "Yeah, I'll bet you will be," Nick said as he moved off to take care of Jeb's request. Returning to Jeb, Nick asked, "Now what, boss?"

"Think you fellows can distract her long enough for me to get the calf? If you can and can give me a head start, we should do just fine."

Roxanne's eyes widened. "Are you crazy? She'll make mincemeat out of you."

"Ah, Princess, I didn't know you cared," he drawled, his dark eyes twinkling.

Roxanne's hand curled into a fist. "I don't," she said in a snooty voice. "I just don't want to hire a bull-dozer to scrape up what's left of you."

Jeb laughed. "Don't worry—I won't put you to that expense."

It took several minutes for everyone to get positioned. Jeb figured the least distance he had to run with an eighty-pound-plus calf in his arms was best and so while he lurked nearby in the underbrush, Acey and Nick gently worked the cow and calf in the direction of the trailer. When the cow was about a hundred feet out from the trailer she started getting stubborn so they backed off and let her graze.

Roman and Roxanne prepared to do their part. Once Jeb snatched the sleeping calf, it was up to everyone to do everything, short of getting killed, to distract the cow until Jeb made it to the trailer. Roxanne was armed with pots to bang and Roman had towels to wave.

The calf slept. The cow ate. The humans eased into position. Standing behind a patch of buck brush, Jeb considered the situation. The calf lay about ten feet in front of him—and almost a hundred feet away from the safety of the trailer. The cow was grazing about thirty feet from the calf; Acey, Nick, Roxanne, and Roman ready to rush between them the instant he grabbed the calf. He took a deep breath, wondering if he was crazy. Looked at Roxanne in those low-rise jeans and cropped top. Her expression was tense and she clutched those two pots of hers as if her life depended upon it. Funny thing—his probably did. No doubt about it—he was crazy—he hadn't showed off for a female since he'd been sixteen.

The cow continued her browsing, putting another six or seven feet between herself and the calf. Jeb waited, his heart thumping. A moment later she was another couple of feet away and her back was to the calf. Now or never, Jeb told himself.

He wiped his hands on his jeans, took in a lungful of air, and exploded out of the brush. Sprinting over to where the calf lay, he snatched it up, surprising a bleat from the animal as he threw it over his shoulder. The next second he was racing toward the trailer.

Even though they knew the plan, Jeb's actions took everyone by surprise and for one almost fatal second, they all just stared. Even the cow who had spun around at the first sound from her calf.

After that, everything seemed to happen at once. The cow let out a bellow and charged. Acey and Nick kicked their horses forward and plunged into the area between the cow and the running man. Yelling and whistling, they swung their ropes in the air. Roxanne and Roman added to the din, Roxanne banging the pots together for all she was worth and Roman waving the towels like a madman. It worked. Confused by all the noise and activity the cow hesitated. A second bleat from her baby, however, was all she needed to send horses and humans scattering and plowed through the ragged line.

Nick swung his horse around and rode hard after the cow, the loop of his rope singing in the air. Acey was a half horse length behind him.

Her heart in her throat, Roxanne stared helplessly as the cow ate up the distance that separated her and her calf as it bleated piteously and bounced on Jeb's shoulder.

It was going to be a near thing, Jeb not ten feet from the trailer and the cow, enormous and black and enraged, five yards behind him—and closing fast.

Half laughing, half swearing, Roman yelled, "Run, Jeb. Run! And don't look back!"

His chest feeling as if it would burst, Jeb hit the trailer in one desperate leap. The trailer shook and rattled. A second later, the trailer shuddered violently and rocked as more than half a ton of furious momma cow plunged inside. Jeb dumped the calf on the floor at the front of the trailer and feeling the hot breath of mayhem on his back, plunged out the safety door at the side of the stock trailer. He misjudged it slightly and, intent on escape, wasn't aware of banging his head on the metal frame or the trickle of blood that ran down the side of his face. All he'd wanted was out. Now. Once outside, he hung on to the side of the trailer and shoved the door shut behind him. Breathless, laughing, and foolishly pleased with himself, he lowered himself to the ground and leaned against the side of the stock trailer as Acey and Nick, right on the heels of the cow, swung out of the saddle and swiftly slammed the two rear doors shut. One cow and calf safely loaded.

Roman and Roxanne ran up to join the others by the trailer. For several minutes, there was laughter, whooping and backslapping and congratulating.

When the initial adrenaline rush had ebbed, his dark eyes dancing with amusement, Jeb said to Nick, "Cut it a little close there, didn't you, boys?"

"Nah," replied Nick, grinning, "for a big guy you ran like a deer and we figured the cow needed better odds."

"Jesus, Jeb," Roman said with a chuckle, "I thought you were a memory for sure. That cow had to be right on your neck when you hit the trailer."

Jeb laughed, absently wiping away the streak of blood. "You're not far wrong. All I could think was don't stumble, don't trip, 'cause if you do, it'll be last thing you *ever* do."

Eyeing the slice through his eyebrow and the blood

on the side of his face, Roxanne felt her heart lurch. What was the matter with her? So what if the big jerk got a cut? He deserved it. It had been a juvenile trick he'd pulled. Picking up that calf and trying to outrun its mother. Stupid. And just like a man.

Acey broke into her thoughts. "Guess we ought to mosey on home," he said, glancing down at the pocket watch he wore. He looked at Roxanne and wiggled his mustaches. "Maria's baking one of her deelicious apple pies for me. Don't want to be late."

Chapter
4

*A*cey, echoed by Nick and Roman, invited Roxanne and Jeb to join them at Nick's place, but Roxanne passed. Tindale was due some time this morning—she had not given him a definite time and didn't know when the architect would likely arrive. "Some other time," she said with a smile.

Jeb waved them on. "Thanks, guys—you know me and Maria's apple pie—never pass it up. Go on ahead, I'll be along behind you in a few minutes."

Roxanne stiffened. "Don't let me keep you."

Jeb looked at her. "Don't start. I just want to have a couple of words with you and then I'll be out of your hair."

With Roman driving and Acey and Nick following on horseback, they gradually disappeared from sight, a cloud of dust churned up by their passing soon the only sign they had ever been there. Roxanne had watched them leave with misgivings. If there was one thing in life that she didn't want it was to be left alone with Jeb Delaney . . . and here she was alone with Jeb Delaney.

The heat was almost suffocating and feeling a trickle of perspiration slide down her back, she took a deep breath and muttered, "Well, hurry up and say what you want to—it's absolutely beastly out here."

Jeb rubbed the side of his jaw. "Now if you were a polite sort of woman, you'd invite me inside."

She snorted. "And we both know, I'm not polite—to you."

"I wonder why that is?"

"Probably because you're not very polite to me."

"Think?"

"Oh, for crying out loud. It's too hot for this sort of argument. Come on inside and I'll give you a glass of iced tea and you can wash that cut of yours." She glared at him. "And don't even mention that I'm being polite to you or I'll take the offer back."

Jeb grinned at her. "Yes, ma'am," he said meekly and followed her inside the A-frame.

Since there was no electricity at present, the cabin had no air-conditioning, but it was much cooler inside. Jeb looked around, noting the signs of vandals from the ripped walls to the patched holes in the floor and the Spartan furnishings. "Not much furniture," he commented as she led him into the kitchen area.

Glad of a safe topic, Roxanne replied, "I'm having a lot of renovations done starting next week so it didn't seem practical to try to move in before they're done."

"You're really going to move in here permanently?"

"Yes, I am," she said, fixing him a tall glass of iced tea. "I have lots of plans for this place." She made a face as she glanced around the tiny corner kitchen. "And one of them is a decent kitchen."

Jeb took the glass she handed him and drank deeply. Putting the empty glass down on the small counter, he smiled at her and said, "Thanks. I enjoyed that."

Fiddling around with the pitcher, more aware of him than she'd like to be, she asked, "What did you want to talk to me about?"

Jeb pulled on his ear. "I wanted to apologize."

Roxanne's lovely mouth fell open. "Apologize? You? To me?"

"Yeah, I know it's hard to believe." He shrugged. "For what it's worth, I'm sorry. I didn't have any business making all those cracks that I did the other day. It's none of my business what you do up here and I don't really think you're going to start growing dope. You got me riled and I just shot my mouth off."

She gaped at him. He was actually apologizing. Jeb Delaney apologizing to her. Would wonders never cease?

"Um, that's OK," she muttered. She flashed him an uncertain smile. "I shoot my mouth off all the time."

"That you do," he murmured, his black-eyed gaze skimming over her. He wondered if she knew how tempting she looked in that skimpy top and those low-cut jeans. Especially those low-cut jeans. His gaze dropped. She had the cutest damn belly button he'd ever seen and it was all he could do to keep from picking her up and putting his mouth right over that spot. And if he did that, he knew he'd have her out of those jeans and flat out on the counter before he could count to three. The picture of Roxanne, sans her jeans, lying on the counter before him, flooded his mind. And he was instantly, immediately, so hard he was certain he'd trip if he tried to walk. He swallowed. Maybe this hadn't been such a good idea. Roxanne was a whole lot easier to deal with when he was angry with her.

"Are you trying to start another argument?" Roxanne asked suspiciously.

He shook his head. "No, ma'am. Absolutely not."

"Well, it's a good thing," she said. "Let's quit while we're ahead. OK?"

"Sounds like a deal."

She gestured toward the sink. "You want to wash that cut?"

"Sure."

She threw him a towel and leaving him to wash at the stainless-steel sink went looking for some first-aid stuff she knew she had in her overnight bag near the bed. It took her a few minutes to find what she was searching for and straightening up, she turned back toward him. She gasped. He'd taken his shirt off and her heart slammed into her ribs at the sight of Jeb standing there half-naked in her small kitchen. His head was hidden in the towel as he vigorously rubbed himself dry, oblivious to her smothered gasp.

Her mouth dry, a prickle of sexual awareness running through her, Roxanne just stared dumbstruck at that magnificent chest. Reminding herself that she had to be crazy, that she didn't like him in the least, didn't cause her to stop looking at all that masculine beauty before her. And Jeb was beautiful—everything about him perfectly proportioned. He was a tall, big man and had the deep chest and wide shoulders that went with his height. He also had powerful, well-shaped muscles, and she watched fascinated at the way those very nice muscles bunched and flowed along his arms and beneath his chest as he moved. She'd never liked hairy men, but the thick mat of black hair that covered Jeb's chest and arrowed down across his lean midriff before disappearing into those tight jeans aroused a funny feeling inside of her. What would it feel like, she wondered, to be crushed against that hard, hair-covered chest? To her horror, her nipples swelled and her breasts ached, moisture pooling between her thighs. Holy Hannah! she thought half hysterically. This is nuts!

She shook her head. Took a calming breath and said brightly, "I don't have much in the way of first-aid supplies, but here's some hydrogen peroxide—it'll do fine as a disinfectant until you get home."

Throwing the towel down on the counter, apparently unaware of Roxanne's reaction to his half-dressed state, Jeb said, "That'll do as good as anything. It's not much of a cut." He must have noticed something though, because he hesitated and said uncomfortably, "Uh, sorry about undressing. I didn't want to get my shirt wet." He smiled crookedly. "I really splashed the water around."

"That's OK," she said in that same bright tone. "Don't worry about it. Here, dab some of this on that cut and you can be on your way." She thrust the bottle of hydrogen peroxide at him and then retreated, her gaze everywhere but on him.

Puzzled, Jeb stared at her. She was skittish as a doe scenting the hounds and he couldn't think of one thing he'd done to cause her to react that way. Surely, she wasn't frightened of him? Shrugging into his shirt and leaving it unsnapped, he turned the situation over in his mind. What the hell was wrong with her? He shook his head. Women. Who knew what went on in their minds? And he sure as the devil wasn't going to solve that age-old question today.

Pushing away the problem, he opened the bottle. "You have any cotton or anything I can use to put it on with?" he asked, looking around.

"No. Use the corner of the towel."

She watched as he dabbed the corner of the towel with a liberal dose of the hydrogen peroxide. Putting the tip of the towel against the cut, he let out a yelp and jumped, banging his hip against the counter and sending the bottle of hydrogen peroxide flying. It landed on the floor by his feet and broke.

Muttering a curse under his breath, he glanced

down at the mess he'd made. "I'm usually not such a bull in a china store," he said with a grimace. "What do you want me to use to clean it up? Got a broom?"

He looked so embarrassed and uncomfortable that Roxanne smiled. "Sure," she said. "I'll get it for you."

Broom and dustpan in hand, Jeb swept up the broken glass and most of the liquid. "Where do you want it?"

"There's a wastepaper basket under the sink."

While Jeb dumped the mess into the wastepaper basket, Roxanne picked up the towel and squatting down began to wipe up what remained of the spilled hydrogen peroxide. Jeb turned around and looked down at her. Her head was bent and he had a wonderful view of that gorgeous neck of hers, especially that delicate spot where it joined her equally gorgeous shoulder. He decided then and there that he'd be hardpressed to choose between her belly button and the area where her neck and shoulder joined as the place he'd like to taste first.

Roxanne glanced up and her breath caught in her throat at the blatant sexuality in his gaze. Desire sizzled through her, her entire body humming with carnal longing. Nothing like this had ever happened to her. Not even in the midst of the mindless affair with Todd Spurling had she been so aware of a man, so needy to feel his mouth on hers, his body against her own. Nothing in her life compared to the hungry yearning that was tearing through her. Nothing.

His eyes locked on hers, Jeb said huskily, "You

know I always wanted a woman at my feet . . ." He reached out a hand to help her stand. He pulled her to her feet and into his embrace. "But I think," he muttered against her mouth, losing the fight to resist her, "that in my arms is a much better place."

Crushed against his chest, Roxanne couldn't think. Didn't think. Didn't want to think. His scent, male and slightly sweaty, flooded her senses; the heat of his body flowed into hers, melting her bones and turning her weak with desire. And when his mouth, when that hard, masculine, taunting mouth, came down on hers, the world went spinning out of control.

There was nothing tentative or gentle about his kiss. He simply took her mouth and did what he wanted with it. His lips fitting hers as if made to do just that, his tongue exploring and tasting, tangling with her tongue. Oh, and his hands . . . his hands cupped that famous Roxanne bottom and pulled her tight against muscled thighs and straining erection.

They kissed for a long time, frantic, mindless, voracious kisses, hands and questing fingers traveling and pushing aside clothing, discovering new delights, new unexplored territory. His mouth slipped to the spot where her neck and shoulder met and Roxanne gasped as pleasure speared through her, her fingers clenching against his hard chest, when he bit down gently and then kissed the stinging spot.

He'd backed her against the counter that divided the kitchen from the main room, his body sliding between her thighs, his hands holding her face to his, as he sought out her lips once more. She was on fire, burning, feverish, aching with need, and when he rubbed his swollen penis suggestively against the junction of her thighs, she thought she'd explode with pleasure. She wanted him. Desperately. She'd die, she was certain, if she didn't have him.

In the grip of a passion that he had no control over, Jeb was aware of nothing but the woman in his arms. Her sweet/salty taste, the intoxicating scent of a warm, willing woman going to his head like potent wine. He'd never felt this way before, never been so out of control, never been *consumed* by such a driving desire. There was nothing in his mind but the joy and pleasure of tasting and touching her soft, silky flesh, of learning the curves and hollows that haunted dreams. He was helpless in his hunger and need, the urgent demand to lose himself in her body pushing him to the edge.

The passion between them was explosive and neither was conscious of anything but the other and the need for a closer contact. Roxanne's top was pushed up around her neck and his hungry mouth teased and nipped at her small ivory breasts, her nipples swollen from his caresses. His shirt had been discarded at some point and she purred like a cat as her fingers explored that hard bristling expanse of his chest, her nails scraping against his nipples eliciting a deep groan from him.

Somehow her jeans and panties were down around her knees, his fingers finding her damp heat; his rigid member was freed from his pants and when her slim hand closed around him, Jeb thought he'd died and gone to heaven. But heaven eluded both of them, the intimate, explicit caresses of their hands and mouths only fueling the fire between them.

The slide of Jeb's fingers against her aching flesh was more than Roxanne could bear, and as desire coiled and tightened in her belly, her body trembled with it and she bit back a moan as his thumb brushed the distended node, there between her legs. She couldn't stand it any longer and helplessly her hips moved against him in a message as old as time, inviting him to complete the act.

Jeb got the message. With something between a groan and a snarl, Roxanne was lifted, her jeans and panties dragged out of the way. Her naked bottom hit the counter and the next instant, Jeb was between her legs, his hands sliding beneath her hips, lifting her to take all of him . . . and there was a *lot* of him to take.

He slid slowly inside of her, the sweet hot depth of her, tight and slick, welcoming his invasion. A shudder went through him and he pulled her even tighter to him, deepening his possession.

Roxanne gasped, the heat and size of him beyond anything she had ever experienced—ever imagined. She was stretched, filled as she had never been before, and the slide of his hard flesh against hers was the most erotic thing she had ever felt in her life.

One of them sighed at that joining, maybe both. Roxanne's arms were around his neck, her breasts crushed against his chest, her mouth wild and eager beneath the demand of his. Seated at the edge of the counter, her legs wrapped around his hips, his hands gripped her bottom and he began to move, heavy thrusts that pleased them both, pleasured them both.

It was fierce mating. Each time his body slammed into hers, the fire between them burned higher, hotter, until there was nothing left but a raging conflagration that sent them hurtling to an explosive climax. Roxanne stiffened as the first wave took her, the pleasure so intense, so powerful, she bit his lip to keep from screaming.

Feeling her body clenching and unclenching around him, the bite of her teeth on his lip, he muttered something, tried desperately to prolong the moment, but lost the sweet battle. Driving urgently into her, he found release, groaning as ecstasy thundered through him.

Roxanne was half slumped on the counter, Jeb lying partially on her. He was lodged between her legs, his mouth buried where her neck and shoulder joined. He didn't think he could move . . . didn't think he *wanted* to move.

A minute passed, maybe two. Reality trickled back. What they had just done hit them both simultaneously. As if jabbed with an electric prod they sprang apart, identical expressions of horror on their faces.

Appalled, Jeb stared at Roxanne's face, knowing his own face wore the same stunned, horrified look that was on hers. Gingerly, he took another step away from her. "Jesus Christ!" he exclaimed, unable to quite believe what had happened. He *never* did this sort of thing—not even when he'd been a hormone-driven teenager. He must have gone crazy. Maybe he'd suffered a stroke. A blackout. *Something* to explain his actions. "Look," he began helplessly, "I never meant. . . ." He swallowed. "I don't. . . ." He looked down at his jeans halfway around his knees and with a muttered curse dragged them up, stuffing himself inside and zipping them closed. He ran a trembling hand through his hair. "Jesus Christ!" he said again, still stunned and thrown off balance by what had happened.

Equally as thrown as Jeb, Roxanne blinked at him. My God! Had they just done what she'd thought they'd done? She glanced down at her half-naked body sprawled on the countertop. Omigod! Omigod! They had.

She jerked upright, dragging her cropped top down over her breasts. Her panties and jeans dangled from one ankle and slipping down from the counter, she grabbed them and, hopping around, forced her opposite foot into the other leg of her clothing. She couldn't look at him, shame and horror roiling through her. Her face was burning, her heart thumping. She must have gone crazy. Crazy as a loon. Lost her mind. Had to have. How else to explain the inexplicable?

Jeb took a deep breath. "Look," he began again. "I don't know what just happened, but I want you to know that I don't go around jumping every available female." So far so good, but then he had to go and put his foot in his mouth. "You may be used to this sort of thing," he muttered, "but I'm not."

Her lips tightened and she shot him an unfriendly look. "I'm not," she said in icy tones, "the slut you seem to think I am. Contrary to the press, I don't usually have sex on my kitchen countertop with a man I don't like."

"Only with those you like?" he drawled, unable to help himself, his eyes cold and disbelieving.

Rage choked her. "Get out of my house, you big ape! Go on—get. And don't you dare come back."

Knowing that he was as much, maybe more, to blame as she was for what had happened—he *had* made the first move—he mumbled, "I shouldn't have said that—it was uncalled for."

"You can say that again!"

Growing a little angry himself, he glared at her. "Look, I'm trying to apologize here—you might be more receptive."

"Apologize?" she asked in a dangerous tone, her eyes narrowing. "For what? And I'd be very careful what I said if I were you."

He look puzzled, then shrugged. "What I'm trying to say is that what happened between us was . . ." He swallowed, memory of the explosive pleasure they had shared flooding his mind. What had happened had been incredible—the greatest sex he'd ever had in his life. To his great dismay, he instantly grew hard. "Look," he said quickly, his one thought to get away before he made a complete fool of himself, "About what happened, I'm sor—"

She slapped him. Hard. "Don't you *dare* apologize for what we did," she snapped, furious and humiliated, her great golden eyes full of fire. "It happened—get over it. And while you're at it—get out of my house."

The sound of a vehicle coming up the road startled both of them.

The argument forgotten, an expression of consternation filled Roxanne's face. The scent of sex was still faintly wafting in the air and she was aware of the damp trickle between her legs. Confident that anyone coming within three feet of her would know precisely what she had been doing very recently, Roxanne exclaimed, "Oh, God! It's Tindale. I can't meet him like this." She threw Jeb a harassed look. "Just leave." And having said that, she sprinted across the room, grabbed her overnight case, and disappeared into the bathroom. A second later, he heard the shower come on.

Who the hell, he wondered, was Tindale? Think he'd stay and find out. He snapped his shirt, shoved it into his jeans, and quickly put himself to rights. Running a hand through his mussed hair, he fingercombed it and hoped that Tindale would think that he normally wore the tousled look. He glanced around, and spotting a bottle of Pine-Sol near the sink, he dumped some of it in the sink and turned on the water. The heavy scent of pine oil filled the air and covered whatever aroma remained of their lovemaking.

Pleased by his quick thinking, Jeb smiled. Yeah. He

could really think on his feet, couldn't he? He looked down at his fly. And with his pecker, it seemed. He sighed heavily, wondering what in the hell had just happened between them—not only the sex, but the slap. What had he said to make her so angry? He'd only been trying to apologize. Women.

He heard the vehicle pull up and park, and a couple minutes later there was a rap on the door. Still puzzling over the situation, he walked to the door and opened it.

A man, a six-footer with a friendly face, stood there, briefcase in hand. Jeb didn't recognize him, figured him from out of town. The guy looked about forty and he didn't wear a hat, his thick wavy blond hair glinting in the sunlight. He was dressed in knife-creased blue jeans, shined shoes, and a maroon shirt with a buttoned-down collar and a dark blue maroon striped tie.

"Come on in," Jeb said, for no obvious reason other than he was standing on Roxanne's doorstep, disliking the man on sight. "Roxanne's in the shower." He smiled, not a very friendly smile, just a faint baring of the teeth that could have been mistaken for a snarl. "We had some excitement around here this morning— a neighbor's cow with a newborn calf showed up. Took all of us a while to get the pair loaded up and on their way home." He stuck out his hand. "I'm Jeb Delaney. You're Tindale, right? Roxanne mentioned that you'd be arriving."

If Tindale got the impression that Jeb was very much at home in Roxanne's cabin and very familiar, quite friendly in fact, with Roxanne, it wasn't from lack of trying on Jeb's part. Precisely why he was creating this impression escaped him. And hey! He hadn't said anything that wasn't true, he thought virtuously.

The two men shook hands, Jeb resisting the urge to let Tindale know just how strong he was.

"Hi, nice to meet you. I'm Sam Tindale—Roxy's architect," he said with an amiable smile. Showing that he was equally at home in Roxanne's cabin, Tindale walked over to the kitchen countertop and laid down his briefcase. Opening it, Tindale took out what were obviously architectural drawings. Glancing back at Jeb, he said lightly, "Like they say, the paperwork is never done. Construction's supposed to start on Monday and Roxy wants one last look at the plans."

"That so?" Jeb replied, bristling at the other man's diminutive use of Roxanne's name. Where did this guy get off calling her "Roxy"? Only family and close friends called her Roxy.

The lady herself appeared just then, looking fresh and downright tasty, Jeb thought, as she came rushing out of the bathroom. Seeing Tindale at the counter, she smiled and said, "Oh, Sam, I'm sorry to keep you waiting. It's been a busy morning and time just got away from me."

"Yeah, that's what I told him," Jeb drawled, bringing himself to her attention.

She hadn't noticed him standing over by the doorway and at the sight and sound of him, she sucked in her breath, her smile slipping just a little. "Oh, ah,

Jeb . . . I didn't realize you were still here." Her eyes angry, she said, "Didn't you say that you had an appointment in town?" Through gritted teeth she added, "An appointment that you're going to be late for?"

"Are you sure?" he asked, all innocent. "Jeez, I don't remember any appointment . . . you must be mistaken. Besides," he continued with a wide smile, "I'd really like to see all the changes you and Sam have planned for the place."

If Tindale was aware of any undercurrent, he pretended otherwise. "Come on over," he said, "and I'll give you the nickel paper tour."

Ignoring the glare Roxanne flashed him, Jeb strolled over and stood beside Tindale at the counter, staring at the sheets of oversized paper that were spread out on the counter. The counter, Jeb thought with a wicked grin, where he and Roxanne had just had the most mind-blowing sex he'd ever had in his life. He glanced at her. Wonder if it had affected her the same way? Her eyes were stormy when they met his and from the set of her jaw, he figured right now that the only emotion she felt was pure fury. Ah well. Served her right. She'd sent him away with a burr up his butt more than once. Turnabout was only fair play.

Jeb's gaze dropped and he whistled at the rendition of the finished house. "Pretty nice," he commented to Roxanne with a raised brow.

"I think so," she muttered, wondering what in the hell he thought he was accomplishing. Why didn't he just leave? Over Tindale's bent head, she mouthed, "Go away."

Jeb just smiled and turned to study the plans, his fingers absently tracing the outlines of the changes.

The plans Roxanne had for the property were indeed "pretty nice." He only half noted the new well house, woodshed, and barn and corrals that would be added at some point. It was the house that riveted his attention. It was, he thought, quite appealing—big, but not huge, nothing pretentious about it. It was stylish and yet there was something very homey, very, he found himself admitting, inviting about it. And he admitted that the whole thing looked like it belonged right where it was.

The original A-frame had been doubled in size and a miniature A-frame now jutted out from the front of the enlarged structure—he assumed it was an entry hall. Two wings with a hipped roof had been added on either side of the expanded building and attached at the end of each new wing was a smaller A-frame, giving the whole house the appearance of an Alpine lodge. The roof was dark green metal with some skylights and there was a series of decks at the back and slate terraces, edged with raised flowerbeds, at the front. A rock-edged slate walkway led from the enlarged parking area; a new three-car garage with the same dark green hipped roof as the wings lay just beyond the parking area, with a long covered breezeway leading to the northernmost A-frame.

He glanced at Roxanne, his finger stopping at the breezeway. "Back door?"

Perplexed at his interest, she nodded. "Yes. The breezeway is also the mudroom." When he continued to stare at her, she added, "From there you enter the laundry area—there's also a half bath and small pantry in that area—a short hall leads to the kitchen."

"And beyond that," Tindale joined in, "will be the dining room, which will be open to what was the original part of the A-frame and the new section—the great room. There'll be a rock-faced fireplace in one corner and floor-to-ceiling windows that give a fabulous view of the valley. Roxy wants the upper floor in the old part torn out—so there'll be open-beamed ceilings in that area." He made a face. "I wanted the open-beamed ceilings throughout the great room, but Roxy said no. The front half, the new part, will have a second floor with a couple of rooms and a bath. It's going to be quite a project—and we want to get it up and closed in before the rains start."

From beneath lowered lashes, Roxanne considered Jeb. What was he doing? Why the hell didn't he just leave? Her mouth tightened. He was probably just hanging around to annoy her. Except, she realized, that she wasn't exactly annoyed. She didn't know what she thought—especially about what had happened between them. She wasn't a prude, but she'd never made love on a countertop before . . . nor, she admitted with a funny feeling in the pit of her stomach, had she ever experienced such a world-shaking climax before in her life. She was thrown off balance, utterly baffled by what they had done. It just wasn't her style to fall into bed with any man that came along, and yet Jeb. . . . She swallowed, her gaze dropping to his strong, tanned hands as they rested on the architectural drawings. All he had to do was touch me, she thought unhappily, and I went up in flames. And I don't, she reminded herself grimly, even like the son of a bitch. Angry with him, as well as herself, Roxanne glared at Jeb's down-bent head. Why didn't he have the decency to leave? Mentally, she slapped her forehead. This was Jeb Delaney she was thinking about—what else could she expect from a cretin like him?

Tindale's voice interrupted her thoughts. "We're hoping," Tindale said, "for six weeks to two months of decent weather."

Jeb nodded, his eyes still on the plan before him. "Rain usually doesn't start heavy until the middle of November, although we can get some fairly good storms before then."

"We're counting on that," Tindale said. He glanced at Roxanne and smiled. "And since Roxy wants it done at the speed of light, I've hired a good-sized construction crew—we're going to move as fast as we can." He sighed. "And as fast as the planning department will allow us."

"What's in the other wing and the A-frame at the end?" Jeb asked, glancing at Roxanne.

Roxanne shot him a dirty look, her expression saying plainly, What's it to you, buster? Aloud she muttered, "It'll be a suite—sitting room, bedroom, and bath for guests and a wide hallway that leads to the A-frame and my bedroom and bath."

"Pretty fancy," he said. "I like the open plan and the use of the space." He smiled guilelessly at her. "I'll sure look forward to the housewarming."

Roxanne smiled at him, showing her teeth. "Well, if that's the case, you'd better be off so Sam and I can get to work."

"No problem," he murmured, a glint in his eyes that made her uneasy.

She was wise to have been uneasy, because he stunned her by walking around Tindale, pulling her into his arms, and dropping a hard kiss on her mouth.

While she stood there frozen, gaping at him, he drawled, "Thanks for, uh, an *interesting* morning. See you around, Princess." He winked and patted her familiarly on the rear. "I'll keep my eye out for that invitation to the housewarming."

Chapter
5

*H*er lips tingling from Jeb's kiss, Roxanne sucked in her breath, uncertain whether to curse or cry. She could do neither, not with Sam Tindale standing right beside her. Her right hand did clench into a fist and the smile she sent Jeb was anything but friendly.

"If you'll excuse us," she said to Tindale, "I want to walk with Jeb to his truck."

"Oh, sure," Tindale said, glancing up from the plan, oblivious to the undercurrents. He sent Jeb an amiable smile. "Nice meeting you. Hope to see you again."

"Same here," Jeb said.

Whatever else he might have said was lost when Roxanne pinched him in the arm and hustled him across the room and out the door. She didn't say anything as they walked to his truck.

Reaching his vehicle, Jeb glanced down at her. "You wanted a word with me? I assume that's why you're being so polite in escorting me to my truck."

She looked up at him, a puzzled expression in her

eyes. "I just want you gone. You don't like me and I sure as hell don't like you." She wrapped her arms defensively across her breasts. "I don't know what happened between us in there, but I want you to know, that despite what you might think of me—th-th-that isn't something that I d-d-do—or have ever done before in my life."

Jeb cocked a brow. "You want me to believe you've never had sex?"

"That isn't what I meant and you know it." She sighed impatiently. "I don't even know why I'm trying to explain myself to a rednecked cretin like you."

Jeb grimaced. The lady sure held a high opinion of him and all things considered, he couldn't really blame her. "Look," he said finally as the silence between them lengthened, "let's just both claim that we went a little crazy or something—jumping the bones of the nearest attractive woman isn't something I do either. I don't know what happened between us. Something in the air. Or maybe there's something in the water. Maybe old Aston smoked a lot of Spanish fly in there and it permeated the walls and we got a whiff of it. Something happened, but what it was I sure as hell can't even begin to guess."

Roxanne felt a little better knowing that he was as baffled as she was by their wild lovemaking. Sex, she reminded herself. Wild sex. The wildest. And Spanish fly worked for her—it made as much sense as anything else did. She half smiled. "Yeah. Spanish fly. I like that. Sounds like as good an explanation as anything I could come up with."

He smiled back at her. "OK. Spanish fly it is." He hesitated, feeling the need to say something else. "I'm not going to risk getting my face slapped again," he began quietly, "by saying, I'm sorry, but I *am* sorry if I've made the situation worse between us." He grimaced. "On a good day we can barely tolerate each other—I'd hate for us to have really bad blood between us."

Roxanne bit her lip. For reasons that totally escaped her, she discovered that she didn't want there to be serious trouble between them either. What she wanted was for this morning never to have happened and for them to go back to their usual exchange of insults. "I know what you mean," she admitted. Thought for a second, then added, "Um, listen, I don't know how to say this without offending you"—she flashed him a half grin—"something I enjoy doing enormously—but not in this case." She hesitated, then blurted, "Do you think we could just pretend th-th-that what h-h-happened, didn't? Just go back to our usual snarling and growling at each other?"

He took in a deep breath. What she was asking was impossible, but probably not for the reasons she thought. He'd never be able to forget the glorious slide of her sleek body against his, the hot glove of her wrapping around him . . . didn't *want* to forget. He looked over at her, saw the embarrassment, the uneasiness, the bewilderment in her eyes. He was com-

forted to realize that she was equally as blown away as
he was by what had occurred on her countertop. But
that didn't mean he was going to wipe out the memory
of the explosive sex between them. He couldn't explain it, but he didn't want to forget it. She obviously
did. Which left him, he thought ruefully, with only one
thing to do.

"OK," he said mendaciously. "We'll forget about it.
Just go back to being what? Enemies? Not friends?
Unfriends?"

She smiled slightly. "We've never been enemies . . .
exactly. I guess 'not friends' works as well as anything."

"Shake on it?"

Solemnly they shook hands, their eyes met, the
same expression of wariness and confusion in both
pairs.

"Not friends," Jeb said.

"Right," Roxanne said, "not friends."

She watched him get into his truck and drive away.
She should have been glad that he was finally gone,
but as she slowly turned and walked back to the house,
she was conscious of a nagging sense that the day had
somehow become duller, that some vitality, some
spark, was missing from it. Hogwash, she thought as
she reached the front door. It would be a cold day in
hell before Jeb Delaney's presence, or lack of it, made
any impression on *her* life.

A careless smile composed on her lips, she pushed
opened the door and walked over to where Sam Tin-

dale was still examining the plans. "So where do you want to start?" she asked brightly.

Unlike Roxanne, Jeb had time to consider the situation as he drove down the twisting road from her place. He wasn't in the mood for pie and chatter at Nick's place. A quick call on his cell phone took care of that. He thanked Nick for the offer but said that he was taking a pass on the pie today. "Tell Maria I'll eat twice as much the next time," he promised as he rang off.

Not in the mood for company, he drove home. He let the dogs out and prowled around with them as they sniffed and marked several intriguingly scented trees and bushes. Inside the house, the dogs sprawled on the cool kitchen floor watching Jeb as he fiddled around, putting away the clean dishes in the dishwasher, wiping down the counter, and folding and tossing the newspaper in the paper recycling bin outside the back door. His housework done for the moment, Jeb sat down on the comfortable blue and green plaid couch near the kitchen table.

He sat there a long time, staring at nothing, his thoughts on Roxanne . . . and the incredible sex they had shared. He shook his head. It was inexplicable. If anyone had asked him to name the woman he'd least like to have sex with, he'd have sworn that Roxanne's name would have been dead last on his list. He grimaced. And now she went right to the top of the list of the women he'd most like to have in his bed. What a hell of a scary admission that was.

He couldn't figure it out. It made no sense. Oh, sure, she was an eyeful and for some reason he believed her when she said that she didn't do that sort of thing. He didn't either, and while the tabloid stories about her would lead one to believe she jumped from one bed to the next as regular as fleas got on dogs, the expression on her face when they came to their senses had reflected the same shock and horror he knew had been on his. He rubbed the back of his neck. What in the hell had gotten into the pair of them? It'd been a while since he'd been intimate with a woman, but he wasn't a teenage sex maniac either. He was long past that stage. And today with all the diseases out there, when he did go to bed with a woman, he made damn sure he knew her sexual history and that he wore a condom . . .

Jeb jerked upright, his eyes going wide. Oh, shit! He hadn't worn a rubber. He swallowed. They'd had unprotected sex. Funny thing though, it wasn't the idea that he might get a disease from her that sent his stomach flipping, it was the knowledge that in those moments of frenzied sex they might have created something else . . . a baby. He swallowed again, his throat tight, his breathing constricted. Oh, Jesus. He really didn't want to go there. Almost hyperventilating, he considered all the reasons why there should be no lasting repercussions from this morning's event. Surely Roxanne was on some sort of birth control?

Yeah. Sure. Had to be. Woman with her past must take precautions all the time. There was nothing to sweat. But just in case she wasn't on birth control, he thought uneasily, luck couldn't have been so against them that they had happened to go crazy just when she was ripe and fertile. But what if she had been ovulating? Feeling like a fist had just slammed into his chest, he groaned and buried his head in his hands. Jesus! He didn't want to think about this. Didn't even want to think for one second about Roxanne having an abortion. Didn't want to think about her bearing his child and tripping off to New York with it. What he discovered to his fascinated horror was that he liked the possibility of the pair of them raising a child together. He froze, his eyes almost starting from his handsome head. The idea that he had actually considered having a child with Roxanne made him break out in a cold sweat.

He sat up and ran a hand across his forehead. He felt a little hot. Maybe he was coming down with something. Summer flu? A cold? Brain fever? Yeah, his brain was all scrambled, fevered. That was it. He was sick. His brain not processing information the right way.

Getting up from the couch, he walked into his bedroom to the master bathroom and opening the medicine cabinet took out a bottle of aspirin. He swallowed two of them, threw some cold water on his face, and accompanied by the two dogs, lay down on his bed. The dogs joined him, Dawg laying her head on his chest and Boss on the opposite side curling up next to his hip.

Both dogs were mixed breeds—Boss part Dobie and shepherd with maybe some pit bull thrown in for good measure; Dawg appeared to be some sort of poodle/cow dog cross and if her wrinkled forehead was anything to go by, sharpei. He'd found Boss five years ago, a half-grown, half-starved black and tan pup prowling around Joe's Market, and even knowing he was being a soft-hearted fool had taken pity on him and brought him home. Even at that young age, from the size of his feet, Jeb had known that Boss would grow up to be a big dog and he'd been right. Boss's back came to Jeb's knee, and he was close to seventy-five pounds. Dawg was smaller, her head barely reached Jeb's knee, and like Boss she'd been a stray. She'd just shown up one day about four years ago, a spotted curly-haired puppy not weaned for very long, starving and dehydrated. She'd been lying in the shade next to Boss's kennel and had met Jeb with a shyly wagging tail when he'd come home from a particularly bad day—a murder/suicide on the coast, father, mother, and six-month-old baby. He'd taken one look at the flea-bitten, mangy little lump of skin and bones and some of the anger and pain of the day ebbed. It had been, Jeb informed her frequently, Dawg's lucky day. Neither dog would ever be called beautiful, neither having picked up the best genes from their respective parents—whatever they may have been—but they suited Jeb just fine.

The familiar weight of Dawg's head on his chest comforted him, as did the warmth radiating from Boss. Absently he scratched Dawg's floppy ears, trying not to think about Roxanne, sex, or the prospect of parenthood. It was difficult. Just about the time his thoughts would be drifting in another direction, like steel to a magnet, they would switch right back to Roxanne and this morning's events.

Finally he gave up trying not to think about it and attempted to consider the situation realistically. After chasing various scenarios around in his mind for the better part of two hours, he concluded that if, and it was a big if, Roxanne did become pregnant, he would support her in whatever decision she made about the baby. He would support her, emotionally, financially, morally, whatever—with no strings. His mouth twisted. That would be the hard part—no strings. And in the meantime, if fate was kind, the question would become moot and he could get his life back on track. He'd have to talk to her, though, at least discuss the possibility of a baby, so she'd know that he'd be there for her if needed.

It was several hours later before Roxanne was alone and able to think about what had transpired on her kitchen countertop that morning. Unlike Jeb, she'd realized almost immediately that they'd indulged in unprotected sex and that had horrified her as much as the fact they'd had sex at all. She had *never* acted in such an irresponsible manner. And it didn't matter that Jeb was probably healthy, it mattered that she hadn't taken the time to find out. But as for a child, she wasn't worried—her period was due any day now and it was unlikely that she'd be in a state to conceive.

Sitting out on her deck that evening, the bowl and plate that had held her dinner at her feet, the thought of a child did cross her mind again, but she brushed it aside. Wrong time of the month. Sipping on a bottle of water, she stared down at the valley, a few lights coming on as darkness fell. Her gaze was drawn to the twinkling lights on the place on the mountain across from her and she smiled. Her neighbor across the way.

She lifted her bottle in a toast. "Dear neighbor," she said softly, "I hope, I really do hope, that your day was less stressful than mine. And makes more sense to you than mine to me."

She shook her head at her silliness and took another drink. Tindale had stayed until almost dark, both of them checking and double-checking the plans for any last-minute changes. Since she was financing the place herself, they didn't have to have any minor changes approved by a lending institution. Beyond discussing the possibility of slate terraces at the back of the house, instead of wood decking, she and Tindale were satisfied with the plan.

"Big day on Monday," he'd said as he'd turned to get into his car.

Roxanne had let out a happy sigh. "Yes, it is. I can't wait. It's like Christmas and birthday and every daydream you ever had rolled into one."

Sam laughed. "Hold on to that thought—once we start tearing the place apart and construction starts—and all the unexpected troubles and holdups that come with it, you may be singing a different tune."

She shook her head. "Nope. I'll just find somewhere quiet and tell myself it'll all be worth it."

"Good plan." He'd slid into his car and pulling away called out the window, "Have a nice weekend. See you Monday."

Alone finally, Roxanne had turned and walked slowly to the A-frame. She'd fixed herself a can of tomato soup and a fried egg sandwich for dinner, concentrating fiercely on the simple tasks to keep her thoughts from dwelling on Jeb Delaney and what they had done together this morning. As she walked out of the kitchen on her way to the deck, her gaze skittered across the countertop and she stopped and stared at its scratched surface, still unable to believe that she'd actually had sex on it . . . with Jeb Delaney. She even managed to keep thoughts of him at bay while she ate outside, but once the food was demolished. . . .

She took another sip of water. She couldn't believe what had happened between them. They'd been like animals. Coupling like minks, she thought with a sour smile. And unprotected. Stupid on both their parts. She bit her lip. She'd have to tell him that he had nothing to worry about catching something from her and find out if she had anything to be concerned over. She grimaced, imagining the expression on his face. Oh, man, she really didn't want to have that sort of conversation with him—with anyone, for that matter, but with him in particular. She touched the cold bottle to her forehead. What had gotten into her? Into them?

One thing was for damn sure—she hadn't come home to start a torrid affair—with anyone. She had no intention of getting herself entangled in a complicated situation with the opposite sex. She wanted to concentrate on her house, her new life; there were many things that she wanted and men were presently at the bottom of the list. And that it had been *Jeb* who'd rocked her socks left her floored.

On one level she'd always been aware that Jeb was an attractive man. OK, very attractive. Very virile. And maybe, before the incident with the marijuana joint, she'd had a few daydreams about him. She made a face. Which put her in league with most of the women in the valley. Maybe that was it, she thought slowly. Maybe because so many females fell all over him, coupled with her chagrin and humiliation over the way he'd treated her involving the marijuana joint, she'd been determined that *she* wasn't going to worship at his feet. Of course, she hadn't been about to forgive him for embarrassing her the way he had and to prove that he hadn't cowed her, that she wasn't the least impressed by him, she'd started sniping at him, letting him know that she didn't think he was so cool and handsome. That he was dirt beneath her feet. All the others could run after him, but not her. Not Roxanne Ballinger.

Her gaze narrowed. Naturally, he hadn't helped

matters, she reminded herself. Calling her "Princess" and looking down that bold nose of his at her like he'd just stepped in a pile of cat shit. He'd always been a bit of a pig with her; the marijuana joint incident had been neither the first nor the last time they'd locked horns with each other. It stuck out the most in her mind, but she could remember other times when he'd ream her out for little infractions, while the other kids just got a smile and friendly warning. Yeah. He'd always picked on her, gone out of his way to be annoying and insult-ing—no wonder she didn't like him. And once she'd become famous and there'd been all those ridiculous stories about her love life . . . The disapproving look he'd get on that handsome face of his whenever their paths crossed had made her want to smack him! You'd think she was a modern-day Jezebel, seducing men left and right and leaving ruined lives and devastated families in her wake. Who the hell was Jeb Delaney to sit in judgment on her?

By the time Roxanne went to bed that night, she was certain she had her head firmly on her shoulders when it came to Jeb Delaney. Lying in her twin bed she stared at the ceiling reminding herself again what a jerk he was . . . But thinking he was an arrogant pain in the ass still didn't explain what had happened this morning on that kitchen countertop. She frowned. Had to be PMS, she finally decided. That worked. Sure. Her period was due and she was a bundle of hor-mones—they'd all ganged up on her and she'd gone sexually nuts. OK. That sounded good. And maybe,

maybe, she thought sleepily, because of all that hormone activity her body had put out an odor that had driven Jeb sexually nuts, too. She nodded and half smiled in the darkness. Yeah. That worked. PMS explained it all. And she'd make damn certain that she was never alone again with Jeb Delaney when her period was due!

Having solved the puzzle to her satisfaction, Roxanne slept deeply and dreamlessly. She was up early Saturday morning and discovered that she'd been right about her period. It had arrived—along with a severe case of cramps. Feeling sorry for herself, and wishing that men had to suffer through the same misery every month, she dragged around the cabin packing up the few things she'd brought with her. As she packed and double-checked the cabin to make certain she hadn't forgotten anything, she marveled again at all the damage the vandals had done.

When she'd first seen the place, the floors had been torn up, windows smashed, cupboards ransacked, holes punched into the walls—it had looked like a cyclone had gone through the place. And if Danny Haskell, one of the resident deputies, was to be believed, the trespassers had come back more than once, doing more damage each time. In a way it didn't matter because very little of the original structure would remain untouched, but the sight of the holes in the walls and the half-ripped-out insulation made her shake her head. All throughout the cabin, upstairs and down, there was the same sort of damage. She hadn't bothered to fix any walls because of the new construction, but she had patched the holes in the floor by nailing down some pieces of plywood—the idea of a snake or a skunk coming up from under the cabin to visit during the night gave her the willies.

After she emptied out the few fresh things from the refrigerator and packed them in a cooler, she loaded everything up in her Jeep. It didn't take long, although she was swearing and sweating by the time she dismantled the bed and had jammed most of it into the back of the Jeep—a few feet of sideboard hanging out the window. The box spring and mattress she wrestled onto the roof of her Jeep and tied it down. She grinned. The Jeep looked like something from the depression era with the mattress on top, the lamp and nightstand perched precariously on the passenger seat, and her suitcases resting haphazardly on the bed rails in the backseat. She shook her head. If her fancy New York friends could see her now.

The Jeep finally packed, she took another walk around the A-frame. The new refrigerator would be moved to the old garage for the time being and just about everything else inside the cabin junked. It made her a little sad, thinking of Dirk Aston, the man who had built the cabin. It was going to be changed all out of recognition and very little of his handiwork would remain.

Telling herself not to get maudlin, she turned her back on the cabin and strolled to the greenhouses. They had suffered some damage from the vandals, too, almost like an afterthought, but it had been minor stuff. They'd torn loose some of the planting trays and benches, knocked some counters over, but hadn't done any serious damage. It hadn't taken long to clean up.

She studied the greenhouses for several minutes. What in the world was she going to do with them? She could have them dismantled, but she resisted that idea. She'd always had a green thumb, although living in New York hadn't given her much chance to use it or prove it, and she decided that maybe, when things settled down, she'd see just how green that thumb of hers was. Maybe start a flower business. Hmm, she'd think about that.

Preoccupied, she walked toward the Jeep. She had just opened the door when she heard the sound of an approaching vehicle. Her heart did a funny little jig at the sight of an increasingly familiar big red truck coming around the turn. Jeb Delaney. Oh, great. Absolutely the last person she wanted to see.

An unfriendly expression on her face, all of her defenses up, she waited for him to get out of the truck, one foot tapping impatiently on the gravel.

Jeb wasn't thrilled to be here either if the look on his face was anything to go by. He'd put off coming out here this morning as long as he could, and he'd been halfway hoping that Roxanne wouldn't be at home. No such luck.

He'd brought Boss and Dawg with him and well-mannered dogs that they were, the moment he opened the cab door, both of them scrambled right over and leaped down to the ground. Smothering a curse, in his sternest voice, Jeb ordered them back into the truck. They both looked at him, wagged their tails, and then trotted over to check out Roxanne.

The frustrated expression on his face made her smile, that and the friendly greeting from the two dogs. Boss checked her out thoroughly before giving her a careless lick on her hand, while Dawg sat at her feet and wiggled all over, one black paw resting on her knee, indicating that a pat on the head would be greatly appreciated. Bending over, Roxanne did just that and got a slobbery kiss on the face for her efforts.

Laughing up at Jeb, she said, "Police dogs, are they?"

Something tightened in his chest when she glanced up at him. She wore no makeup this morning and her skin was glowing, her hair waving around her shoulders. She was very, very appealing, he thought uneasily, in blue jeans and red gingham shirt as she laughed at him and ruffled Dawg's ears. Her eyes were dancing and that fabulous mouth of hers . . . . Jeb swallowed. She looked good. Too good. And he was a damned fool. This was Roxanne, remember? The infamous, half-naked model who posed so provocatively in countless magazines. Darling of the jet set. Used to living the good life—changing her men like she changed her sheets. The topic of every tabloid in the nation. His mouth tightened. How could he forget? Or that he was just some country yahoo, a two-time loser, who thought pizza-to-go was living high. He scowled, disgusted with himself.

Aware of his gaze and feeling shy, she buried her head in Dawg's fur and asked lightly, "So, are they police dogs or not?"

Jerked back to the present, and glad to be, Jeb shook his head. "Nope, not these two. What they are is a pair of ungrateful mugs who think their mission in life is to eat me out of house and home."

She asked their names and for a few minutes they talked about the dogs, watching the pair of them as they raced around to sniff and dig at various spots that appealed to them.

"I always wanted a dog," Roxanne admitted, "but living in New York and all the traveling I did didn't make it possible."

"Well, I wasn't looking to be a dog owner when these two showed up. I don't know, for some reason— I just couldn't turn them away." That sculpted jaw of his hardened. "If I hadn't taken them, I knew that they'd starve or get killed or end up in the pound and be put down."

Roxanne glanced at him, liking this side of him. She'd never figured him for a soft touch, but to have adopted two such unlikely creatures as Boss and Dawg showed that he might be human after all. OK, *almost* human, reminding herself that it was in her best interests to keep thinking of Jeb Delaney as a big jerk. Much, much safer.

Nodding toward the stuffed Jeep, he asked, "Moving?"

"Yes. You know construction is going to start on Monday. It wouldn't be practical for me to try to live in the place with all the work that is going to be going on."

"Practical," Jeb murmured, "now that's a word I wouldn't normally associate with you."

His words stung and her eyes narrowed. "I know that we decided to be 'not friends' yesterday, but don't tell me you drove all the way out here just to insult me."

He held up his hands. "Hey, I'm actually here on a friendly mission."

"Oh, really?"

"Yes, I am." He took off his black Stetson and ran a hand through his hair. He hadn't slept much last night, thinking about yesterday and all they hadn't discussed—diseases, babies . . . He'd woken up determined to speak with her, but he wasn't enthusiastic about it. In fact, he'd rather leap from a plane into a forest fire than talk about it. Still he had to do the right thing. He took a deep breath.

"About yesterday . . ."

"I thought we decided that yesterday didn't happen," she said sharply, her eyes fixed somewhere over his shoulder, embarrassment and shame roiling through her.

His mouth tightened. "I know. But there's a few

things that we do need to talk about before we forget about it."

She glanced at him, her expression wary. "Like what?"

Bluntly he said, "Diseases and babies."

Startled, she looked at him. "Oh," she said, feeling embarrassed for different reasons. "You're right," she admitted, "we should talk about those things." She hesitated, not comfortable with blurting out to him that her period had just started. Mortified by the entire situation, especially yesterday's madness, her cheeks burning, she muttered, "About babies—you have nothing to worry about—I won't get pregnant. And as for the other"—her chin lifted and there was a challenging glitter in those lovely eyes— "I'm not as promiscuous as you'd like to believe. You don't have to worry about catching anything from me."

"Good. Good," he replied awkwardly, wishing he were ten thousand miles away. As she gazed at him expectantly, one slim brow arched, he added, "Uh, um, and you don't need to worry about anything from me."

"Well, good," she said briskly. "Since that's out of the way, can we forget about yesterday now?"

"Sure, sure, whatever you want."

The sound of a vehicle grinding up the hill made them both look in that direction. The dogs heard the sound too and enthusiastically began to bark, running

over to the blue pickup as it pulled up next to Roxanne's Jeep.

Jeb had recognized the truck immediately and he
growled, "What the hell is he doing here?"

Her spine stiffened. "Since when is it any of your
business?"

Oblivious to the man staring down at the leaping
dogs, Jeb grabbed her arm. "Listen, Milo Scott is no
good—he's not someone you should be hanging
around with."

She glared at him and said, "I've known Milo since
we were in school together. I know he's supposed to be
a bad boy, but trust me, he's a cupcake compared to
some men I've met."

"Oh, yeah, I forgot," he drawled, her words reminding him again of how different their lives were,
"you would know all about bad boys, wouldn't
you?"

It was amazing, she thought with a pang, how easily they slipped into their old confrontational mode.
She smiled icily. "Indeed, I would—after all, the
tabloids are always right, aren't they?"

"How the hell would I know?" he snapped, furious
and not knowing why. "I don't read the damn things."

"Oh, no. Then how come you know so much about
all the bad boys in my life?"

He stifled the urge to shake her. "OK, I was out of
line. But not about Scott. You may have known him in
high school, but that was a long time ago. He runs with
a nasty crew these days."

"So what? And if you're talking about dope—forget about it—he was selling it back then." Flippantly she added, "I even used to buy some from him."

His grip on her arm tightened. "I don't give a damn what you did back then, this is now and I'm telling you that Scott is someone you should avoid. Tell him to get lost."

She jerked her arm out of his grasp. "And who," she grated, "gave you the right to decide who I see and who I don't see?"

He'd gone about this all wrong, he could see that now. If he'd kept his mouth shut, even acted friendly to Scott, Roxanne probably would have sent him on his way. But no, what did he do? He told her, almost ordered her, to have nothing to do with the guy. He scowled. A surefire method to have her greeting the creep with open arms. Damn! He was dumb sometimes.

And sure enough, when Milo Scott finally decided that the dogs were greeting him and not thinking about eating him and risked getting out of the truck, what did Roxanne do? After throwing him a challenging look, she turned on her heels and just walked right up to Milo, gave him a big hug, a kiss on the cheek, and exclaimed, "Milo! It's great to see you."

Disgusted with himself, Jeb whistled to the dogs. To his astonishment, for once they obeyed. Loading them into his truck, he climbed in behind them. Rolling down the window, he said, "Guess I'll be on my way."

"You do that," Roxanne murmured, her eyes glittering. "Milo and I have tons to catch up on." She smiled warmly at Milo. "Don't we?"

Milo put an arm around her shoulder. "Sure do," he said with a smirk in Jeb's direction. "Roxy and me will be seeing a lot of each other."

"Is that so?" Jeb asked in a dry tone.

"Yeah," Milo drawled. "I'm the cement contractor on the house." He grinned at Roxanne. "We'll be spending lots of time together out here."

Chapter
6

Jeb's truck was hardly out of sight before Roxanne slapped Milo's arm off her shoulder. "Knock it off," she said irritably. "We're not *that* good of friends."

Milo cocked a sandy-colored brow. "Hey, you were the one that came over all friendly-like."

"My mistake." She flashed him a hard look. "Despite what just happened, don't get any ideas—anything between us is strictly business."

"No problem." He nodded in the direction Jeb's truck had disappeared. "So what is it with you and macho-man."

"None of your business."

"Hey, I only asked."

"Well, don't ask anymore." She frowned. "What are you doing out here anyway?"

It wasn't that she didn't trust Milo Scott exactly . . . Despite her act in front of Jeb, she didn't care for Milo all that much. Never had. Not even in high school. There had always been something furtive, creepy about him and the years hadn't changed that aspect of him, she thought as she studied him. He was considered an attractive man with even features and a head full of wavy sandy-blond hair, but she'd never found him particularly appealing. Something about those flat dark blue eyes and his thin-lipped mouth gave her the whim-whams. Almost six feet and slimly built, he still exuded a wiry strength that she remembered from high school. Milo had been two years ahead of her and as a giggly freshman she had looked up to the school's star quarterback. In a small town like St. Galen's, Milo had been a very big fish, but even then there'd been rumors of dope-dealing and word among the kids had been that if you were looking for a score, go see Milo Scott. She hadn't smoked a toke in over a decade, and as for any other drug, she'd passed them by—she'd seen too many lives and careers ruined by drugs. And Jeb hadn't told her anything new—she'd come back to the valley enough times to know that Milo Scott was still selling dope and had expanded his, ah, area of expertise.

"So," she asked again when Milo remained silent, "what are you doing out here?"

He shrugged. "Just thought I'd take another look before Monday."

She frowned again. It would be several days yet before Milo's company could start pouring cement and she didn't really see the need for him to be out here today. If he wanted to waste his time, it didn't matter to her. "OK, I'll walk you through it."

He hesitated and she got the distinct impression that he'd rather have been alone. Her eyes narrowed. "Did you know Dirk Aston?" she asked abruptly.

If he was startled at the change of topic, he gave no sign. Just shrugged again and said, "Sure. Everybody knew Dirk." He nodded in the direction of the A-frame. "I helped him build the place." He smiled, showing very nice, very even white teeth, but Roxanne noticed that the smile didn't reach his eyes. "Dirk and I were good buds. We did some business together."

"Drug business?"

"Maybe." He glanced at her, those flat blue eyes watchful. "You working for the sheriff's office these days? Doing a little investigating for Jeb?"

Roxanne snorted. "Get real. I was just curious. You know St. Galen's—there are so many rumors going around, I just thought I'd get things clarified . . . from someone who might know the true story."

Milo looked off. "Well, about half the stories are true. Dirk did grow a little pot up here, but he wasn't one of the big growers. He grew a little for himself and sold a little to buy himself a few, er, necessities of life." He shook his head. "Sure was a shame him getting offed like that in Oakland. But that was poor stupid Dirk—too damn dumb to know he should have stayed in Oak Valley and kept his nose clean."

The contempt in his voice was obvious and his comment about Dirk keeping his nose clean made her wonder if he knew more about Dirk's death than he was letting on. She considered pumping him some more, but something about his expression told her he'd said all he was going to say on the subject.

"So you're a cement contractor these days," she said by way of changing the topic.

He grinned. "Yep. Sure am. Do lots of work all over the county. Got myself a couple of different businesses. You know, keep the cash flowing."

And how much of that cash, Roxanne wondered, was actually generated by those companies. Again it wasn't a subject she was going to pursue. None of her business.

"Well, good for you," she said. "It's always nice to see someone become successful."

"Hey, babe. I'm successful, but nothing like you— you're *Roxanne*."

She wrinkled her nose. "I *was* Roxanne. Those days are over. I'm home to stay. I may still do a few special jobs just to keep my hand in, but as of the first of September, I'm retired."

His jaw dropped. "You're shitting me, right? You've giving up all that fame and money to come back to St. Galen's? Are you nuts?"

Laughing, she linked her arm in his and said, "No, I think for the first time in a long time, I'm thinking straight. Now come on—I've got a copy of the plans in the Jeep. Let me grab them and then we can do that inspection of yours."

Once she had unearthed the architectural drawings, side by side they walked around the house, Roxanne pointing out the changes that would take place. For someone whose sole purpose for coming out was to inspect the place, Milo didn't seem to be all that interested. She knew he'd already seen and studied the plans—after all, he'd made a bid on the job, and won it for that matter, but his disinterest bothered her. While she was talking, she noticed that his gaze drifted away in the direction of the outbuildings, the garage, the dilapidated pump house, and the falling-down woodshed.

Again she considered calling him on it, but figured he'd just give her some song-and-dance, so she let it go. But he was wasting her time and rolling up the drawings, she said, "I think that's it, don't you?"

"Yeah. Sure." He glanced at her. "Don Bean's doing the tractor work, isn't he? Leveling and digging the foundation?"

She nodded. "Yes, he is. He starts bright and early Monday morning. It'll probably be at least a week or two before your part of the job will start."

"That's OK. My crew will be ready." He took in another encompassing gaze around. "Well, guess I'll be on my way. Nice seeing you again."

Roxanne watched him drive away with a frown between her brows. What, she wondered as she slid behind the wheel of the Jeep, was that all about? He'd barely looked at the house site and he'd agreed way too quickly when she'd called it quits. She bit her lip. If she knew Milo, and she rather thought she did, she'd lay odds he was just waiting for her to leave and then he'd come back and check out what was really on his mind. She'd always considered him a slippery bastard.

It bothered her, the possibility of his sneaking around the place, but there was nothing she could do about it, unless she was going to stay in the cabin twenty-four hours a day. She shook her head. Nope. She wasn't that interested in the games that Milo Scott played. She took one last look at the A-frame and then turned on the ignition.

The Ballinger family mansion was located off Adobe Lane in the middle of the valley. Driving down the mile-long driveway lined with wide-spreading century old oak trees, she could imagine for just a minute that she was in Louisiana. Gray-green moss even hung from the heavy limbs of the trees, but it wasn't as luxurious or ghostly as found in the South. The sight of the three-storied house with its ten magnificent Doric columns marching across the front and the pair of circular freestanding staircases always made Roxanne's heart leap. Today was no different. It didn't matter that she'd grown up in the house, didn't matter that she was as familiar with it as one could be, it still gave her a thrill to see it.

Wide, shady verandas on the first and second stories surrounded the house on all sides and its style was such that it would have looked perfectly at home perched along a grand vista overlooking the Mississippi River. York Ballinger, the first Ballinger in the valley, had commissioned the house to be built in the late 1860s. Roxanne had always wondered why York, a Yankee from Boston, who had fought for the Union during the Civil War, had chosen such an obviously southern-styled home. Maybe he'd fallen in love with the gracious southern mansions he'd helped sack and burn? She shook her head. Nah. Probably something to do with the feud with the Grangers. Probably thought it was the style of house old Jeb Granger would have built so York had wanted to beat him to it. She nodded. Yeah. That sounded like the Ballinger/Granger feud.

Bypassing the broad circular driveway in front of the house, she took the narrow offshoot that angled to the back. A minute later she was bounding up the wide steps to the screened-in veranda at the rear of the house.

Walking through the spacious wash/mud room, she entered the big country kitchen her mom had insisted upon remodeling about ten years ago. No one had blamed her—the last time it had been done had been sometime in the fifties or sixties and the whole family had been pretty sick of the gold and avocado color scheme—especially the avocado linoleum on the floor.

Roxanne automatically glanced toward the huge family room that opened off the kitchen—a favorite gathering place. It was a sunny, casually elegant room with an impressive rock-fronted fireplace in one corner. These days it sported a brass and bronze enameled fireplace insert and with the wide glass front, it was as cheery and inviting as a regular fireplace. The room was filled with windows and two pairs of French doors opened onto both the screened-in veranda at the rear, and the veranda on the south. Her mother, Helen, and younger sister, Ilka, were sitting there, her mom in a comfortable recliner done in a vibrant shade of striped wine-colored velvet and her sister on a pillow-backed couch covered in teal leather. They were both reading and looked up when the back door slammed shut.

"Oh, good, you're home," her mother said, smiling. "I didn't know whether to plan on you being here for dinner tonight or not."

At sixty-two years of age, Helen Ballinger was still a beautiful woman. Thanks to excellent genes, she easily looked a decade younger and even possibly younger than that—on a good day, her children teased her. It helped that her hair had been a lovely ash blond in her youth and had just grown lighter as she had aged until it was a gorgeous shade of champagne blond. Roxanne had never seen her wear it in any other style than the one she currently wore, a short bouncy pageboy. As always, she looked elegant, even in blue jeans and a sapphire-blue shirt that deepened the hue of her stunning silvery-blue eyes.

Ilka looked like her mother's twin. She had the same ash-fair hair and cool blue eyes. Unlike Ilka, Roxanne, Sloan, and the others took after the Ballinger side of the family, having inherited from their father tall, lean bodies, black hair, and amber-gold eyes. Like her mother whom she so resembled, Ilka was small, delicate, and ethereal, and most people unfamiliar with the family couldn't believe Ilka was related to the others . . . until they met Helen. There were almost five years between Roxanne and Ilka and they had never been particularly close. Roxanne had left home just as Ilka was entering her teens and while they had some fond childhood memories of each other, they weren't exactly easy with one another as adults. Their lives, so far, had been very different and it had always been difficult to find common ground. Roxanne was hoping that now that she would be living in Oak Valley she could get to know all of her siblings better, including Ilka. Ilka would turn thirty-three in October, and Roxanne figured if they were ever going to forge some bonds, it would be now, since age wasn't an issue anymore—they were all adults. She hoped. Sometimes she worried about herself and if her actions lately were anything to go by, she had reason to be worried.

Flopping down in a matching chair to her mother's, Roxanne said, "Yep, I'm home." She laughed ruefully. "Something I find hard to believe."

"Why?" asked Ilka, looking up from the book she'd been reading. "You've been home before—several times."

Roxanne shrugged. "Yeah, I know, it's just that this time is different, I'm home for good. And if you'd asked where I would spend the rest of my life, even two years ago, I'd have sworn it would be anyplace *but* Oak Valley."

"Oak Valley's not so bad," Ilka said defensively. "There're a lot of people, even wealthy sophisticated people, who wouldn't live anywhere else. They adore the valley—even its isolation and remoteness. Not *everybody* considers it the back of beyond, you know."

"Hey, I'm not arguing with you, I wouldn't be here if I didn't love the place, too, I'm just saying that life's funny, the twists and turns it takes."

Ilka's face closed down. "Yes, it is," she said flatly, her eyes dropping to her book.

Oh, damn, Roxanne thought, I've put my foot in it again. She sighed and glancing across at her mother made a face. Her mother looked sympathetic and shrugged.

The thing about Ilka, Roxanne reflected, was that it was so difficult to remember that at one time, Ilka had been the real rebel in the family—with tragic and disastrous results. It wasn't that Roxanne didn't think that what had happened to Ilka was a terrible, horrible tragedy, it was just that it *had* happened over a decade ago, almost fourteen years ago, and Ilka acted, sometimes, like it had just happened a year ago. Losing your children, your babies, wasn't something a person would ever forget, she didn't blame Ilka for mourning their loss, but she thought that it was time Ilka quit punishing the rest of them for innocent remarks. Besides, if Ilka had followed the advice everyone had given her and listened to the pleas of her parents and had left the son of a bitch the first time he'd raised a hand to her, there would have been no tragedy. Better yet, Roxanne thought grimly, never married the bastard, then none of it would have happened. But then, who was she to make judgments, she thought glumly,

God knew her life hadn't always been something to brag about. But still, Ilka should never have married Delmer Chavez. Her mouth tightened. Never. Ilka's husband, his whole family in fact, had been known for ugly tempers, heavy drinking, and drug use—they were considered shiftless layabouts by most residents of the valley and were prone to stealing for a living rather than working. But had Ilka listened to her worried, frantic parents? Her friends? Nope. She had horrified everyone by running away with Delmer and marrying him on her eighteenth birthday in Reno, Nevada.

It wasn't enough, Roxanne reflected sourly, that Delmer had brutalized Ilka during two years of marriage, but when she had gathered her tattered courage to tell him she was leaving him, he'd extracted a horrifying revenge. On that terrible October night, high on drugs, at gunpoint, he'd loaded the little family into his truck and roared down the twisting Oak Valley road. Despite Ilka's tears and pleas, ten terrifying miles later, he had plunged over the road and plowed into a tree. Ilka, though badly injured, had been the only survivor; killed in the crash had been her three-month-old daughter and fourteen-month-old son. Just twenty years old, she had lost her husband and her two infants.

The community had been horrified and torn between fury at Delmer and grief at the terrible, senseless loss of the two innocent lives. As the lone survivor Ilka became the focal point of the valley's emotions and attention; even strangers approached her to express their sorrow at the tragedy that had overtaken her. Hardly anyone mentioned Delmer and only his family and friends grieved over his death.

It wasn't, Roxanne admitted, as she shot Ilka a considering look from beneath her lashes, that she didn't feel wretched about what had happened—her heart still ached for her sister, but she wished that Ilka would snap out of it and stop being so sensitive and prickly. Of course, part of the problem was that they all tended to pretend it hadn't happened, all of them trying to ignore the fact that Ilka had been married to a creep who had beat her and kept her pregnant. Roxanne grimaced. She could be compassionate forever about the babies, Bram and tiny Ruby, but she found it hard to be sympathetic about the choice Ilka had made to marry a guy from one of the worst families in the valley—a family known for violence and drugs. Jesus! Delmer Chavez. What had Ilka been thinking of? Then she sighed. There she went again, judging—and who was she to talk after what had happened between her and Jeb Delaney? She scowled. Hormones, she decided, could be blamed for a lot of ills in the world.

As if becoming conscious of Roxanne's stare, Ilka looked up. "What?" she asked.

"Uh, nothing," Roxanne answered. "Just thinking."

"I know what you're thinking," Ilka snapped. "You're thinking, 'Oh, poor Ilka. She's being *sensitive* again.' I'm right, aren't I?"

Roxanne scratched her chin, trying to decide

whether to be honest or avoid a confrontation. If she and Ilka were ever going to find common ground the first thing they had to do was to stop pussyfooting around each other. "Yeah, you're right. I was."

Ilka stood up. "Well, thank you very much. You try losing everything you love and see how you cope with it."

Her chin set, shoulders stiff, Ilka stalked from the room.

Feeling like a heel, Roxanne looked at her mother and muttered, "I was only being honest."

Helen sighed. "Don't worry about it, honey—and I think you did the right thing. It's not your fault she's so touchy." She looked unhappy. "It's this time of year. Most of the time, she deals pretty well with life, but as October approaches. . . ."

Roxanne was stricken. "Oh, Jesus! I forgot. It's only a couple weeks until. . . ." She swallowed. "Me and my big mouth." She bounded to her feet. "Listen, I'm going to go talk to her. Try to smooth things over."

"Be careful and don't feel bad if she rebuffs your overtures. Mostly she'll just brood in her room for a few hours and then come out and act as if nothing happened." Helen made a face. "And your father and I go along with it—we know we shouldn't, but there are times that it just seems simpler than calling her to account."

The back door slammed and they both looked in that direction. A big, burly man sauntered through the kitchen and seeing Helen and Roxanne in the family room, halted in his tracks, grinned, and clutched his heart. "Man, I don't know if I can take the sight of so much beauty under my own roof," Mark Ballinger said. "And how is my favorite wife and favorite famous daughter."

Both Roxanne and Helen rolled their eyes.

"Since Mom's your only wife, and at present I'm your only famous daughter, that compliment doesn't hold the punch it could," Roxanne murmured, her eyes dancing.

After walking into the family room and dropping a kiss on his wife's cheek, he straightened up and said, "Well, there is that. I keep forgetting. Age you know. Old-timer's disease, I can feel it coming on."

What a hoot, Roxanne thought, Dad still had a mind like a steel trap and you only needed to try to pull a fast one on him to discover it. Though he had just turned sixty-five, Roxanne still considered him one of the handsomest men she had ever known. Tall, like most of the Ballingers, he was a brawny man, his shoulders wide, his chest deep, and his arms strong as an oak limb—a large oak limb. How well did she remember giggling and screaming with laughter as he had swung her up into those powerful arms when she'd been a child and how gently those arms had comforted her when she'd awakened from a nightmare. He'd been, she realized, a great dad. Tough exterior, marshmallow inside—after coolly pulling out her first tooth, at her insistence, he'd cried right along with her when she discovered that it hurt.

Mark Ballinger was not traditionally handsome, his face too craggy, his jaw and chin stubborn, and his mouth too wide, and yet the only word that really applied was "handsome." His sun-bronzed face reflected years of being outdoors, several little creases radiating out from the corners of his dazzling amber-gold eyes, and there were pronounced laugh lines near his mouth. The still-thick black hair now sported several strands of silver in their depths, his temples almost totally silver, but Roxanne thought that age had only added to his attractiveness.

"Old-timer's disease? Who are you trying to kid?" Roxanne asked.

"Obviously not you," he replied. Sitting down on the couch that Ilka had just vacated, he stretched his booted feet out in front of him. Sending Roxanne a sleepy look he murmured, "You know it'd be just about perfect if someone would bring me a tall icy glass filled with some of that Ruby tangerine juice your mom keeps in the refrigerator."

Chuckling, Roxanne turned to do just that, calling over her shoulder, "Do you want some, Mom?"

"Yes, I would."

Roxanne fixed her parents their drinks and after handing them tall blue glasses, she said, "Guess I better go take care of things."

"What things?" asked Mark.

Helen sighed. "Ilka. She took offense at something Roxanne said in all innocence. You know how she gets."

Mark looked down at his drink. "Yes," he said in a soft voice, "I know." He glanced over at his wife. "And you know what? Even though it'll be fourteen years, I'd still like to wipe up the ground with that son of a bitch."

"Me too," said Roxanne, her hands unconsciously clenching into fists. Then she relaxed and added, "But right now, I think I'd better go make peace with Ilka."

Her dad nodded and she left, heading in the direction Ilka had taken.

All of the bedrooms were situated on the second floor and Roxanne quickly made her way up the handsome sweeping staircase that led to the upper floor. The stairs ended in the middle of a wide hallway lined with a carved mahogany railing that overlooked the spacious entry hall below. Decades before, the second story had been extensively remodeled and where once the house had boasted over a dozen bedrooms, dressing rooms, some with sitting rooms, the upper floor now only held six bedrooms, all of them with large walk-in closets, sitting rooms, and private baths.

There had been no room sharing for the Ballinger kids, they'd each lorded over their own little kingdoms and Roxanne remembered fondly slumber parties with her friends. Loaded down with goodies from the well-stocked refrigerator and cupboards, eight or ten teenage girls had scampered upstairs and into her rooms, locking the door behind them to spend the night giggling and talking about school, boys, clothes, boys and boys.

As the children had grown and left home, the rooms became guest rooms; Mark had taken Sloan's old rooms and turned them into a neat little gym, even installing a sauna. The others had been updated with carpets, wallpaper, and paint but when she came to visit, Roxanne used what had been her old room. Of course, Ilka still occupied the set of rooms she had always had—except for her brief marriage.

Stopping before the door to Ilka's rooms, Roxanne took a deep breath. Be nice. Be compassionate, she told herself. Don't get impatient. This is your sister. The sister you want to be friends with.

Her knock was met with silence. She waited, then knocked again, harder. She was just preparing to give the door a third and more determined rap when it was flung open. Her expression sulky and unhappy, her face and eyes showing signs of tears, Ilka stood there.

"What do you want?" Ilka demanded, angrily wiping away a tear that streaked down her cheek.

She looked so small and woeful that Roxanne's heart melted. "Oh, honey, I just wanted to say that I was sorry. I didn't mean to be so unfeeling."

Ilka hiccuped back a sob. "Don't apologize," she said thickly. "I was being a bitch—as usual." She looked up at Roxanne and her beautiful eyes filled with tears. "I don't know what's wrong with me— other people cope, but I just can't seem. . . ." She wiped her nose. "I just need some time alone. I'll be OK."

"Probably," Roxanne said stoutly, "but this time

you don't have to be alone—big sis is here." And having said that, she put her arms around Ilka's slender shoulders and pulled her close.

Roxanne's touch unleashed a flood and Ilka sobbed into her shoulder as if her heart would break. Roxanne felt helpless, she wasn't good with dealing with this kind of wound. She patted Ilka's back and feeling useless muttered, "There, there, honey, don't cry."

To her amazement it seemed to help and a moment later Ilka stepped away, wiping her face with both hands. "Come on in—I don't want Mom or Dad to see me like this—it makes them feel terrible and they start blaming themselves."

Roxanne followed her across the room and joined her on the white, yellow, and black plaid sofa that had been placed near one of the windows that opened onto the upper veranda. The room was cozy, the walls painted a soft yellow, wooden shades adorned the windows, and a thick-piled rust-colored rug covered the floor; a pair of French doors led to the veranda.

Seated on the couch beside Ilka, Roxanne held her sister's hand and said, "I'd forgotten how close it is to the date that. . . ." The words froze in her mouth, the horror of what had happened roiling over her.

Ilka sniffed, wiped her nose again, and said, "I know. Everybody does and I don't blame them. I wish I could forget it too." Her eyes filled again and fighting back tears she choked out, "But if I did, it would mean forgetting my babies." Her voice hardened. "As for *him* . . . I pray every night that he burns in the deepest pit in hell."

Roxanne perked up. Dealing with tragedy wasn't her best suit, but cursing and trashing men . . . Oh, yeah. She could do that. "Especially his balls," she blurted. "Men hate anything happening to their balls."

Ilka's tears stopped. She looked at Roxanne, her eyes widening. "You know, I never thought of that. What an excellent idea! His balls. Burning in hell. For eternity."

They stared at each other. Then smiled and a moment later they were laughing.

"Oh, Roxy," Ilka exclaimed. "I *am* glad you're home. I wasn't sure how I'd feel about it, having you around all the time, but I think maybe I'm going to like it."

"Don't get carried away," Roxanne said. "It's going to be a lot of adjustment for all of us." She wrinkled her nose. "Really an adjustment for me—I'm used to being alone and on my own. It's going to be strange falling all over family all the time." She cast a glance at Ilka. "How do you stand it? I mean still living at home and. . . ." She made a face. "Put my foot in it again, didn't I?"

"Not really," Ilka said slowly. "It's an honest question. And I guess the answer is that I never considered doing anything else. A-a-after the . . . a-a-accident, when I first got out of the hospital there was no place else for me to go." Her voice grew bitter. "His family certainly wanted nothing to do with me. I still needed some nursing and Mom and Dad were right there. Once I got well. . . ." She hesitated. "Once I recovered it just seemed easier to stay right here."

Roxanne frowned. "Yeah, but, Ilka, that was almost fourteen years ago."

"I know, but it's not hurting anything is it? I mean Mom and Dad don't mind that I'm still living here." Earnestly, she added, "We have a lot of fun together. Did you know that we all went on a cruise this spring? We enjoy each other."

"Yes, but that's not my point. My point is that you need a life of your own."

Ilka seemed to freeze, to shrink inside herself. "I don't want a life of my own," she said in a small voice. "I had my own life once and look what happened." She sent Roxanne an anguished glance. "I couldn't bear it, Roxy, to go through that sort of pain again."

"What makes you think the same thing would happen? You're older now. Wiser. The odds of you hooking up with someone like Delmer again are astronomical."

Ilka frantically shook her head. "No. I couldn't risk it."

Roxanne let go of her hand and sat back. Thoughtfully she studied her sister. "Did you love Delmer that much?"

Ilka frowned. "What do you mean? I loved him, or thought I did, when we married, but in the end . . ." Her eyes grew icy and hard as steel. "In the end, I hated him more than I've ever hated anyone . . . or ever will."

"Then why are you letting him still rule your life?" Roxanne asked quietly. At Ilka's expression of outrage, she added, "You are, you know. As long as you remain hiding here at home with Mom and Dad, hiding from life, you're letting him win. You're letting what he did to you dictate your whole life."

Ilka opened her mouth. Shut it. Stared at her sister. "That's not true," she finally managed. "Not true at all."

"Isn't it?"

"What do you know about it?" Ilka demanded. "You've never even been married. You never had children . . ." her voice choked, "or buried them. Just what the hell do you know?"

Deciding it was time for a retreat, Roxanne rose to her feet. "You're right. I don't know what you experienced. But I'll tell you one thing, little sister: no man would ever keep me chained and imprisoned like Delmer has you. Every day, every hour, you hide out here is an hour, a day, that he's stolen from you." Ilka's hurt expression almost undid her, but keeping her voice firm, she added, "Are you going to let him steal your whole life?"

"You don't understand! It isn't like that!" Ilka said shrilly.

Roxanne shrugged and walked to the door. Her hand on the knob, she glanced back at her sister. "You can deny it all you want, but if you think about it, really think about it, you'll see that I'm right. Mourn your children, Ilka, but for God's sake, get a life of your own. Don't let Delmer take that away from you, too."

She shut the door on Ilka's protests and hurried to her own rooms, just down the hall. Slipping inside, she closed the door. Her head resting on the door, she stared blankly into space. Since when had she turned into such a know-it-all? Had she done the right thing? Should she have kept her mouth shut? What if she was wrong? What if she had made things worse instead of better?

All I was trying to do, she reminded herself unhappily, was be a sister. A wise, understanding sister. Who knew it would be so complicated?

Chapter
7

Despite a few setbacks, construction on Roxanne's house proceeded smoothly. Well, except for the break-ins and vandalism. She frowned. It was hard to figure out why the kids, and she and the sheriff's office were certain it was older teenagers, kept coming back and wreaking such destruction. What puzzled her was that there had been three more break-ins after she had moved back into her parents' home. Walls and flooring had been torn up and even the old cupboards and counter ripped out, but after the first two weeks of construction there had never been any more of those kinds of problems. She'd wondered if the deputy had been wrong about it being kids and that the perpetrators weren't members of the construction crews working on the place—there were several. But if she was honest, and Roxanne usually was, brutally, her suspicions focused on Milo Scott. She'd automatically dismissed Jeb's comments (what did *he* know, anyway?). Her own memories of Milo, however, and the scowl on her father's face when she mentioned that he was doing the foundation work on her house made her wonder if it had been wise to hire him, and more troubling, if he hadn't been behind the vandalism. The first day of construction, she had expressed her worries to Sam Tindale, keeping quiet about her suspicions on the break-ins, but he had vouched for Scott Construction.

"I know he has a reputation, but believe me," Sam had said earnestly, "I've used him on other jobs and he's been dependable and does fine work."

She'd decided that if Tindale trusted him, so could she . . . with cement. Once the work started, she had to admit that Milo and his men had been professional and that they'd done a great job. After watching him supervise his men for a few days it was obvious he knew a lot about cement. Then she thought about the ways he could have become such an expert, such as casting cement boots and burying bodies in cement, and decided that maybe it wasn't such a great thing that he was *so* good with cement.

As the days grew shorter and September drifted into October and October became November, Roxanne found herself watching the weather reports with rapt fascination. There had been a few showers, some wet days, no serious storms yet but she knew that sooner or later they'd receive a drenching that could be, and most likely would be, followed by days and days of rain.

The weather cooperated. By the end of November,

the entire shell of the house was up and closed-in and the new dark green metal roof was in place. Even the flagstone terraces in front and at the rear of the house and the mudroom walkway had been laid—mainly to keep from tracking the expected mud into the house.

The second week of December arrived and with it the first real storm of winter. The forecasters had predicted two or three days of rain, but Roxanne no longer cared. There was still much work to be done, but except for landscaping, and some other outside work, it was the interior of the house that took precedence over everything else these days. Spring would be soon enough to worry about the barn, new well house, and garage.

Driving up that Tuesday morning, as she pulled into the newly graveled parking area, she turned off the ignition and sat and stared through the gray light and rain at her house. From this vantage point it looked wonderful. The rising foothills to the west made solar panels on the front impractical and she was just as glad—if she squinted, and ignored the southern solar panels, the house had an ageless look. The stonework foundation and the mullioned windows coupled with the steep roof gave the place the impression of an Alpine chalet—just what she'd been aiming for. A charming flagstone walkway edged with gray, pale green, maroon, and white jagged rocks wandered its way to the wide terrace at the front of the house. A couple of irregular-shaped flowerbeds had been put in along either side of the walkway and a few evergreen bushes had been planted so the front didn't look raw and unfinished. That fall she had spent hours poring happily over bulb catalogs and then in early November stuffing the beds full of multicolored daffodils, hyacinths, and tulips. She could hardly wait until spring to see the fruits of her labor.

From here, the house looked as if it had been there forever and no one would ever guess that inside it was mostly an empty echoing shell with two-by-fours still showing in some of the rooms and the flooring just sheets of plywood. But it was taking shape. The electricians and plumbers would be through any day now; kitchen cabinets were scheduled to be hung at the end of the week, the tile countertops put in soon after that, and appliances would go in once the floor was laid.

Despite the rain, the thought of actually having a real kitchen within a few weeks had her grinning and skipping up to the front door, a big brown bag in her arms. She was early, it wasn't yet 7:30 A.M., but she couldn't seem to stay away from the place. Unlocking one of the new hefty wooden double doors, she walked inside, the heat from the fireplace insert she'd crammed full before leaving last night, still radiating some warmth. It was dark inside the house, but the scent of new lumber and paint wafted to her nose. She took in a deep breath. God, she even loved the smell of the place. Quickly crossing through the large entry hall, she walked to the far end of the great room, guided by the faint light seeping in from the two pairs of French doors at the rear and the arched windows above the doors. She poked around in the new brass and bronze fireplace insert and threw on an armful of wood, watching as the flames licked at the oak logs. The fireplace insert had been located in one corner of the great room and the area behind it, floor to ceiling, as well as the wide hearth upon which the insert sat, was faced with a carefully selected array of river rock. It was a stunning focal point and had turned out just as she had envisioned it.

Heat taken care of, humming to herself, she walked through her dining room, empty and hollow right now, to the back of the house and into the kitchen. There was a makeshift counter in the kitchen with room for a hotplate, a coffeepot, and nearby the refrigerator. A small generator gave her enough electricity to run a few things in this area and in a second she'd flipped it on and had a pot of coffee brewing. She unloaded the items from the brown bag, putting some in the refrigerator, the rest near the coffeemaker. As the scent of coffee mingled with the other odors, she took in another deep breath. Perfect! The best perfume in the world—fresh perked coffee and new lumber.

Some minutes later, her outer clothes hung up on hooks on the wall in the mudroom, only needing the flooring, plumbing, and wiring to be completed, mug of hot coffee in hand, she walked through the house, imagining how it would look once it was finished. She'd been amazed at how quickly the shell had gone up, and hadn't really believed her contractor, Theo Draper, when he'd warned her that when they started on the interior things wouldn't move so swiftly. She made a face. Darn. He'd been right, too. Who knew that it would take so long to put in wiring, plumbing, insulation, and sheet rock? And that didn't count the taping and texturing and painting and paneling and all the finishing touches such as light fixtures and kitchen and bathroom fixtures and last but not least rugs and floor coverings. Some days she thought that the house would *never* be completed.

Today wasn't one of those days—although it could turn out that way, if someone or something was delayed. Telling herself not to run down the road to meet trouble, she took her coffee and with a sense of anticipation walked toward the other end of the house.

Light drifted in feebly from the bank of arched windows and glass sliding doors that formed the wide hallway that led to her bedroom. She stopped to admire the mist-covered mountains across the valley, but the view didn't hold her attention for long. She hurried past the doors that led to the guest suite and halted before the door that opened onto her suite.

Roxanne pushed open the broad carved oak door and a sigh of pleasure escaped her. The rest of the house might still be under construction, but this part was complete.

It was a huge room, bedroom and sitting room all in one; the western wall broken by two doors. One door led to a handsome bathroom, the other to an impressive walk-in closet. Even on this gray, rainy day the room was full of light: floor-to-ceiling windows, broken only by a pair of French doors, faced the eastern mountains; luxurious drapes in wine-colored brocade framed the windows. Roxanne smiled. Now those were probably wasteful—she'd probably never pull them shut. A gleaming dark blue enamel wood stove was situated on the wall across from her; the hearth and back finished with large, pebbled rose-tinted tiles. The open-beamed oak ceiling soared overhead and contrasted nicely with the soft white she'd chosen for the walls. The flooring for this room had given her fits and in the end she'd decided to be practical, or as practical as she ever was, and had followed the contractor's suggestion of a new product for her oak parquet floor. It looked like wood, wore like wood, but was actually a type of linoleum. She shook her head as she studied the gleaming floor. Who would ever guess?

Because she'd wanted these rooms finished as soon as possible, and because she did not have conventional electricity, this area had its own generator and propane water heater. She flipped the switch that started the generator and a moment later the light switch. Brilliant light cascaded down from the track lighting along the walls and the two large brass and etched glass chandeliers overhead. She listened intently for a second, pleased to hear no drone from the generator. It had been enclosed in its own soundproof box so that when it was running, the noise wouldn't intrude. Glancing around at the lights and the sweet sound of silence, she smiled.

Walking past the stack of cardboard boxes and

rolled-up rug in the center of the room, she went into the bathroom and was thrilled when she turned on the hot water faucet and actually got hot water. She flushed the almond-colored toilet and watching the water swirl away she laughed at the pleasure it gave her. Who would have ever guessed she'd be delighted by a working toilet? Ah, the simple joys of living in the country. Spinning one of the crystal handles of the huge pale aqua, almond, and rose tiled walk-in shower she was equally delighted when water sprayed out from a half-dozen heads.

At the sound of an approaching vehicle she shut down the shower and left off her inspection. After switching off the lights and generator, she shut the door behind her and walked down the hall to the great room.

The front door opened and she heard the stamping of feet and smiled a second later when Theo Draper, her contractor, walked into the great room. He stopped, surprised to see her there, and then shook his head.

"I thought for sure, with the nasty weather, that I'd beat you here this morning," he said in his slow, soft-spoken way. He sniffed the air. "And coffee already done, too."

She grinned. She liked Theo. He was cagey about his age, but his thick thatch of white hair and sun-wrinkled face made it apparent that he was no spring chicken. The best estimate anyone came up with was that he was somewhere between sixty-five and eighty.

He was a small, quiet man, built like a piece of barbed wire, all tough, wiry strength, and indefatigable—as Roxanne knew to her cost. She'd observed him working men half his age into the ground and more than once he'd done the same to her. What she found amazing was that the next day she'd be dragging around, while Theo would be bright-eyed and bushy-tailed and ready to do it all over again. So far, she'd never seen him in a hurry; he worked at the same slow steady pace in the morning as he did at the end of the day. She'd been at the site just about every day since construction had begun and over the course of the months, she and Theo had become friends. She had been surprised to find out that Jan, his wife, dead these past five years, had been a valley girl, related to the McGuires, and that Theo was very familiar with Oak Valley. "We'd even planned to retire here," he'd told her once. His face had grown sad. "But then Jan died and I just didn't have the heart. Still own the property though, so who knows, maybe one day I'll get tired of living in Ukiah and build myself a house and move up here. I feel as at home in the valley as I do there. Jan's relatives are always after me to do just that."

Motioning toward the kitchen, she said, "There's a fresh pot waiting for you . . . and I even baked some cinnamon rolls last night after I left here."

His gray eyes gleamed. Heading in the direction of the kitchen, he said, "You know you've about got me spoiled for any other job. After working for you, I'll expect to be served snacks and coffee on a regular basis." He pursed his lips, but his eyes were dancing. "And my men will, too, that's the hard part."

"Life's tough," Roxanne said teasingly, following behind him. "You'll just have to endure."

Pouring himself a mug of coffee and selecting one of the rolls, he took a bite. Closed his eyes in bliss and chewed. Swallowing, he grinned at her and said, "Yes, ma'am, I think in my next contract, I'll have it written in that refreshment has to be served or I just can't do the job."

They could hear the sound of the rest of the crew arriving and a few minutes later the kitchen was filled with half a dozen men. And ten minutes after that, the plate of two dozen cinnamon rolls was empty and a second pot of coffee had been put on and they had all dispersed and Roxanne had disappeared into her bedroom.

She spent the morning happily unpacking the boxes and unrolling the rug. The boxes contained some clothes, towels, sheets, blankets, and items for the bathroom, and she tackled those things first. Stacking the empty boxes out in the hall, she turned to the rug. It was oriental in pattern, woven in shades of gold, ruby, and emerald against a sapphire-blue background. Flexing her toes in the thick, almost velvety weave, she glanced around the room, visualizing how it would look with furniture. The furniture for the bedroom was scheduled to arrive later in the week, but the mattress and box springs were *supposed* to be delivered this afternoon. She stared out at the rain and sighed. But that, she reminded herself, was before the storm. She grimaced. Another night at home wouldn't kill her. . . .

It wasn't that she didn't adore her parents and that she wasn't grateful for their unstinting hospitality, it was just that it had been a long time since she'd lived with anyone or had had to consider other people in her plans. Her parents didn't pry or intrude . . . very much . . . or make terrible demands on her, at least no more than was normal, it was just that sometimes she felt like a teenager again, making certain Mom and Dad knew where she was, who she was with, and when she'd be home. She realized it was only polite to give them some idea of her comings and goings, but after so many years of being answerable only to herself, it grated. She desperately wanted her own space. Having her own space again, being able to arrange her own life in her own way, had become an urgent priority. She adored her parents. She loved her parents. But she could hardly wait to get away from them. And Ilka. She sighed. She and Ilka were getting along— sort of.

It had been a bit bumpy after their conversation that night, but Helen had been right. After the anniversary of the tragedy, Ilka became less moody and touchy, but it bugged Roxanne that her sister still made no effort to get on with her life. It was beyond her comprehension, no matter how wonderful their parents were, that Ilka could actually be happy living at home. And, of course, she admitted wryly, *I just can't seem to keep my big mouth shut about it either.* She sighed. What business of mine is it anyway if Ilka wants to hide at home and become a crabby old spinster?

OK, she'd admit it wasn't any of her business, but it still bugged her. Ilka had so much to offer. She was smart. Funny. Warm. Loving. Roxanne's face softened. Ilka had been a great mom—when Bram had been born, she'd flown home to see her sister and the baby and she remembered vividly the expression on Ilka's face as she had looked down at her son. Maybe Ilka had dragged her feet when it had come to facing up to Delmer, but no one disputed that Ilka had adored her children and had tried to do her damnedest for them. It wasn't that Roxanne necessarily wanted Ilka to run out and marry and have more children, although she suspected that being a wife and mom was probably what suited Ilka best, she just wanted her sister to have a life again. To *do* something that was separate from their parents, even if it was nothing more than showing and raising yippy little schnauzers like Sam did. She grinned. Oh, and wouldn't her parents love that! They loved animals, dogs included, but Roxanne didn't think they'd be exactly thrilled to have a pack of always-looking-for-trouble schnauzers underfoot all the time. Her grin faded and a steely glint entered her fine eyes. Whether it was any of her business or not, somehow, she was going to shake Ilka out of her shell.

She brooded over Ilka as she moved about the room. She'd invited her to see the progress on the house several times, half hoping that seeing the house would spark some desire to have a home of her own.

It hadn't. She'd even torn herself away from the house and endured a couple of overnight trips to San Francisco, dragging a reluctant Ilka along with her. They'd spent the time shopping and wandering around downtown, finally eating lunch at the Japanese Tea Gardens, staying that time in Sausalito across the bay from the city. Roxanne had made plans with a couple of male models she liked and knew in the area and had invited them out for dinner. Ilka's date, Charles Blackman, had been utterly smitten. But had Ilka been the least bit flattered or interested in one of the most eligible bachelors, and nicest, that Roxanne knew? Nope. Ilka had been totally unfazed to be the object of interest of such a charming, stunningly handsome man. Poor Charley, Roxanne thought. He'd tried several times after that to see Ilka but her sister always said no. Politely. But no. The next time they'd stayed in San Francisco itself, at the Top of the Mark, browsed through the museum, and lunched at Fisherman's Wharf, then explored Pier 39 before dining in regal splendor in the hotel. Ilka went along, but didn't seem to care one way or another. Desperate, Roxanne had suggested they spend a weekend in the Napa Valley. Ilka dutifully accompanied her, but seemed happiest when they were heading home. It wasn't that Roxanne really thought any of those things would necessarily set Ilka on fire. She was just trying to find her way, trying to understand her sister, working at getting to know Ilka and trying to find a clue, a hint of something that interested her sister other than living quietly at home with their parents. She'd hoped that spending time together exploring all the little shops, that she would have discovered some topic, some activity, that would put a spark in Ilka's eyes. Nothing had. Ilka seemed perfectly content to live with Mommy and Daddy and arranged her life around theirs. It drove Roxanne nuts. Ilka had her stumped.

The rumblings of her stomach interrupted Roxanne's thoughts. Looking at her watch, she realized it was long past lunch, almost two o'clock. She took one more glance around the room and decided she'd done what she could for the present.

Shrugging into her jacket, she said to Theo, who was busy putting up the last of the sheet rock in the great room, "I'm gone for now. There's supposed to be a furniture delivery this afternoon. Tell them the mattress and box springs go in my room and the other stuff in the spare bedroom for now."

"Will do." He cocked a brow. "You still planning on staying out here tonight?"

"Yes. Mattress or not. If it doesn't arrive I'll sleep on the floor. Another night at home will probably drive me 'round the bend."

He chuckled. "You know what they say—you can't go home again."

She shook her head. "No. You can come home again—I'm proof of that. You just can't go home to your *parents* again."

His laugh rang in her ears as she left the house and sprinted to the Jeep. A few minutes later, she was pulling into the parking area of The Blue Goose. When she'd left home, the place had been named The Stone Inn and had been in a state of disrepair. That was no longer the case. About six or seven years ago, Hank O'Hara and his sister, Megan, had bought the place, renovated it, and presently served breakfast and lunch.

Stepping out of the Jeep into the steady downpour, Roxanne scurried to the door of the restaurant. She'd noted that the rain had brought in several patrons and recognizing a couple of the vehicles, she wasn't surprised to discover the place half full and several people she knew seated at the big table in front of the wood stove at the side of the room. Her heart took a nosedive right down to her toes when she caught sight of the tall, dark man seated at one end, then returned to normal when she realized that it was Mingo Delaney and not Jeb. Thank God.

She had been doing a very good job of avoiding Jeb—she didn't think it was solely because of her efforts either that they hadn't run into each other. She'd be willing to bet money that he was doing his best to avoid her. Oak Valley was a small place, but it helped that she was out at the construction site most of the time or at home and that Jeb's work kept him out of the valley most days. Still, she never knew when their paths might cross and she'd gotten into the habit of always checking out vehicles before venturing into Heather-Mary-Marie's or McGuire's Market or any of the places she *might* run into Jeb. So far, she'd been lucky, but the sight of Mingo had given her a start.

Spying an empty table near the window, she scooted into it, waving to Mingo, Don Bean, who had done the tractor work on her place, Profane Deegan, who sometimes worked with Don, and Danny Haskell, one of the local deputies. She recognized the other three men, too. One was a local volunteer fireman named Monty Hicks; the other was a retired logger, Hugh Nutter, who was a friend of her parents'. The last man, wearing the ubiquitous baseball cap, was Hank O'Hara.

The moment she sat down, a wide smile on his comfortable face, Hank jumped to his feet. "I'm on my way, darlin'," he called, and grabbing a menu hustled over to her table.

Roxanne grinned at him. "You didn't have to leave your friends for me," she said.

"Ah, now darlin', why would I stay with a bunch of raunchy men when I can have your charming company?"

There were some catcalls and hoots from the table containing the raunchy men. Hank laughed and said, "Just ignore them. What can I get for you on this cold rainy day?"

"What have you got that I'd like?"

Hank tugged at his gray goatee. "Megan cooked up a nice thick cream of potato soup for today. And a hearty stew—lots of meat and vegetables."

"The soup sounds wonderful. I'll have a bowl of it and a green salad. Garlic dressing. And coffee to drink."

Megan came out of the back room and seeing Roxanne greeted her through the glass divider that separated the cooking area from the main part of the restaurant. "How are you doing today?"

"Fine. I guess I'm glad to finally see some real rain. We need it."

Megan nodded. Several years younger than her brother, Megan was small and blond, her hair worn short and tidy, and looked to be in her forties. Hank was probably on the shady side of sixty, a tallish, slim man with laughing brown eyes. Roxanne liked them both and thought they'd done a marvelous job with the restaurant. Food and decor.

The Blue Goose had a cozy air about it. A black wood stove at the far side of the room heated the place. The main room held perhaps ten tables of various shapes and sizes and was capable of seating about forty people. The tables were made of thick redwood slabs and the flooring was a bright blue carpet. The walls were white and white lace curtains hung at the windows; fat geese strutted and cavorted on pale blue wallpaper edging near the ceiling. And the food was great as far as Roxanne was concerned.

Her meal arrived and she busied herself with eating, only half listening to the bursts of laughter and teasing that were coming from the table containing Mingo and the others, her gaze on the weather outside. It was really pouring, the day becoming darker and darker. But not my mood, she reminded herself sternly. Tonight she would sleep in her own house—on the floor if necessary and despite any protests her parents might make. I just hope, she thought mournfully, that they don't get those "oh, but honey, we'll worry about you out there all by yourself . . . and we're hurt that you don't want to stay with us" looks on their faces. If they did, she'd just have to harden her heart or she'd be sunk. An Ilka I am not going to be.

A vehicle door slammed outside and there was the stamping of feet and the next second the door to the restaurant flew open. Jeb Delaney, his black Stetson dripping water, his maroon leather bomber jacket speckled with rain, and his black western boots muddy, filled the doorway. The room seemed to compress; it was as if he were larger than life, and had brought the storm inside with him, the scent of cool wet weather, a hint of the winds of winter overpowering the warmth of the wood stove and the smell of cooking food.

A spoonful of Megan's thick, chunky soup half lifted to her lips, Roxanne froze, her eyes on Jeb. Oh, God! He looked so good, so virile and masculine that her heart pounded with excitement despite her best intentions. And he's still an arrogant obnoxious dickhead, she reminded herself. You don't like him. Remember? He doesn't like you. Remember that, too? OK. OK. We hate each other. But, why, oh, why, does he make me feel so alive? And why, dammit, can't I forget how great it was to make love with him? You had *sex* with him you did *not* make love. For that, she reminded herself grimly, you had to have respect, admiration, liking, and love. . . . None of which you have for him. He's a creep. A bossy Neanderthal. The sort of man you can't stand. Remember? Right. I remember that.

It was a good thing she did, because Jeb's eyes unerringly met hers, and her silly little heart almost jumped right out of her chest. She wanted to look away but she couldn't and when he began to walk toward her with that sexy long-legged stride, tight black jeans molded to his muscular thighs, his dark face intent and those black eyes of his fixed on hers, she thought she'd have an orgasm right then and there. Uh-oh. I'm in trouble. There is something very strange going on. This is Jeb Delaney, not my favorite person. This is the man I've been avoiding for weeks, months. The man I always get into a fight with. So why am I tickled to death to see him? Boredom, she thought desperately. Yes. Yes. That's it. I'm bored. And he's here. Right here in front of me.

Jeb's face was expressionless as he nodded to Roxanne and slid easily into the seat across from her. He took off his hat and put it on the empty seat next to him. "Afternoon," he said softly.

Angry at the jumble of emotions that just the sight of him created, she put down her spoon and said with saccharine sweetness, "Now why don't I remember inviting you to join me?"

Amusement glimmered in the depths of his dark eyes. "Now, Princess, why do you have to get all frosty with me? Can't a fellow just sit down and have a chat with a pretty girl?"

Her chin lifted. "I was never just 'pretty' and I haven't been a 'girl' for a long time."

"Yeah, you're right about that. Guess you are getting a little long in the tooth." He cocked a brow. "That why you retired? Too many younger, prettier, ah, forgive me, more beautiful women climbing over your back?"

Roxanne waited for the surge of outrage to come, but it didn't. And surprising herself as much as him, she muttered, "Yes. That's exactly why I'm sort of retired. It was getting harder and harder to stay on top. And since I knew I was going to lose the battle and that I'd had a good long run, I abdicated while I still could." She grinned. "Abdication is much easier on the ego than an overthrow."

His eyes roamed over that lovely, untamed face of hers, the elegant cheekbones, eagle eyes, and the flyaway mane of black hair. He'd known she was in here. He'd recognized her Jeep and instead of continuing on his way home, like some poor, lovesick schmuck, he had pulled off and come inside to find her. And at the sight of her just sitting there at the table, something fierce and wild had happened in the region of his heart—that and the odd sensation that he'd found something he'd been looking for all his life. He wasn't exactly happy or thrilled about any of it and it proved that he'd been wise these past weeks to stay clear of her. The woman, he thought grimly, was just plain trouble. And he sure as hell didn't want her to be *his* trouble. Why in the devil couldn't she just have *stayed* in New York? Why did she have to come back here and mess up his perfectly nice life?

His mouth seemed to have a mind of its own, because he said none of those things. Instead to his horror he heard himself saying, "They're crazy to have let you go—at sixty you'd still be lovelier than any twenty-year-old . . . girl."

Roxanne blinked. Her heart pounded. Her gaze dropped to her bowl of soup and for one of the first times in her life, she found herself speechless. Jeb Delaney thought her lovely. Now why did that warm her as nothing ever had in her life?

Jeb was wondering if he could rip his tongue out by the roots. A flush stained his cheeks and the collar of his shirt felt as if it would choke him. What a weapon he had just handed her. She'd stab him with it every chance she got. Why in the devil had he ever stopped? He took a deep breath. Of course, he remembered gratefully, he did sort of have a reason for seeking her out. And it wasn't just because he'd been hungering for the sight of her. It absolutely was *not* because of that!

The situation was saved by Hank. "Well, well, look what the storm blew in," Hank said, brown eyes twinkling as he walked up to the table.

Jeb mumbled something about finishing up early and deciding to head home before the weather got any worse.

"Don't blame you," Hank replied. "Supposed to be a big storm. Was the road bad when you came in?"

Recovering himself, Jeb shook his head. "Not yet. There were some rock slides along the river stretch, nothing very big, but come nightfall . . ."

Rock slides were a constant danger anytime on the winding, twisting road to Oak Valley, but they were much worse and more prevalent during stormy weather. The rain turned the steep ground to mud and the rocks and boulders buried within it tumbled regularly onto the road. During the day, it wasn't so bad, but at night, on wet slick pavement, the pavement shiny from headlights, a driver could come up on a slide in a heartbeat. Sometimes the slides were small, other times. . . .

"Remember that night, that big boulder came down? Big as a Volkswagen?" Hank asked.

"Yeah. Just glad that there was only pavement beneath it when it landed and not a car. Would have been nasty," Jeb answered.

Hank agreed and then asked, "So what can I get you?"

"Just coffee and some of Megan's walnut cake."

Roxanne and Jeb said nothing while Hank bustled around filling Jeb's order. By the time Jeb's coffee and a three-layered slice of cake exploding with walnuts was put in front of him, Roxanne had managed to regain some of her poise.

Pushing her spoon around in her bowl of soup she

muttered, "Thank you for the compliment." She risked a glance at his face. "It *was* a compliment, wasn't it?"

The suspicion in her voice made him smile. He nodded. "Yeah, it was a compliment. But don't let it go to your head—there are a lot of uncomplimentary things I could think to say about you instead."

She smiled, but it looked more like a dog lifting its lips in a snarl. "And I about you."

They ate and drank in silence for a moment. Then unable to stand it any longer, Roxanne demanded, "Why are you here? And don't try to tell me it's to pay me compliments."

"OK, I won't," Jeb replied equitably. He hesitated. Took a sip of his coffee. Fiddled with his fork. Finally when Roxanne was on the verge of smacking him, he looked at her and said, "It's about Ilka."

Chapter
8

Roxanne frowned. Jeb and Ilka? Now that was a depressing thought and she didn't want to discover why either. "Ilka? What about her?"

Jeb smiled wryly. "I know it'll come as a shock to you but Ilka and I are good friends. She actually thinks I'm a nice guy and happens to like me—we enjoy each other's company."

"Gee, I find that hard to believe," Roxanne muttered, ignoring the cold creeping into her heart. If he told her that he and Ilka were lovers, she'd just die. Right here. Right now. "Beats me what she sees in you."

"Maybe it's my kind nature," Jeb drawled, enjoying the exchange, enjoying watching her lively features, the glint in her eyes, the ebb and flow of color in those elegantly sculpted cheeks. Yeah. He did enjoy watching her, no denying it. The only thing he'd enjoy more at the moment, he admitted, was kissing some of the sass off that smart mouth of hers.

"Kind? Doubt it. At least I've never seen any sign of your being kind." She stopped, honesty forcing her to admit, "Well, that's not exactly true—it was kind of you to adopt Dawg and Boss, so I guess you do have *one* redeeming feature."

"Thank you," Jeb said dryly.

Roxanne fiddled with her soup spoon. "So what is it about Ilka that you want to talk about?"

His eyes dropped to his coffee cup and a mixture of sadness and anger crossed his dark face. Roxanne's heart stopped. Oh, God, she prayed more fervently than she ever had, please don't let him apologize again for what happened between us . . . but most of all, please don't let him tell me that he's in love with Ilka.

His eyes fixed on the cup, he said slowly, "Did you know that I was one of the first deputies on the scene the night that Delmer wrapped his truck around that tree?"

Roxanne started. "No. I didn't." She swallowed. "It must have been terrible."

"It was. I still have nightmares about it. Especially finding those two little babies. . . ." A shudder rolled through him and he looked across at her, a terrifyingly savage expression in those black eyes. "You know," he said with an equally terrifying quiet, "I always thought that it was a good thing that Delmer died instantly. In my mind, I've killed him with my bare hands a dozen times . . . and I like to think that if he'd still been alive when I reached the wreck that my training and duty would have held me back from breaking his miserable neck right then and there."

Instinctively Roxanne reached over and laid her hand on his. Their eyes met and she said softly, confidently, "You would have done the right thing." She smiled crookedly. "Your kind always does." Her face grew grim. "Now if it had been me. . . ."

He smiled. "I know—you have all that outlaw blood in you, all the way back to old black-hearted York Ballinger himself."

She cocked a slim brow. "Don't forget you have some, too. Isn't your mother part Ballinger and part Granger?"

"In this valley, I'm not allowed to forget it."

"Probably not." Her gaze fell on her hand still lying on his. She started to withdraw it, but he turned his hand and caught hers in strong fingers. Since it would be a useless struggle, she let her hand stay—or so she told herself.

Trying to ignore the pleasurable tingle it gave her to feel his warm hand around hers, she asked, "So tell me about you and Ilka."

He sighed. "That night, the night of the tragedy, I was the one who got her out of the truck just before it exploded. And I was the one who had to tell her that Bram and Ruby were dead." He looked away. "The ambulance had arrived, and they were trying to calm her down, trying to stop the bleeding, but she kept fighting them, kept screaming that she had to get her children. The only way we could stop her was to tell her the truth, that her babies were dead." He shook his head. "That was back in the days before mandatory safety seats for kids. . . ." He swallowed. "They both went right through the windshield and looking for those little bodies was one of the worst, if not the worst thing, I've ever had to do in my life. I'll never forget it. Never."

His words touched a cord inside of her and she absorbed the fact almost absently that there was a lot more to tall, arrogant, tough, good-looking Jeb Delaney than most people realized. He really was a cupcake. She scowled. Well, when he wasn't being an overbearing jerk.

Jeb took a drink of his coffee. "Anyway, the events of that night formed a bond between the pair of us— probably to do with the drama and tragedy of the moment. I was in to see her several times when she was in the hospital recovering and after she got out I don't know, the visits just continued. Your mom told me that Ilka always seemed to cheer up after I'd been to see her. More importantly, I was one of the few people she would talk to about what had happened." He looked embarrassed. "And somewhere along the way, we became friends. Good friends. I guess I consider her one of my best friends."

Friends. Hmm, that didn't sound too bad. Even best friends. In fact, friends was a whole lot better than lovers, Roxanne thought, wondering why it should matter to her what the relationship was between Jeb and Ilka. After all, she couldn't stand Jeb Delaney . . . right?

She cleared her throat. "Um, so you two have been friends, best friends, since then?"

He nodded. "Yeah. And as best friends, we talk about a whole range of things." He scratched his cheek with one hand. "And lately, she's been talking an awful lot about all these trips the two of you have been taking. . . ."

Roxanne stiffened. "Oh, really? And what has she told you about them?"

Jeb grinned. "Well, first of all, she says that she's enjoyed them tremendously, including the date with the handsome cover boy that you set up. Claims that it's been fun getting to know her famous big sister. She likes you, you know, admires you—apparently always has." His eyes gleamed. "Although, I can't imagine why."

Roxanne sniffed and Jeb laughed, adding, "She thinks that you have a lot more depth than most people realize. Of course lately, she's mentioned that she really hopes that you'll find someone else to save soon, so she can relax and get back to her normal life."

Humiliation at the idea of Jeb and Ilka having cozy little chats about her washed through Roxanne. Hurt and angry, she caught him by surprise, jerking her hand out of his. "Is that so?" she asked in frosty tones.

"Afraid so, Princess," he said gently.

"Did she ask you to tell me this?" Roxanne demanded, her eyes fierce.

Jeb looked uncomfortable. It suddenly dawned on him that he might have opened his mouth when he should have kept it shut. He winced. Not only did it appear that he'd put his foot wrong with Roxanne, but he had a powerful hunch that Ilka was going to be livid when she learned what he'd done. I should have kept going. Never should have stopped, he thought uneasily. Certainly never should have mentioned a private conversation with Ilka. Oh, man, I'm in for it now. Both of them are going to be after my scalp. He winced again. What had he been thinking of? He knew better. He wasn't a blabbermouth. He could keep a secret. Hell, he kept them all the time. It was just that he'd seen Roxanne's Jeep parked out there and had wanted an excuse to see her. And that, he realized, was the scariest admission he'd ever made.

"Did she?" Roxanne demanded again.

"Uh, no," he muttered.

Roxanne smiled thinly. "I see. So it was your very own omniscient decision—without finding out if Ilka even wanted you to open your big fat mouth—to share this little bit of information with me?"

"Uh, yeah."

Roxanne rose regally to feet. Her face full of contempt, she snapped, "Well, thank you. I appreciate it. I'm sure Ilka will, too. I can hardly wait to tell her how kind you have been to speak up for her."

There was an icy draft as Roxanne swept past him and he winced for the third time when the door slammed shut behind her with a ferocious bang. He buried his head in his hands. Not one, but two women were going to be after his hide. Two Ballinger women. And he didn't blame either one of them. He was dead meat. *Very* dead meat.

Hank walked over to the table. "I take it," he said dryly to Jeb's down bent head, "that you're going to pay the lady's bill?"

Jeb lifted his head and looked at him. "Yeah. I guess so."

Hank took the seat Roxanne had vacated. Crossing his legs, he asked, "Lovers' quarrel?"

"Are you crazy? Me and Roxanne? Hell, I'd rather mate with a grizzly bear with cubs than tackle that firecracker."

Hank chuckled. "She was pretty mad, wasn't she? For a minute there I thought she was going to dump her soup on your head. What'd you say to her anyway?"

"Now, Hank, you know that a gentleman never tells," Jeb quipped, thinking he'd opened his mouth once too many times already.

"Yeah," Hank said, rising. "But who ever said that you were a gentleman?"

Jeb laughed and, getting to his feet, grabbed his mug and walked over to the table that held Mingo and the others. Greetings were exchanged as Jeb took a seat with his back to the wood stove. The heat felt good and the fresh coffee Hank poured tasted just fine.

He took some ribbing from the guys about Roxanne's sudden exit, as well as the fact that he had joined her at the table in the first place. Eventually, since at least two of the men in the group had worked on her house, conversation drifted to her house.

Don Bean ran heavy equipment among other things and had done all of the site preparation. He was a brawny, barrel-chested man only a couple inches shorter than Jeb. Like the others at the table, except for Hank, they'd all grown up together in the valley: Don had been two years ahead of Jeb in school. Wearing worn, grease-stained blue jeans and a striped long sleeved chambray shirt, having a big round friendly face, his hamlike hands bearing some recent nicks and scrapes, he looked like what he was—a hardworking, honest good ole boy.

"I can't believe that *Roxanne* is actually going to live up there," Don exclaimed. "I mean, it's gonna be a great house, nice, you know, but not a mansion. Not the kind of place you'd think someone as famous as she is would live in. No wine cellar. No swimming pool. No servants' quarters. And the house isn't even that big— it's good size, probably thirty-five hundred square feet, maybe a little bigger, but it's not one of those ten thousand square feet plus places you hear about celebrities buying and building. And there's no gold-plated faucets or inlaid Italian marble or things like that. Nice stuff, but nothing outrageous." He grinned. "Sort of disappointed me—I was hoping for a bunch of half-naked models hanging around and seeing things I've only read about in magazines." He shook his head. "Can you believe it? She's gonna have a barn built next spring—wants a couple of horses and chickens. Now I ask you, can you picture Roxanne feeding chickens, picking eggs, and scooping up horse shit?"

Jeb wasn't surprised by Don's words. If he hadn't already seen the plans, he would have assumed Roxanne would build a manison that would have looked more at home in Beverly Hills than Oak Valley. And a barn with horses, well, yeah, he could see that—provided she had a stableman to handle all the messy work and she could just stroll out now and then and find her horse all groomed and saddled and waiting for her. Chickens gave him pause and he did have a little trouble seeing her clucking as she threw out feed and then picking eggs from the nest. But from what Don had said, it appeared he was wrong about that, too. He frowned. So what *else* was he wrong about? It made him uncomfortable to think that he'd been so busy coming up with reasons to dislike her that maybe he hadn't seen the real person.

Mingo grinned, sending a sly look at his brother. "I can picture her doing lots of things, but I don't think chickens and horse shit fit."

There were a few grins and a laugh or two, but there was nothing salacious or unkind about it. The valley took great pride in Roxanne's accomplishments and there wasn't a man gathered around the table who would have stood for her to be insulted—teased some, but not insulted. And that was whether they approved of her lifestyle or not. Roxanne was valley born and bred and that said it all . . . which didn't mean they wouldn't speculate or gossip some—they were, after all, men.

"Me neither," said Don. "I'm to do the site work for the barn, too, and she's talked to me about putting in a couple of ponds for her come spring and some roads so she can get around the place." He shook his head. "I'd have thought that someone like her would have chosen somewhere rich and fancy, like San Francisco, or Marin County, or even Sonoma County. Not Oak Valley." His blue eyes danced. "Plays hell with my image of her to think of her living here just like a regular person."

"I'll say," said Monty Hicks, an expression of awe on his boyish face. Monty was a newcomer to the valley. About six or seven years ago, he'd come to visit a friend he'd met at Junior College in Santa Rosa, fell in love with a local girl, and never left. Married these past five years to Gloria Adams, and the father of two lively boys, he was considered a welcome addition to the valley. He'd worked awhile at McGuire's but four years ago he'd taken a job at Western Auto—better hours than a grocery store and better pay. He trained as an EMT and was also a volunteer fireman. At twenty-eight years old he was the youngest of the men seated at the table and with his blond crew cut and slim build, he looked even younger.

"The first time she came into the store, I thought I was hallucinating," Monty continued, his voice as awed as his face. "I blinked and nearly had a heart attack when I realized it was really her standing right in

front of me. She was really nice, too—acted just like a
normal everyday person." He looked rueful. "When I
went home that night all excited and told Glory, she
just stared at me and said so what, her older sister,
Sandy, had gone to school with Roxanne. It was no big
deal." He shook his head. "To me it was a big deal and
I just couldn't get over how real, how normal she
was."

Annoyed, Jeb said, "Come on, Monty, she *is* a normal person. Just because she's a famous model doesn't
mean she isn't just like the rest of us."

"Goddamn prettier," chimed in "Profane" Deegan,
so named for obvious reasons. Next to Hank and Hugh
Nutter—who wouldn't see seventy again—he was the
oldest of the group, being somewhere in his fifties. He
was noted for three things: he was a hard worker, willing to tackle any job; he could hardly complete a sen-
tence without some sort of profanity in it; and his
T-shirts. The T-shirt he wore today was black and
stated in big, bright orange letters, "Save a Horse, Ride
a Cowboy." Profane glared around the table as if daring anyone to disagree with his statement. When there
was a general nodding of heads, he added, "And she's
a hell of lot nicer than some of the women in this damn
valley. Shit, I've worked for some of them and I'd
bake in hell before I'd ever do that again. But
Roxy . . ." His weathered face softened, which was
quite a sight considering that he sported a salt-and-
pepper beard that seemed to have been electrified and
sprouted wildly in all directions. "I'll tell you one

thing—she's a goddamn nice person. When I was helping Don at her place, and we had that hot spell—I'd look up, certain I'm one damned degree from turning to toast and there'd be Roxy. She'd be walking out in that heat, smiling that sweet smile of hers, and bringing me a big, icy glass of tea, or a Pepsi or a bottle of water. Nice lady. A real nice lady." He looked ferocious. "And if I ever find out which of those little sons of bitches were that broke into her place and trashed it, I'll put their asses in their mouths. See if I don't."

"Count me in," growled Don. "You should have seen the place. We'd done some initial work that first Monday and came back the next day to find someone had gone in and had a party tearing some of the walls out and even ripping down the few cupboards in the kitchen."

Jeb frowned. "Are you talking about something that happened recently? You're not referring to the vandalism that was done this summer, are you?"

Danny Haskell, the local deputy, spoke up. "No. This happened back in September."

Jeb glared at Danny. "Why didn't you tell me?"

Danny looked taken aback. "Hey, she didn't report it, OK? I only heard about it from these guys." More curiosity in his voice than complaint, he asked, "And since when do I report to you? Last I heard you were the detective around here, and that robbery and vandalism was my bag."

Jeb shrugged and sent Danny a rueful glance.

"Sorry. Stepped out of line. Hard to remember sometimes that I'm not in uniform."

Danny was a good kid. Well, not a kid anymore, Jeb admitted, since he'd attended Danny's thirty-fifth birthday back in September. But he had trouble remembering that fact sometimes—he was just enough older to remember when Danny had been a rambunctious, gangly teenager with a goofy smile and *he'd* been the local deputy. He shook his head. Some days he just felt old.

Looking at Don and Profane, Jeb asked, "Any trouble since then?"

"Nope," Don said. "Theo was fit to be tied though—after that he had one of the younger guys on the crew sleep out there in a camper. Theo was pissed about the break-in, but since the inside was going to be torn out anyway, he got over it—but he was worried about all the equipment stored out there and the damage the kids might do to the new construction. Never had any more trouble after that."

"Milo Scott do a good job on the concrete?" Jeb asked.

Don grinned. Everyone knew how Jeb felt about Milo. "Hate to say it, my man, but yeah, he did." Tongue in cheek, he added, "Hung around a lot, too—*after* the job. Theo finally had to tell him that if he didn't have work to do to kindly get out of his way."

Hugh Nutter spoke up. "When are you guys going to arrest that guy anyway?" Hugh was bald, stood about five feet five, and was almost as wide as he was tall. He belonged to another old valley family and had spent his days in the logging business. Hadn't made a fortune, but retired comfortably enough. These days he hung out at The Blue Goose or sometimes during the summer across the street at The Burger Place—when he wasn't busy helping with community affairs. Now that Hugh was retired and his passel of six kids was grown, he and his wife, Agnes, were big on community affairs. His eyes boring into Jeb, he muttered, "Seems like you'd make more of an effort to get scum like that off the streets."

Danny looked at Jeb, a grin on his handsome face, his black eyes, inherited from his Indian great-grandmother, dancing. "Yeah, when are we going to arrest him?"

Jeb made a face. "Not my department. Milo Scott's got juice and there's someone higher up who's just as happy to let him play his games. Besides, we've never been able to really pin anything on him. He always manages to weasel out of it."

Heads nodded and the conversation slipped onto other topics.

It was several minutes later that the sound of vehicle doors slamming outside signaled the arrival of someone else seeking a late lunch. Hank glanced at the clock on the wall and jumped up. "Wouldn't you know it, you guys distracted me and now it's past closing time." He said over his shoulder to Megan, "Sorry, Meggie, but we'll have to stay open a little longer than usual."

Megan sent him an exasperated look and he grimaced. "I know. I know. I'll lock the door behind them."

Crossing the room, he met the two new arrivals as they poured into the room shaking the rain from their jackets and hats.

"Damn, it's wet out there," said Morgan Courtland.

"You can say that again," replied his fraternal twin, Jason.

Recognizing the pair of them, a gleam of anticipation entered Hank's eyes. The Courtland boys were always good for a laugh. He pointed to the clock and said, "Ah, now, me boys, you're too late. It's after 2:00 P.M. We're closed."

Morgan grinned, his blue eyes glittering in his dark face. He pointed to the lighted sign in the window. "That says you're still open."

"Come on, Hank, don't give us a bad time," Jason added, smiling. He glanced over at the group of men around the table. "And half the valley is here anyway." He saw Megan behind the counter, the big black grill and stove behind her. "Hey, Megan, say something to your brother—he's trying to throw us out."

Megan smiled. "Now do you really think Hank would do that to the pair of you?"

They looked innocently at Hank and he burst out laughing. "Go on, the pair of you. Tell Megan what you want." While they walked over to the counter and ordered, Hank turned off the open sign and put the closed sign on the door and made a big production of locking it.

Room was made for the twins at the table and after hellos were given and they shrugged out of their wet jackets and hats and Hank had poured them coffee Jason said, "Can you believe Christmas is in two weeks? Think we'll have a white one this year?"

"My kids are hoping," said Monty. "Although I don't think the youngest really understands what all the fuss is about."

Hugh chuckled. "Just wait 'til next year—he'll be three then, won't he?" At Monty's nod, he went on, "My youngest grandkid is three and believe me, he knows *exactly* what it's all about."

Emerald eyes dancing, Jason flashed a glance at Jeb. "Well, I know someone who's going to get switches and a sack of coals for Christmas this year— if my cousin Roxy has anything to say about it."

Morgan laughed, almost choking on his coffee. Looking at Jeb, he asked, "Man, what did you say to her? Sam and Ross are home for the holidays and we'd stopped by to see them. Just as we were getting ready to leave, Roxy came tearing in the back door, spitting fire. Your name was mentioned frequently, along with some language that I won't repeat before such tender ears."

A burst of laughter greeted that statement.

"That so?" Jeb murmured, smiling. "Can't imagine why she'd be upset with me. Everyone knows that I am always the epitome of gentlemanly behavior."

Mingo and Danny hooted insultingly, the twins grinned, Hank and the others just laughed out loud.

"You should have seen her when she left here," Hank said, his expression amused. "She was sure mad then—thought she'd dump her soup over his head. Left him to pay her bill."

"So what'd you do?" demanded Morgan. "Pat her on the butt? Make an obscene offer? I'm telling you, Jeb, she was *pissed*!"

Jeb liked the Courtland twins—it was hard not to—they were both charming and likable. He just wished they'd keep their damn mouths shut about Roxanne. Related to the Ballingers on their father's side—Helen Ballinger was his older sister—they came from old valley stock. Their grandfather had been a big cattleman and the family still owned a nice chunk of land in the area. Their father, Steve, had left the valley as a young man to make his fortune in Hollywood, even married a gorgeous starlet. After acting awhile, mostly small parts, he'd eventually become a very successful producer. The twins had grown up in Hollywood, but they'd spent summers and as many school vacations as they could with their grandparents in the valley. As adults they'd spurned the glamorous life of their parents and had returned to the valley. Morgan opened a real estate office, sold a little insurance, and ran a small herd of cattle on some of the family's land. Jason followed a more artistic bent and was noted worldwide for his exquisitely handmade furniture. There was currently a two-year waiting list of eager clients who just had to have a Courtland table or armoire. Thirty-six years old, unmarried, and considered by many women to be as handsome as any two devils, next to Jeb and Mingo, they were the most highly sought-after bachelors in the valley.

"You can tell us," Jason urged, his lips twitching with laughter. "You can trust us—you know that."

Jeb cast him a dry look. "But why would I want to?"

"Because we'll tease you unmercifully and hound you to death until you do?" quipped Morgan.

Jeb smiled, asking gently, "Now do you really think the pair of you could do that?"

They eyed him a long moment. Then grinned, Jason admitting, "Probably not, but it sounded good."

Hank rose from the table. "Well, it's been fun, folks, but I better go help Megan cook or I'll be in the doghouse for sure."

Hank's departure gave Jeb the excuse he needed. "Think I'll head on home. See you guys later."

A couple of the other men followed Jeb's lead. Seated in his truck, watching the others disappear into the rainy afternoon, Jeb considered driving to the Ballinger mansion and trying to head off Roxanne from telling Ilka about his flapping tongue. He shook his head, still unable to believe he'd been so indiscreet. Groveling was his only option, but he didn't think it would get him out of the doghouse. Apologizing to Ilka might help, but he doubted it. The more he thought about it, the less the idea appealed. Roxanne was furious with him and he suspected that Ilka soon would be. Nope. He'd leave it alone and be wise . . . for once.

By dinnertime that night, Roxanne was still stewing. The worst of her temper had abated though, and upon reflection, she'd decided that there was nothing to be gained by telling Ilka of Jeb's indiscretion. Nobody liked a tattletale. It killed her to keep her mouth shut, but she'd never been a troublemaker and telling Ilka that her *best* friend had diarrhea of the mouth would certainly cause trouble. Not only between Ilka and Jeb, but probably Ilka wouldn't be happy that Roxanne was privy to things that were meant to be private.

The worst of it was that Jeb's words had given Roxanne food for thought. OK, maybe she had been pushing Ilka a little too hard. Maybe she'd been a little too enthusiastic about wrenching Ilka out of her cozy, boring life. She made a face as she descended the stairs for dinner. Of course, that was just her opinion. Her bottom lip drooped. She'd only been trying to help. She wanted Ilka to be happy. She sighed. Being a big sister, she decided, wasn't all that it was cracked up to be.

Roxanne took some teasing of her own that evening at the dinner table. Since everyone had seen the fury in her eyes when she had come home and heard some of the curses she'd called down on Jeb's head, they were all curious.

"I can't stand it a moment longer . . . what did Jeb

do to put you in such a snit?" asked Ross, seated across the table from her. After Sam, the baby of the family, he was the next youngest. With his height, dark hair, and amber-gold eyes, he was clearly a Ballinger. As with all of her younger siblings, Roxanne didn't know him very well, but what she had learned about him during visits at home and brief telephone conversations, she liked.

Toying with her baked potato, she mumbled, "Private stuff. Not for the ears of children."

Sam and Ross exchanged laughing glances. "Come on, Roxy," Sam coaxed, her big golden-brown eyes dancing, "we're all grown-up now. You can't get away with that children designation anymore. What did Jeb do?"

"You're always going to be children to me," said Mark, cutting his broiled swordfish with a fork.

All four of his children groaned. "Don't we know it," said Roxanne. "If it was up to you, we'd all still be living at home and you'd be driving us everywhere we wanted to go."

Mark chuckled. "Unfortunately, that's probably true."

"Yeah," added Ross, "Mom was much better about cutting the apron strings than you were." He looked at Sam. "Remember when I moved to Santa Rosa to attend college? You'd have thought there was a death in the family."

"And when I announced that I was getting married," Sam said, "I thought you were going to hire the CIA to look into Mike's background."

"And I should have," growled her father. "Denning was no good."

Sam laughed, although there was a shadow at the back of her eyes. "Oops. Wrong example. My ex-husband is definitely a sleazebag, but"—and she pointed her finger at her father—"even if he'd been perfect, you'd still have been unhappy about my leaving home."

Mark looked pained. Glancing at Helen who sat at the other end of the table, he said, "I could use a little help here. They're ganging up on me."

Helen shook her head. "Sorry, dear. I side with the children." She flashed him a loving smile. "You really did take their leaving home hard. You wanted to wrap them in cotton wool and keep them safe from harm."

"Well, it's hard to have done just that for eighteen or twenty years and then all of the sudden, they're out there on their own, and you can't protect them anymore," he said gruffly.

"It's called growing up, Dad," Roxanne said softly, her eyes tender.

He grimaced. "I know." He glanced around the table. "And you've all done a fine job of it. I'm proud of you." A sly look crossed his face. "Of course, a few more of you could follow in your brother's footsteps and get married. A grandchild or two would be nice before I drop dead."

Roxanne sent a worried look at Ilka, who sat beside

her. Would their father's careless words hurt Ilka? Bring tragic memories to the surface? They didn't seem to. Ilka joined in the laugh that followed and Roxanne relaxed. Maybe she *was* getting too protective of Ilka.

Dinner was over and Roxanne had just shut her suitcase when Ilka tapped on her bedroom door and peeked inside. Seeing Roxanne's two suitcases all packed, she muttered, "You're really going to move out there, aren't you?"

"That's the plan," Roxanne said cheerfully. "Can't wait. Tonight I sleep under my own roof, if I have to sleep on the floor."

Sam stuck her head around the door. She was almost an exact replica of Roxanne—same wild black mane of hair, same glittering eyes, and the same stubborn chin. There were differences, Sam was an inch shorter, her cheekbones were not quite as sculpted as Roxanne's, her nose shorter and her figure a bit more curvy, but they had been mistaken for each other more than once. Even though Sam was seven years younger, they still bore a striking resemblance to each other.

"I don't suppose," Sam asked hopefully, "that you'd like some company?"

Ilka's face lit up. "What a great idea! We can help you celebrate. Like a slumber party. Just the three of us. Ballinger girls' night out."

Roxanne's heart sank. She couldn't very well tell the pair of them that she could hardly wait to get away from them, not that she didn't love them or enjoy them, it was just that she needed the privacy and solace of her own space. All day she'd been looking forward to having her house all to herself. Gleefully anticipating. Looking forward to being alone, able to consider just her own wants and not worry about anybody else. Did she want her sisters' company? Absolutely not.

She glanced from one face to the other. There was a touching eagerness on both faces that stabbed her heart. Oh, what the hell. "Sure," she said, smiling. "Grab what you need and let's go."

Chapter
9

*A*s she looked back on that first night in her new home, Roxanne was glad that she'd given in to her heart's prompting and invited Sam and Ilka to share that time with her. They had a ball. They drank wine and munched on pretzels, crackers, and cheese pilfered from home. Camped out on Roxanne's mattress on the floor of the bedroom, they laughed and giggled and told "do you remember" stories until the wee hours of the morning. Half tipsy, standing at the French doors in the great room, they looked out and oohed and aahed at the sight of the glittering lights of the valley floating below them and later ran through the house shrieking with laughter for no reason at all. It was, Roxanne decided, a bonding experience. A soft smile curved her mouth. A "do you remember" story for the future.

Christmas came and went. Roxanne enjoyed spending the holidays with her family. It was the first time she'd done so in probably a decade and so it took on special importance. She even relented and came down from "Roxy's Roost" as Ilka and Sam had christened her house and stayed the night on Christmas Eve at the family home. They exchanged small gifts from each other that night—long ago a twenty-five-dollar limit having been set. Christmas Day had always been reserved for the expensive gifts from Santa. Roxanne had bought the women in her family earrings made from delicately twisted gold wire by a friend of hers in New York, the men receiving handmade bolo ties fashioned out of silver and braided horsehair. She might have fudged on the cost, but not too much. She was touched that as a group they had all gotten together and purchased her an industrial-sized bright red wheelbarrow and an assortment of tools—shovels, rakes, and a couple of different pairs of pruners. She guessed that they had gone way over the limit, but she wasn't going to ruin the moment by talking about such a sordid thing as money. A lump filled her throat and looking at their grinning faces, she said, "I take it you all plan on me working in the yard . . . a lot." She smiled mistily. "Thank you. You couldn't have given me anything I'd have liked better."

Christmas Day Sloan and Shelly drove in from their place in the mountains to join in the festivities and for the first time in ages, except for his indefatigable eighty-seven-year-old mother, currently tearing through . . . er, touring Europe, Mark had his entire family safe under his own roof. He beamed.

Accepting Shelly into his family had been difficult for Mark; she was, after all, one of those Grangers. But once Sloan had taken him aside and informed him that his marriage to Shelly was the *only* way he'd ever get a grandchild from his eldest son and that if he so much as looked cross-eyed at Shelly, it'd be the last time his son set foot in his house, reluctantly he set aside his prejudices. It helped that his son was madly in love with his new wife and that Shelly obviously felt the same way about Sloan. That Shelly had a warmth and charm all her own helped alleviate some of Mark's prejudices against the Granger family—and as Sloan had reminded him, Shelly was a Granger no longer, she was now a Ballinger. There was a glow about the pair of them that only someone a lot more hard-hearted than Mark would have wanted to destroy. As long as Sloan was happy his father would put up with anything—even a Granger daughter-in-law.

As the year drew to an end, except for a few minor things, Roxanne's house was completed. She had unpacked some of the personal belongings she'd had shipped from New York and now had some furniture and a kitchen that worked and had pretty much settled in. She loved it. The quiet. The spaciousness. The privacy.

Sipping coffee this rainy morning in late December, she stared out of her front kitchen window, picturing how the yard would look in a few months. The stiff green foliage of the bulbs she had planted was beginning to push up through the damp earth and she could hardly wait for the first bright yellow daffodil to bloom. And for construction on the barn to begin. And the new well house and new garage. All the improvements she had planned in her head. Impatience gripped her. Oh, for spring.

She was happy. Almost contented. She wished, not for the first time, that Roman hadn't returned to New Orleans. To everyone's surprise, he'd flown home to Louisiana in early October, promising to return for a visit after the first of the year. Business, he explained, could only be left on automatic pilot for so long and he'd been in Oak Valley for almost five months. Any decisions that had needed to be made had been done via phone and fax, but as he'd said, it was time for him to make his presence felt. He had fitted in so well in the valley that it was a shock for everyone to realize that Roman's life was not centered in the valley. That he had family and a whole different life waiting for him in the South. Roxanne missed him more than she had thought she would. Not in a romantic way—she simply liked Roman. He made her laugh; she enjoyed his company and she would have liked his opinion about the house and what she was doing with it. Not, she thought with a grin, that she would have done anything different. It just would have been nice to hear his comments— good and bad.

The house still dominated her thoughts; it still needed all those finishing touches, still felt new and unfamiliar—there were times she couldn't find common, ordinary things in her own kitchen or bathroom, but she didn't care. Most of the time, she hugged the solitude and reveled in it. And if she wanted company, it was waiting for her just a few miles away on the valley floor. She was almost totally content. She frowned. That "almost" bothered her. Then she tossed her head. So what if now and then the thought crossed her mind that it might be nice to have someone special, someone other than friends and family to discuss plans with and to share the pride in the place? Big deal. She didn't *need* anybody. A scowl crossed her face. Especially a man.

Flouncing out of the kitchen, she spent the rest of the day hanging a couple of pictures and trying out different arrangements of furniture. She'd sold most of her furniture before leaving New York and since arriving in Oak Valley, she hadn't done much about replacing it, but she'd gotten the basics, with a few treats she just couldn't resist like the large screen television for the living room and the huge, ornate cherry-wood armoire that matched her equally large canopied bed and nightstands. Eventually, she planned on a small table and chairs to place near the windows, maybe a desk and another chair for her bedroom, but for now, she was satisfied. And of course, the guest bedrooms, the dining room, and the great room would require more furniture, but she wasn't in a rush. She was too busy savoring the quiet pleasure of owning and living in her own home. No place she had ever lived, no matter how elegant and costly, had filled her with the same possessive joy. She loved her house!

She frowned. And she resented anything that took her away from it . . . such as Sloan and Shelly's impetuously planned New Year's Eve gathering tomorrow night. She sighed. She'd been looking forward to spending New Year's Eve in solitary splendor—she'd already selected the crimson silk lounging pajamas she'd wear, even the perfume—Red to match the pajamas. She'd planned to put on the latest Gipsy Kings CD, open a bottle of really good wine, red naturally, bake an artichoke frittata and sitting on the floor before the fire in the great room, revel in her privacy. And if she spied the lights from her neighbor across the way, she'd drink a toast to him or her. She'd be alone, but not lonely. Big difference, she thought. She'd dreamed of waking up on New Year's Day in her own bedroom, of later pouring herself a cup of coffee, and then if it wasn't raining or snowing as predicted, walking out on the half-completed terrace at the back and looking down at the valley. She wanted to savor the moment as she stood there on her own terrace and stared down at the valley, St. Galen's spread out below her like a child's toy village. She pictured standing there enjoying the simple pleasure of a hot cup of coffee as she reflected on all that had been accomplished these past months and all she hoped to accomplish in the coming year.

Her lips twisted. But that wasn't going to happen.

Not this year anyway. No, just as the bonds that bound families together had changed her plans for her first night in the house, so had her plans for the New Year's holiday been changed. Shelly and Sloan would have been hurt if she had refused to attend *their* first New Year's gathering. Since that had been something she had been loath to do, she had cheerfully pushed aside her own plans, besides baking the frittata to take to the party, and reminded herself that this was one of the reasons she had come back to the valley—family. She shook her head. Living in New York, for years all she'd had to consider was whether or not *she* really wanted to do something—not the feelings of others. It was weird the way that affection impacted your life. Not, she told herself hastily, that she was going to be at the beck and call of the family at a drop of a hat—she wasn't that selfless. She grinned. Hardly. Honesty made her admit that she was going to have a good time at Shelly and Sloan's and it would probably be more fun. Besides, there would be other New Year holidays to celebrate . . . . Who knew, maybe this time next year, there would even be someone special to share the day with . . . Her nose wrinkled. Nah. Never happen. She'd been her own woman too long.

She wasn't due at the party until six o'clock, but Roxanne gave herself plenty of time and left the house for the drive out to Sloan and Shelly's place just after five o'clock. Shadows were beginning to creep around the buildings and trees and she enjoyed the almost spooky drive to the valley floor, watching as her headlights turned ordinary objects like crooked snags and manzanita bushes into goblins—at least to someone with an active imagination, she thought with a giggle.

Sloan and Shelly only lived about fifteen, sixteen miles away, but taking in the rugged terrain between here and there it wasn't just a simple drive. They lived about ten miles out the Tilda Road, up in the mountains at the north end of the valley. The Tilda Road itself was a good five or six miles from her place and once she reached the valley floor, she was able to make good time . . . until she reached the Tilda Road and the pavement stopped. In a series of hairpin curves, the road rose steeply in front of her, and leaving the valley behind, she grimaced as the Jeep hit a hole that shook the entire vehicle. From here on out it would be slow, careful going. The rough, graveled Tilda Road was littered with pot-holes, some Sloan swore were the size of Delaware, and twisted like an angry snake—it made the road to Oak Valley seem like a four-lane freeway. All part of its charm, she told herself as the Jeep rattled and protested when she hit one of those Delaware-sized potholes.

She hadn't driven more than three miles up in the mountains when huge, wet snowflakes began to splat against the windshield and float in the air. Gee, for once, she thought, smiling, the weathermen actually got it right. Then she sighed. Oh, how she would have loved being all snug and warm in her own house watching the snow fall, instead of driving out to her brother's place. What we do for love, she thought ruefully.

She had barely completed that thought when the Jeep gave a cough, a lurch, and stopped. Just stopped. The lights still shone brightly, the dash was lit up, but there was no go.

Puzzled, she turned off the ignition, then on again, trying to restart the vehicle. Nothing. She stared at the gauges, her heart sinking when she noticed the gasoline gauge; the needle rested firmly on empty.

Biting back a curse that would have made an iron-worker blush, she frowned at the gauge. How could that be? Why, she'd filled the gas tank only. . . . She grimaced. When had she last filled the Jeep? She couldn't remember.

Staring accusingly at the gas gauge, she considered the situation. Not good. She glanced outside. In the glare from her headlights only encroaching blackness and swirling snow met her gaze and mindful of the drain on the battery, she turned off the lights. Darkness closed down on her.

Nibbling at her bottom lip she considered the situation. The Tilda Road was *not* a busy thoroughfare. It wasn't a heavily populated area either, not even sparsely populated. A few people lived out here, but well off the road, like in *miles* off the road, with miles between neighbors. It wasn't as if good neighbor Sam was suddenly going to appear with a gas can

or that she could just scamper down a handy driveway and find shelter and a phone with an obliging
homeowner. She groaned. And brilliant woman that
she was, she'd left her cell phone back at the house.
It was just a short drive out to her brother's . . . why
would she need a phone? Ha! She was stuck. In the
middle of nowhere, in the dark, in the snow, and the
only creatures she was likely to meet except *maybe*
someone else on their way to the party, were cougars,
bears, foxes, and skunks. On New Year's Eve.

She looked down at her snug-fitting black suede
jeans, matching vest, and leopard print silk shirt
she'd chosen to wear tonight. Large gold hoops
swung from her ears, a delicate multifaceted gold
chain hung around her neck, and a snappy pair of
leopard-printed microsuede boots with gold heels
completed the outfit. Not what she would have selected to wear while tramping through the snow and
the wilderness that lay outside the Jeep's windows.
But help was at hand. Since it was planned for everyone to stay the night, she'd packed a couple of
changes of clothes—heavy socks, boots, jeans,
blouses, and sweaters—and a jacket. She didn't look
forward to adding clothes, but with no gas, there
wasn't any heat in the Jeep and she sure wasn't
dressed for the weather.

OK, she could bundle up and put on every piece of
clothing she'd brought with her. Maybe she wouldn't
freeze. She flicked on the lights for a moment, trying

to get her bearings, wondering if she was really considering trekking for help.

The Tilda Road wasn't a full two lanes wide; it was wide enough to pass, barely, in most places, provided the meeting vehicles dove instantly to their side of the road. Because of the narrowness of the road, it was customary to drive pretty much down the center—until and if you met an oncoming vehicle. Following normal practice, Roxanne's Jeep was stopped almost in the middle of the road. The only good thing she could see in the situation was that it was on one of the few fairly straight stretches; anyone coming up on her would have warning and not just come barreling around a curve to smash into the back of the Jeep. Remembering the flares in the back, she scrabbled around and found one. Heedless of the icy weather, she jumped out of the Jeep, got the flare lit, and threw it on the ground in back of the Jeep.

Shivering, she hurried back into the relative warmth of the Jeep. Inside, she grabbed her suitcase and dragged it to the front seat. Getting and keeping warm was imperative. Ten minutes later, a pair of denim jeans pulled over the suede ones, another blouse and two sweaters added to what she was already wearing, two pairs of socks and her hiking boots on her feet, she figured she was as prepared as she was going to get. Her heavy leather jacket lay on the seat beside her—she was saving it for when it got *really* cold—like around two o'clock in the morning.

Arms wrapped around herself, she stared out at the

blackness, wondering if she shouldn't try to find help before it got later . . . and colder and the snow deeper. She bit her lip. Leaving the safety and confines of the Jeep was not appealing and she was conscious of her lack of knowledge of the area. Sure, she'd grown up around here, but that was twenty years ago and those intervening years had been spent where takeout was only a phone call away, neon lights came on at sundown, and there were people *everywhere*.

The fact that she'd be missed gave her some comfort and there was the distinct possibility that help would arrive in the form of another partygoer. She brightened. Of course. She couldn't have been the last person on the way to Sloan and Shelly's. Ilka or Ross or Nick or someone else invited to the party was bound to drive up any minute now.

That thought had just crossed her mind when the sweep of lights behind her caught her attention and the soft growl of another vehicle seeped inside the Jeep. Elation swept through her. Help had arrived— and before she really became worried or really cold. Was she born under a lucky star or what?

The other vehicle stopped and there was the slamming of a door. A big bulky male form appeared at her window and tapped impatiently on the glass.

Rolling down the window, she smiled brilliantly up at Jeb Delaney. She was even happy to see him. Any refuge in the storm, she reminded herself.

Jeb did not appear happy to see her. "What in

hell," he demanded, "are you doing stopped in the middle of the road?" He glanced back at the shimmering flare. "At least you had the brains to put out a warning."

She kept her smile in place, although it took an effort—a big effort—and said politely, "No gas."

His black brows snapped together and he glared down at her. "Are you telling me," he snarled, "that you've run out of gas?"

Roxanne smiled even more brilliantly. "You got it, big guy. Flat out empty. Bone dry. Not a drop in the tank."

"I suppose it would do me little good to remind you that this isn't New York—that gas stations do not abound, nor is there help ready on every corner?"

She opened her eyes very wide, her smile even brighter. "Gee, you know, I never noticed." She fluffed her hair. "Silly little ole me."

"Knock it off," he growled. "You could have been in trouble. Real trouble if I hadn't come along."

Her jaw hardened. "I would have been uncomfortable and probably not happy with the situation, but I was not in any danger—except of spending a cold, miserable night in the Jeep." Her eyes burned like amber fire. "Why don't you just buzz off? I'll wait for a more congenial rescuer."

"And that's another thing," he began, the snow dusting his black hat and broad shoulders under the black leather jacket he wore, "you shouldn't have opened your window to just anyone. We may not have the sickos that frequent the big cities, but there *are* guys around here that you really don't want to meet alone on a night like this. You were a damned fool to have opened your window like that."

"I know," she snapped, and promptly rolled it back up.

Hands on his hips, growing colder by the moment, Jeb glared at her. She glared back, her chin set at that stubborn angle that drove him nuts.

It was a standoff. Muttering under his breath, Jeb knocked on the window. "Open it," he mouthed when she just stared at him. Her chin went up a notch higher.

He closed his eyes, counting to ten. He'd probably strangle her one of these days. He took a deep breath. OK, maybe he'd come on a little strong. But Jesus! The fright she'd given him when he'd rounded that last bend and spied the jaunty little black Jeep sitting forlornly in the middle of the road. Of course, he recognized it immediately and the shot of pure fear that had gone through him wasn't something he wanted to experience again anytime soon. His imagination working overtime, terrified that she'd been hurt, or worse, wasn't in the vehicle, had him flying out of his truck before he'd had time to think. The relief that had gone through him when he realized she was safe had left him, he'd admit, a mite testy.

He opened his eyes and stared at her stony profile. He took another breath and, tapping the window, shouted, "I'm sorry. Can we start again?"

She eyed him. Sniffed. And slowly rolled down the window.

He bent down, his hands firmly on the door of the Jeep . . . and the window. "Ran out of gas, did you? Bad luck," he said. "Were you on your way to Sloan and Shelly's?"

She nodded, not giving an inch.

He smiled and she blinked, her heart behaving erratically as he leaned there, the snow falling gently around him, giving her the full benefit of that mesmerizing smile. His teeth gleamed whitely beneath the heavy black mustache, faint attractive lines crinkling near his long-lashed eyes, and she looked at him, really looked at him for the first time. Why, he's handsome, she thought stupidly as her gaze roved over his craggy face. Very, very handsome. Her gaze dropped to his mouth and she suddenly remembered what those lips had felt like on hers. Breathing became difficult. She swallowed. Uh oh. She was in trouble. Bad, *bad* trouble.

She cleared her throat. "Uh, yes. I was. On my way to Sloan and Shelly's." Her eyes locked on the snap at the top of his jacket, she asked, "Is that where you're headed?"

"Yep." He glanced around. "Cold night and all . . . good thing I came along, huh?"

She smiled faintly. "Yeah. A good thing."

"Well, before I freeze my balls off," he said with a grin, "let's get you off the road and your stuff transferred to my truck—we have a party to attend. We can worry about your Jeep tomorrow."

Roxanne couldn't think of one objection. With Jeb's truck pushing her, they managed to get the Jeep to a wider spot and she was able to park it off the road. A minute later, her suitcase and the ice chest with the frittata in it were tossed on the backseat of the truck and she was sitting in the warm cab of Jeb's truck.

As they pulled away from the Jeep, Jeb said, "I don't want to start another argument, but come on, Roxy, you know better." He shook his head. "Running out of gas. Jesus."

She sent him a look and he shut his mouth, his eyes on the road, but she noticed he was smiling. They made conversation for the first mile, both of them being very polite, talking about the weather, the Christmas holiday, and the coming New Year.

The warmth of the truck soon became too much for Roxanne and she began shedding her clothes. Jeb tried not to gawk, but it was hard when one of the most beautiful women in the world was sitting right beside you taking off her clothes.

He didn't say anything when the sweaters were discarded and she had struggled with her boots and socks and put them in the suitcase, but when she began shimming out of her jeans, he cleared his throat and croaked, "Uh, what are doing?"

She grinned. "Getting rid of all the extra clothing

I put on in anticipation of spending the night in the Jeep."

She pulled on a pair of leopard-patterned boots with gold heels that sent the most lascivious visions through his brain. One in which she wore nothing but the damn boots had his breathing coming in faint gasps. Staring fixedly out of the windshield, he finally managed to say, "The extra clothes—smart thinking."

"Why thank you, Mr. Delaney. That's probably the first compliment you've ever given me."

"That's not true," he protested. "I've said nice things about you before."

Jeans, sweaters, and blouse safely packed along with the rest of the extra clothing, she looked over at him. "Name one."

"Uh, well, um. . . ."

Roxanne chuckled, a warm, husky sound that did something to his diaphragm . . . and lower. He felt his sex swell—or rather swell even more and he moved uncomfortably. He'd been in a state of half arousal from the moment he'd caught sight of her face inside the Jeep and having her this close to him, the scent of her perfume tangling in his nose and the intimacy of the cab and night did nothing for his unruly hormones.

Roxanne had seldom seen Jeb at a loss and she shook her head, laughing softly to herself. He wasn't such a bad guy, she thought as she finished repairing the damages of the past several minutes. As the truck bumped and lurched down the road, she combed her hair and, using the lighted mirror on the sun visor, touched up her makeup. She flicked the dangling gold hoops. There. She looked just as she had when she left the house.

She glanced at Jeb, startled to see him looking at her, a funny expression on his face. The truck slowed, until it was barely crawling down the narrow gravel road. There wasn't much light in the cab, only what came from the dash lights, but it was enough to illuminate all the contours and angles of Roxanne's face framed by a cloud of black hair.

"God, you're beautiful," he said almost on a note of reverence, the truck almost coming to a full stop.

Roxanne was not vain. She took no credit for her looks—she'd had nothing to do with the mix of genes that had given her the face and form she possessed and she never quite knew what to say when people complimented her on her beauty. And because her beauty was none of her making, she usually dismissed such comments, but Jeb's remark was important to her, although why totally escaped her. She knew that her looks shouldn't matter, that it was her brains and intelligence that she wanted to be noticed, but right now, she was glad she had been blessed to be born beautiful.

She smiled uncertainly, her heart fluttering oddly in her chest. "Why, thank you." She swallowed, the flutter in her chest growing stronger, as his eyes remained fixed on her face. "That's twice," she said nervously. At his incomprehensible expression, she muttered, "Twice that you've paid me a compliment. Keep it up and it might become a habit."

How he wrenched his gaze away from those mesmerizing features, he never knew. He just did it and felt as if his heart had been ripped from his chest. Eyes on the road, he pressed down more firmly on the gas pedal. "Yeah," he muttered. "Wouldn't want that to happen now, would we?"

"I don't know," she said, "I might find it enjoyable, but . . ."

He glanced at her. "What?" he asked warily.

Laughter bubbled up out of her. "But you'd probably choke to death before twenty-four hours went by."

He joined in the laugh.

An easy silence fell between them and before hostilities could break out again, they had turned off the Tilda Road and were on the final leg of the journey. Five minutes later they could see lights gleaming through the forest and a moment after that the truck was pulling into the wide graveled area at the side of Sloan and Shelly's place.

Hearing the vehicle, Sloan had appeared at the door, the light from within outlining his big frame. Tumbling from the truck, Jeb hoisting a duffel bag over his shoulder and Roxanne clutching her suitcase, they hurried through the increasingly heavy snow up the wooden steps and into the cabin.

The warmth felt heavenly and after kissing her

brother on the cheek and giving Shelly a hug, Roxanne asked, "Don't tell me we're the first ones here?"

Shelly laughed. She was a tall, striking woman
with tawny hair and emerald eyes, just a few years
younger than Roxanne was. Like Roxanne, Shelly
had been born and raised in the valley, but an
abortive love affair with Sloan when she was eighteen had sent Shelly fleeing to New York and New
Orleans and she had not returned to Oak Valley for
seventeen years. Because of that and the family feud
that had existed between the Grangers and the
Ballingers since the days just following the Civil
War, Shelly and Roxanne hadn't gotten to know one
another until Sloan and Shelly had settled their differences and to everyone's surprise had married.
They had been a little wary of each other at first,
mainly Shelly, but during the past six months, they'd
discovered that they genuinely liked each other.
While the remainder of the Ballingers remained just
a trifle aloof, Roxanne, right from the beginning, had
happily welcomed Shelly into the family. They had
become not only sisters-in-law, but friends, too.

"Yes, as a matter of fact you are," Shelly said. "I
expect the others will start arriving any minute now—
although I know that M.J. and Tracy will be late.
M.J. has to close the store and Tracy has a sick calf
she's going to check on before leaving town—they'll
ride out together—provided Tracy doesn't get called
out on another emergency. But the others—Ilka,
Ross, and Sam ought to make it with no trouble."

"And God knows," said Sloan with a grin, "nothing stops the Courtland twins from reaching a party."

"Good thing you suggested we all stay overnight," Jeb commented as he handed Sloan his jacket. "The way the snow is falling, I wouldn't relish trying to make it out of here at one, two o'clock in the morning."

"I just hope everyone gets here," Shelly said worriedly. "Nick, Acey, and Maria were supposed to be here early." She glanced at the clock. "They're running a little late—I expect the weather is slowing them down." She sighed. "When we planned the party we weren't expecting it to snow." Glancing at Roxanne's suitcase she said, "Oh, enough of that. Come on, let's get you settled."

Leaving Jeb and Sloan talking in the main part of the cabin, Shelly and Roxanne walked to Shelly's studio to stow Roxanne's suitcase. As they entered the room, Shelly made a face. "Sorry that you'll be sleeping on the floor. And once M.J., Ilka, and the others pile in here, you're probably going to think you've moved into a sorority."

The cabin wasn't large; Sloan had built it for a bachelor—himself—but his marriage to Shelly in June had changed all that. Since Shelly was an artist of some repute, a studio had been mandatory. The studio had been completed a few months ago and was a large, pleasant, open room with lots of windows and a rock fireplace in one end. There was little furniture in it; a red plaid couch and a couple of small occasional tables with fat china lamps made up the majority of the furnishings. All of Shelly's supplies were put away in the oak cabinets that lined one wall and her easels and canvases were stacked in a corner out of the way. The cabinets were broken by a long countertop with faucets and a sink; a compact refrigerator sat at one end of the counter. A can of coffee, mugs, a coffeemaker, and other coffee odds and ends were set neatly in the middle of the counter. Mattresses had been flopped on the floor with sheets, quilts, and pillows piled on them for later use. Looking around, Roxanne thought that the studio would serve admirably as an extra bedroom for tonight. There was even a small bathroom. Perfect.

Dumping her suitcase on the floor near one of the single bed mattresses, Roxanne laughed. "Don't worry about it, Shelly. We'll have a ball. A slumber party for grown up women—who could ask for anything more." A sparkle lit her golden eyes. "And to make it even better . . . who knows, the guys might stage a panty raid. Poor you. You'll miss all the fun snuggled up in bed with Sloan."

Shelly chuckled. "You make it sound tempting. Maybe I'll join you." Mischief dancing in her eyes, she murmured, "I wonder if Sloan would like to bunk with the guys tonight in the barn?"

They exchanged looks and burst out laughing. "Not!" they said in unison.

Putting her arm through Shelly's, Roxanne said, "Come on, let's see what the men have been up to in our absence. Didn't you mention something about hot buttered rum tonight?"

They walked back into the main part of the cabin to find Sloan and Jeb sitting in front of the fire. A little black and silver ball of fur was curled up near by. At Shelly's entrance, it jumped up and trotted over to Shelly. Sitting on the floor at Shelly's feet, the tiny miniature schnauzer gave Shelly a pitiful look, her luxurious mustaches quivering. Shelly laughed and bending down picked up the dog and gave her a cuddle. "That look doesn't fool me, Pandora," she said with mock sternness to the dog. "I know what you're up to. The only reason you're even noticing me is because Sloan wouldn't let you in his lap."

Melting black eyes stared back at her from beneath long, shaggy silver eyebrows. A quick flip of a pink tongue on her cheek made Shelly laugh again. "I'm still not fooled. But since you've pulled out all the stops, I'll let you sit in my lap."

Roxanne grinned. "Looks like she's finally accepted the fact that you're not going to go away."

Sloan looked over at them. "For a while there I thought I might actually have to choose between my wife or my dog." His warm gaze rested on Shelly. "Would have been a hard choice."

Shelly sniffed, though her eyes were smiling. "Keep talking like that and you *will* end up sleeping in the barn with the rest of the guys."

"Hey, hey, I never said I wouldn't have chosen you in the end," Sloan drawled, a grin tugging at the corners of his mouth. "I only said it would have been a hard choice."

Before Shelly could reply they all heard the sound of another vehicle. Shelly put down Pandora and said, "Looks like we have more arrivals."

Chapter
10

*L*aughter and conversation could be heard above the shutting of vehicle doors and Sloan strolled over to the front door. Opening it, he glanced outside, then said over his shoulder to Shelly, "You can stop worrying— it's Nick and his mother and Acey." He looked outside again. "And it looks like they've brought a couple of stragglers with them."

Acey and Maria, Nick's mother, laden down with grocery sacks and a heavy cardboard box from which emanated the most delicious smells, entered the house first. Both Acey Babbitt and Maria Rios had worked for Shelly's family almost as long as she could remember. She'd grown up around both of them and since the death of her brother, Josh, in early March and her return to the valley a few weeks after that, she looked upon them as her only remaining family. And then there was Nick, Maria's son . . . Nick who looked at times very much like Josh. . . .

Nick, carrying a small ice chest, followed his

mother and Acey and as his eyes met Shelly's, they softened, affection deepening their emerald color—the exact shade of green as Shelly's own. Brushing a kiss on her cheek, he asked softly, "You still want to do this? Tonight?"

Shelly clutched his jacket, nodding. "Yes. You?"

He took a deep breath. "Yeah. Been a secret too long."

There was a loud clearing of the throat behind Nick. He grinned. "Oh, I forgot—the reason we're late."

He stepped aside to reveal the couple standing on the deck behind him. Shelly took one look and rushing outside with arms spread, squealed, "Roman. And Pagan! What a lovely surprise."

Jeb looked at Sloan. "Pagan?" he murmured out of the side of his mouth.

Sloan grinned. "Shelly says it's a southern thing—she's got an Uncle Fritzie and an Aunt Lulu—Pagan and Roman's parents. Tom, the eldest, is the only one with what you could say is a 'normal' name. There's another brother named Noble and another sister named Angelique—I met the whole lot when Shelly and I were in New Orleans for our honeymoon. There's a ton of other cousins, too . . . let's see, uh, Storm, Hero, and, oh, yeah, Wolfe. There's more but their names escape me at the moment."

"Jesus. And Mingo thought he had a weird name," Jeb said with a shake of his head. He got his first look at Pagan just then as she entered the room and shrugged out of her coat. His eyes widened and he whistled under his breath. "Uh-oh, she looks like trouble for all the males in the valley—and, unless I miss my guess, a hundred miles beyond."

Being introduced to Roman's youngest sister, Roxanne was thinking much the same thing. Having lived and worked with some of the most celebrated beauties in the world, Roxanne was used to beautiful women, but Pagan had to be, she admitted, one of the most stunning females she'd ever seen in her life.

Pagan Louise Granger was not a tall woman. She stood only five feet six in her bare feet, but there was a lot packed in between the top and bottom. A lot. She was daintily made but with a bust that usually occasioned a second look by most males. For her height her legs were long and shapely and her hips slim and taut. Like Roman she had a feline grace.

But despite that perfect body of hers, it was her hair that usually caught most people's attention. Pagan had been blessed or, as she often suspected, cursed with the most incredible shade of red hair ever seen by man; that it was natural only made it more incredible. Tonight that burgundy-red hair was worn loose around her shoulders like a cloud of dark fire. Her hair was clearly red, but of such a deep shade that in certain lights you'd almost swear that there were strands of plum and claret mixed in.

The heart-shaped face that hair framed was equally remarkable. The impact of her wide-spaced, long-lashed almost lilac-hued eyes had been known to make strong men tremble. She had an elegant little nose that

Helen of Troy would have killed for, a generous mouth that made even puritanical males think lascivious thoughts, and cheekbones that sent master sculptors scrambling for their tools. Alabaster skin and a smile that had enough wattage to light up a midsize city completed the package.

Being the object of that smile, Roxanne almost blinked. Oh, my, she thought, amused, aren't the boys going to fall all over themselves trying to impress you. She glanced up and saw the way Jeb was staring at Pagan and her amusement fled. Not *Jeb*, she thought, oddly panicked at the idea of him falling for this southern beauty. Upset and not knowing why, she quickly turned Pagan over to Nick who had just come back out of the kitchen.

Roxanne disappeared into the kitchen, needing a moment to get her thoughts under control. She was so used to having men fall at her feet, that jealousy was an emotion she had seldom experienced. So what exactly was she feeling right now? I can't be jealous—not about Jeb. I mean, come on, so we had a tumble together, it was no big deal. It had been a *physical* thing—her emotions hadn't been involved. Right? She bit her lip. That frenzied coupling on the countertop shouldn't have made a difference in her feelings toward him—it certainly shouldn't have made her feel all green-eyed with jealousy when Jeb just looked at another woman. I'm not jealous, she told herself firmly. Oh, but you are, whispered a voice slyly in her brain. Maybe he means more to you than you realized—have you considered that? Maybe what happened back in September *hadn't* been just a mindless, hormone driven sexual act. She shook her head, trying to silence the voice, but it continued. Maybe somewhere down deep inside, crooned the voice, you're actually attracted to Jeb Delaney—and not just physically. Maybe there's something more going on between the pair of you. Roxanne almost moaned aloud at the idea. Oh, please, I don't have time for this! Shut up, she hissed to the voice in her brain, and go away—I don't want any serious involvement right now and certainly *not* with Jeb.

Her emotions in a jumble, Roxanne strolled out of the kitchen and over to where Jeb was standing, his gaze still fixed on Pagan who was laughing at something Nick said as he handed her a mug of hot, mulled cider.

Roxanne gave him a sharp jab in the side and muttered, "Put your tongue back in your mouth. Didn't anyone ever tell you that it's impolite to stare?"

His attention immediately settled on her and Roxanne wished she'd kept her mouth shut. God. She'd sounded like a jealous wife. To make it worse, there was something very male and satisfied in Jeb's eyes as he looked at her. It unsettled her even further. A lazy smile curved his mouth. "Jealous, Princess?"

"When hell freezes over," she snapped, thoroughly ruffled, and spun on her heel intending to put as much room as possible between herself and a certain Neanderthal.

She only took half a step before a strong male arm wrapped around her and jerked her back. Jeb grinned down into her stormy face. "Come on, Roxy, you've got to admit that the kid's gorgeous." He lifted a mocking brow. "And the last time I checked, I was single and fancy-free. I'm allowed to look—or more if I want to."

Her eyes shooting gold flames, her hands clenched into fists, she snarled, "Be my guest. Go ahead. Rob the cradle if that turns you on."

He laughed and uncaring who saw it brushed his lips against hers. "My point exactly. She's an eyeful, but she's just a baby." His gaze rested on the lips he had just touched. "My taste tends to run to more, ah, mature women." Ignoring her outraged stare, his face laughing down at her, he murmured, "Just to put your mind at rest—she's not my type." He glanced over to where Pagan stood and added, "But Jesus, Princess, even you must see that she's one incredible package." Before Roxanne could reply, he turned back to her and his lips touched hers again, longer this time. When he lifted his head, his eyes were no longer laughing. "Not," he said huskily, "that she holds a candle to you. No one could."

"As if I care," she muttered, wishing his words didn't send a flash of warmth through her. What in the world was wrong with her? Jealous wasn't a word she would have ever applied to herself, but she was honest enough to admit that when she'd seen Jeb staring with such open admiration at Pagan, she'd felt something perilously close to it.

At the moment everyone else was taken up with greetings and unpacking the food that had arrived with Nick and the others, leaving Roxanne and Jeb isolated in a little circle all their own. They were standing off a ways from the others, almost hidden in a corner. As had happened before that veil of intimacy seemed to wrap around them, everything fading away until they were only aware of each other.

His expression unreadable, Jeb said slowly, "I think you do."

"What?"

"Care."

Roxanne reared back to glower up at him. "Are you nuts? You know I can't stand you—and you don't like me very much either."

"Then how," he asked quietly, "do you explain what happens between us? Something does. It has ever since that day. Whether you want to admit it or not, something changed between us then."

Roxanne froze, wishing she had kept her mouth shut and never started this conversation. She was so confused. She wasn't a jealous person, yet she had felt jealous only a few moments ago. She didn't like Jeb, yet she couldn't forget those moments in his arms and the very last thing she ever wanted to talk about was *that* day. Escape seemed her only option, but when she tried to leave, his arm tightened around her waist.

"Things changed. Admit it," he demanded.

Her chin lifted. "Are you referring to that time . . . we, uh, you know . . . in my house?"

"Made love on your countertop?"

"We didn't make love. We had sex," she said through gritted teeth.

"Now why, I wonder, is it so much easier for you to call it sex than making love?"

Roxanne ran a trembling hand through her hair. "Because that's what it was." Almost desperately she added, "It couldn't have been anything else." She took a deep breath. "Look," she said, "I don't want to talk about this. And certainly not here."

"OK," he said affably, removing his restraining arm. "We'll do it later."

Roxanne left his side as if shot from a gun, his words sounding ominously like a warning.

Seeing that Maria and Shelly were setting out food on the table, Roxanne leaped in to help. Not only had Shelly and Sloan prepared a slew of finger food, but everyone else had brought along a little something extra. Soon enough the dining-area table was straining beneath the array of food, plates, napkins, and utensils. There was a big red Crock-Pot filled with tiny sweet and sour meatballs, Roxanne's artichoke frittata cut into dainty squares came next, stuffed mushrooms, and then a large tray brimming with crudities, carrots, broccoli, cauliflower, cherry tomatoes, and the like. A warming tray kept cheese puffs, mini spinach quiches, Maria's chili-cheese triangles, and bite-size barbecued spareribs hot; a creamy olive-nut spread with small rounds of rye and onion bread sat nearby and scattered in between were several different kinds of chips and, of course, dips galore. To drink there was hot buttered-rum and spiced, mulled apple cider and wine or beer. And for the sweet tooth . . . . Ah, Maria had baked four of her apple pies—much to Acey's unabashed delight. But if apple pie didn't suit, there were also lemon bars, cream cheese pies, and Pagan and Roman had brought a huge platter of melt-in-your-mouth pralines direct from New Orleans. It might not be a sit down dinner, but no one was going to go hungry.

The last of the food had just been set out when the Courtland twins arrived, bringing more food—pretzels, crackers, and a chunky guacamole made by Jason and corn salsa made by Morgan. The food was given into Shelly's waiting hands and Sloan dispensed with their jackets.

Roxanne had been waiting for their introduction to Pagan and she almost laughed aloud at their expressions. Watching their eyes glaze and their faces go slack, Roxanne's sense of humor came back. Jeb was right. Pagan was one incredible package. But what impressed Roxanne most was that Pagan seemed totally unaware of the effect she had on the opposite sex.

As expected, M.J. and Tracy were the last to arrive. Ilka, Ross, and Sam had driven up shortly after the Courtland twins and Shelly had been anxiously awaiting the last of her guests. As the two women, one blond, one redhead, piled into the house, Shelly rushed up to them and, giving them a hug, exclaimed, "Oh,

I'm so glad you got here. I was worried with the snow and everything."

Sloan came up to stand behind his wife, one hand resting on her shoulder. "And I'm doubly glad you're here," he said. "She's been fussing for the last half hour and any second I've been expecting her to send me out to look for you." Amid the laughter and Shelly's halfhearted protests, the two women were divested of their heavy jackets and urged to join the others.

As they started away, Sloan glanced at Tracy and asked, "Calf OK?"

Tracy nodded, smiling. Tracy Kingsley was the local vet and worked for both Shelly and Sloan. While Tracy had a small clinic on her property and did tend to dogs and cats, her specialty was horses. Sloan had been elated when she had moved to the valley about ten years ago, since he bred and raised very, *very* expensive American paint horses. Until Tracy's advent, the nearest big animal vet had been, at the least, over ninety minutes away. When you had a mare foaling and a problem arose, there wasn't a moment to waste—having a vet in the valley had been a godsend as far as Sloan was concerned.

Tracy wasn't fond of cows—and made no bones about it—but since she was a vet and had a living to make, she had quite a few cattle ranchers as clients, Shelly and Nick among them. Tracy had been one of the first "new" people Shelly had met when she had returned to the valley and had liked the other woman on the spot. In the ensuing months they had become good friends.

It was a great party. The food was plentiful and there were just enough differences among the guests to make the conversation interesting and the evening lively. Of course, everyone was happy with Roman's return and Pagan provided a magnet to the men, which gave the women a moment or two to speculate about the newcomer.

"God. She's gorgeous!" said M.J. for perhaps the tenth time that evening. Sitting on the hearth, a plate full of nibbles in front of her, she looked at Pagan's lovely face and sighed. "Guess I might as well wear sackcloth and ashes as long as she's in the valley. No one's going to be looking in my direction."

"Oh, come on," said Roxanne. "You've got a lot going for you. You're cute as a button and you know it. Don't tell me that the men don't like those big brown eyes of yours and that mop of blond hair." She cocked a brow. "And you've got curves—something I'd kill for."

M.J.'s mouth fell open. "You're kidding, right?"

"Nope. Trust me, being tall and slim has its disadvantages."

"She's right, you know," offered Tracy. "I'm five-nine and I remember what it was like to be the tallest girl . . . in the school." She grinned at M.J. "I'd have hated you in high school—you'd have been the cute little cheerleader all the guys on the football team would have gone after. Tall skinny girls like me didn't stand a chance."

M.J. made a face. "I never got a chance to be a cheerleader—Shelly and I went to a private girls' school, remember." She glanced over to where Pagan was standing surrounded by the Courtland twins, Ross, and Nick and sighed heavily and looked glum—as glum as someone with her lively gamine face could.

Shelly laughed—she and M.J. had been friends practically since birth and she knew that look. "Come on, M.J. If you'd wanted one of those guys, you'd have done something about it months, years ago. Don't tell me you're going to act like a dog in a manger?"

M.J. gave that infectious little giggle of hers. "You're right. It's hard to get excited about men you've known all your life."

"Besides, I thought, like me, you were off men," commented Sam, sitting on the floor beside M.J.

M.J. and Sam were both divorced. Both divorces had become final in 1999 and both divorces had been painful. Married for less than four years, Sam thought she had been lucky that she'd found out what a scumbag her husband had been before they'd had children. M.J., on the other hand, married for over ten years and with two young sons, was grateful every day for her two children. She shared joint custody with their father, a highway patrolman, and treasured every moment she was able to spend with the boys. While Sam had remained in the Novato area after her divorce and raised champion miniature schnauzers—Pandora was one of hers—M.J. had returned to the valley and since her family owned the largest grocery store in the valley, she had found a job ready-made for her.

Ilka, wearing an icy blue silk shirt and tailored dark blue slacks, was sitting like a small fey cat on a footstool across from M.J. "I don't think you really have anything to worry about with Pagan," Ilka said thoughtfully. "First of all, she's only here for a visit, and second of all, she seems friendly and nice."

"I saw you two chatting away earlier," said Roxanne. "What was that about?"

"Oh, just polite talk, the weather, the differences between here and New Orleans. But she seemed genuine, maybe even a little shy, and not at all like a man-killer." She looked over to Pagan. "In fact, I'll bet, she'd be delighted if one of us rescued her about now."

"Think so?" asked M.J. doubtfully.

Ilka nodded. "I know I would—wouldn't you? New girl in town, all the guys rushing you and the other women staying off in a corner all cozy by themselves to talk about you. Pagan's no dummy, she knows we're talking about her."

A collective pang of guilt went through the group and they all looked over in Pagan's direction.

"Ilka's right," Roxanne said with surprise. "Pagan does seem a bit beleaguered. I'll go rescue her."

"Wait, I'll go with you," said M.J., jumping to her feet.

"And me," chimed in Sam. "Us women have got to stick together."

The men never knew what hit them. One minute they were clustered around Pagan and the next she was whisked right out from underneath their noses and hustled away to the female group by the fire. None of them were brave enough to try to wrest her away.

Making room for Pagan next to her on the hearth, Shelly said, "We thought you'd like a break from your adoring public."

"Are western men always so kind and charming?" Pagan asked in a warm brown sugar drawl, a twinkle in those incredibly hued eyes of hers. "Now I thought that southern men had all the moves down, but those guys. . . ."

"Pretty slick, huh?" asked M.J., grinning.

Accepting a glass of wine from Ilka, Pagan nodded. "Indeed yes. My mama warned me about Yankees, but she never breathed a word about westerners. Whew."

She smiled at M.J., Sam, and Roxanne. "Thank you so much for inviting me to join you."

Naturally they all pestered her with questions. How long would she be visiting? About two weeks—depended upon Roman. Where exactly did she live? New Orleans. What did she do? Computer programmer.

At that M.J.'s ears perked up. "I don't suppose you'd like to make it a working holiday and maybe help me out in the store? We put in a new computer system this fall and it's about to drive me around the bend."

"Sure," Pagan said easily. "I wouldn't mind a bit." She grimaced. "I'll confess it—I'm a computer nerd and I get all twitchy and weird if I don't get my hands on a computer every few days."

That brought out protests, but the conversation moved on, the collective opinion being that while Pagan was definitely a stunner, she was intelligent, too, and didn't take herself or her looks very seriously. And while a definitive decision couldn't be made on a half hour or so of conversation, the group decided that so far Pagan fitted right in.

M.J. looked around the room, a puzzled expression on her face. "Where's Mingo and Danny? I don't see them anywhere."

"Mingo had a hot date with a woman in Santa Rosa and Danny's on patrol tonight," Shelly replied. "I asked Cleo to come, but she only looked smug and said she already had plans."

"Really? You think she and Hank are finally getting serious?"

"With Cleo you never know," Roxanne said, grinning. "And since she's been married five times, nothing would surprise me."

"And Bobba? What was his excuse?" M.J. asked quietly, her brown eyes troubled.

M.J., Shelly, Danny, and Bobba had been best friends practically from birth. Their families had been friends and as small children they had always been in one another's company. The bonds forged in those long-ago days still held, but Bobba seemed to be drifting away.

Shelly sighed. "I asked, but his wife informed me that they had already made plans to attend some gala event in San Francisco."

"Bobba's going to hate that," remarked Ilka. "Bess should know that he'd have preferred being here than hanging around with her friends and family."

M.J. looked fierce. "Bess doesn't care what Bobba wants. Haven't you ever listened to her? Everything is about her and for her and she's been doing everything she can to keep him away from his own friends and family. They spend every free moment with *her* family and *her* friends—and as for seeing any of Bobba's friends, why, they're always just *so* busy. And Bobba, stupid cluck, thinks she's just wonderful."

"Well, she is his wife," Ilka said gently. "Most men do tend to think their wives are wonderful."

M.J. glared at her. "Don't remind me. And what he ever saw in her but a pretty face is beyond me."

Tongue in cheek, Shelly murmured, "She has culture, don't forget."

Intrigued, Roxanne asked, "Culture?"

Shelly nodded. "Um-hmm. And, of course, as she informed me the first time I met her—Oak Valley has absolutely none. Not a speck of culture. According to her, the valley is a dreadful place and just as soon as her daddy arranges it, Bobba is going to be offered a *real* job in San Rafael, where they can attend just all sorts of cultural events."

"And Bobba, the sweet blockhead, will take the damn job for her and be miserable," M.J. said mournfully. "He loves the valley. It'll kill him to leave, but for her, he'll do it."

"You can't live someone else's life for them," Pagan offered gently, her eyes kind. "Maybe making his wife happy means more to him than his own happiness."

M.J. and Shelly looked at each and sighed heavily. "You're probably right," M.J. admitted. "It's just that we've known him for so long. . . ."

"And you can't stand his wife," Roxanne murmured, a slight smile curving her mouth.

"You're right," M.J. said glumly. "We can't."

The conversation became more general and a few minutes later the women were talking about the Super Bowl playoffs, everyone having their favorites. Except for Pagan who naturally wanted the Saints to make it and Shelly and Roxanne being die-hard Raiders fans, everyone else was rooting for the Forty-Niners.

"You've got it all wrong," said a male voice. "My money's on the Broncos."

Almost as one the women looked up at Acey. Blue eyes brimming with laughter, white hair gleaming silver in the light, he wriggled his handsome handlebar mustaches. "I'd hate to take your money, but if you're gonna bet on them other teams, so be it. Broncos it is."

There was a mutual booing and hooting at Acey's words, but he only grinned and took a seat in the only empty chair near the fire. Looking at Shelly, he said, "Nice party. Glad you and Sloan thought of it."

Maria walked up and, taking the place Shelly offered her, sat down on the hearth. She looked at Acey and snorted. "Any time there's apple pie in the offing is a nice party for you."

Acey appeared thoughtful. A sly smile on his wrinkled face, he murmured, "But only if it's one of yours."

"One of whose what?" asked Sloan, dragging a couple chairs up for himself and his wife.

"Maria's apple pies," replied Sam, smiling up at her eldest brother.

"Not dessert, already," said Jason as he and the other men invaded the area. "I still haven't sampled everything on the table yet."

They all found places around the fire, some of the men sprawling on the floor, others drawing up odd chairs as Sloan had done. Full of good food, warm and comfortable, everyone was in a relaxed, lazy mood. The conversation jumped around as they told tales on each other, or expressed concerns about the economy and how it would affect livestock production and life in the valley. A moment later it would veer off into a different direction, focusing on Roman and Pagan, then about Morgan's real estate business, how many foals Sloan expected in the spring, was Nick and Shelly's cattle operation doing OK, and then back to telling outrageous stories about each other. There was the easy camaraderie of people who had known one another a long time. And liked each other.

Sloan got up and grabbed a couple pieces of oak firewood from the front deck. "Brrrr," he said as he came back inside. "Man, it's cold out there." He tossed the wood on the fire and reseated himself next to Shelly. "Glad you're all staying the night—it's still snowing and accumulating out there."

"Yeah, but you're making us sleep in the barn," teased Nick. "How come you get to stay in here with all the women, while we're banished to a freezing barn?"

Sloan smiled sleepily. "My house, my rules. Besides, the barn is heated and you know it. You won't freeze."

"Yeah, but I might damage my delicate skin," drawled Jason, green eyes gleaming.

"Jason's right," said Ross, grinning. "Putting us in the barn just isn't fair. Why, who knows, we might get chapped lips or something."

"I knew a guy had terrible chapped lips once," said Acey. "Worst case I ever saw in my entire life."

Shelly rolled her eyes. "And you're going to tell us about him, aren't you?"

"If you'd like me to."

Sloan chuckled. "Please, we can hardly wait."

"Well, it happened this way," began Acey. He looked around to make certain he had everyone's attention. "This was back in the old days, you understand, before we had all these fancy lip balms and such available today. And being as how we all worked out in the weather, rain or shine, chapped lips could be a problem. Anyway, I was working for the old Bar T then and I'd gone into town to get me a beer and a sandwich for lunch. Wasn't a bad day for January, sun was out, so I was sitting out on the front porch of the old hotel with a couple of other guys when we see this old cowpuncher ride up on his horse. We all said hello and watched as he got off his horse and tied him at the rail." He stopped and looked around at his attentive listeners. "We still had hitching rails in town in them days."

"When was this?" Nick drawled, smiling. "In the prehistoric age?"

"Nick!" scolded his mother. "You let Acey tell his story."

Acey beamed at Maria. "Thank you. Well, anyways, as I was saying, this old cowboy got off his horse and tied him to the hitching rail. And then right before our very eyes he did the most amazing thing I've ever seen. He walked around to the back of his horse, lifted the animal's tail, and stuck his arm half up . . ." He glanced at the women and hesitated. "Well, you know where he stuck his arm up. And danged, if he didn't take what he'd just pulled out of the back end of that horse and wipe it on his lips."

There was a chorus of ughs and eewws, from the women.

"You're making that up," accused Roxanne.

"Nope. I ain't. I saw it with my own eyes. Fellow

wiped horseshi-, er, horse manure right across his lips."

"Why?" demanded Roxanne suspiciously.

"You know I asked him that very question," Acey replied earnestly. "I said, 'What'd you do that for?' and he said that he had a bad case of chapped lips. Well, naturally I was plumb curious so I asked him if it worked. He admitted as how he didn't know if it helped his lips or not . . . but that it sure kept him from licking 'em."

There was a burst of laughter and smiling. Roxanne shook her finger at Acey. "You're an evil man, Acey Babbitt."

"Got ya, didn't I?" Acey chortled, his blue eyes dancing with glee.

"Bull's-eye," replied Jeb, still chuckling.

They spent the time waiting for midnight, laughing and talking, telling more stories on each other. As midnight rang out, there was a chorus of "Happy New Years," hugs were exchanged, and Sloan offered a toast welcoming in the New Year.

As their glasses were lowered, Shelly stood up and stepped to Nick's side. They stood side by side with clasped hands, their resemblance suddenly very marked. Shelly glanced over at Sloan and he nodded encouragingly. Nick looked at his mother. Maria sighed and slowly nodded. Acey came to sit by her, his gnarled hand covering hers. She smiled gratefully at him.

Shelly cleared her throat. "Uh, we have an announcement to make. We thought since it was a New Year that we'd start it out with a bang."

She had everyone's attention and somewhat nervously, she said, "As you all know there have long been rumors that my brother Josh was Nick's father. We decided that tonight would be a good time to set those rumors to rest. We invited you here, first of all because you're our friends, and second, because we wanted you to know the truth and to help us make it public."

Shelly took a deep breath. "Josh, at his wish, was cremated, so we had no way of obtaining any of his DNA to prove or disprove that Nick was Josh's son. Last summer, determined to settle the matter once and for all, Roman, Nick, and I had our DNA samples taken. Mine alone would have been enough to prove a relationship between Nick and me. But I felt we needed a bit more—Roman had volunteered to give his DNA and we'd had all of our samples taken when I decided to have my father's body disinterred to try to get a sample of his DNA from his remains." She smiled faintly. "Fortunately Dad didn't believe in embalming and despite the odds, we were able to obtain a good sample."

Nick swallowed. His face was pale and he was holding on so tight to Shelly that his hand nearly crushed hers. He'd waited years for this moment and now that it was at hand, he was almost overwhelmed and anxious. Did he really want to lay his past bare? Have people looking at him? At his mother? Whispering about the two of them behind their backs? Once

Shelly made her announcement, there would be no more secrets and . . . no turning back.

Sensing his turmoil, Shelly squeezed his hand and smiled at him and that smile, so warm and affectionate, calmed him.

She glanced back at the intent group gathered around them. "It took a while to get the results and when they arrived, they weren't what we expected. We were stunned, hardly able to believe what those DNA samples revealed. But even though they didn't prove what we expected, they were wonderful." She looked at Nick, her eyes full of love. "I'd like to introduce you," she said softly as she turned back to the group, "not to my nephew as everyone thought, but to my *brother,* Nick Rios."

Chapter
11

There was a second of silence and then the room erupted into a babble of gasps, exclamations, and questions. Sloan raised a quieting hand.

"OK, OK, everybody, pipe down." When the noise subsided, he said, "I told Shelly and Nick and Maria that there were going to be a ton of questions." He smiled crookedly. "You can't just toss out that sort of information and *not* have a lot of questions. But we decided early on that there was no reason for the public"—he flashed a hard look around the room—"and that includes you, to know *all* the details. What you need to know right now is that Nick *is* Shelly's brother—we have proof of it. Shelly is publicly acknowledging that Nick Rios is her brother. And before you ask, no, Nick isn't going to change his name to Granger." He grinned at Nick. "As he said from the beginning, he's been a Rios too long to change. What he was always after was simply the truth. That it turned out to be more than any of us expected is just one of life's little surprises. And yes, Shelly is splitting the Granger estate with him. And no, he didn't ask for it and has been arguing with his sister not to do just that. But stubbornness runs in the family and Shelly is determined that he should have what is morally his." His gaze swept the room again. "As for the secrecy all these years, I think that's self-explanatory. Now as for what you tell anyone else, that's your business—and we want you to tell everybody. That's the point of this. We wanted to get the truth out, but we didn't"— Sloan's mouth twisted slightly—"want to take out a full page ad in the newspaper. We figured if people we trusted knew the truth and they treated it as if it were nothing out of the ordinary, that we might brush through this with little more than a few weeks of rampant curiosity on the part of the valley inhabitants."

Sitting on the arm of the couch, Jeb scratched his chin. "So just how do you expect us to handle this? Are we all just supposed to march into town tomorrow and start shooting our mouths off?"

"Not exactly," Sloan replied with a glimmer of a smile. "I figured you'd probably tell Mingo, your sister and your dad first. Then they'll mention it to someone else and so on. Shelly and I will tell my folks—and Cleo. They were supposed to be here tonight, but for various reasons they couldn't make it. They'll be told tomorrow, or just as soon as we can arrange it."

A chuckle rippled through the group. "Once it

reaches Cleo," murmured Roxanne, "it'll be all over town."

"My point exactly," Sloan drawled. "We *want* it all over town, but the truth, not gossip and innuendo, even though there will be a lot of that anyway, no matter what we do."

There was a collective nodding of heads. "Sounds like a plan to me," said Ross, rising elegantly to his feet and walking over to where Nick and Shelly stood. He reached out and offered his hand to Nick. "Since your sister is married to my brother, I think that makes us in-laws of sorts. Welcome to the family."

"And to ours," said Roman, following Ross's lead and clapping Nick on the back. "I should warn you," he said with a smile, "that you might find being a member of this family a bit overwhelming . . . and that a family can be a curse, as well as a blessing." With that leopardlike grace of his he turned to Maria who had said little. "And Madame Maria, as Nick's mother, may I welcome you also to the family." He smiled whimsically down at her. "Since we are related, dare I call you Cousin Maria?"

Maria looked uncomfortable, but she nodded. "Yes, I would like that." Her eyes dropped. "Thank you for being so kind." Her voice was thick and it was clear she was on the verge of tears.

Roman frowned, started to say something, but Shelly nudged him and shook her head. "Later," she mouthed to him.

Acey, who had stood on the sidelines observing

everything, ambled up with that rolling gait of his that bespoke a lifelong horseman and thumbs hooked into the waist of his new, knife-edged creased Levi's, grinned at Nick. "Does this mean," he demanded with a glint in his eyes, "that I have to call you *Mr.* now?"

Nick smiled at the old man. "Would you?"

"Hell, no," replied Acey with relish. "But considering my age you could call me Mr. Babbitt."

Nick laughed. "And would you answer?"

"Course not. You know I don't hold with all them fancy manners." Grinning from ear to ear, Acey pumped Nick's hand enthusiastically. "Congratulations, son. I'm damned happy for you. This is something that should have happened a long time ago." He cast a chiding eye in Maria's direction. "And would have if certain people didn't have such a misplaced sense of loyalty."

Her voice wounded, Maria protested, "I promised. Josh promised. We swore to Señor Granger that we would never tell." She glanced unhappily across to Shelly. "You understand?"

Aware of the curious eyes, Shelly smiled gently and put her arm around the other woman, deftly maneuvering her away from the crowd. "Yes, I understand. Don't worry about it," she said when she felt certain they would not be overheard.

Her head half-hidden against Shelly's breast, Maria murmured, "I'm so ashamed. Everyone will be looking at me, thinking that I was Señor Granger's woman." She raised tear-filled eyes. "I was not. There was only that one time, I swear to you."

Sloan walked over and positioning himself so that Maria was hidden from the rest of the room, he said, "We believe you. We knew there would be talk, but you said that you wanted no more secrets. There's going to be gossip and a ton of speculation, but it'll pass. It's a brave thing you're doing for your son—remember that. You keep that chin of yours up. We're behind you. You don't have to face this alone."

Maria took a deep breath and stepped away from Shelly's comforting embrace. "I know what you say is true, it is just that it is going to be hard to pretend I don't see the looks or hear the whispers." Her mouth drooped and her hands twisted together. "I knew it would be hard, I just hadn't realized *how* hard, how naked and exposed I would feel." She smiled weakly. "And this is in front of people of who are sympathetic—how is it going to feel when I face those who have ugly hearts and minds?"

Roxanne met Jeb's eyes. Both of them thinking the same thing. Gossip was going to run rampant, with Maria's relationship with Shelly's father getting the juiciest play. As the news spread—and it would—like wildfire—the valley would be electrified. Very few people would have the nerve to ask Maria about the situation, but it was certainly going to be the topic of conversation and speculation all through the valley for weeks to come and they all knew that it would never entirely go away. Someone would always bring it up.

Nick would come into his share of it, too, but since he was the innocent product, except for the spiteful and mean-spirited, there would be few slurs cast his way. Not so for his mother. Nor so for Shelly's father or even her mother—there would be people who would wonder if Catherine Granger had known the truth, if she had condoned the situation or been completely ignorant of it.

Shelly hugged Maria closer, wishing there had been an easier way to handle this. Since her parents were both dead, she hadn't worried about what the gossips would say about them. She might not like it, but they were beyond being hurt by busy tongues. Maria's case was different. They had discussed it at length and had tried to find a way to avoid Maria being thrown to the wolves. Beyond extending their protection and the protection of their family and friends, Sloan and Shelly just hadn't seen any other way to protect her. They had considered keeping Nick's parentage secret—Nick's own suggestion. All he'd ever wanted to know was the truth. He didn't care who else knew— and he wasn't keen on people speculating about his mother. Shelly and Sloan would have respected his wishes and kept it private if Maria hadn't insisted that there be no more secrets. Though she had tried desperately to keep the vow she had sworn all those years ago, it was a relief to finally admit the truth. She had denied her son the name of his father all his life and had watched him suffer because of it. She had suffered, too, her heart bleeding every time Nick had begged her to tell him and she had pushed him away. "It was shameful what happened between Señor Granger and me, but Nick has nothing to be ashamed of. The sin was Señor Granger's and mine. If we continue to keep it a secret to protect me, then we are still punishing Nick." She had smiled tremulously at Shelly across the oak table in the kitchen in what had been Josh's house. "I should face up to the past." She had glanced at her son, her face full of love. "He should be known as Señor Granger's son. After all these years and all the lies, he deserves it. It is his right."

Once Maria had given the go-ahead, they'd had to come up with a way to make the announcement. Shelly and Nick had both thought that New Year's Eve was an excellent time. "A new beginning," Shelly had said. "Off with old and on with the new," Nick had added. And so it had come about. There was no going back now.

After the first storm of astonishment died down, Sloan, aided by Roman and Acey, tactfully turned the conversation toward a less personal topic, and though eaten up with curiosity, everyone politely followed their lead. Roman launched into an explanation of the southern custom of eating black-eyed peas on New Year's Day; Jeb told a story about Mingo waking up with a skunk in his sleeping bag, and Acey reminisced about some of the early cattle gatherings on the Granger ranch and the awkwardness passed. Several people were yawning and beginning to think of bed when the stories gradually wound down and it was almost as if Shelly's big announcement had never taken place. Almost.

Before departing for their various beds, despite Shelly's protests, everyone had pitched in and helped clean up. Since paper plates and napkins had been the order of the day and all the cooking had been done ahead of time, it didn't take very long. Twenty minutes later, the house was quiet, Sloan having gone with the men to get things set up in the barn and most of the women busy making their beds in Shelly's studio.

Roxanne had stayed to help Shelly wrap and put away the last of the leftovers. They worked amiably in the kitchen together for several seconds, until Roxanne couldn't stand it anymore and asked, "Weren't you shocked?"

For a second Shelly looked blank. "Oh, you mean about Nick?" When Roxanne nodded, she said, "Maybe. But at first I was just so happy to find out that I had a brother that I didn't even think about what it really meant. By the time I did think about it, I didn't care." She laughed. "Finding out that Nick Rios is my half brother is one of the best things that's ever happened to me. And as for the circumstances—it happened a long time ago. My dad's dead. My mom's dead. And Josh is dead. Maria was the only one left alive who knew the facts. If it weren't for DNA we might not have ever known." She shook her head, a sad smile curving her generous mouth. "Poor Josh.

Dad wasn't fair about that—letting Josh take the blame and swearing him to silence."

Roxanne raised a brow. "I'd say that Josh wasn't the only one he wasn't fair to—what about your mom? And Nick? And Maria?"

Shelly made a face. "Them, too. He acted badly, no denying it—it was a terrible thing and he comes out of it looking tawdry and spineless—which he wasn't . . . not really. Except for this one mistake, he lived a pretty honorable life. And Maria . . . I don't really blame Maria for what happened—don't forget she'd only been in this country nine, ten years—she didn't even speak English fluently then—she was young and naive."

Roxanne snorted. At Shelly's look, she added hastily, "OK, I'm sorry. I know she practically raised you and that you're fond of her, but the fact remains she did sleep with your dad."

"Did you know that as a young woman her mother worked for a wealthy patron in Mexico?"

Roxanne shook her head, wondering where this was going.

"Hmmm, well, she did—before she was married. It seems that some old ways die hard and, remember, we're talking Mexico and over fifty years ago. In those days work at the hacienda was greatly desired—it was that or in the fields. Everyone considered it an honor to work in the hacienda. When Maria's mother was hired, her own mother took her aside and explained that it was understood that sooner or later El Patron might seek out her bed. Like many Mexicans, her family was very poor, desperate—they needed every peso Maria's mother earned. She was told that if she wanted to keep her job, that she would submit to whatever El Patron demanded and keep her mouth shut. So she did." She turned to stare hard at Roxanne. "When Maria began working for us, she was told something similar by *her* mother."

Roxanne's mouth fell open. "You mean her mother told her that your dad would hit on her and that she had to put up with it?"

"Something like that. Maria didn't really believe her—after all, this was America, not Mexico, and her memories of Mexico were vague. She thought her mother was being old and silly. Señor Granger, she told her mother, was nice to her, he would never ask her to sleep with him." Shelly made a face. "And it probably never would have happened if my folks hadn't had some problems—which isn't an excuse, but I suppose you call it an extenuating circumstance. I was too little to remember it, but my folks separated for a while and Mom and I went away for four or five months and lived in Ukiah. Anyway, Maria says one night Dad came home half swacked and found her in the kitchen in her nightgown—she'd gotten up for a glass of milk . . ." She wrinkled her nose with distaste. "Anyway, they did the deed and that was that, until Maria turned up pregnant."

"One time?" Roxanne asked sarcastically.

"According to Maria . . . and I believe her. Maybe

I'm trying to make excuses for my dad, and her. Maybe I just don't really want to believe that my dad was a tomcatting bastard. Knowing everyone involved, I have trouble believing he was the kind of guy to be diddling the Mexican housekeeper or that Maria was some sort of vamp seducing the master of the house. Don't forget how young and naive she was." A wistful expression crossed Shelly's face. "Dad always seemed a stand-up kind of guy. I think he slipped one time, for whatever reasons, and bitterly regretted it. And begging Josh to take the blame, wrong as it was, seemed the only way to save his marriage. I mean I don't agree with it, but I can't let this color all of my memories of my dad. Maria said he adored Mom and that he would have done anything to prevent a divorce. She swears, except for that one time, that he never touched her again. The very next morning, she says, he apologized and begged her to forgive him. According to her, he was horrified at what had happened."

"I dunno, Shelly, it sounds pretty thin to me."

Shelly nodded. "Probably. I'm not going to argue with you about that. But unless something else pops up, and I doubt it will, I'm going to believe Maria." She sent Roxanne a steady look. "And if we're going to remain friends, I would advise you to do the same."

Roxanne grimaced. "OK, OK, I'll back off and fall in line." She grinned at Shelly. "After all, what are families for?"

"Thank you. I was hoping you'd agree."

"Well, hey, it's pretty clear it's either that or you'll make certain that I disappear never to be seen again."

Shelly grinned. "Maybe not that drastic, but close."

Roxanne returned her grin, and having put the last of the leftovers in the refrigerator, she asked, "You want a glass of wine? I think I'd like one. It was a great party, but I always think the best part is after everyone has left and you can just relax and reflect."

It was cozy and intimate in the small kitchen, the snowfall closing them in, blocking out any sound, and Shelly agreed—she was waiting for Sloan to return from the barn and was glad of the company.

Shelly poured Roxanne a glass of wine and opted for a glass of milk for herself. "No wine for me. I'm in training to get pregnant, remember?" she said as she sat down across the table from her.

Roxanne hesitated, then took the plunge. "How's that project coming anyway?"

Shelly's face clouded. "No luck yet, if that's what you want to know."

"Hey, you've only been married for six months. It's no big deal. I had a friend who was married for three years before she got pregnant."

"I'll be thirty-eight in three years," Shelly said hollowly. "I don't have three years to wait."

Her words slammed into Roxanne. Having a family, a baby, wasn't something she had ever worried about—it was something she'd take care of in the future—when she found the right man and was ready to settle down, but it dawned on her that *she* was thirty-

eight with nary a papa prospect in sight. The thought
that time might run out for her had never crossed her
mind. She made a face. She'd been too busy being
Roxanne, romping through life as if there were no tomorrow. Well, tomorrow had just walked up and
slapped her in the face. While having a baby still
wasn't high on her list of accomplishments, she suddenly understood the anguish and worry in Shelly's
voice.

She fiddled with her wineglass. "I think you're putting too much on yourself," she finally said. "You've
had so much to deal with in the last eight, nine months.
Josh's death. Coming back here. Starting up Granger
Cattle Company. Sloan. Marriage. Nick." She grinned
at her. "Meeting my folks. All of that is bound to have
been stressful. Maybe you're not giving yourself
enough time."

Shelly sighed. "You sound like your brother. That's
what Sloan says. He says that I'm impatient and that
I'm pushing too hard." She took a sip of her milk.
"Maybe I am. It's just that every month when my period comes, I want to die. I feel so useless, so, so *bar-
ren.* You don't know what it's like." Her voice
wavered. "I feel like a failure, as a woman, and a wife,
and worse, like I'm failing Sloan."

"Whoa. Stop right there. Why do you feel it's your
fault? Sloan could be shooting blanks, you know."

Shelly gave a watery laugh. "That's exactly what he
says."

"Well?"

Her eyes on her half-empty glass, Shelly admitted, "He's made arrangements for us to see a fertility expert in Santa Rosa next week. Says first thing we need to do is run some tests and make certain that there is nothing wrong with either one of us. Then we'll know what we're dealing with and can take the next step."

"Gee, I never knew I had such a smart brother." She smiled at Shelly. "Normally, just on principle, I would tell you to ignore anything he says, but this is one time he's hit the nail on the head."

"I know . . . it's just. . . ."

Roxanne leaned forward and put one of her hands over Shelly's where they rested on the table. "Honey, I think you're beating yourself up for no reason—and running down the road to meet trouble. Have the tests. And I'll bet they're going to come back that everything is fine. I'll bet the doctor will tell you the same thing that Sloan and I have—you're too impatient."

Shelly made a face. "Probably. But I'm still scared and anxious."

"Anyone would be—it's only natural. Hell, I sweat my Pap test every year, even though I know the odds are that everything is normal. *Everybody* does—it's called being human."

"You're right. I'm just being a worrywart." She smiled at Roxanne, her hand turning to clutch Roxanne's. "Thanks. I think I probably just needed someone else to tell me that I'm being silly."

The conversation with Shelly troubled Roxanne, niggling at the back of her mind. Acting her usual charming self, Roxanne got through the night and the following morning, even eating a spoonful of black-eyed peas Roman lovingly prepared for brunch, but despite her best efforts, there was a constraint, a preoccupation about her.

No one else noticed it, but Jeb. But then there wasn't much about Roxanne that he didn't notice. He knew something was bothering her, but he didn't have a clue. One thing he knew—it wasn't any worry about getting gas for her Jeep.

Like many ranchers, Sloan had his own gas tank on the place. An outfit from Ukiah came by regularly and kept it filled. Getting gas for Roxanne's Jeep had been simply a matter of walking out to where the cylindrical, silver-painted, thousand-gallon tank sat on its stand and filling a five-gallon gas can. Jeb and Roxanne had been among the last to leave and her vivacious manner vanished the moment they'd driven away from Sloan and Shelly's. It was a quiet drive to her Jeep; the only sounds inside the cab were the purr of the engine and the crunch of the truck's tires on the snowy, frozen ground.

Even while he filled the Jeep and helped transfer her things, Roxanne didn't say much. She seemed in her own world, hardly even aware of him.

She thanked him politely for his help and climbed into her Jeep. The engine turned right over and she smiled at him through the window. He motioned for her to roll it down, which she did.

A faint frown on his face, he asked, "You OK? You've been awfully quiet."

"Just tired, I guess—we all were up late last night and it seemed like it was the crack of dawn when you guys came tramping into the house this morning."

He nodded, not believing a word. He tapped a gloved finger on the roof of the Jeep. "I'll follow you home."

Roxanne lost her preoccupied air. "Look," she said firmly, "that isn't necessary. I appreciate all your help, but I'm fine now. The Jeep is fine. I promise I'll get gas before I drive out to the house."

He shook his head. "Can't, Princess. New Year's Day. Like I told you, this isn't New York. The only gas station in St. Galen's is closed." He flashed her a smile that made Roxanne's teeth ache. "But don't worry— you have enough gas to get home and back into town tomorrow. Besides, like I said, I'm following you home."

She began to get angry. "Why?"

His smile widened, his teeth very white beneath the black of his mustache. "You and I, Princess, have things to talk about." He looked around at the snowy landscape, then back at her scowling face. "New Year and everything, I thought today would be as good a time as any other for us to have that little talk I mentioned last night."

"Suppose I don't want to talk to you?"

"Well, since I intend to stick to you like glue to paper until you do, you'll just have to get used to me hanging or sticking around until you do decide to talk to me."

"Have I ever told you that I despise you?" she said through gritted teeth.

He grinned and ran a finger down her nose. "Frequently."

Growling under her breath, Roxanne rolled up the window and stepped on the gas. She would have liked to speed away from him, but the icy road put paid to that idea—that and the hairpin curves. The snow had only fallen in the higher elevations, not reaching the valley floor, but even leaving the snow and curves behind, it did Roxanne little good; Jeb stayed right on her tail as she hit the pavement and increased her speed. She glared at him in her rearview mirror half a dozen times as they sped across the flat paved roads of the valley, racing toward her place.

Roxanne barely slowed when they left the pavement and began the climb on the gravel road that led to her house. About the two-thousand-foot level, they hit snow again; the tire tracks made earlier by Nick's truck the only disturbance in the smooth icing of snow on the road. At the turnoff for her place, she punched the Jeep and like an angry cat the vehicle snarled up the curving incline, coming to a screeching halt as she whipped it around and into the parking area in the front of her house. Intent on reaching the house before Jeb, she took no time to admire the pristine snowfall. It was a breathtaking sight; the ground blanketed in white, the tree limbs hanging low, iced in snow, and the house with its peak roofs and mullioned windows looked like a frosted gingerbread cottage.

Ignoring Jeb, who pulled in right beside her, she jumped out of the Jeep, grabbed her things, and stalked to the front door. He was right behind her, admiring the angry movement of her hips in the tight blue jeans. No doubt about it—she had quite a swing in that fine backyard of hers.

He was so fascinated by her movements that he didn't realize that Roxanne had stopped dead in front of him, until he plowed into her. His big body slammed into hers and he clasped her shoulders to keep from knocking her down.

"Uh, sorry," he muttered, "wasn't watching where I was going."

Roxanne remained frozen in front of him, her shoulders rigid beneath his hands.

He frowned. "What's the matter?"

"The front door's open . . . I locked it before I left," she said uneasily. She glared at him over her shoulder. "And before you ask, yes, I'm sure that I locked it."

"OK," he said softly, moving around to stand in front of her. "You wait here, I'll check it out."

She gasped when he reached around behind him and from beneath the black leather jacket pulled out a pistol.

He glanced back at her. "What?"

Eyes worried, she asked, "Do you always carry a gun?"

"Pretty much." He grinned at her. "I'm a cop, re-member?"

She rolled her eyes. "I remember."

He started down the path and Roxanne was right on his heels. He looked back at her and muttered, "I thought I told you to wait."

She smiled. "Well, you know how I feel about being ordered around. Besides, it's my house. I have every right to go inside it."

"Yeah, well, Princess, stop and think about this: there could be a guy inside with a gun or knife, just waiting for you to come home. If you want to barge right in there, be my guest."

Roxanne paled, her beautiful eyes huge in her face. She swallowed. "I wasn't going to 'barge' inside. I was just going to follow you."

"Don't. I don't want to be worrying about you. Just stay here—better yet, go back and get in the car with the engine on—if I run into trouble, you get that sweet little butt of yours into town and get me some backup. OK?"

She stood her ground. "Do you really think there's any danger? Isn't it more likely that whoever was here has already left?"

He stepped aside. "Like I said, you want to go first?"

She bit her lip, eyeing him and then the shadowy porch and the half-ajar front door. "No," she said sullenly. "But I think you're making too big a deal of this."

"I agree, but until I check it out, we don't know that, do we?"

She made a face. "Point taken. I won't follow you inside, but I'm not going back to the car."

"Fine. Just make damn sure you *do* remain right here."

Roxanne watched him as he carefully approached the front porch. She was suddenly grateful that he'd been such a jerk and insisted upon following her home. If she'd been here by herself, she'd have taken one look at the half-opened door and wheeled on her heels and headed straight back to her Jeep and town. Stupid she was not and there was no way that she'd have entered that house by herself.

She glanced around, noting that they had made the only footprints in the snow, except for a few animal tracks, birds and squirrels. Which meant that whoever had been inside her house had left before much snow had accumulated on the ground. But even telling herself that the house was empty didn't still the knot of anxiety that tightened in her breast when Jeb disappeared inside.

She waited for what seemed an eternity, even taking a few tentative steps toward the house as the minutes passed and Jeb did not reappear. She didn't like standing out here, but she wasn't foolish enough to go traipsing inside after him like some silly female in a melodrama. Besides, dammit, she'd given her word. Her chin set. And she wasn't running back to the Jeep either, though she did send a longing glance or two in that direction.

In spite of the weak sunshine, it was cold outside and Roxanne stamped her feet now and then to keep them warm. She kept her eyes on the doorway where Jeb had disappeared, all sorts of grim and grisly pictures floating through her mind. The only good thing that she could think of was that at least there'd been no gunfire. But then that made her recall several movies wherein bloody murder had been done silently with a knife. . . .

When the door was suddenly shoved open, she let out a half-muffled shriek and went weak with relief as Jeb's familiar form filled the doorway. He grinned at her. "Come on, it's OK. No one here but us chickens."

She scurried up the path and brushed past him. Dumping her suitcase on the floor of the foyer, she asked, "How bad is it?"

He shrugged. "They didn't trash the place if that's what you're worried about. And if they stole anything, I can't at first glance spot it. You'll have to check it out yourself."

She frowned. "They?"

He pointed to the floor. "Two sets of muddy footprints—which means they came in while it was still raining, before the snow. And since there didn't appear to be any sign of them outside, they had to leave while it was still raining, or at least before too much snow had fallen. The tracks inside the house are pretty easy to follow—especially since it seems the only room they entered was the living room. If they went anywhere else, they either removed their boots or the mud dried, because the only place I find any sign of tracks is in that one room."

Frowning, Roxanne followed the footprints that Jeb pointed out. Both sets were large, obviously male, and as he said, they only seemed to have been in the great room, the dried mud on the wood floor and carpet signs of their passing.

She looked around. Beyond a crooked picture on the wall, nothing seemed out of the ordinary; on the surface the house appeared as it had when she had left less than twenty-four hours ago. A quick search of the rest of the house confirmed Jeb's assumption that the only room the intruders had entered was the great room. Standing in the middle of that room several minutes later, feeling vulnerable and uneasy, Roxanne wrapped her arms around her waist. "This is creepy," she said. "I just don't understand it. There hasn't been any more trouble or break-ins for months. Why now?"

"Well, first of all, they didn't 'break in'—or at least, there's no sign of it. Looks as if they had a key to the front door . . . or you made a mistake and left it unlocked."

"I did not," she said sharply, "make a mistake. I know this is Oak Valley and all that and that some people still leave their houses unlocked, but not me. I lived in New York too long. I know the door was locked when I left."

"Anyone else have a key? Your folks?"

"No. Besides, they wouldn't just come inside my house without my permission."

Jeb looked skeptical. "Maybe you've forgotten someone. Construction hasn't been completed that long ago. Maybe a tile guy or painter had a key."

Roxanne shook her head. "No. The front door was one of the last items installed. And once it was installed, I made certain that I had all the keys. I didn't loan them to anyone either." Earnestly, she added, "Believe me, no one came inside the house when I wasn't here. A couple guys even got a little irked when they had to wait for me to get here to let them in."

Jeb studied her face for a moment. He walked back to the front door and stared at it, the smooth brass surface of the lock plate showing no signs of tampering and the door itself sporting not so much as a scratch.

Walking back to stand in front of her, he sighed. "Well, since there seems to be no simple answer, you've got to ask yourself, who else has a key to your house and how did they get it?"

Chapter
12

Roxanne ran nervous fingers through her mane of black hair. "Oh, that's just great. Not only do I have trespassers and housebreakers, but somehow they've managed to get a key to my house."

"That's simple enough to fix," Jeb said. "First thing tomorrow morning you call a locksmith and have the locks changed. That'll eliminate one problem."

Roxanne's face brightened for a moment, then fell. "Yeah, but it won't tell us who they were or what they were after," she said gloomily. "Besides which, it'll probably take him a week to get here and get the work done."

Jeb smiled. "Haven't you learned yet that you can't have everything just when you want it, Princess?"

"I'm beginning to but I can't say that I like the process." She slid a look in his direction. "Well, thank you for seeing me home. I appreciate it—particularly in view of the housebreaking."

"Ah, I'm supposed to go my way now like a good boy, is that it? Well sorry, but it's no go. We have things to discuss, remember?"

Roxanne sighed. She wasn't in the mood to fight, she wanted to unpack, take a shower, and sit down with a cup of hot chocolate and enjoy the view out of her windows . . . and consider the implications of the housebreaking incident. What she definitely did not want to do was embark on an emotional, and probably embarrassing, discussion with Jeb. She eyed him, the thrust of his chin, and the way his thumbs were shoved into the front pockets of his black jeans, making it clear that Jeb wasn't about to leave until he got what he was after.

Giving in, she said, "OK, but I'm going to unpack and shower and change clothes first. Why don't you go home, do the same, and come back in forty-five minutes or so? I'm sure you have things to do at your place, like checking on Dawg and Boss?" She smiled sweetly. "I'm sure that they missed you."

He studied her face, his expression suspicious. "You won't hightail it out of here the minute I drive away?" She shook her head. His eyes narrowed. "You're not going to try to lock me out, are you?"

She laughed. "No. I promise to be here."

He thought about it a moment. "OK if I bring Boss and Dawg with me when I come back?"

"Sure. I might even ask to borrow them for a few nights until the lock gets changed."

Something moved in the back of his eyes. "Oh, that

won't be necessary," he drawled, strolling up to her and cupping her chin. "I intend to see that you have your very own private security system on the premises until the lock gets changed."

"Uh, that's not necessary," she replied uneasily, having a good idea what he meant. "The dogs will do me just fine."

He stepped nearer, his gaze locked on her mouth as he reached out and his thumb moved softly over her full lower lip. He seemed hypnotized by the movement of his thumb, his lips taking on a sensual curve that did nothing for Roxanne's peace of mind. As the seconds passed her breathing became difficult, the heat of Jeb's body flowing warmly against hers and the touch of his thumb on her lip was driving her nuts, arousing sensations she could do well without.

She took a step away from him, relieved when he let his hand drop. "I think you'd better go," she said huskily.

Jeb jerked, as if he had suddenly come awake. "Yeah," he muttered. "I think I'd better."

He strode away from her, but stopped at the door and looked back. "Don't," he said quietly, "try any tricks. We're going to have that discussion. I'd just as soon have it privately, but if you force the issue . . ."

The threat was unspoken but Roxanne had no doubt that if she was foolish enough to try to run, that Jeb would track her down and that it wouldn't matter where he found her—he'd have his damned discussion. Her fingers closed into a fist, but she said, "I'll be here."

"Good."

Even though he infuriated and annoyed her, Jeb's departure made the house suddenly seem awfully big and empty. Angry with herself for feeling that way, Roxanne gave herself a shake and stalked over to the wood stove. Poking around in the ashes, she was pleased to find a few coals still burning. The house was chilly and she set about stoking up the fire. Several minutes later, watching the leaping flames behind the glass door of the wood stove, she decided that the fire was doing nicely and she could leave it. She picked up her suitcase and walked to her bedroom.

The bedroom door had a lock on it and she didn't hesitate to use it. Her suitcase unpacked, she got into the shower trying not to think of a certain Neanderthal with an overdeveloped sense of his own appeal. Where did he get off demanding that they have a "discussion" about a subject she had pushed to the back of her head? Oh, hell, she thought glumly as she washed her hair, maybe once they discussed it, hashed it to death, they'd be able to go on the way they had for years. Except she knew in her heart that her feelings for Jeb Delaney had changed. She might call him names. She might act furious with him, but a part of her knew that it was exactly that: an act.

She wasn't a novice when it came to the games that the sexes played with each other, but she had to admit that she had entered new territory, unknown territory when it came to Jeb. And it terrified her.

Over the years, she'd had a couple of long-term relationships. There'd been a guy when she'd been in her early twenties that she'd lived with for three or four years before the romance had ended. Their breakup hadn't been explosive, they'd just discovered that the spark that had brought them together had died and they drifted apart. A few years after that, there'd been another man who had shared her life, the actor, Shane Michaels. They actually got around to discussing marriage, but his trips back and forth to Hollywood and her trips to location shoots, as well as his, had put a strain on their relationship. They'd been together for five years and Shane was pushing for marriage and children. But marriage she thought of as the final commitment, and it wasn't something that she'd been ready for so she'd held back, coming up with excuses and postponements, and eventually the relationship ended . . . badly. There had been a few other lovers along the way, but after the breakup with Shane, she'd taken a vow, no more live-ins. Her mouth twisted. Yeah, but what about what's his name, ole married tight-buns? Did three weeks count?

Her thoughts moody, she stepped out of the shower and after drying and wrapping her wet hair in a towel spread perfumed lotion over her body. A spritz or two of the same scent in cologne, Red, and she was ready for clothes. Slipping into a loose-fitting burgundy velour pantsuit, she tackled her hair, quickly fashioning a French braid out of the wet strands. She looked at herself in the mirror, frowning at her fresh scrubbed face. Makeup? No. Jeb might be coming back, but it wasn't going to be *that* sort of evening. She was shocked to feel a pang of disappointment. Dammit! What in the hell was wrong with her?

Grumbling, she wandered out of the bedroom and eventually, after checking on the fire and flicking on a few lamps, made her way into the kitchen. Glancing at the clock in the shape of a rooster that hung over one of the kitchen doorways, she frowned. It was approaching 2:00 P.M. and the rumblings in her stomach let her know that it had been several hours since she'd eaten at Sloan and Shelly's. She poked around in the refrigerator, but didn't see anything that took her fancy. Sighing, she shut the door and checked her cabinets. The cupboards were full, but nothing appealed to her. Probably, she thought with a grimace, because I know that Jeb is coming back and that the conversation isn't going to be fun. Anything but.

She poured herself a glass of nonfat milk and sipping it strolled back to the great room. Standing at the French doors, she stared down at the valley below her. It was weird. All around her, the landscape was white and dusted with snow, a winter wonderland, and yet a scant five hundred feet below her, the snowline stopped. At that point a steady progression of green-needled firs, pines, and shiny-leafed madrones intermixed with the stark, naked limbs of the oaks led to the valley floor. Untouched by snow, the various rooftops of the houses in town in colors of blue, green, and beige looked almost like a patchwork quilt and the fallow fields lay brown and rust-colored in the winter sunlight.

Roxanne sighed again. She supposed she was suffering from the usual letdown after a party. The house seemed quiet, lonely almost after all the laughter and conversation at Sloan and Shelly's place.

She prowled around the great room, double-checking her belongings, wondering who had broken in and why. Nothing seemed to be missing, but she frowned as she straightened a couple of pictures. Now why would someone move her pictures? Surely they hadn't been looking for a safe behind one of them? She shook her head. Odd. She followed the muddy footprints back and forth, studying them, trying to make sense of them. Jeb was right, whoever had broken in—her mouth twisted, OK, whoever had managed to get a hold of a copy of her key and opened the front door—didn't appear to have left the great room. Unless they'd taken off their boots? But that didn't make sense either. Why leave muddy footprints in the great room and nowhere else? Unless, she thought with a chill, they didn't want her to know that they'd been through the entire house?

Creeped-out and restless, she wandered around, wishing that Jeb would get back—and angry because she felt that way. All right. Maybe she wasn't the brave, independent woman she thought she was—as long as no one else knew that, it was OK. And right now fighting with Jeb seemed a much pleasanter way to spend the afternoon—besides, she admitted, smiling, she was looking forward to seeing Dawg and Boss again. To kill time, she cleaned up the muddy tracks and checked out the phone book, looking up the names of locksmiths. There wasn't a large selection and she'd bet that precious few of them would be eager to travel to Oak Valley to change one measly lock. She stopped, frowning. But suppose it wasn't just the front door key? Suppose they had copies of all of her house keys? That tears it, she thought grimly. There is no way I'm going to sleep easy wondering if someone is going to slip in my back door—or any other door. Tomorrow morning, I'm buying all new locks and getting them installed. The hell with waiting for a locksmith.

Before she actually began to pace, she heard the sound of a vehicle climbing up the road and a few minutes later the slamming of a door and Jeb's voice.

"Goddammit," he yelled. "Boss! Dawg! Get back here. Right now!"

Roxanne popped her head out the front door and grinned. Boss and Dawg, in typical dog fashion, were paying no attention to their owner; heads down, wagging tails up, they were busy sniffing and checking all the new and exciting smells. She glanced at Jeb as he paused and stood in the middle of the pathway. Except for a red shirt, he was all in black—jeans, leather jacket, and boots, his black cowboy hat pulled low over his face—and he held a brown paper grocery bag in one arm. There was an expression of resigned affection on his face as he watched the antics of the dogs. He was such a strong man, some would say a tough man, and yet it was obvious that he could be a gentle and caring man. How many men, she thought, suppressing a giggle, would open their hearts and homes to a pair of butt-ugly dogs like Boss and Dawg? No doubt about it, Jeb Delaney had unexplored depths to him. Her heart leaped as two things struck her: one, she wanted to be the woman who explored those depths, and two, how absolutely *right* he looked standing out there on her walkway. Almost as if he belonged, as if he were coming home . . . to her. She swallowed the lump that formed in her throat, trying to ignore the rush of tenderness, the storm of fierce emotion that flooded through her. Jeb Delaney touched something deep inside of her, a part of herself she had always kept inviolate and she was frightened by the new feelings rushing through her body. Oh, lust was there, no denying it, but something else . . . some deeper, more powerful emotion struggled to break free. It was exciting and unnerving, scary and delightful at the same time, and she knew that she'd never, *ever* felt this way before. . . .

Roxanne jumped as if shot. Oh, shit. Shit. Shit. She thought, not Jeb Delaney. Please, oh, please don't let me be falling in love with him.

Sensing her presence, Jeb glanced at the door. "Hi," he said, a grin breaking across his dark features. "I'll be in in just a minute—the dogs decided they needed to explore. Is it OK to lock them in your mudroom as soon as they've taken care of business?"

"You don't have to lock them up—they can come into the house with us—and I'm sure they'd be much happier there than in the mudroom," Roxanne said, opening the door wider and standing on the porch.

At the sound of Roxanne's voice, Dawg's head jerked up and she gave a joyful bay. Leaving off the interesting exploration, Dawg came flying through the snow toward her. Jeb yelled, but as she had earlier, Dawg just ignored him and leaped up on Roxanne, nearly knocking her over with an enthusiastic welcome. Tongue hanging out the side of her mouth, paws resting on Roxanne's velour-covered thighs, she grinned up at her, clearly pleased with herself.

Roxanne laughed and ruffled her ears. "You're a very bad dog and I'm sure that I should scold you, but I'm very happy to see you, too." For her efforts, she got a sloppy kiss on the wrist and an adoring look. Having greeted Roxanne, Dawg jumped down and trotted confidently into the house. Roxanne sent a laughing glance over at Jeb. "Guess that settles it, don't you think?"

"You don't mind?"

She shook her head. "No. I intend to get a dog eventually—Dawg and Boss can give me a taste of what it'll be like."

"If you're sure . . ."

Dawg settled the matter. As if she owned the place, she came back to stand by Roxanne and barked at Boss. The black and tan mixed breed heeded Dawg's call and coolly jogged over to where Roxanne stood. He gave her a polite sniff and then ignored her, following Dawg back into the house.

Her eyes dancing, her cheeks rosy, Roxanne said, "I think you've been outvoted here. Might as well give in gracefully."

Jeb shook his head, smiling back at her. "I really should enroll them in obedience training, but I never seem to find the time—and they don't bother me so I never think about how they might affect someone else."

Dawg came back just then and gave an imperious bark, clearly indicating that they should stop wasting time and get inside. Laughing, Jeb and Roxanne followed the dog into the warmth of the house.

The scent of fried chicken filled the air and Roxanne looked appraisingly at the bag Jeb still carried. She sniffed the air. "Is that what I think, hope, it is?"

"Yeah, I was getting kinda hungry as I went through town, so I swung by McGuire's and grabbed some of their Chesterfried chicken. They were the only eating place open, or I'd have brought hamburgers."

Taking the bag from his arm, Roxanne said, "Fried chicken is just fine." She peeked inside the bag. "Ooh and Jojos, those fried potato things, too.

We'll probably die of an overdose of cholesterol, but hey! I'm hungry."

I am too, Jeb thought ruefully as he watched the movement of her buttocks beneath the velour material as she walked toward the kitchen. I am so hungry, Princess, that it's all I can do to keep my hands off of you. And don't you just look tasty—all scrubbed and smelling like heaven—I could gobble you up in one bite. He glanced down at the front of his jeans. Yep. Someone else had the same idea. He jiggled a bit to make his swollen penis less noticeable and then walked after her.

Followed by the dogs and Jeb, Roxanne walked to the kitchen. Soon enough, the humans were eating at the painted dark green wooden table in one corner of the cheerful kitchen and the dogs were scarfing up skin and bits of chicken from the floor. Roxanne had fixed a green salad to go with their meal, telling herself at least that much of the meal wouldn't give them heart attacks. She'd opened bottles of Carta Blanca to drink with the meal and had put up some coffee for afterward.

The conversation had been general as they'd eaten, both of them careful not to stray into heavy topics. They talked about the party, Shelly's surprise announcement about Nick, and the break-in. Jeb agreed with Roxanne's plan to replace all the locks on the doors that opened to the outside.

Pushing back from the table, he said, "The glass doors won't be a problem, since they all lock from the inside, it's just the main doors you have to worry about." He moved aside his empty bottle of Carta Blanca. "I'm off tomorrow—we could drive to Ukiah and buy the locks and I can install them. You won't need a locksmith since you're going to replace the complete units."

Roxanne hesitated. She didn't know where this thing with Jeb was going and while one part of her liked the idea of the two of them driving to Ukiah and shopping together, she wasn't certain that it was a smart thing to do. She found him too attractive— and sexy, far too sexy, she thought as she squirmed in her seat, desire shimmering low in her belly. She fiddled with her glass of beer, trying to think of a polite way to refuse his company. A rueful smile curved her lips. Since when had she started being polite to Jeb Delaney? That she was even trying to be polite showed how far they had come in a short while.

Her thoughts scattered when Jeb reached across the table and ran a finger across her hand. She looked at him, her heart pounding at the serious expression on his dark face.

"I'm not asking you for a lifelong commitment," he said carefully. "All I'm suggesting is that we drive to Ukiah together."

Her eyes were huge and golden as she stared back at him. She nodded slowly. "I know," she said, "it's just that it's so weird—you and me doing anything together except fighting."

He smiled crookedly. "Fighting isn't the only thing we've done together . . . remember."

The problem was that she did—too well, and if she weren't careful they'd do it again. She'd been fighting the sexual awareness that hummed between them ever since she'd seen him out front standing there as if he owned the place, as if he belonged. Being alone with him in the cozy setting of the kitchen wasn't such a good idea, she decided. She needed space—breathing room. This was too intimate and if she sat here a moment longer, she was likely to fall on him like a ravening beast . . . and they'd end up coupling like minks in the kitchen again. She jumped up from the table and began to clear away the signs of their meal. Jeb said nothing, just watched her dash around the kitchen. Even when she cleaned up the tile floor after the dogs, he didn't say anything, but when she strayed near him, his arm shot out and he scooped her onto his lap.

"I'm not going to bite you," he muttered, his lips near her ear, "although it is tempting. Roxy, honey, we've got to talk about what's happening between us." He gave her a little shake. "Something is and you damn well know it."

Her heart banging painfully in her chest, she slowly turned her head in his direction. Her gaze searched his face, noticing the fine lines at the corner of his eyes, the bold nose, and the strong jaw. That face, powerful and unforgettable, haunted her—as did that equally powerful and beautiful body.

"OK," she said shakily, "I'll admit that lately there's . . . *something* between us."

He smiled, such a tender smile, that Roxanne was stunned to feel tears fill her eyes. "See," he said, "that wasn't so bad, was it?"

The problem was that it wasn't so bad. In fact, it was wonderful, especially being in his arms, feeling those hard, warm thighs beneath her bottom. They were only inches apart and she was conscious of the sexual pull. Her eyes dropped to his lips and she actually bent toward him, before she caught herself. She leaped off his lap and onto her feet, putting distance between them. "No, but it doesn't settle anything," she murmured.

Jeb sighed. "Princess, there's nothing to settle, except for the fact that strange as it may be, you and I are attracted to each other. We've both been trying to pretend otherwise, but it's an inescapable fact and I'm tired of this game we're playing."

She shot him a resentful look. "I don't play games."

"OK, you don't play games, but admit it—if I hadn't forced the issue, you'd have driven away from me as fast as that excuse for a vehicle would go and never looked back. And the next time we met, you'd act as if nothing had happened . . ." His voice lowered. "You'd be the same old snooty Roxanne and pretend I hadn't had you on that countertop back in September."

"That's crude," she said in a very snooty voice, her nose in the air, her back ramrod straight as she poured them mugs of coffee from the coffeemaker.

"Yeah," he said with a slow grin as he took the mug from her, "but it's true. And you know it."

She wanted to fight with him, and she fought to resist that grin of his, but she couldn't. She giggled. A very un-Roxanne giggle.

His grin widened.

She shook her head at him, and said, "Oh, come on, let's go into the other room where it's warmer." And bigger, she thought to herself.

Accompanied by the dogs, they walked into the great room. The dogs immediately walked over to the wood stove and flopped down in front of it, sighing contentedly. There wasn't a great deal of furniture to choose from so Jeb and Roxanne sat down on the couch, sinking comfortably into the soft cushions. They sipped their coffee in silence for a moment, Roxanne curled up like a cat at the far end of the long couch, her bare feet tucked up under her; Jeb was at the other end, his lean muscled legs sprawled out in front of him.

"Do we really have to talk about this?" she finally asked.

He considered her, thinking that he'd like nothing more than to find out what she was wearing under that velour material. "Probably not," he admitted slowly. "As long as you don't backtrack and start trying to pretend that when we made love"—she made a sound of protest and he sent her a hard look—"that it was just sex. Get it through that beautiful head of yours—it wasn't *sex,* we made love, wild and incredible love, at that."

Roxanne wanted to argue. She really did. Admitting what had happened between them hadn't been just some inexplicable mindless drive for sex made what they had shared all the more important, made what she was feeling for him all the more real. She bit her lip. Took a sip of her coffee. Looked at the dogs lying in front of the wood stove and all the while Jeb waited patiently at the other end of the couch. He was such a stubborn prick, she thought. She took another sip of coffee, stalling, but knowing she was running out of time.

"I've already admitted that there's something between us," she finally replied, not looking at him as she put her mug on the end table. "What more do you want?"

"Loaded question, Princess."

"You know what I mean."

He put down his mug on the floor and to her absolute terror scooted to her end of the couch. Too close, she thought hysterically. He's too close. Don't touch me. Oh, please don't touch me.

But he did and it was like flame to gasoline. The instant his hands reached out for her, Roxanne could have sworn that she heard an explosive whoosh and that was her last coherent thought for a long time.

Jeb hadn't meant to start anything, at least not then, but the moment his hands closed around her shoulders, his brain turned to mush. He no longer wanted to talk; he didn't want to reason with her, didn't want to explore what was happening between them. All he wanted was her naked and beneath him.

Their mouths met, melding together, the slip and slide of lips and tongues stoking a fire that was already burning out of control. Her fingers tangled in his hair, her body arching up next to his; his hand captured her chin, holding her mouth just where he wanted as he tasted and explored.

The delving of his tongue deep into her mouth sent fire ripping through her body and Roxanne shivered with anticipation of even more explicit caresses to come. When Jeb broke the kiss and lifted his head, she moaned in frustration, following his lips with her own.

He laughed huskily, pleased at her response. "Hold my place, Princess, I'll be back. But right now I think we need to get rid of some encumbrances."

She stared blankly at him and he laughed again. "Clothes," he said softly, tugging impatiently at his belt buckle.

"Oh, those," she murmured, a seductive smile breaking across her face. With a careless flick of her hands, she tossed aside the top of her pantsuit.

His breath caught at the sight of her delicate

bosom, the hard nipples standing upright from the rosy aureoles that surrounded her small milky breasts. And that smile . . . that smile promised heaven. He kicked off his boots and with fingers that fumbled, he dragged off his jeans and underpants, his shirt landing somewhere nearby.

Roxanne's eyes ate him, tasting every inch of his powerful body. He was, she decided dreamily, absolutely perfect, from the crown of his arrogant head to the soles of his feet. And in between was everything a woman could want. Her gaze dropped to his rampant sex. Everything and *more,* she thought breathlessly.

They stared unashamedly at each other, the sight of each other's body exciting, the look in the other's eyes arousing. Reaching out, Jeb cupped one of her breasts, his thumb moving slowly over the nipple, making her arch like a cat under a caressing hand.

His mouth hovered over hers and he bit gently at the corners. "You're still wearing more clothes than I am."

Her arms went around his neck and she smiled, her eyes teasing him. "Well, I guess you better do something about that, hadn't you?" she murmured, her lips traveling along the length of his jaw.

"Yeah," he muttered, "I'd better."

He swept her out of the lower half of her pantsuit so fast it was a wonder it hadn't ripped.

The room was in shadows, the mauve and indigo shadows of the winter evening already sliding across the sky. It was quiet inside except for the occasional pop and snap of the fire in the wood stove—and the faint, excited sighs that came from the region of the couch.

The couch was wide and long, the cushions yielding, and until that moment, Roxanne hadn't realized how perfectly it could hold two naked bodies almost side by side. Face-to-face, their bodies nearly touching, they looked wonderingly at each other. Feeling as if she were in a trance, Roxanne brushed her fingers over his brow, his extravagant eyelashes, down to his wide, sexy mouth. At the touch of her fingers he gently nipped the tips. She purred, feeling a jolt of desire clear down to her toes.

"Yeah, me too," he murmured, his heavy-lidded gaze moving over her slender length, making her tremble.

They came together as one, their mouths seeking the heat and pleasure of the other's. Jeb's fingers skimmed over her breasts, tantalizing her, making her ache. Reluctantly leaving her sweet mouth, he bent down, his teeth closing gently around one pink nipple, and Roxanne shuddered, delight sparking through her. She moved restively, her thigh brushing against his hot, hard sex, and it was Jeb who ached now, the sensation of her warm limb touching his flesh an exquisite torture.

They had both been celibate since that last time and the clamoring of their senses was overwhelming. Despite his best intentions, Jeb couldn't seem to hold back and when he touched her between her legs and discovered that she was already slick and wet and ready, he nearly went crazy with the need to plunge immediately into her.

His mouth found hers and he kissed her urgently, the thrust of his tongue and the slide of his fingers into her hot depths crowding Roxanne, pushing her to the edge. An orgasm, hard and powerful, ripped through her, and she bucked and shuddered in his arms, biting down on his shoulder to keep from screaming her pleasure.

He felt her response and his own body tightened and for one awful moment, he feared that he would lose it right there. He gulped in a breath, his hand moving slower more gently between her legs, concentrating on slowly bringing her down, forcing thoughts of his own pleasure away.

With dazed, slumberous eyes, she stared at him, smaller shocks of ecstasy still flowing through her. "I think I got ahead of you," she murmured huskily.

He grinned tightly. "Don't worry, Princess, I'll get mine . . . and take you with me," he muttered thickly, his mouth brushing hers, his fingers beginning a new dance, a new foray between her legs.

She gasped, feeling the pressure begin to build almost instantly, the need to taste again the joy he could give her urgent and demanding. Her hand clasped him, pulling slowly on the swollen, hard length of his organ. Jeb groaned, trembling under her touch. His mouth crushed hers, his kiss passionate and excited.

His caresses became frantic and Roxanne moaned, the violent writhing of her hips urging him onward. She was already on the brink when he parted her thighs and thrust deeply into her hot depths. The sensation of him buried within her, the heat and size of him, the fevered pumping of his hips, sent her over the edge. Her arms tightened around him and she threw back her head and gave herself up to the carnal glory, the world exploding in crimson and gold behind her lids.

Feeling her body quake with the force of her orgasm, Jeb lost control, his pace urgent as he raced to join her, to find the same blinding goal. He grasped her hips, plunging heavily into her. Her flesh tightened around him, frantically milking him, and with something between a groan and a growl, he joined her in paradise, his fingers digging into her hips, his big body pumping wildly into hers.

It was a long time before either one of them moved. And then it was with the slow, languid movements of bodies well satiated. His body gradually slipped from hers and they lay side by side on the couch, their arms entwined, their lips touching now and then, their hands and fingers lightly caressing the other.

They didn't speak, their eyes and hands and mouths did it for them, moving sweetly and tenderly over the other one. There was a rightness, a magical completeness about what had just happened, and Roxanne felt none of the panic and horror she had that first time they had made love. She didn't know if what she felt for Jeb was really love, the kind the poets sing of, or just an aberration, but she wasn't going to fight him any longer. She wanted to discover just what it was they shared. Primitive lust? Or love? She was still wary of it, still frightened by it, but she wasn't going to run from it. Not this time. Not now.

Jeb slid a finger down her nose. "What are you thinking?" he murmured against her ear.

"If I told you," she said with a smile, "you'd be even more conceited and arrogant than you already are."

"That good, huh?" He grinned at her, his black eyes soft and warm.

His expression changed in an instant and he leaped up from the couch as if he'd been hit with a fiery poker. "Jesus H. Christ!" he yelled, spinning around.

Alarmed, Roxanne sat up. "What? What's wrong?"

Jeb glanced back at her, a smile now on his face. "That's the problem," he said, pointing to Dawg, who stood in front of him wagging her tail. "She just put her wet cold nose on my butt—you try it and tell me you wouldn't jump."

Roxanne burst into laughter.

Jeb's heart turned right over in his breast as he

stared at her lying there, her pale skin almost glowing against the dark material of the couch, her face still soft from the passion they had shared. His eyes darkened and his sex twitched. He knelt down on the edge of the couch. "Laugh at me, will you," he murmured, his hands reaching for her. He pulled her up into his arms and kissed her with explicit thoroughness.

Desire blasted through them and as he pushed her down onto the couch, following her body with his, he muttered, "Let's see how long you laugh now, Princess . . ."

Roxanne didn't laugh for a long time. A very, *very* long time . . .

Chapter
13

They made it to Roxanne's bedroom and bed . . . eventually. A makeshift dinner of leftover fried chicken and anything else that looked interesting that night was eaten in barbaric splendor among the piled pillows and quilts of Roxanne's bed. They couldn't seem to bear to be out of each other's arms, although Jeb did scramble into some clothes at one point and go to his truck for food for the dogs and of course, later, he'd had to take the dogs outside.

Despite supposedly being banished to the great room for the night, the dogs pushed open the door to Roxanne's bedroom and followed them inside. After waiting patiently for the humans to quit squirming and wiggling around on the king-size bed, they joined them, Dawg curling up hard against Roxanne's back, Boss staking out the foot of the bed. Jeb and Roxanne looked at each other. Jeb shrugged and Roxanne laughed. "Leave them," she said. "We'll see how it goes."

It wasn't a restful night for any of them. At least three times the humans woke and kicked the dogs off the bed and proceeded to do more of that squirming and wiggling around before allowing the dogs to rejoin them. But all in all, everyone enjoyed themselves. Immensely.

Roxanne woke slowly the next morning, savoring the heat radiating from Jeb's big body on one side of her and the warmth of Dawg's body on the other side. She lay there a long time, a smile on her lips, her thoughts wandering to the night that had just passed. A faint flush rose in her cheeks. The things they had done, together and to each other . . . she could hardly wait to do them again.

She glanced across at Jeb lying beside her and a wave of tenderness swept over her. He was asleep, his black hair tousled, those incredible lashes of his lying like black fans on his cheeks, and that mouth . . . . Her gaze lingered, remembering the feel of those knowing lips on her body. Whew! He was good. Very, very good.

Ignoring the tingling warmth spreading through her body, she stretched and immediately winced, places and muscles she hadn't known could ache, aching. She smiled. Oh, but it was such a pleasant, marvelous ache.

Careful not to wake Jeb, she pushed Dawg off the bed and padded to the bathroom. Five minutes later, teeth brushed, the remains of her French braid undone, she stepped into the shower.

She heard the bathroom door open and a lazy masculine voice say, "Got a toothbrush I can borrow?"

She peeked out from the shower, her pulse leaping at the sight of Jeb standing there in all his naked glory. Oh, and he was glorious. Those wide shoulders. That flat, hard stomach and broad hair-covered chest. And then there were those powerful thighs and legs and of course that wonderful source of pleasure hardening beneath her very eyes. She grinned at him and said, "Sure, look in that right-hand drawer—there should be half a dozen."

He quirked a brow. "You planning on entertaining a lot of men?"

"What do you think?" she asked, the expression in her eyes hard to define.

What he thought was that he'd like nothing more than waking every day for the rest of his life and finding Roxy Ballinger in the shower. Not *Roxanne* of fame and fortune, but Roxy, the sweet, generous, giving lover of last night. Instead, he forced his thoughts in a different direction and said, "That living out here it's practical to stock up on things and save a trip to town."

She smiled. "Smart man. So smart in fact, I might just even fix you breakfast."

The sight of one rosy-peaked breast slipping into view made him forget what the conversation was about, until Roxy said gently, "Toothbrush. Right-hand drawer."

"Oh, right," he mumbled and turned around, giving Roxy a wonderful view of his splendid ass. Oh, my.

Teeth brushed, water thrown in his face, Jeb felt more awake, as did another part of his body. One part in particular seemed *very* wide awake, standing stiffly up from his body. He glanced at his jutting penis and shook his head. God, he was insatiable. The sound of the running shower was irresistible and before he knew what he was doing, Jeb joined Roxanne in the shower.

She didn't seem surprised. She smiled limpidly at him, and handing him a soapy sponge, murmured, "Oh, good. I need you to wash my back."

He not only washed her back, but also very thoroughly washed her front; she returned the favor, paying special attention to his groin area. One thing led to another and it was quite some time later before they stepped out of the shower.

Breakfast was a comfortable meal and there was none of that morning afterward awkwardness. The new door locks were on the top of their agenda, and after a leisurely breakfast and the dogs' needs were seen to, dogs and all, they piled into Jeb's truck and headed for Ukiah.

Roxanne enjoyed the day. They bought the locks at Friedman Brothers, an impressively sized box of condoms at the local drugstore, and then grabbed sandwiches at Subway, including two plain roast beef ones, for Dawg and Boss.

It was a quick trip and despite the distance involved, they were back at Roxanne's place by 2:00 P.M. and fifteen minutes later Jeb was busy changing the lock in the front door.

Watching his deft movements as he took out the old lock and replaced it with the new one, she said, "Gee, I wonder what this is going to cost me?"

He glanced over his shoulder at her, his black eyes full of sensual promise. "I think I'll be able to, ah, come up with an appropriate payment."

She walked over and kissed him on the mouth, her lips clinging. "Oh, I sure hope so."

Jeb stayed the night again. Roxanne thought that she could really grow to like waking up with him in her bed each morning. She even liked the feeling of security it gave her to have Dawg curled up at her back and Boss at her feet. The dogs had just naturally assumed that they belonged on the bed too.

Thursday, Jeb rose with the dawn. It was back to work for him and after dropping a kiss on Roxanne's shoulder and telling her he'd call her later in the day, he'd dragged on his clothes and taking the dogs with him departed for his house.

Pleasantly exhausted from another night of fevered lovemaking, Roxanne barely mumbled a "good-bye" when he left, but when she arose a couple of hours later, she was conscious of being lonely and feeling slightly deserted. Standing under the hot spray of the shower, she decided morosely that he could have at least left her the dogs. He didn't have to take *everything* with him, did he? She'd have liked the dogs underfoot for company.

That thought brought her up short. Since when did she need company? Hadn't she left her parents' home because she wanted to be alone? Hadn't she complained that she'd felt smothered with people all around her, constantly underfoot?

Dressed in jeans and a lavender sweatshirt embroidered with white and purple tulips, she wandered into the kitchen. She started the coffeemaker and fixed herself a piece of whole wheat toast.

A few minutes later, nibbling on her dry toast and sipping her coffee, she stared out the French doors in the great room at the valley below. It was a slightly overcast morning, a bit gloomy, and Roxanne decided that the weather fit her mood exactly. The snow was beginning to melt on the mountainside, more and more areas of green and brown showing up here and there. Even at this elevation, the snow on the ground rarely remained for more than four or five days. Oh, in the shady areas, there would still be patches of white that hung on for a week or two, but most of it disappeared before wearing out its welcome.

Having finished her toast, Roxanne turned away from the French doors and heaved a heavy sigh. She missed Jeb. She missed the dogs.

She made a face. Get over it. The man's got a job to do and the dogs are his, not yours. Get your own damn dog if that's what you want. But she didn't want a dog—she wanted Jeb!

Annoyed with herself for mooning over him, Roxanne threw herself into an orgy of housecleaning. She tidied the great room, swept the kitchen, made the bed, cleaned the bathroom, and washed clothes.

By noon the overcast had vanished and the sun was out. It was one of those crisp, bright, cool days for which northern California was noted. She ate a cheese sandwich and an apple with a glass of milk for lunch and after checking out the state of her cupboards, decided that some grocery shopping was definitely called for.

Scolding herself for not shopping yesterday when she and Jeb had been in Ukiah, she got in the Jeep and resigned herself to picking over what was on the shelves at McGuire's Market.

Actually, she was pleasantly surprised at the variety of items that the store now stocked and she suspected that M.J.'s fine hand was behind the additions. The vegetable section had a small amount of just about anything a shopper could want, from limes to Chinese green beans. Impressed in spite of herself, Roxanne loaded up on cauliflower and broccoli, some fruit and other things before splurging on vineripened tomatoes and avocados. It had been years since she had really shopped at McGuire's and she spent several minutes just wandering around the store, familiarizing herself with the layout and just being curious. The meat counter impressed her the most and after picking up a package of boneless center-cut pork chops, a couple of New York steaks, four pounds of ground round, some lean stew meat, and a pot roast, she studied the neck bones. Now if I were dog, she wondered, which ones would I like? Finding two packages of big meaty neck bones that satisfied her requirements, she tossed them into the cart. Dawg and Boss were gonna love 'em. Just as she was preparing to move on, Tom Smith, who had been managing the meat department ever since Roxanne could remember, walked up to her. As a child she remembered the Tootsie Rolls he passed out to just about every kid in the valley and she almost expected him to hand her one.

"Howdy, Miss Roxanne. How're you doing?" he asked in his soft voice. He was a tall man, thin as a rail and bald as a cue ball. He was also one of the kindest, gentlest men Roxanne had ever known. He glanced into her cart and, seeing the neck bones, murmured, "Going to use them for a broth base?"

"Uh, no," she mumbled. "I got them for some dogs."

He smiled, his blue eyes twinkling. "Well, if that's the case, let me go in back and bring you out some nice knucklebones—dogs really love 'em."

A few minutes later, two gargantuan knucklebones resting in her cart, a small Tootsie Roll having mysteriously appeared in her hand, she moved on, smiling as she did so. Passing the mirrored window she knew opened to the store's tiny cramped office, she tapped on it. A second later M.J.'s face popped into view. Seeing who it was, she smiled.

"Hi," M.J. said. "How's it going?"

"Fine," Roxanne replied. "I didn't mean to interrupt you, I just wanted to tell you what a great job you've done with the market. It's certainly changed in twenty years." She waved a hand. "New, bigger building. More freezer cases. Lots of things."

M.J. beamed. "Thank you! Most of the time all I hear is complaints. It's wonderful to receive a compliment."

A gorgeous redhead squeezed next to M.J. in the small opening. "Hello, Roxanne," Pagan said shyly.

"Don't tell me," Roxanne said with a laugh, "she dragooned you into helping her with the computer."

"Guilty," replied M.J., her brown eyes dancing. "And man is she *good!* I've already told her that she can't go back to New Orleans—I'm going to chain her to the computer and keep her here forever."

The three women chatted for several moments, just innocuous conversation, until M.J. asked, "Have you heard any rumors about Nick yet?"

A pang of guilt struck Roxanne. Nick and his relationship to Shelly had been the last thing on her mind the past few days. "Er, no," she admitted. "Is the news all over town?"

M.J. nodded. "You bet. Sloan told your parents New Year's Day, as well as Cleo, Mingo, Danny, and Bobba. Hank and Megan know too. Shelly asked Hank not to be the one to introduce the topic at the restaurant, just for him to make certain that when everyone else is gossiping about it that the story stays straight. Hank loves it. He says there's half a dozen blowhards that he's wanted to correct for years. Says he's really going to enjoy pinning their ears back. I told most of my family." She grinned. "And you know how my grandpa loves to talk—he had coffee at The Oak Valley Inn the other morning with his group of cronies, so you know that the news has traveled far and wide by now."

"That's great!" Roxanne said. "How're the reactions going?"

"Beyond shock, just about everyone is falling in line. Sloan said your folks were taken aback, but with Shelly being their daughter-in-law, they have to support her—even if your dad would like to do differently just on principle. Some of the older folks, like Cleo and Judge Delaney, admitted that they always sort of suspected something like that. All in all, I think Shelly's plan is working." M.J. made a face. "Of course, there's always going to be mean-spirited and petty people who'll give Nick a hard time. And I worry about Maria. She's so scared and embarrassed. It can't be easy knowing that everyone is looking at you and gossiping. But we're all rallying around her and considering that the people behind her represent some of the oldest and most respected families in the valley, I think we'll be able to keep her from taking a drubbing from the more vicious tongues. Judge Delaney told Mingo to let him know if he needs to drop a warning in anyone's ear."

Mingo and Jeb's father was a retired Superior

Court Judge for the county and though he'd not sat on the bench for ten years or more, he was still called "Judge." His word was law in the valley—and having him drop a warning in your ear was tantamount to an order. Few disobeyed.

Another stab of guilt went through Roxanne. Jeb was supposed to have told his parents, not left it to Mingo. She fiddled with the handle of her cart. "It's good that Mingo told the Judge right away."

Tongue in cheek, M.J. said, "Speaking of Mingo—he was in earlier today and says that his big brother has been curiously absent from home ever since New Year's. Even took his dogs with him." Innocently she asked, "You wouldn't know anything about that, would you?"

Roxanne had forgotten how swiftly news spread in the valley. Oh, damn. Did everyone know that Jeb had spent the last two nights at her house? She suddenly felt very young and vulnerable. As quickly as that feeling had come, she shook it off with a toss of her head. What did it matter? Hadn't her love life been splashed all over the television screen and *The Enquirer* for years? She should be used to it by now. Besides, she was a big girl now, a grown woman, answerable to no one. There was no reason why she couldn't have a gentleman stay the night . . . or two, without turning it into a big deal. Except, she admitted, biting her lip, this was Oak Valley . . . not New York. She knew she was being silly, overreacting even. Men and women had sex in Oak Valley just as they did anywhere else, and men and women stayed overnight with each other here just as they did other places. So what was the problem? The problem was that this was home, these people had known her since she was an infant, and Oak Valley was definitely *not* New York. To her amazement, she felt two spots of color burn in her cheeks. Flustered, she muttered, "Uh, er, is that so?"

"That's what I heard," M.J. said, grinning at Roxanne's discomfiture. Sloan had mentioned that Roxanne hadn't been seen or heard from either and it didn't take a rocket scientist to put two and two together.

Fighting to regain her composure, Roxanne shrugged. "Detective Delaney is a big boy. I'm sure he'll turn up. Somewhere."

"Yeah, I'll just bet he will," murmured M.J., her pansy-brown eyes dancing.

Trying to divert M.J. Roxanne smiled at Pagan and asked, "Now that you've been here a few days, how are you liking it?"

Pagan grinned. "It's been great! Everyone is so friendly"—she winked—"especially the men, and the valley is beautiful. Shelly says now's not the best time to see it, that if you see it in the spring, it'll capture your heart forever. I think the whole valley is just gorgeous. So different from Louisiana—I love the nip in the air."

"So how long are you staying? Roman seemed vague on that the other night."

Pagan looked wry. "I don't know. The date has been sort of left open. If Roman had his way, I think he'd move here permanently, but the family relies on him to run the agricultural part of Granger Industries and Roman has this huge sense of responsibility, even though one of my other brothers, Tom or Noble, would take on that part of the company without complaint." She made a face. "He doesn't feel it's fair to ask them to take on any more than they already have. Besides, like he said, he's got really great people to run everything while he's gone and with E-mail, fax, and computers, there is a bunch of stuff he can do from here, but he admitted it's not the same as being there. So when guilty conscience strikes, we'll probably go home. I'm hoping we'll be able to stay for at least a couple weeks." She grinned. "And if his conscience strikes too soon, I may just stay by myself— although I'd have to find someplace else to stay—don't know how it would look with Nick and me living in that house together by ourselves—right now, Nick's got enough on his plate."

The three women talked for several more minutes and then Roxanne walked to the checkout counter.

Debbie Smith, Tom's wife of more than forty years, was standing in her usual place behind the register. She had been McGuire's first full-time employee and remembered the days when the store had been a little hole-in-the-wall and only a meat market. With her steel-gray hair and round little form, she looked exactly the opposite of her husband. Next to Cleo, she was the best source of gossip in the valley.

"Well, hi there, stranger," Debbie said with a friendly smile as she began to unload and ring up Roxanne's groceries. "Haven't seen you in a coon's age. Your folks well? How's that house of yours coming along? Heard that it's very nice. You really going to be living here all the time now? Retiring, I hear. Aren't you kinda young?"

Roxanne laughed and proceeded to let Debbie pick her brains. She often wondered why the valley even had a newspaper—Cleo and Debbie did an excellent job of spreading the news.

Sacking up Roxanne's groceries, her blue eyes alert, Debbie leaned forward and asked in a low voice, "You heard the news about Nick Rios? About him being Shelly's brother?"

Roxanne nodded. "I was there when she announced it."

"Well, it's a good thing the truth is finally out in the open. I always wondered about Nick—especially as he grew older. Looked too much like Josh for it just to have been an accident and I never believed the gossip about Josh being his father." At Roxanne's raised brow, she went on, "I know there're a lot of people who didn't like Josh Granger and I can't say as how I blame some of them—he could be a son of a bitch when he wanted to be, but in his own way he always struck me as an honorable kind of guy. I had trouble believing that he wouldn't acknowledge his own son."

Roxanne didn't know what to say. She hadn't known Josh—he was a Granger, she was a Ballinger, so they never had much interaction with each other. And deciding that it would be better to keep her mouth shut, she just nodded and said, "I feel sorry for Nick and Maria. They'll be the talk of the valley for a while."

Debbie's blue eyes twinkled and she chuckled. "Oh, don't worry about it—in two weeks, tongues will be wagging about something else."

Debbie's words didn't comfort Roxanne. She knew exactly upon whom the valley's interest would next focus. Her and Jeb.

Back at the house, she unloaded and put away the groceries. Checking her answering machine, she was disappointed that she'd missed a call from Jeb. Just the sound of his deep voice sent a thrill through her and she wished she hadn't lingered in town—she'd only missed his call by minutes. But she perked up. He'd said that he'd bring dinner, Chinese food from Willits, and the dogs, and they'd be at her house tonight. About 7:00 P.M. If that was a problem, leave a message on his home phone. A problem? she thought with a grin. Who does he think he's kidding?

And just about at 7:00 P.M. sharp there was a rap on Roxanne's front door. She opened it, her heart leaping at the sight of Jeb, a paper bag holding Chinese food in his arm and the dogs leaping around his feet. They managed to get the food to the kitchen before they fell into each other's arms as if they'd been separated for a month.

The days passed Roxanne in a blur of passionate nights lost in Jeb's arms and happy hours settling into her house. By tacit consent, the first weekend in January, Jeb constructed a small enclosed dog run at the side of the old garage and placed a new doghouse and pad he'd bought in it, along with a big water pan. From then on the dogs spent their days following Roxanne around and taking long walks with her as she explored the property. There was never any question of the dogs actually spending the night in the dog run—it was for those times when they couldn't take the dogs with them and didn't want them running loose. At night, the dogs were confidently curled up on the bed, Dawg a warm bundle at her back, Boss doing a fine job of keeping her feet warm—except of course when she and Jeb were lost in each other's arms. Jeb still slipped out of her bed and left to shower and dress on workdays, but other times, he was at her house and spent most nights. And while he was practically living with her, he was very careful to keep up the pretext that he still lived in his own house on the other side of the valley—neither one of them seemed inclined to formalize the situation.

And while she and Jeb easily talked about many subjects, they studiously avoided any serious conversation about the future, both of them wary and not quite certain just what direction and just how far this relationship was going to go. To their astonishment, despite some differences, they discovered that they enjoyed each other's company—a lot. It was a comfort to both of them that excellent sex wasn't their only area of agreement.

It was a dry January and as it drew to an end, there was increasing talk of drought. The days were reasonably pleasant—for January—and though they'd had some rain, it had been more in the form of misty showers than the good winter downpours everyone was hoping for.

Roxanne was so immersed in her life in Oak Valley that it was as if her days as a model had never been. A phone call in late January from a fellow model and friend, Ann Talbot, evoked only the tiniest pang of regret that she had given up her career. Or most of it—she had told her agent, Marshall Klein, that she'd be willing to do the occasional charity gig and once in a while a brief shoot—provided it was somewhere in the Caribbean or Hawaii. Marshall was Ann's agent, too, and over the years the two women had frequently shared assignments and at the beginning of their careers had shared an apartment together. Ann was a tall, striking café au lait–skinned woman with almond-shaped eyes that were a mysterious shade of pale blue-green. "I probably," Ann often said with a laugh, "got those from some white honky plantation owner who couldn't keep his hands off the slave women. Only good thing the bastard ever did for my people was pass on these eyes."

Ann was full of news and gossip and they laughed and talked for nearly two hours. "So how're you doing out there in the wilderness, girlfriend?" Ann asked toward the end of their conversation. "Missing the excitement of the Big Apple, yet? Or have you gone totally back to nature?"

"Not totally but almost. Oh, Ann, I do love it here. I'd forgotten how much. It's so wonderful to wake up to the sound of absolutely *nothing*. And the air! Terrific. And when I look out my windows all I see are blue sky, and miles and miles of wilderness. The lack of stress is unbelievable. You should try it sometime." Roxanne laughed. "Of course, there's no takeout—in fact a couple nights of the week, there isn't even a restaurant open. There are no clubs or theaters—we're so small and far from civilization we don't even have a *movie* theater. No taxis. No buses. No delivery, except mail, UPS, and FedEx. No doormen. No adoring fans. There's just cattle, horses, sheep, and big empty fields and mountains of forest filled with wildlife. It's wonderful—if it doesn't bore you to death."

"Sounds pretty nice," Ann said, a note of wistfulness in her throaty voice. "Some of those luxurious resorts I escape to, ostensibly, mind you, to rest, just wear me out. Now I'm not saying I'm ready to give up the high life, but a weekend now and then away from all the hustle and bustle would be welcome."

Roxanne understood the wistfulness. She'd always had Oak Valley to escape to, but not everyone else did and more than once she'd thought that some of her friends could have done with a week of peace and quiet in the valley. "You know you can come and stay with me anytime," Roxanne offered warmly. "I'd love to have you come visit." She laughed. "It'd give the natives no end of excitement."

"You be careful passing out invitations, honey bun, there's probably a dozen of us that would descend on you like locust. In fact, if I didn't have this assignment this weekend in Greece, I might take you up on it."

"What assignment is that?"

They talked shop for a few minutes longer and shortly thereafter they hung up. Stepping out onto the rear terrace, Roxanne stared down at the valley. She took a deep breath. For just a second there at the end, she'd been aware of feeling left out, of being passed by, and it troubled her. Then she laughed. Guess she now knew what an old retired fire-horse felt like when the whistle shrieked and the fire engines roared away from the station. But even though she'd suffered that little pang, she was happy with her decision. Less than twenty-four hours back in New York and she'd be clamoring for home.

The dry weather held and the grumblings of drought grew louder, but while there were those who complained about the lack of rain, Roxanne wasn't one of them. Her daffodils were growing taller and taller by the day and a few had tiny buds. She checked them eagerly almost every day, trying to decide if the buds had gotten bigger overnight.

Watching her one sunny Saturday afternoon as she bent over and closely examined the plants, Jeb laughed and shook his head. "Trust me, Princess, they haven't grown since last night."

Roxanne no longer took offense at the name "Princess"—especially not when it was said in that soft, almost tender tone of his. These days she nearly purred aloud when he called her Princess. She turned a laughing face to him and said, "I know, but it's so much fun to check on them." She pointed to a clump of the stiff green fronds. "Look, there are more buds—and I'd swear they weren't apparent last night."

He gravely examined the clump in question. "Well, I don't know about that, but there are certainly more buds than the last time I looked . . . about two weeks ago."

Roxanne put her arm through his and she lifted her face to the winter sun. "God! It's a gorgeous day. The sky is so blue, the trees so green. It seems as if everything is so much more intense here than anywhere else I've ever been."

"Now you wouldn't be prejudiced, would you?" he asked with a smile.

"Nah."

With the dogs set free and gamboling around their

feet, they started on a leisurely hike. It had become a habit of theirs when the weather was good.

Today, as they tramped along what looked like an old skid road when the place had been logged thirty or forty years ago, Jeb asked, "How much land did you say you bought?"

"It's a section. A mile square. Six hundred forty acres." She spun around, a grin on her face and her arms outstretched. "And it's all mine. Mine. Mine."

"So Madame Land Owner, what are you going to do with it?"

They were climbing a particularly steep section of road. Nature was doing a fine job of obliterating the road. What remained was rutted from years of storm runoff and there were small slides here and there; everywhere they walked, firs and pines some ten feet tall had staked a claim, most growing right down the center, and of course there was the inevitable brush— manzanita, madrone, and buck brush.

Winding her way around one of the smaller firs, her hand lingering on the soft green needles, Roxanne admitted, "I don't know yet." She made a face. "Obviously running cattle isn't an option, nor is raising horses, except on a very limited scale." She glanced around at the stunning views. "This is a great piece of recreational land, but it doesn't have much value beyond that. I do have several ideas though, but nothing's set in concrete yet."

"Care to share?"

She brushed her lips across his cheek. "I always share with you."

A distinctly carnal curve to his lower lip, he pulled her against him and murmured, "Oh, really. Wanna do some 'sharing' right now?"

She chuckled and pushed him away. "None of that. But I will share some ideas I have about this place."

Hand in hand they traversed the rough ground. "I've been thinking of putting those greenhouses to use." At his raised brow, she pinched his arm. "And not as you so nastily suggested once to grow marijuana. I'm going to be talking to some of the local florists within the next few weeks and see if I could create a niche market with my own flowers. Try to grow some of the more exotic flowers and shrubs and vines and grasses used in making bouquets. Not a big operation but enough to make a profit and keep me busy. These past months have been nice, but I can't imagine not working at something."

"You know anything about growing flowers?" His expression was dubious.

Roxanne made a face. "Not commercially, but a green thumb does run in my family and my apartment in New York was like a jungle—I had it stuffed with plants. I even had a window box. I love growing things and there's not too many things I like better than having my hands in rich warm dirt."

Jeb nodded thoughtfully. "Sounds like a possibility. If you're serious, I could repair some of those old plant benches, make new ones if you need them, and check out the water lines for you." He wiggled his brows. "I'm real handy with my tools."

Spying what looked like flat areas of ground off to the side, they whistled for the dogs that had gone on ahead of them and climbed up the steep banks of the road. Following the gentle slope of the land, they eventually reached an area that was relatively flat. Scattered trees and brush made it hard to estimate its size, but after trampling around and pushing through stands of fir and pine, Jeb said, "I'd guess there's about two acres of fairly level ground here. Be a dandy place for a small hunting cabin or a weekend getaway if you needed one."

Roxanne agreed. "Hmm, yes it would. Lots of privacy. Water and power might be a problem. And access, but it could be done." She looked around again. "I haven't explored very much of the property yet, but on our walks the dogs and I have run across a couple of areas like this—I was surprised because when you look at the property, it looks like it's just a perpendicular hillside."

"You may be on the side of a mountain, but on a big piece of land like this, unless it's in a canyon, you're bound to find some areas that are fairly level." He cocked a brow. "You've got a great house, you're not really planning on building a cabin, too, are you?"

Her conversation with Ann at the back of her mind, Roxanne said slowly, "I might be." As she studied the area, picturing it without the brush and only the nicest trees left and trimmed up, a charming cabin nestled in the center of the trees, an idea began to take shape. "In fact," she said, "I might be planning on having three or four built."

"Why?" he asked, startled.

"Well, for one thing, just think of the fun we'd have making love in all those different cabins . . ."

Chapter
14

The sun was beginning to slip behind the mountain above them and a chill was seeping into the air. Jeb's arm thrown over her shoulder, they slowly made their way back to the house, the dogs, tired out from futile pursuits of anything that moved, ambling at their heels, tongues hanging out.

"You really serious about this?" he asked, after she had explained the idea that had come to her as she looked around the clearing.

Roxanne hesitated. "Maybe. I don't know." She looked over at him. "I need to do something and while I don't object to volunteer work and plan to do some of that, it's not how I see myself spending the rest of my life. I like to work and I'm lucky that I can choose and pick what I want to do." She spread her arms indicating the land around them. "I've got this great piece of property that isn't really good for anything but recreation, why not turn what might be thought of as a negative into a positive?" Her face full of excitement, she looked at him. "Think about it, Jeb. I'm not just talking about my celebrity friends needing a place to get away to now and then for some serious R and R. What about a writer on a deadline? Any kind of writer—screen, song, books. Wouldn't this place inspire you?" She grinned. "And the best part—no distractions."

Jeb rubbed his chin, nodding thoughtfully. "Yeah, I can see for certain people that it might be an option."

"*Certain* people is right! Over half the people I know from New York would freak out at the sight of a dirt road and just the thought of being away from neon lights and pavement would send them shrieking for their shrink. I'm not talking about them. I'm talking about people who really do need some peace and quiet. The kind of jaded celebrities who'd like to spend a week or two in their own little hideaway. Even if I built half a dozen cabins, each person would have over a hundred acres to call their own—and that's if every cabin was filled." Bubbling over with enthusiasm, she went on, "And remember, we may be remote, but we have our own airport. They could charter a plane from SFO, fly in, be met by me, or whoever, and whisked away before anyone has any idea that they're here."

"You gonna run this enterprise single-handedly, Princess?"

"Nope. That's the beauty of it. If I were to do it, and if it proved successful, I'd be creating jobs for at least three or four people in the valley." She frowned.

"Honest, *discreet* people. And even better, I can pick and choose my clients. I could close down for the winter if I wanted or limit the business to just certain weeks out of the year. So what do you think?" She glanced in his direction, wondering when his opinion had come to matter so much to her. She'd be crushed, she admitted, if he ridiculed her idea. Her jaw tightened. His disapproval wouldn't stop her, but it might put a very big crimp in their relationship. She'd learned the hard way that some men could be controlling in not so subtle ways—constantly giving negative feedback and putting up roadblocks was one manner of keeping the little woman in her place. Time and again she'd run into men who were threatened by a successful woman and their way of dealing with it was to crack jokes about achievements or belittle the accomplishments. She didn't expect Jeb to just jump for joy with every idea she had, but she wanted him to take it seriously and if he saw problems, real, honest problems, say so. Constructive criticism she could take—provided it *was* constructive. It occurred to her that a great deal suddenly hung on Jeb's answer and reaction. Unaware and unexpectedly, they'd come to a very big fork in the road of their relationship.

Jeb was silent as they walked, turning the idea over in his mind. He had to confess that on the surface it didn't sound bad. It wasn't likely to be as easy as Roxanne seemed to think, but then it was just off the cuff and for a working premise, it seemed pretty damn good to him. There'd be problems along the way, of that he had little doubt, but he was confident that Roxanne would find a way around them. She was stubborn. She was smart. And she had guts.

He grinned at her. "Sounds like a plan to me, Princess. There'll probably be some snags, but overall, I think it could work—and if anybody can make it work—it'll be you."

Roxanne's heart soared and she let out the breath she hadn't even been conscious of holding. Stepping in front of him, her hands clutched the lapels of his black leather jacket, halting him in mid-stride. Her expression dead serious, she asked, "That's your honest opinion? You're not humoring me? Or petting me on the head?"

He looked insulted. "Since when have I ever humored you? And as for petting you on the head . . . if I dared, I'd pull back a bloody stump." He caught her shoulders and shook her slightly. "Come on, Roxanne, think! Why would I not be honest with you? And when have we ever pulled our punches with each other? If I thought it was a stupid idea, I'd say so. I think it's a great idea! At least," he added cautiously, "on the surface."

"Really?" she couldn't help asking, her eyes glowing. So what if his approval pleased her? Did that make her less a modern woman? She didn't think so.

He smiled crookedly at her and brushed a strand of hair from her cheek. "Really. Honest. And all that crap. Now can we please go home? In case you haven't noticed the sun's gone down and it's cold and I'm freezing my ass out here."

When they made the last turn before the house, the dogs suddenly lifted their heads, sniffed the air, and then baying like bloodhounds took off at a dead run. Jeb's voice, a note in it they seldom heard, stopped both dogs in their tracks. Chastened, they hurried back and in spite of raised hackles, and a soft whine from Dawg and an ominous low growl from Boss, kept pace with Jeb and Roxanne.

Jeb and Roxanne both recognized the blue pickup and the wiry man half out of the cab. Milo Scott didn't look happy; in fact, he looked as if he was of a mind to get back inside the truck. The dogs had obviously made an impression.

"What the hell is he doing here?" Jeb demanded, his mouth setting in grim lines. "You hire him to do more work?"

"Hey, don't get mad at me. I don't control Milo, he goes where he wants—invited and *un*invited."

"Point taken." Jeb stared at Milo through narrowed eyes. "I wonder how long the little bastard has been here and what he's been poking his nose into."

Pushing past Jeb, who looked like he might grind Milo between his teeth, Roxanne walked up to the side of the truck and said, "Hi, Milo. What brings you out here?"

Keeping a wary eye on the two dogs, who remained at Jeb's side, Milo said, "Oh, nothing much. Heard in town that you might be doing some new building.

Barn. Garage. Was wondering if I could get the specifics and put in a bid on the project?"

"Sorry," she said in a voice that indicated just the opposite. "Don Bean and Profane are doing the entire project. Don made me an offer I couldn't refuse. You could talk to him if you want to."

"Nah, that's OK. Bean generally only works with Profane and a couple of other guys he knows." He got back in the truck. "Well, I'll be going. You hear of any jobs around, you be sure and let me know."

"Drugs not paying these days?" Jeb drawled, strolling up to stand beside Roxanne.

Milo gave an exaggerated sigh. "How many times do I have to tell you—I don't know what you're talking about. I'm a cement contractor, not a drug dealer."

"Yeah, right, and I'm Santy Claus."

Ignoring Jeb, Milo smiled at Roxanne. "I'll be off. See you around, Roxy."

"Not if I see you first," Roxanne muttered under her breath as the blue pickup pulled away.

Jeb surveyed the area. Nothing looked out of place. Of course, that didn't mean anything; with Milo Scott sometimes you didn't find the damage right away.

"I wonder what he was up to?" Roxanne mused. "I made the deal with Bean weeks ago. *If* Milo heard about the job, he has to have known that Bean's handling the whole thing and that there wouldn't be any work for him."

"Used it as an excuse to drive out here. And I'll lay money on it that if we hadn't shown up, he'd do whatever it was that brought him out here and have left without a word to you."

Roxanne shrugged. "Probably. Now let's get inside and see about warming up those freezing buns of yours."

Jeb didn't forget about Milo Scott's visit. In fact, now that he thought about it, Scott seemed to prowl around Roxanne's place more than warranted. Even taking into account that the creep might be trying to make the moves on Roxanne didn't explain his frequent appearances. It wasn't a far leap to wonder about Scott's connection to Dirk Aston, the previous owner of the property. Dirk and Scott had been friends and sort of colleagues after a manner of speaking.

Sitting at his desk on the last Monday in January, Jeb considered the situation. Dirk Aston had been murdered in January last year. He had died suddenly and without warning. At least, it had appeared that the shooting in Oakland had been random and unexpected. It hadn't had the earmarks of a hit. Just one of those senseless killings you see on television and read about in the paper. So maybe, Dirk and Scott had had some unfinished business? Some business that was tied to Roxanne's property?

Jeb scowled at the pile of paperwork in front of him. The only business those two butt-wipes had shared had been drugs. So that left only two things that Scott could be looking for: drugs or money. His scowl deepened. Yeah. All those break-ins and the damage done to the original A-frame began to make sense. It had been teenage vandals, but not *just* teenage vandals—someone had been looking for something . . . looking damn hard.

His fingers steepled in front of him, Jeb leaned back in his chair. Since Milo Scott seemed to be still hanging around, it was pretty obvious that he hadn't found the object of his search. Jeb would be willing to bet that by now Scott had decided that, wherever and whatever Dirk had hidden, it wasn't in the house. Practically the whole interior of the original cabin had been gutted and Scott had been there during most of the project. As someone working out there, he'd been free to come and go and would have had plenty of time to snoop around when no else was about.

OK, Scott hadn't found anything, but he kept coming back. So that meant whatever Dirk had hidden was still out there.

He hadn't paid much attention to the Aston shooting at the time. The murder had happened out of his jurisdiction and the death of one more dirt bag hadn't caused him to lose a great deal of sleep. But he was curious now. He looked up and dialed the number of the Oakland Police Department. He knew a guy who worked as a detective in the Homicide Department—they weren't exactly friends, but they'd taken some advanced criminology classes together years ago and had kept in touch with each other. They'd been known to empty out a bar simply by walking inside—Gene Cartwright had a scarred and battered face that would give a mother pause—he'd paid for his way through college by being a semi-pro heavyweight boxer. When you added that he was as big as Jeb and black as the ace of spades, the reason was clear. No one wanted to tangle with someone Jeb's size, let alone *two* some-ones. Gene was also one of the good guys and Jeb liked and respected him.

Jeb was lucky. Cartwright was in.

"Hey, white boy," Cartwright greeted Jeb. "Long time no hear. How's everything up there in the boonies?"

Jeb laughed. They spent a few minutes catching up with each other's news and then Jeb said, "Listen, I'm curious about a murder that took place last January. Dirk Aston. Shot in a drive-by in one of your less law-abiding areas. Ring any bells?"

"Jeb, you know how many murders we have in a year down here? Don't answer. Right off, I don't re-member the case, but I'll poke around and see what I come up with. This a priority? You got a connection or something new on it?"

Jeb grimaced. "No, not really. I'm just grasping at straws, trying to tie up some loose ends."

They talked a bit longer and Gene promised to call Jeb back as soon as he had the time to drag out the file and read it.

The dry weather held and Roxanne noticed that al-ready the days were getting longer. By the first week of February her daffodils had begun to bloom and she filled the house with small bouquets of white and yel-low blossoms, their sweet scent filling the air.

She hadn't planned anything special for Valentine's Day. In fact, to her embarrassment she'd forgotten all about it. On a whim, only a trip to Heather-Mary-Marie's to check out some cute kitchen towels she'd noticed a couple weeks ago saved her from ignoring the most romantic day of the year. Reminded by all the Valentine's Day cards prominently displayed, after careful selection, she picked one out that wasn't too mushy. She'd dawdled over a couple fantastic cards declaring lasting love and reluctantly had put them back. She sighed. Maybe next year. . . . As for a present, Heather-Mary-Marie's had a fine selection of The Mountain T-shirts and sweatshirts and spying a T-shirt in a beautiful tie-dyed deep green with a snarling black panther on the front, she grabbed it from the rack and put it on the wooden counter with the card.

Red hair bright enough to blind, big hoops of beaten gold dangling from her ears, Cleo glanced from the card to the T-shirt. Cleo Hale was actually Heather-Mary-Marie—her grandfather, Graham Newel, had named the store for his three daughters, Heather, Mary, and Marie, around the turn of the century when he first opened a dry-goods store in the valley. At a time in life when she had long been considered on the shelf, Heather Newel had astounded everyone by marrying Sam Howard and producing a daughter whom she had named Heather-Mary-Marie. Cleo had endured being called Heather-Mary-Marie Howard until she turned eighteen and then she had decided that she was more a Cleopatra than a Heather-Mary-Marie and had run away with her first husband, Tom Haggart.

Cleo was not a beauty; she had more of a plain face than a pretty one, had shoulders that would have done a lumberjack proud, and stood six feet tall. None of that had stopped her from marrying five times over the course of almost sixty-six years. The Hale name came from her fifth husband and since she thought it went well with Cleo, she didn't bother to change back to her maiden name when she'd kicked old Charley Hale out for fooling around with the widow Brown about fifteen years ago. She was a mainstay in the valley, both beloved and reviled—depending on which end of her tongue you got, and known for not being shy about voicing her opinion.

A gleam entered Cleo's clear blue eyes as she looked at Roxanne's purchases. Cleo believed that a woman should make the most of what she had—no matter her age—and lowering eyes lavishly covered with lavender eye shadow, she murmured, "For anybody I know?"

Roxanne smiled. "As if I would tell you. It would be all over town within five minutes."

Not offended, Cleo grinned. "Hmm, make that three." She winked. "Got my reputation to think of, girl. Sure you can't give me a hint? Something for me to throw to the piranhas?"

Roxanne looked thoughtful. "Well, it's a man. A handsome man. He fills out his pants and shirts very nicely. And he's older than I am. Oh, and taller." Her eyes laughing she asked, "How's that?"

"Cute, very cute," Cleo said, ringing up the two items. "Want me to wrap them for you?"

"Sure."

While Roxanne waited, Cleo set about quickly wrapping the T-shirt, they talked idly and eventually the subject of Nick and Maria came up. Her scarlet lips tight with disapproval, Cleo muttered, "Some folks ought to be horsewhipped. Reba Stanton and Babs Jepson were in a few minutes ago . . . so was Maria Rios." She shook her head. "Those two harpies stared her up and down, stepped back ten paces, and then began to whisper." Cleo snorted. "Didn't take a fool to know they were gossiping about Maria and not making any attempt to hide it. Maria looked stricken, put down the card she was going to buy, and scuttled out of here like she'd been beat. I'd have liked to have given those fat cows a talkin' to, but I had a lot of customers and by the time the place was clear, they'd sashayed out and gone across the street to The Blue Goose for lunch."

A hard light in her eyes, Roxanne drawled, "Is that right? You figure they're still eating?"

Cleo nodded. "Yep, that's Babs's black Caddy parked in front of the restaurant. They meet every Wednesday for lunch—probably enjoying tearing Maria from limb to limb with their salads."

"No doubt. Think I'll go join them," Roxanne said, picking up her brightly wrapped package and card.

Cleo looked at her, frowning. "Now why would you want to do that?"

"Because dear Cleo, I went to high school with them, and I know where all the bodies are buried. I have some very clear memories of things I'm sure the pair of them would like forgotten." She smiled tightly. "Think I'll go remind them."

Roxanne pushed open the heavy door of the restaurant and instantly spotted her quarry. The two women were seated near one of the windows, their fashionably coiffed heads together.

Waving to Hank who flashed her a wide smile, she motioned to the table where Reba and Babs sat unaware of the thunderbolt about to descend upon them. "I'll be joining my friends," Roxanne called out gaily to Hank.

Reba and Babs looked up startled when Roxanne pulled out a chair and sat down at their table. Her eyes bright, Roxanne looked the pair of them over. "My goodness, but you two haven't hardly changed in twenty years. However do you do it?"

Reba and Babs had been three years ahead of Roxanne in school. Usually, lordly juniors wouldn't have given a lowly freshman the time of day, except when the lowly freshman just happened to be the daughter of one of the leading families in the valley and was also one of the most popular kids in the small high school. Reba and Babs had also been friends with Sloan's first wife, Nancy—Nancy had been the ringleader of the trio, but even then Nancy had had her eye on the

Ballinger fortune and she had quickly swept Roxanne up in their exclusive little circle. Roxanne had been flattered, but it didn't take her long to decide that she didn't really like Nancy, Babs, and Reba very much and she drifted away. But not, she thought grimly, as she faced the two women, before knowing quite a few things they'd rather she didn't.

It was Babs and Reba's turn to be flattered. After all, this was *Roxanne* complimenting them and like a pair of plump pigeons in the sun they preened and cooed.

"What a nice thing to say," said Reba with a pleased smile.

"Why thank you," added Babs. "That's a real compliment coming from *you*."

"Yes, it is," Roxanne said. She hadn't been lying: Babs and Reba did look great for having passed their big 4-0 birthdays. The two women complemented each other, Babs was dark-haired, dark-eyed, and Reba was blond and blue-eyed. They had kept their figures, although neither was as slim as they had been in high school—and their vicious tongues.

Roxanne glanced at the menu that Sally, the main waitress in The Blue Goose besides Hank, gave her, and asked, "So what would you recommend for lunch?"

"Oh, well, we both have to watch our weight so we ordered the grilled chicken salad," Babs said. Her gaze envious, she assessed Roxanne's weight to the pound. "You can eat anything you want."

"Don't you believe it—I didn't get this way pigging out on ice cream and chips." She smiled at Babs. "The way you did when you were pregnant in high school." Ignoring Babs's gasp, she went on coolly, "Whatever happened about that anyway? Abortion? Or adoption?"

Having vanquished Babs, she turned her icy golden eyes on Reba. "And you, whatever happened with your first marriage?" She frowned prettily. "Don't I remember something about you running away with a Mexican kid? Oh, yeah, that's right—your folks caught up with you before you actually got married."

Roxanne smiled into the two stunned faces. "Funny the things you remember from high school, isn't it?" Her face fierce, she bent closer to the two women. "And if you two bitches don't hold your tongues and treat Maria Rios kindly, I'll just have to share my memories with several folks in town. In fact, I think as a sign of good faith, you should invite Maria to have lunch with you next week. Sort of show the community that you're rallying behind her. A good idea, don't you think?"

Reba swallowed. "Uh, why, yes. Excellent. I'll call her this afternoon."

"Oh, yes, we'd be more than happy to throw our support her way."

Roxanne stood up. "See that you do. Otherwise . . ."

Turning her back on them, Roxanne strolled up to

the counter. "Hey, Hank, could I have one of your half-pound hamburgers to go?"

Ten minutes later, her hamburger resting in its foam carton, Roxanne smiled and walked out of the restaurant.

Back at the house, she split the hamburger with the dogs, signed the card, left the package and card in the middle of Jeb's pillow. It might not be a particularly romantic present, but, she thought with a grin, she'd make it up to him.

Jeb showed up earlier than usual and if Roxanne was disappointed that *he* hadn't remembered Valentine's Day, she didn't show it. After the dogs had given him a welcome worthy of someone returned from the dead, the same as they did every night, Jeb pulled Roxanne into his arms and kissed her quite, quite thoroughly.

"Happy Valentine's Day," he said as he lifted his mouth from hers.

Heart thumping madly, nearly swooning from his kiss, she arched one brow and murmured, "And that's it? A kiss?"

He grinned. "What a mercenary little witch." He dropped a kiss on her nose. "No that's not it." He swept low in a bow and said, "If the princess will come with me, I'll show you your present."

Mystified, she linked her arm in his and followed him out to the truck. Lifting up a folded cloth, he said, "I know this will sound kinky, but would you mind putting this on like a blindfold. I don't want you to see it until I have you in the right position."

Muffling a chuckle, she put on the blindfold.

Jeb started the truck and drove down the winding gravel road that led to her place. A couple of minutes later, he turned the vehicle around so that it was pointing in the direction that they had come from.

"Not yet," he said as he turned off the ignition. "Let me get you outside."

Eaten alive with curiosity, Roxanne waited impatiently as he got out of the truck and came around to open her door. His hands around her waist, he lifted her from the truck and set her on the ground. "Turn around. But don't look yet," he said softly in her ear.

He hesitated and muttered, "Christ, I hope this isn't a bust. It took me weeks of tramping the woods to find the right piece of wood and then you don't want to know how many nights I was late because I'd spent a couple of hours working on it. I wanted to make something for you and this was the only thing that I could think of that you didn't already have."

He whipped off the blindfold.

Roxanne stared, feeling a lump forming in her throat and tears almost spilling from her eyes. In front of her, fastened to a stout wooden post newly cemented into the ground, was the most romantic gift she'd ever been given in her life.

It was a wooden sign. Not just any old sign, but one lovingly made from oak burl wood. Jeb had smoothed out the edges until the large slab was almost in the shape of a heart. With a router, he'd carved out in large letters, ROXY'S ROOST: there was an arrow beneath the name, pointing in the direction of the house. The letters were painted in bold black and then coat after coat of urethane had been lovingly applied until the sign glistened in the fading sunlight.

"Uh, I know it's not much. And some women wouldn't think it was very romantic," he began in an apologetic voice. "But I thought, if you started that business of yours, you'd want a sign or something. . . ."

She turned around and flung her arms around his neck. Raining kisses on his face, she cried, "It's perfect. Perfect! And I think it's the most romantic thing in the world."

"You do? I mean really? You like it?"

"I love it." And she kissed him.

The weather was nice enough that night that she and Jeb decided to barbecue T-bone steaks outside on the rear terrace. They'd shared a very nice, very long shower together after viewing the sign so dinner ran a little late. And since they had no plans for the evening, they hadn't bothered to fully dress after the shower. Roxanne wore an apricot silk caftan and Jeb had shrugged into a loose pair of sweatpants and his new T-shirt—the new T-shirt and card had caused more delay as Jeb had thanked her so explicitly that another shower was called for.

They had lingered over the meal and now the remains of their dinner was spread out on the cheerful yellow and green tiled table in front of them. Dawg and Boss were gnawing noisily on the bones under the table. The two humans were loafing in their chairs, talking idly.

Roxanne took a sip of her wine and looked across in the direction of her neighbor. At this distance the only sign of the house had been its lights and while she hadn't been keeping score, she realized that she hadn't noticed the lights on in a long time. She frowned.

"You know just about everybody in the valley, don't you?" she asked Jeb.

"Yep. Just about."

She motioned toward the area where she usually saw the lights across the way. "Do you know who lives over there? That house about halfway up the foothills? Almost directly opposite of mine?"

Jeb knew exactly which house she meant. "I might. Why?"

She smiled, that warm, beguiling smile that made his toes tingle . . . and other parts, too. "Promise you won't laugh?" she asked almost shyly.

"Promise."

She took another sip of wine. "It's silly, but I call him, although I don't know whether it's a he, she, or a whole family, my neighbor. One of the first nights I was here, I looked out across the valley and there it was, his light shining like a beacon in the darkness." She giggled. "It was like a welcome light. I started talking to him whenever I notice the light on and I've even shared a toast or two with him. He's like, I don't know, a secret friend or something."

Jeb looked at his glass of wine and smiled. Roxanne hadn't been to his house yet—there'd been no need. He remembered looking out and seeing her light and cursing the day she'd returned to the valley. Funny how things change.

"So whose house is it?"

"Come here," he said, pushing back from the table and indicating his lap.

She complied, saying as she settled down against him, "Ooh, are you going to tell me a story? About the deranged dope dealer who lives across the way?"

He laughed. "Nope. Sorry to disappoint you, primrose, but no deranged dope dealer. The house belongs to a really great guy. Handsome, charming—everything a maiden could wish for."

Roxanne looked at him, her expression skeptical. "Why don't I believe you?"

"Honest," Jeb said, nipping her ear with his teeth. "He's a real prince of a guy. Kind to animals. Hardworking. You can ask Mingo if you don't believe me."

Ignoring the flash of warmth that slid through her at his touch, she stared at him. "And who is this paragon? Have I met him?"

Jeb grinned. "Oh, Princess, you've done more than meet him—you've been screwing him blind for several weeks now."

Roxanne sat up, her eyes wide. "You? It's your

house? You're my secret friend? You mean to tell me I've been pouring my heart out to you all this time?"

Jeb spread his hands. "You got it, sweet-cakes."

"Well, I'll be damned." She squirmed around to look across the valley. "You really live there?"

"Not much lately, as you may have noticed— there's this insatiable siren who keeps me occupied. But yes, that's my house over there. I bought it about five years ago—thought it was time I settled down and had my own place instead of renting all the time."

Roxanne didn't know what to say. It gave her a funny feeling to realize that all those times she'd looked wistfully across the valley and babbled like an idiot that it had been to Jeb of all people. Of course, he hadn't *heard* what she'd said, but still!

"Do you see my lights?" she asked.

He nodded. "Sure do."

She swung around to face him, her legs hanging on either side of him. Arms around his neck, she sent him a sly glance. "You ever talk to my lights?"

He cleared his throat, looking uncomfortable. It was hard to think when Roxanne was sitting in his lap, her breasts inches from his chest and her lower body was pressing against his growing erection. Jeb was not a stupid man. And admitting that he, yes, he had talked to her lights, had *cursed* her lights, seemed like a very stupid idea right now. She brushed her lips across his and he groaned. It would be, he decided, the height of stupidity. So he did what any not-stupid guy would do: he lied.

"Uh, no," he muttered. "Never did."

Her eyes gleamed and she wiggled on his lap. "You're lying. You did. And I'll bet you said something horrible and nasty."

"Why would I do that?" he demanded in an injured tone.

"Because you didn't like me very much then," she breathed against his mouth, her lips teasing him. "I'll bet you hated the sight of my lights burning up here." She ground her hips against the solid length of him. "I'll even bet that you cursed the day I returned to the valley." Her tongue slid between his lips and she kissed him deeply, crushing her breasts against his chest.

Jeb's brain turned to mashed potatoes. His arms went around her and he returned her kiss with interest. "God!" he said against her mouth when he could. "You feel so good."

"I do, don't I?" she purred. She wiggled around on his lap, stretching and pulling her caftan free. A flick of her hand and it went flying. Running a finger down his chest, she said, "Your turn, big boy. Off with your clothes. I have to punish you for being such a bad, bad boy and not telling me sooner that you're my very, *very* special neighbor."

Like a madman Jeb struggled out of his clothes. When he was naked, she caught his swollen, aching

penis between her legs. She hovered over him and then
inch by sweet inch she sank down on him.

His mind blurring, his fingers tightened around her
hips. "You're right—oh please, please punish me for
being such a bad boy," he muttered thickly. "Please,
please punish me . . ."

Chapter
15

*L*ong after Roxanne had gone to sleep that night, Jeb lay awake beside her in their bed. His thoughts were not comforting. He was in trouble. Big bad trouble. And he was scared. He wasn't quite certain how it had happened, but somewhere along the way, he'd broken his own commandment: Do Not Get Serious. He wasn't ready to swear his undying devotion, but he was bleakly aware that he wasn't far from it. And that a declaration of love was probably the last thing that Roxanne wanted to hear from him.

He shifted slightly in bed, his gaze falling on Roxanne as the faint moonlight streamed in and illuminated her sleeping features. As he stared at her, at that arrogant little nose and sassy mouth, something almost like pain moved in his chest. How had she slipped under his guard? *When* had she slipped under his guard?

After Sharon had left him and he'd shaken himself out of the morose pit he'd fallen into, he'd sworn that from then on he was going to be a love 'em and leave 'em sort of guy. He'd kept that vow. There had been many women in his life during the twelve or so years since his second divorce and he liked them all, enjoyed them all, and parted from them without a backward glance. Maybe there had been one or two he might have considered weakening his resolve for, but he always managed to pull back in time.

He grimaced in the moonlight. Ha! Pull back in time. What a laugh. He'd never stood a chance with Roxanne. One day she had been that smart-mouthed little brat just daring him to do anything about her wayward ways and he'd had to take up the dare. He smiled. And by God, hadn't she just hated him for that! She'd barely grown out of that stage and then suddenly she'd been the sassy, chic, the world is my oyster *Roxanne*. Those two incarnations hadn't caused him to lose any sleep, but just when he thought he had a handle on her, right before his eyes, she'd turned into the warm, intelligent, funny, and wonderful lover who lay beside him. She charmed him, disarmed him, and he'd been a lost soul ever since.

His quest was hopeless, he knew that. No way was Roxanne ever going to settle for a bucolic life in Oak Valley—no matter what she claimed to the contrary. And after Sharon there was no way he was going to run the risk of tying himself to a woman who'd eventually grow bored with valley doings and be off like a shot for new and greener, more exciting pastures.

Nope, he wasn't about to take the chance—not even for one that *seemed* to be currently happy as a bug in a rug living in the valley. Sharon's words still had the power to hit him like bullets and he was never going to leave himself open to that kind of pain again and another failed marriage. Nope. Uh-uh. Not him. No way. No how. Been there, done that.

It wasn't easy keeping his relationship with Roxanne on a light level—not when every instinct urged him to deepen what they had and take it to the ultimate conclusion—marriage. He sighed. Nope. Marriage wasn't for him. He was determined to revel in this time with her, however long it was, and let her have her head. And when she left him, he swallowed painfully, and when she left him as she would inevitably do he'd take comfort from his memories.

He brushed a kiss across Roxanne's nose and even in her sleep she seemed to sense him and turned to him, snuggling even closer. Her simple act made him feel like a heavyweight fighter had just punched him in the chest and for a moment he couldn't even breathe. Oh, God. He was definitely in trouble. Big time.

Roxanne was surprised that no one in the valley had yet discovered that she and Jeb were lovers. She knew that particular state of affairs wasn't going to last for very long and every day she braced herself for a phone call or a visit from a friend or relative demanding to know if the latest rumor was true.

She and Jeb hadn't been secretive, but because of

his job he was gone most days and some nights and the rest of the time, they were either alone together at the house or out of town. It was winter, a quiet time in the valley and most people weren't out and about, everyone tending to stay home near the fire, and the people most likely to tumble to the brewing romance had been busy with their own lives. Her folks had come to inspect the new house and to visit a couple of times, but each time they'd come, Jeb had been conveniently away. She made a face. Convenient, hell—she'd made certain he and the dogs were gone when they came. Ross and Samantha had both returned to their respective homes in Santa Rosa and Novato so she didn't have to worry about them, and Sloan, Shelly, Nick, Acey, and Roman had been taken up with various winter ranch projects. Roxanne had talked to all of them from time to time or bumped into them in town by herself, but so far no one had made an inopportune visit. It was almost like the gods were watching over them, keeping them cocooned and protected in their own little world. It was a miracle that no one had seen them when they had driven to Ukiah after the door locks. Ukiah was a large town, but since it was also the county seat and the town where most people in Oak Valley did their major shopping it was a rare trip that you saw no one from the valley.

She treasured this interlude, hugging the knowledge of their relationship to herself. She didn't want to share it with the world just yet—as much because she wanted no outside intrusion as the realization that she didn't quite know what to make of it.

Jeb seemed satisfied with the way things were and Roxanne, for the first time in her life, was so uncertain that she just drifted, unwilling to do anything to change their relationship. They were not exactly living together, although Jeb slept at her house most nights. There were a few times due to the pressures of work that he'd either stayed in Ukiah or had simply fallen exhausted into his own bed for a few snatched hours of sleep before returning to the field. Neither one of them appeared to want to formalize the living arrangements. Jeb kept only the minimum possessions, besides his dogs, at Roxanne's house: a couple changes of underwear, a jacket, a razor, two shirts, and a well-worn pair of jeans.

Roxanne wasn't certain how she felt about the whole situation. Having him actually move in with her was a step she wasn't certain she wanted to take and yet she knew that she cared far more deeply, more passionately for him than she ever had for any man. She'd lived with a man before—two in fact, not counting Todd Spurling, but she easily dismissed him. What she felt for Jeb was so different, so much more powerful and intense than those affairs that it was like comparing tap water to a rich, full-bodied Cabernet Sauvignon. She smiled. No doubt about it—she was drunk on Jeb Delaney.

The amazing thing was how much they both enjoyed each other's company, in and out of bed, and she found it hard to believe that El Jerko himself had turned into a nearly irresistible Prince Charming. During the past six weeks or so since New Year's Day, she'd seen many sides of Jeb Delaney and with each one, she slipped a little further under his spell. He was dedicated to his job—they'd spent hours discussing it, the pros and cons of recent court decisions, the death penalty, the politics, and the day-to-day boring drudgery of just being a cop. A lopsided smile on his tired face, he'd said one night after a particularly brutal day, "Trust me, Princess, glamorous it ain't. But I can't imagine myself doing anything else, or doing it"—he'd shot her a long look—"*any*where else. The valley's my home. My roots are here. My family's here. I've got no plans of moving on."

She'd felt that he'd been trying to tell her something, something, she thought ruefully, she didn't need telling. It was clear that Sergeant Jeb Delaney had no plans of making use of any of those advanced criminology classes he'd taken to push himself up the advancement ladder. He was an ambitious man, but, and it was a big but, he had no ambition to become a big hotshot in law enforcement somewhere *else*. His heart was here in Oak Valley and he wasn't leaving— he'd used those classes and his years of knowledge for the betterment of *his* county. He'd even fought old Bob Craddock, the current sheriff, to keep from moving from the valley once he'd become a detective. Technically he was supposed to live in Willits or

Ukiah. The sheriff grumbled but Craddock left it alone—Jeb was too well connected politically—retired judge for a father; an uncle on the Board of Supervisors, and a sister in the DA's office—had made Craddock think better of fighting about it. But Craddock's main reason for letting it go had been because Jeb was too valuable to the department to lose over a little thing like his choice of residency. And Jeb had been adamant: he wasn't moving from the valley. Neither was Roxanne, although sometimes she suspected that Jeb didn't really believe it. He was careful about it, but it was apparent sometimes that he thought her return to the valley and the building of the house might just be a rich celebrity's whim. She didn't try to disillusion him. She knew she was home to stay and in time he'd come to realize that fact himself.

Another astonishing facet of their relationship was that they seldom seriously argued. Oh, they had some heated discussions, but when the debate was over, most times with neither one of them changing the other's mind, there were no hard feelings. She liked that about him. She liked a lot about him.

Roxanne didn't examine her own feelings too deeply, but she knew that what was happening between the two of them was like nothing she'd ever experienced in her life. The depth of Jeb's feelings for her, she couldn't guess. Sure, she knew he cared for her—the Valentine's Day sign had been a dead giveaway that he felt something for her besides pure lust. The tenderness with which he made love to her, the dozens of thoughtful acts—bringing dinner home when he was running late, picking up a magazine he knew she liked, or surprising her with a huge bouquet of flowers all showed his feelings. And yet, they were both wary, as if they were balancing on a tightrope, neither one wanting to be the one to push them over the edge.

Roxanne's problem was that she didn't think she wanted to continue on the tightrope, wonderful and exciting though it was. On the other hand, she didn't think she was ready for the next step. Once that step would have been to simply formalize their living together, but this time, once or twice to her bewildered shock, she had caught herself thinking of what it would be like to be married to Jeb Delaney.

That she even considered the idea of marriage indicated that she was well and truly trapped. She was still fighting the knowledge that she was wildly, passionately, deeply in love with Jeb Delaney of all people. The thought was at once wonderful, terrifying, exciting, and appalling. Marriage had never been on her agenda, well, maybe, when she grew up. She sighed. Problem was she'd never seemed to grow up, she'd floated through life, gaily tripping along figuring that someday. . . .

Standing in front of the French doors in the great room, midmorning on a gray Monday, she sipped a mug of coffee and stared at the valley below. Fog obscured large parts of the valley floor, but occasionally she could see several fields that were beginning to show that almost blinding green of new growth. Above the valley, in the foothills, here and there the pink and gray buds of the oak trees were beginning to swell and at this time of year the manzanita bushes had boughs of tiny white flowers standing out above the stiff green leaves. She was restless, but she couldn't put her finger on the reason. There were tons of things that needed doing—she and Jeb had gone shopping in Santa Rosa over the weekend and she'd bought a gazillion items for the house—and they all needed putting away. Except for a few personal things and closets full of clothes, she'd simply locked her apartment, put it in the hands of an agent, and walked away. While glamorous and expensive, her apartment in New York had only been a place to entertain, eat, and sleep to her—she'd enjoyed living there, but those rooms, that space held no special meaning for her. She'd had an interior decorator furnish it and the elegant decor and furnishings were just part and parcel of being *Roxanne*. None of it mattered. But this house . . .

This house was *home*. Not just a place to sleep and eat. It was important to her and she wanted it to reflect who she was and what she liked. And if the choices she made sent an interior decorator yelping into the night . . . big deal. It was *her* house. She bit her lip. And maybe, she thought uneasily, Jeb's. He'd certainly had a hand in picking out bathroom accessories, kitchen stuff, and even some of the furniture.

She glanced into her empty dining room. They'd chosen a dining suite this weekend at Ethan Allen's that would be delivered on Friday. For reasons that escaped them, both had fallen in love with an exotic black and gold lacquer Chinese set with scarlet satin seats. Jeb had winked at her and murmured, "Must have been all that Chinese food to go." She smiled at the memory, but it made her anxious. They'd been almost like a married couple. . . .

They were a couple, yet they weren't and she supposed that was what was bothering her; she felt she was in some kind of limbo—an exciting and delightful limbo, but limbo none the less. She bit her lip again. That was the problem; she thought she might want out of limbo and yet she was frightened of taking the next step. What if she was wrong? What if Jeb was simply a nice, charming guy who thought she was a great lay? It wouldn't be the first time a woman had misread the situation . . . but it would be for me, she thought unhappily—she'd never fully risked her heart before. Of course, I could flat out ask him, she reminded herself. Just force the issue. Demand to know where this was all going. She smiled bleakly. Demand to know his intentions.

The ringing of the phone interrupted her thoughts. Picking it up, she was pleased to hear Shelly's voice. They talked for a few minutes, then Shelly said, "I'm up at Nick's and since we haven't seen each other in a while, thought I'd stop by before I head back to the house. Is that OK with you?"

"Sure. Great. Listen, why don't I fix us something to eat? I'm bound to have something in the refrigerator."

"Sounds good. I'll be over in about an hour. Expect me when you see me."

In the kitchen Roxanne threw together a green salad, scrubbed two red potatoes, seasoned some chicken breasts with wine and garlic, added the potatoes, and popped them in the oven. No dessert, she told herself virtuously. She might not be modeling full-time anymore, but there was no reason to throw away a lifetime of watching what she ate. As she moved around the kitchen, Boss and Dawg were constantly underfoot, hoping for a handout, and scolding them, she put them in the mudroom with their favorite blankets and water . . . and a pair of beefy neck bones she just happened to have in the refrigerator. Shutting the door behind her, she realized another benefit of locking the dogs away; she wouldn't have to explain to Shelly what she was doing with Jeb's dogs.

The kitchen was cozy and warm on this dreary day; cheerful, ruffled curtains in a bright green and gold country print hung at the windows that faced the front and the long banks of maple cabinets gleamed pale amber. Roxanne hummed to herself as she set the table and put out the new tan and orange place mats, using the matching napkins on opposite mats. She and Jeb had purchased the set this weekend at Macy's in the Coddingtown Mall in Santa Rosa. The mats and napkins looked nice against the dark green painted wood of the table just as she had known they would. Opening a cupboard, she took out plates and mugs and put them on the table. She'd ordered them from the Wildlife Federation catalog and had been thrilled with them. The background was almond with each piece of the set bearing one of four different animals—bear, fox, moose, and wolf done in soft shades of brown, russet, and gold. She thought they looked charming.

The crunch of tires on the driveway about forty minutes later let her know that Shelly had arrived. Meeting her at the door, Roxanne smiled. "Welcome to Roxy's Roost," she said almost shyly.

Shelly laughed and hugged her. "I saw the great sign. Wherever did you get it? It must have cost you a fortune—burl wood is hard to come by."

Roxy sidestepped the question. "Thank you. I'm very pleased with it."

Shelly stepped into the great room and stood there gaping at the wonderful space, the soaring handsome open-beam ceiling overhead, the French doors with their commanding views, and the birch floors. "Omigod! Wait until Sloan sees this. It's gorgeous!" She glanced back at Roxanne. "Did you know he's building us another house?"

"No." Roxanne's face lit up. "Expansion room for a growing family, I hope?"

Shelly's smile faltered. "Not yet—we're still 'practicing' to get pregnant," she said brightly. Turning away, she added, "Sloan says that the cabin was built with a single guy in mind and while we've added on my studio and another bathroom, he says if we keep making it bigger, it's just going to end up being a hodge-podge of cobbled together rooms. Better we start from scratch with a new house entirely."

"But what about the cabin? You're not going to just abandon it, are you?"

Shelly shook her head, her shoulder-length tawny hair flying. "Oh, no, nothing like that. We figure we'll either use it as a guest cabin, or more likely Sloan will hire someone to help with the horses and they can live there. It won't remain empty, believe me. Now show me around this fabulous place, but I warn you, I'm going to steal all sorts of ideas."

They spent several minutes wandering from room to room, Shelly eagerly asking questions and admiring and cooing over the view from the various windows that faced the east and the barbaric splendor of Roxanne's bedroom. To Roxanne's relief, when Shelly peeked into the bathroom, there was no obvious sign that she shared the room. It wasn't, she scolded herself, that she was trying to hide the relationship with Jeb, she just wasn't ready to announce it. Back on that damned tightrope, she thought grimly.

She'd forgotten about the dogs and pushing open the door to the mudroom a few minutes later to show it to Shelly, she was greeted by Dawg who rained slobbery kisses on her hand and Boss who sent her a reproachful look as he brushed past her. One minute she was confidently balancing on her tightrope and then the next she had stepped off into space.

"Oh, you got yourself some dogs," Shelly exclaimed, immediately dropping to her knees and promptly having her face washed by Dawg. "You darling." Shelly laughed, pushing Dawg away. "I think you're adorable but I have a rule about kissing on the first date." She ruffled Dawg's ears and stared down into her wrinkled face. Rising to her feet, Shelly stared from one dog to the other; Dawg wiggling slavishly at her feet and Boss sprawled like a sultan on a satin couch in front of the cabinets near the sink. As if aware of Shelly's interest, Boss yawned hugely, showing how indifferent he was to Dawg's unseemly display of affection.

"Where did you get these guys?" Shelly asked, a little frown on her forehead. "I swear I know them." She blinked. "Why, they're Dawg and Boss, Jeb's dogs."

Roxanne remained frozen in the doorway. Numbly she thought, Oh, God, it's out of the bag now . . .

Shelly smiled uncertainly at her. "What are you doing with Jeb's dogs? Did he lend them to you because of all the break-ins?"

Roxanne would have loved to grab the excuse, but she knew it would only postpone the inevitable.

Shutting the mudroom door, Roxanne muttered, "Uh, no, not exactly." Her cheeks were flushed and she looked much like a Christian facing the lions.

While her scrambled brains hunted for a way out, Shelly stared at her, dawning excitement in her green eyes. Shelly was no dummy and Roxanne could almost see her working out the explanation.

"So this is why Jeb seemed to have disappeared lately," Shelly said thoughtfully. "Mingo was complaining about it just the other day. Said his brother seemed to have vanished from the vicinity." A big grin broke across her face. "Oh, wow! You and Jeb. I thought he might have a new lady friend, but I never suspected that the woman would be you." She shook her head. "You and Jeb—that's a pairing I never considered—and believe me I've paired you with just about every single guy in the valley." She hugged Roxanne's limp form. "This is just great! I always knew that sooner or later my favorite cousin would find the right woman. Those two wives of his were idiots—they didn't deserve him anyway. And as for all those other women—don't worry about any of them, he was just marking time." She hugged Roxanne again. "Now tell me all—every lurid detail."

Roxanne stared dazedly at Shelly's smiling face. How much to tell? Just as important, how was Jeb going to react when he found out that their affair was no longer secret? And where to begin? Oh, God! She wasn't ready for this. Or was she? Maybe she'd subconsciously planned for Shelly to find the dogs and leap to the right conclusion. It made Roxanne uncomfortable to think that she could be that sneaky

and underhanded—even if she hadn't been aware of
it.

"Um, well, ah, I guess you could say we started,
um, thinking differently about each other after your
party," she managed, still trying to avoid the moment
of truth. The timer on the oven went off and swing-
ing in that direction with relief, she babbled, "Our
lunch is ready. Let me get that served first."

If she thought she was going to deflect Shelly she
sadly underestimated her opponent. Shelly didn't
press while Roxanne busied herself putting out the
green salad and ranch dressing and then serving the
baked chicken breasts and red potatoes. Shelly even
managed to hold her tongue when Roxanne fussed
over selecting something for them to drink, finally
settling on tall glasses of milk, when Shelly passed
on white wine.

"Practicing to get pregnant, remember?" Shelly
said quietly.

"Oh, right. Sorry."

When Roxanne finally sat down at the table,
Shelly picked up her fork and said, "OK. I've been a
wonderful guest and sister-in-law, I haven't pushed,
but you start talking right now or I'll just have to go
back to Sloan with all sorts of wild suspicions and
guesses." She grinned. "You might as well tell me—
I'm going to keep asking until you do. And once I tell
Sloan . . ." She giggled. "Well, you know your big
brother."

Roxanne stared at her, wondering when Shelly had become so practiced in the arts of the Inquisition.

"So, give," Shelly prodded when Roxanne continued to stare at her like a bird paralyzed by a snake. While she waited, Shelly took a bite of her chicken, closed her eyes, and gave a blissful moan. "Hmm, this is good—I didn't realize how hungry I was." She swallowed the chicken. "So," she said, deciding to give Roxanne a shove, "are you and Jeb living together or what?"

Roxanne started, and as if coming out of a daze, muttered, "Uh, not exactly. Sort of. He stays here a lot."

Shelly smiled kindly at her. "See, that didn't hurt. Now tell Auntie Shelly the rest of it."

Roxanne laughed weakly. "Shit, Shelly, I don't know what the rest of it is."

Shelly nodded. "I know what you mean. For a time there, I couldn't decide about Sloan and me either. I knew I loved him, but I didn't know if I could trust him." She took another bite. "Then I decided that I loved him and the only way I was going to find out if I could trust him was to love him. Simple when you think about it. You just follow your heart."

"Easy for you to say," Roxanne grumbled, picking at her food. "You and Sloan had a history together. Jeb and I . . . Well, I've spent most of my adult life thinking he was an arrogant jerk—and that was only when I wasn't thinking he was the biggest prick I'd ever known."

"Obviously you've discovered you were wrong, right?"

Reluctantly Roxanne admitted, "Yes. I was wrong. He's not a *complete* jerk."

Shelly laughed. "Oh, that's good—you've not gone all soft and silly over him. It's bad for them when they think we adore them—even when we do." She eyed Roxanne, her expression suddenly serious. "You *do* adore him, don't you?"

Appalled, Roxanne heard herself say, "Yes, yes I do. I'm so in love with him, I don't know what to do about it."

"What's his take?" Shelly asked, her green eyes full of curiosity. "He's serious, I know that much."

"You just found out about it, how can you possibly know that?"

"Easy. You say this has been going on since New Year's Day. It's now the end of February. Never known Jeb to hang around for more than two weeks. A month tops. And if you don't believe me, ask M.J." Shelly grinned. "M.J. keeps track of that sort of thing. She says it keeps her from forgetting that all men are scum and that once they've gotten what they want from a woman, they're movin' on down the road. Fast."

"Thank you, I needed to hear that," Roxanne said dryly.

Shelly leaned forward, her voice sincere. "Oh, Roxy, don't you see, they only do that while they're looking and waiting for the right one. You've done it yourself. You can't hold it against them. Besides, the poor dears are just men." She grinned. "Once they find the right one, they're hooked—even if they struggle a bit before they give up and admit it. And remember M.J.'s opinion is colored by that nasty divorce of hers."

Roxanne nodded. "Yeah, that'd do it for me." She took a bite of salad and chewed. Swallowing, she looked across at Shelly. "And that's all I can tell you, because I haven't a clue what comes next."

"OK, I accept that. You two need to work out your feelings. You're probably both scared. I know Jeb must be."

Exasperated, Roxanne snapped, "And how do you know so much about him?"

"Come on, Roxy, use your head. The man's been married and divorced *twice*. There's probably all kinds of baggage he's carrying around. He's what, forty-five? He's been single for years. This will be a big step for him. He's bound to be gun-shy and cautious. And what about you? You've got some baggage of your own. What about that actor you almost married? And what about that photographer you lived with when you first went back to New York? Don't you think Jeb is wondering how he stacks up? You know women aren't the only ones who are uncertain when they fall in love. Think about it from his point of view. You're this glamorous world-famous model just returned from New York. Could have just about any man you want. How do you know he doesn't think you're just toying with *him*?"

Roxanne stared at her thunderstruck. "You think Jeb is afraid that I don't love him?" Her voice rose indignantly. "That I'm playing a game?"

Shelly shrugged. "Could be." She looked at her. "Have you told him how you feel? Let him know that this means more to you than just playing house?"

"No . . . not exactly . . ." Roxanne swallowed, looking miserable. "I just can't come out and say 'I love you.' "

"Why not? Assuming you do? This isn't the Victorian Age, you know. Women are allowed to express their feelings."

Roxanne looked away, played with her spoon. "What if he doesn't love *me?*" she asked in a low voice. "What if he's just passing time? What if I'm the only one thinking what we share is forever?"

"Well, first of all, Jeb never struck me as a dunce—he's a smart man and, in my humble estimation, a smart man would reach out and grab you with both hands. You're a catch. And so is he. He's crazy if he doesn't realize how perfect the two of you are together."

"Yeah, but . . ."

Shelly leaned forward. "All right, let's assume the worst. Let's assume that he *is* playing with you. That he doesn't love you. Wouldn't you rather know that than live in a false world?"

Roxanne nodded. "I know you're right but I'm

still scared to death—guess because it never really mattered before." Roxanne looked at her plate. "It's funny," she said ruefully, "I've never been shy when it came to men. Never had to be—they just fell at my feet and I decided which one I wanted."

"And Jeb doesn't appear to worship at your feet?"

Roxanne grinned. "Are you kidding? Absolutely not! And the interesting thing is that I wouldn't want him if he did." She grimaced. "It's awfully hard being put on a pedestal and being adored."

"OK, so what are you going to do?"

Roxanne took a deep breath. "I don't know. It all happened so fast—one minute I hated his guts and the next I'm hopelessly in love with him." She eyed Shelly. "I don't suppose I could convince you to keep your mouth shut for a while?"

Shelly's eyes gleamed. "Oh, wow, are you going to owe me big time. Sure. If I can tell Sloan—and as you know your big brother is good at keeping secrets. He won't let the cat out of the bag."

Roxanne didn't like it, but she figured it was the best she was going to get. "Thanks. And when I've resolved the problem, you'll be the first to know."

They finished their lunch in perfect harmony, talking about the weather, the worries about the lack of rain, Shelly and Nick's Granger Cattle Company, Sloan's budding paint horse operation, and Roxanne's ideas for growing flowers and maybe having a place for harried celebrities to hide away. Shelly was enthusiastic about both projects.

"You know," she said, "you might even be able to drag Ilka into it. She needs something to do besides living in your parents' shadow and volunteering at the high school and Willits Hospital."

"I know." Roxanne made a face. "I suppose you've heard about my attempts to pry her loose from her veil of sorrow?"

Shelly nodded. "I thought it was great, but Sloan wasn't so sure. He says that Ilka is going to have to make the break all by herself. That we can provide the opportunities, but she's the one who has to take them."

"I said it before and I'll say it again, how did my brother get to be such a smart man?"

They both laughed.

"Don't heap too many praises on his head—he's puffed up enough with himself as it is," Shelly said wryly. She took a deep breath. "We've gotten the fertility test results back."

"And?"

"And you and Sloan were right. According to the tests there is no obvious reason why I shouldn't get pregnant. We're both healthy and fertile."

Roxanne smiled happily. "What great news! Aren't you thrilled?"

Shelly shrugged. "Yes and no. I now know there's no physical reason for me not getting pregnant, but here it's seven, eight months later after we got married and I'm still not pregnant."

Roxanne reached across and laid her hand on

Shelly's. "Maybe you need to take another approach."

"If you say relax and enjoy it. Or take a second honeymoon. Or have some wine and Valium, I'm going to hit you."

"Nope, nothing like that. Let's take a dark view. Let's suppose, for whatever reasons, you *never* get pregnant. How would you feel about that?"

"Like a failure," Shelly said in a low voice. "Like I cheated Sloan. Denied him something he desperately wanted."

"Would Sloan feel that you've cheated him? Is he making you feel guilty?"

Shelly looked shocked. "Oh, good God, no! He feels like he's denying *me* something that I want desperately. He's as eaten up with guilt for his part in this as I am." She laughed unhappily. "He feels that he's denying me—he wants me to have anything I want and I feel the same about him."

"OK, let's go a step further. If there was only yourself to consider, don't think about him, just you, how would you feel if you never had a child?"

Shelly frowned. Thought for several minutes, then said slowly, "I'd be disappointed, shattered even, but it wouldn't be the end of the world . . . as long as Sloan loved me."

"Maybe it wouldn't be the end of the world for Sloan either. Maybe he feels that as long as you love him, that life's pretty damn good. Maybe you two need to talk about that."

Shelly squeezed Roxanne's hand, their eyes meeting. "You know, your brother isn't the only one in the family who's smart," Shelly said. "You're pretty damn smart yourself." She grinned and added, "For a Ballinger, that is."

"Yeah, well, for a Granger, you're not so dumb yourself."

Chapter
16

With Shelly's words about Ilka buzzing in her brain, after Shelly had driven away that afternoon, Roxanne called her sister.

Helen Ballinger answered the phone and Roxanne and her mother spent a few minutes catching up on the latest family news.

"Have you had that terrible flu virus that's going around the valley?" Helen asked eventually. "Your father had it two weeks ago and Ilka the week before that. So far I've escaped, but it's awful and seems to hang on forever. Your father still isn't up to par, but Ilka seems to have bounced back. I understand that Cleo was out almost a week with it at the end of the January and at the Lioness meeting last night, nearly everyone was complaining about it—they'd all either had it or someone in their family had."

"Knock on wood, so far, I haven't caught it." Roxanne laughed. "Probably because I'm isolated up here and not mingling with you sickly valley folk."

"Probably," Helen agreed. "But if you do come down with it, don't be foolish and try to tough it out by yourself. Let us know so someone can come and stay with you for the first couple of days—that seems to be the worst patch. And don't tell me that you're a big girl and can take care of yourself—you're always going to be my little girl—whether you like it or not."

Roxanne chuckled, touched by her mother's words. "OK. OK. Mom, I surrender. If I get sick, I'll call. I promise. Now let me talk to Ilka."

To her astonishment, Ilka was not home.

Helen laughed. "I know, I know. We all expect Ilka to always be around, but Pagan Granger talked her into driving to Santa Rosa to look at computers today."

"Computers?" Roxanne repeated blankly.

Her mother laughed again. "Yes, computers. I understand that M.J. grabbed Ilka at the store one day when Pagan was there and they all got to fooling around on the Internet. Ilka is hooked—now she wants a computer of her own and for Pagan to tutor her. I think they may stay at Ross's place tonight before heading back tomorrow. Ilka said to expect her when I saw her. Such a refreshing change—and you can take some of the credit for that."

Roxanne made a face at the phone. "Maybe. I think all Ilka needed was just a little push."

"Well, how about you give your baby brother a push? Did you meet his latest Barbie doll?"

"Er, no, I haven't. Did he bring her to St. Galen's? That sounds serious."

"No, thank God. I guess I have that to be thankful for. We met his latest little bimbo over the weekend when we drove to Santa Rosa to visit some friends. This latest one is stunning, I'll give you that, but if she has two brain cells to rub together in that gorgeous blond head of hers, I'll be surprised." Helen sighed. "I like to tell myself that Ross is too smart to actually marry one of these women. In fact, for a long time, I just thought it was a stage he was going through, but he's not a kid anymore and he still seems fascinated by these women whose bust size is larger than their IQ. I'm terrified that he's going to show up at the door one day and say, 'Look who I married, Susie Brain-dead.'"

Roxanne choked on a laugh. "Come on, Mom, Ross has got more sense than that. He's just, uh, having fun."

"And that reminds me . . . when are you going to stop having fun and start thinking about marriage and children?"

Roxanne grimaced at the phone. "Uh, um, gee, I gotta go right now, Mom—someone's at the front door. Love ya. Bye."

Hanging up from her mother, Roxanne stared down at the phone as if it might bite her. Oh, great! Just what she needed—her mother quizzing her about her love life. She gave herself a shake and sinking down onto the sofa in the great room, stared off into space.

Her thoughts were scrambled for a while, but eventually they cleared and she began to think about what her mother had said about Ilka. It was good that Ilka was taking an interest in something new, but Roxanne didn't know that surfing the Internet was necessarily the best new hobby for someone who was already inclined to solitude. Then she shrugged. She'd see how it went before she started meddling—at the moment, the way she was handling her own affairs didn't instill within her a great deal of confidence that she knew the answer to everything. If she didn't know what she was going to do in her life, how the devil could she go around telling someone else what to do with *their* life? Her lips quirked. Well, hell, when had she ever let a little thing like that stop her?

She'd enjoyed the visit with Shelly. She genuinely liked her sister-in-law and hoped that when Ross left behind his Barbie doll toys and finally settled down that he'd choose someone who fit into the family as well as Shelly did—even if she was a "hated" Granger. Thinking of the long-standing enmity between Granger and Ballinger, she shook her head. What a crock! Probably the only ones who thought that way these days were her father's generation. Listening to tales around the campfire about the wicked Grangers and the evil things they did to the angelic Ballingers might make for an interesting evening, but Roxanne suspected that in the light of day, the stories were only half right: no one ever mentioned the equally wicked and nefarious deeds the Ballingers executed against the Grangers.

She was restless for the rest of the day, the conversations with Shelly and her mother never far from her thoughts, though she tried hard to shove them out of her mind. Since the weather was not conducive to wandering around outside, she headed for the kitchen. After putting on a pot of coffee and putting a Gipsy Kings CD on the player at full blast, she dragged out a cookbook she'd bought in New Orleans once and a few minutes later was busily trying her hand at making chocolate eclairs. It didn't seem too hard although there were several different steps. The whipped cream filling was a snap and even the dark chocolate frosting for the top wasn't difficult. The pastry part of the eclair wasn't difficult either but it was messy, she decided, as she delicately pushed the spoonfuls of goopy dough into an oblong shape. Shutting the oven door on the pastry, she crossed her fingers. The dough bore little resemblance to the plump eclairs she pictured in her mind, but she'd followed the recipe so they *should* turn out OK. Not a whiz in the kitchen—as she used to say with a wicked smile, her talents lay in a different direction—Roxanne had great faith in cookbooks.

Taking a sip of coffee now and then, halfway dancing to the primitive beat of the Gipsy Kings, she puttered around the kitchen, cleaning up the mess. When the bell rang signaling that the pastries were done, she took a deep breath and peeked.

A squeak of pleasure came out. "Ooh, you little darlings! Aren't you just beautiful," she exclaimed as she opened the oven door and took out a dozen or so perfectly risen and delicately browned pastry puffs.

Pleased and proud of herself, she set them on the rack to cool.

Dawg and Boss were at her feet and she gave them a stern look. "Touch one and you're dead."

"Now that's a greeting I don't expect very many men want to come home to at night," said Jeb from the doorway of the kitchen.

Roxanne jumped and spun around to face him. Her heart leaped as it always did at the unexpected sight of him. The kitchen suddenly became small, Jeb's big frame filling the doorway, making everything shrink around him as he stood there, that half smile she'd grown to love on his lips.

She laughed and rushed to him. "That wasn't for you," she said as his arms closed around her. Her hands cupped his face and her lips brushed his. "*This,*" she breathed against his mouth, "is for you."

Bodies locked together, they kissed deeply, passion humming between them. When Jeb finally lifted his head several moments later his eyes were glazed and his brain mush. With an effort he focused on Roxanne's flushed features. "Now that," he finally managed, "is a welcome home a man would walk through fire to get."

"I should hope so," Roxanne said saucily as she turned away and went back to admiring her pastries, turning the racks of pastries this way and that. "It isn't every man that I turn up the wattage for."

Jeb walked up behind her. His hand resting possessively on the back of her neck, he bent and bit her ear gently. "I'd like to think that I'm the *only* guy you kiss like that."

Roxanne's hands stilled, her heart skittering around in her breast like a rabbit chased by a very large, very hungry fox. Now how did she reply to that statement? she wondered, breathless. Turn around, fling her arms around him, and exclaim, "Oh, you are, you are!" or give him a smart-mouth remark? Funny thing, she seemed fresh out of smart remarks.

The silence spun out and she was increasingly aware that Jeb was waiting for a reply. She swallowed. She loved him. Loved him as she had never loved anyone before in her life and it scared her to death. She knew Jeb enjoyed screwing her blind and seemed to equally enjoy her company. Did that add up to love? This was all uncharted territory for her. Conquests had always come easy for her and it had never mattered a great deal whether the man of the moment was "in love" with her or not. If he professed to be, well, that was very nice, but as long as they had taken pleasure in each other's bodies and company, that had been enough for Roxanne . . . then. But this was now and it mattered more than anything ever had that Jeb loved her. Loved her as deeply, as fiercely, as she did him.

Roxanne took a deep breath. OK. She was a modern woman, right? And being a modern woman meant that she didn't have to wait for a man to ask her out anymore—she was perfectly free to do her own asking. Right? Yeah. Of course. And being a modern woman meant that she could make all the moves first, could even admit her love first—she didn't have to be an old-fashioned wilting-lily pining for the man to declare himself before she did. She could just say it. I love you. Right? Uh, well, no. To her dismay she discovered that she wasn't quite as modern as she'd always thought. The idea of telling Jeb that she was wildly, passionately in love with him, without knowing the depth of his feeling for her, was the most terrifying thing she had ever contemplated doing. She made a face. What a wimp, she was. She was letting the sisterhood down. Setting modern womanhood back thirty years. She shrugged. Screw the sisterhood, this was her life and she desperately wanted to know what Jeb really felt for her. He *liked* her, she knew that . . . but did he love her? Love her enough for them to make a life together?

When Roxanne remained silent, Jeb sighed and, turning away, asked, "So how was your day? Anything interesting happen while I was away fighting the minions of evil and injustice?"

Relief flooded through her . . . and the tiniest regret that she hadn't taken the opening. "Uh, no," she said, pushing the racks of pastries away for further cooling. "Talked to my mom—Dad and Ilka have had the flu—apparently it's going around the valley. Pagan and Ilka went computer shopping in Santa Rosa. Oh, and Shelly came by for lunch." Her voice faltered as she recognized the canyon opening beneath her feet. She bit her lip. Telling Jeb that Shelly knew about them was another topic she'd just as soon avoid right now.

You yellow-bellied coward, she thought contemptuously.

Jeb snagged a beer from the refrigerator and sat down at the kitchen table, his long legs crossed at the ankles. He caught the pause in her voice and shot her a sharp look. "And?"

"Um, nothing. She just came by and we had a nice visit. Those fertility tests she and Sloan took in January came back just fine. She's fretting though that she still hasn't conceived."

"And?"

She turned and glanced warily at him. "And? What? I've told you everything."

He contemplated her. She looked tasty enough to eat as she stood there at the kitchen counter and his body was still sizzling from that welcome home kiss. In the months they'd been together he'd become a pretty good judge of Roxanne's moods and right now she was as nervous as a hen eyeing a chopping block. He'd been a cop too long not to know when someone was lying to him. Most times, they were simple, unimportant lies. But sometimes, they were important lies and something told him that he needed to know what Roxanne was trying to hide from him.

"More to the conversation than that," he murmured. "You're twitching and squirming like a worm on a hook. What else did you two darlings discuss?"

Roxanne glared at him and put her hands on her hips. "If you must know," she snapped, "she found out about us."

"Really?" he asked, lifting a brow. So *that's* what had her all in a twitter. Now this was very, *very* interesting. And so goddamn important, he thought his heart was going to jump out of his chest and lay its silly self right at her feet. His face revealing nothing, he inquired further. "And what exactly did she find out about us? Something I should know? Something you want to share?"

"She saw Dawg and Boss and recognized them and one thing led to another and I told her. . . ." Roxanne swallowed, looking very young and uncertain. "I, um, told her that we were sort of living together."

"Sort of?" Jeb asked, taking a long swallow of his beer. Ah hell, Princess, he thought moodily, there's nothing "sort of" about it—at least for me there isn't. And if I thought for one second that you weren't going to run off to New York or some other damned foreign place like that one of these days and take my heart with you, I'd make damn sure you understood that I'm not "sort of" living with you. That I don't "sort of" live with anyone. Especially not you.

"Well, it is, sort of, isn't it? You still keep all your clothes and stuff across the valley. I mean it's not like you moved in or anything."

He looked at her, something in his eyes making her heart race and her breath catch. Then his gaze dropped and the moment was gone. "Yep, guess you're right. We are sort of living together."

Unhappily Roxanne stared at him. A perfect opportunity to take their relationship to the next step had been handed right to him and he neatly sidestepped it. Maybe he *didn't* want to move in with her; maybe an enjoyable romp was all she meant to him. A little angry, she glared at him and muttered, "She's going to tell Sloan. It won't be a secret forever."

He took another swallow of his beer. "You ask her to keep it a secret?"

Roxanne flushed, her cheeks burning bright pink. "Uh, well, yeah, I did. I didn't know how you'd feel about it."

He glanced at her, that disturbing look in his black eyes again. "Question is, how do you feel about it?"

Of all the unfair tactics, Roxanne thought, outraged. She'd thrown the ball in his court and damned if he hadn't just tossed it right back at her. She narrowed her gaze. It was almost as if he were toying with her, trying to trick her into revealing her feelings first. Well, damn him!

"It doesn't matter to *me* who knows about us," she said snippily and went to the refrigerator to get a bottle of water. "It's bound to get out sooner or later. You know the valley." She shot him a glance over her shoulder. "And, remember, I'm used to having my private affairs splashed all over the place."

He nodded. "Yep. Forgot about that."

She could have slapped him. Those lovely eyes of hers sparking like firecrackers, she demanded, "Will it bother you? People knowing about us?"

Jeb laughed, reached out a long arm, and pulled her onto his lap. "Now what do you think?" He nuzzled her neck. "Have my name linked with the prettiest woman around? What's to mind?"

It was a very unsatisfactory answer. Bewildered and angry, Roxanne shot up from his lap. "Well, good," she snapped, "I'm glad we have this settled."

But it wasn't good and Roxanne was in an irritated mood for the rest of the evening. She couldn't figure him out any more than she could figure out her own reluctance to lay her cards on the table and find out what was going on between them. She knew her feelings. Her heart. But when it came to Jeb, she hadn't a clue. He was playing his cards too damn close to his chest. That he felt something besides lust for her, she didn't doubt, but there were times she sensed that part of him was closed off from her. Not often, but now and then. It was almost, she thought miserably, as if he was deliberately keeping her at a distance . . . as if he was just fine with things the way they were and that he had no intention of seeing what lay beyond their initial attraction to each other. It terrified her to think that she might be in this all by herself. All the gossip about his other women flitted through her head. Was that what she was? Just another woman in a long line?

If Jeb noticed that she seemed moody that evening he didn't mention it. He had enough troubles dealing with keeping things light and easy when every instinct he possessed screamed for him to grab her and pour out his heart. Nope. He wasn't traveling down that path. Light and easy. That was the way and he had to keep reminding himself of that fact every second of every day.

For all her moodiness, when Jeb reached for her that night and kissed her, she went flying into his arms, aware that at these moments, these moments of passion and desire, precious moments of intimacy and tenderness, that she had no doubts. No doubts at all.

By morning, even though she had resolved nothing, Roxanne's sunny nature reasserted itself. She hummed in the kitchen as she put on a pot of coffee, took some eggs and shredded cheddar cheese out for an omelet, and cheerfully began to chop some green pepper, onions, and Canadian bacon. Her good mood might have had some basis in the fact Jeb was going to go in late to the office this morning and that they could share a leisurely breakfast together.

It was still raining lightly and the day wasn't appreciably more appealing than yesterday had been, but somehow this morning it didn't seem quite so bad. In fact, as she and Jeb sat down at the kitchen table and ate the omelet and whole wheat English muffins she'd toasted, it was a great day as far as she was concerned. They took their coffee mugs into the great room and lingered over coffee, talking easily as they usually did. Dawg was resting at her feet as she sat on the couch and Boss had taken up his place near a corner of the couch that Jeb had claimed as his own. Their conversation wasn't important; it consisted of simple things as they talked about this and that, enjoying the moment and each other's company.

The phone rang and Roxanne sent it an irritated look. Rising to her feet she walked over and answered it, her expression of irritation disappearing the moment she recognized the voice. "Marshall," she cried, "what a surprise to hear from you. How are you doing?"

Jeb set his mug down and cocked an ear. Marshall? Who the hell was Marshall? His stomach suddenly knotted. Oh, yeah. Her fancy, famous New York agent, Marshall Klein.

Jeb tried not to listen to the conversation, contenting himself with scratching Boss's ear, but since she was less than ten feet away from him, he couldn't help overhearing. From his end, it sounded as if Marshall was trying to convince Roxanne to take a modeling job in Bermuda next month. Roxanne appeared to be listening, to be considering it, and Jeb's heart nosedived. He'd known she'd leave sometime. Known that sooner or later the bright lights and pavement and glamour would lure her away from the valley. Away from him. He'd known all along that this time with Roxanne was just a taste of paradise. That it wouldn't last. He thought he'd accepted the idea, but as he listened, everything within him rebelled. It was all he could do not to leap up, march over to where she stood, and slam that phone down and tell her in blunt terms that she wasn't leaving the valley . . . and him. He fought his primitive impulse and kept right on scratching Boss's ears, dying a little inside.

Forcing a smile, when Roxanne put the phone down

and turned around to face him, he said, "I couldn't help overhearing. Sounds like a pretty plush assignment. Bermuda, sun and surf."

It did sound like fun. At least it had until she considered that accepting the assignment would mean leaving Oak Valley. Her home. Dawg and Boss . . . and Jeb. If she'd never tasted the heady brew of fame and fortune, she would have jumped at the offer. The money was great. The locale was great. The photographer, Gabriel, was a leader in the industry and a favorite of hers. The assignment was short—she wouldn't be gone more than a week. It would be a perfect opportunity to rub shoulders again with friends she'd made in the industry. Put her toe back in the water for a bit. But Roxanne knew in her heart that the life she'd left behind no longer appealed—one of the reasons she was standing where she was right now, trying to decide if she *really* wanted to step back into the limelight—if only briefly.

Roxanne shrugged. Seating herself on the couch, she picked up her mug of coffee and took a sip. "When you've seen one sandy beach, no matter how beautiful, you've seen them all."

"You're *not* going to accept the assignment?" he asked incredulously.

Roxanne looked at him across her mug. "Would you mind if I did?"

Jeb sat back and scowled at her. "Is this a test?"

Roxanne smiled. "No. I'm just curious how you'd feel about me taking off for a week or two to do some modeling." She wiggled her eyebrows. "Making oo-dles of money."

His first response was to roar that you bet your sweet ass he didn't like the idea one damn bit. That hell, no, he didn't want her traipsing off to Bermuda and cavorting around half-naked before a guy named Gabriel and who knew how many other men. Christ, what did she think he was made of?

He opened his mouth. Shut it. Thought about it. This was her career. She must love it—she stayed in it long enough. How would he feel if she asked him to give up his career in law enforcement? He knew the answer to that one. He swallowed. Ah shit. Sometimes life was just too complicated.

Jeb rubbed his hand over his face. Wearily he said, "If that's what you want to do, then I've no right to put obstacles in your way."

"That's true," Roxanne agreed, not certain whether to be happy or upset with his words. It was nice that he was being so "modern" about it, but she thought she'd prefer it if he'd at least act as if her absence would bother him. "But would you be happy about it?" she persisted.

Jeb's look burned her. "Hell, no." Feeling he'd re-vealed too much, he growled, "What about the oppo-site? What if I was gonna be gone for a week? Going back to Washington, D.C., for a seminar or something? Would you be happy?"

Her eyes danced, her heart nearly flying out of her

chest. "Hell, no," she said. "I'd make you take me with you."

Jeb grinned, his dark mood vanishing. "Sounds like a plan. So you gonna take me to Bermuda with you?"

Roxanne stood up. "Nope." At the expression on his face, she didn't know whether to run for her life or burst out laughing. "I don't think that Bermuda holds much interest for me these days."

"You're going to *pass* on this job?"

She nodded. "Hmm, yes, I think so. Marshall will understand. I told him when I left New York that while I was going to be semi-retired what I really meant was that I'd be *mostly* retired and that the assignment would have to be something really special." She shrugged again. "This one isn't. It'd be fun and I'm sure I would enjoy myself—Gabriel is a great guy, and an even greater photographer, and my friend Ann Talbot is going to be one of the other models on the shoot. It would be pleasant and no doubt fun, but . . ." She looked around her, at Dawg at her feet, Jeb and Boss across from her, and the view of the valley right outside the French doors. "But I'd have to leave all this behind and this means more to me now than a week in Bermuda ever could."

As he drove down the twisting road, heading for work, Jeb kept turning Roxanne's words over and over in his head. Maybe she really was back in the valley for good. Maybe she *wasn't* going to go flying back to the glamorous world she'd left behind. Of course, that "now" was the tricky part. Maybe next time Marshall called she wouldn't feel the same way.

As he turned onto Highway 101, Jeb was frowning, his thoughts on Roxanne. He really wouldn't mind if she took the occasional modeling assignment, he wouldn't like it, but he wouldn't mind. He was a big boy. He could endure a week or two without waking up beside her in bed every morning. Just. But he could handle it. He'd be miserable, probably grouchy as a bear with a festered paw, but he'd be OK. What he feared was that if she did take those intermittent assignments and traveled to all those fascinating and enchanting spots all over the world, sooner or later the simple charm of the valley would pall and there'd be a time that she didn't come back. That she disappeared into the sophisticated hustle and bustle of New York, or Madrid, or London, or any one of a dozen more exotic cities and he'd never see her again except smiling from the pages of a magazine.

His heart turned into a lump of ice and there was a desolate twist to his lips as he considered that idea of Roxanne gone from his life. He didn't think he'd survive it. He'd thought he'd been in love before, thought that he'd found love everlasting, but comparing what he felt for Roxanne to the emotion he'd felt for his two wives made him realize what a pale thing those emotions had been. Christ. No wonder his marriages had failed. He'd only given half his heart and it had taken falling violently in love with Roxanne to show him the difference.

Jeb's eyes were bleak as he drove toward Willits. So what the hell was he going to do? Somehow he had trouble believing that Roxanne would be happy for very long simply being the wife of a deputy in a mainly rural county in northern California. She was used to the glamorous life. Oh, sure, she seemed to be happy right now, but what about a year from now? Two years from now? What then?

Jeb was in a thoroughly bad mood when he finally arrived at work. Like a wounded cougar, he hid out in his cubicle at the office and kept his head down, reading and writing reports, trying to keep focused on the job and not his personal problems. It was difficult, but somehow he managed and the stack of paperwork on his desk gradually shrank.

He was just getting ready to leave to drive home that evening when the phone on his desk rang. It was Gene Cartwright.

They exchanged greetings and bullshit for a few minutes and then Gene said, "You know that murder you asked me to look into? Guy by the name of Dirk Aston? Killed back in January of last year?"

"Yeah. Anything interesting about it?"

"A lot more interesting than I thought it would be."

Jeb sat up, his eyes alert. "What do you mean?"

"Well, it's still technically unsolved, like most drug-connected crimes, but we think we know who did it—and why. Word on the street is that it was no accident that your guy got clipped. It *was* an accident that he died, but not that he got shot. Word is that he'd been skimming money and drugs and his employers took a dim view of it—they wanted their belongings back. According to street gossip, some kid was supposed to *wound* Aston, frighten him, let him know just exactly what a dim view they took of his pilfering. Wasn't meant to be a hit. At least not then. I don't doubt that once they got back their belongings Mr. Aston wouldn't be long for this world. He crossed the line and there was no way they were going to let him live. But first he had to cough up the goodies."

"Aston? Skimming? Christ. I always thought of him as a small-time marijuana grower. Real low echelon. Not the brightest bulb in the lamp."

"Yeah, he was that too, but apparently, he also acted as a mule between Oakland and your neck of the woods. If my information is correct—and remember it's mostly street gossip—now and then he carried cocaine and other drugs into your area and money back to Oakland. Wasn't a regular, but was trusted enough to do the job upon occasion."

Jeb felt stupid. He'd known Dirk Aston and dismissed him as a nuisance. And even though he investigated mainly homicides in the county, he kept his ear to the ground and his eyes wide open for intriguing bits of information that might come in handy down the road. There'd never been a whisper that dirty ole Dirk had been more than just another low-life subsistence grower.

"So, what about this kid? Was he picked up? Questioned?"

Gene sighed. "Nobody connected it at the time, but two days after the Aston hit, a black kid, name of Leroy Seely, was found floating in the bay—shot in the back of the head. Same caliber gun that killed your guy."

"The kid messed up by killing Aston by mistake so they took care of him," Jeb said flatly.

"Yeah, that's our read. Can't prove it. But we're pretty certain that's what happened. Doesn't mean your guy wouldn't have bought it eventually, just not then and probably not in Oakland." Gene chuckled but there was no humor in it. "Once they'd gotten their money and drugs back, you'd probably have had the pleasure of investigating Mr. Aston's death."

"Probably." Many things were coming together for Jeb. "The money and drugs were never recovered, were they?" he asked after a moment.

"Nope, not as far as I know, but you gotta know, there's only so much information circling on the street. Bastards don't tell us all the gossip. Just what doesn't matter anymore. You know, throw the poor bumbling cops a bone now and then."

"What kind of money are we talking about, Gene?"

"Best estimate, relying on our informants, is around a hundred thousand, maybe a little less. Part in cash and part in actual drugs."

Jeb whistled. No wonder Roxanne's place had been broken into time and again. The damage was now easily explained and it hadn't been just your garden-variety trespasser either. It had been someone dangerous; someone who didn't think twice about murder, someone searching desperately for a hundred-thousand-dollar stash they thought was hidden in or around Dirk's old place. A chill snaked down Jeb's spine. Dirk's old place, the place Roxanne now called home. . . .

Chapter
17

*J*eb's first instinct was to drive like a maniac to Roxanne's. Then common sense asserted itself and he realized that Aston's old place had been searched and re-searched numerous times during the past year. The place had been deserted for over six months—anyone looking for drugs and money had had plenty of time to do so. New construction had been going since last September and structures had been torn down and rebuilt; by now it was highly questionable that anyone would still be nosing around. Logic said that the people Aston had double-crossed must have given up on ever finding his stash, or at least decided that Dirk hadn't hidden it on his own place. Roxanne was in no danger, he repeated to himself several times. No danger at all. Trouble was, he couldn't quite completely convince himself and calling himself all kinds of a fool, he picked up the phone.

Roxanne answered the phone on the third ring and at the sound of her voice the gristle of fear jammed in his throat disappeared. He didn't really have a reason to call except to assure himself that she was all right and since the last thing he wanted to do was alarm her, he fumbled through their conversation. They talked for a few minutes until Jeb had the bright idea to ask if she'd like him to bring home Chinese food for dinner tonight.

"Sounds like a plan to me," Roxanne said cheerfully. "I've spent the day on the phone and computer trying to find out if my idea of growing flowers and plants for resale locally has any merit—and what the start-up costs would be. Until you mentioned it, dinner never crossed my mind."

Jeb glanced at the clock. "I'll be leaving Willits in an hour or so, so expect me home sometime around eight."

It gave him a thrill to say those words to her. Almost like they were married or something.

"Got it. After I hang up from you, the dogs and I are going to take a quick hike to the greenhouses before it gets dark. There's a couple of measurements I want to make."

Jeb didn't like that idea at all and he muttered, "Look, I know you're used to taking care of yourself, but be careful, OK? Bad things happen even in Oak Valley and you're out there all by yourself. Keep your eyes open and it wouldn't hurt if you kept in mind some of the safety principles you used in New York."

Roxanne was touched by his concern. "I will," she

said softly. "And don't forget that I have Dawg and Boss. Besides, you're the one fighting—now what did you call it—ah, the minions of evil. *You* be careful."

Wearing a silly smile, Jeb hung up the phone. Man, he had it bad. Just the sound of her voice and he was floating on air. He gave himself a shake and turned his mind back to the conversation with Gene Cartwright.

A grim smile crossed his face as something occurred to him. Bet he knew the name of the fellow overseeing the search of Roxanne's place. Milo Scott. Yep. Good old Scott strikes again. Not only had Scott had months to hunt for Aston's stash but getting the contract for cement work had given him free rein to continue searching. Had he found the money and drugs?

Jeb didn't think so. Not only did Gene's street gossip not give any hint of success in the search for the stolen goods, but the fact Milo Scott was still sniffing around would indicate that the stash hadn't been found. Jeb shook his head. By now someone had to have realized that the stuff couldn't have been hidden in the house or the outbuildings. Besides, had Dirk really been dumb enough to hide the stuff on his own place? Knowing if his thievery was discovered that his property would be the first place anyone looked?

Before talking to Gene this afternoon, Jeb would have said yes, Dirk was that dumb, but now he wondered. Aston had been smart enough to skim off almost a hundred grand in money and drugs before his theft was discovered. Maybe Aston was smarter than he gave him credit for, and yet it didn't feel right. Just the fact that Aston had thought he could steal from his employers and that they wouldn't find out showed that Aston had been as dumb as Jeb had always thought. Smoked one joint too many, Jeb mused, and came up with a wild-assed plan that got him killed. Yeah, that sounded like the Aston they all knew and loved.

So. Was the money and drugs still hidden on Roxanne's place? And if it was, where in the hell was it? Couldn't be in the house. Whatever secrets the original A-frame had held had been lying right out in the open all during construction. Someone was bound to have stumbled across it. The dilapidated garage had been demolished. Don Bean was ready to start building the new garage and woodshed any day now. The pump house had been pretty well vandalized, too, so it wasn't likely that the stuff had been concealed there. Which left the greenhouses. But the greenhouses were, well, clear as glass. Their floors were dirt, however . . . . Jeb grimaced. Unless a backhoe was brought in and the floors dug up, no one would ever know if Aston's stash was buried there. He pictured the expression on Roxanne's face if he asked if she minded if he looked for stolen money and drugs in her greenhouses—with a backhoe.

He sighed. Even if his actions enraged Roxanne, now that the possibility existed that her place was the likely site for a cache of stolen drugs and money, he was going to have to investigate. Or at least talk to the drug guys in the department and get their take on the situation. He looked thoughtful. He didn't have anything concrete. When you boiled it all down it was just street gossip from a fellow cop in Oakland. They might dig up the floor of Roxanne's greenhouses and find nothing. Zip. Nada. Squat. Maybe he'd wait a few days. Aston's stash had already been hidden for more than a year. A few more days wouldn't hurt.

An abstracted expression on his face, Jeb left the Willits substation and drove to the Chinese restaurant. Pulling into the parking lot, he recognized Sloan's black and silver Suburban parked in front of the long redwood-sided building.

Entering the restaurant, he smiled as he walked up to Sloan, where the other man stood waiting at the small counter just to the left of the double-glass doors. "Takeout?" Jeb asked.

Sloan nodded. "Yes. I had to go down to Santa Rosa today. Shelly wanted to get some painting done so she stayed home, but pleaded that I bring home dinner." Sloan shook his head, adding, "When she gets in her studio and gets lost creating magic with brushes and paints, food becomes an abstract idea."

The waitress came up just then and Jeb placed his order: chicken and black mushrooms; sweet and sour barbecued pork; beef and green beans, and shrimp and snow peas.

"My four favorite food groups: chicken, beef, pork, and shrimp," Jeb said as the waitress turned away and headed to the kitchen.

Sloan glanced around the restaurant and said, "There's still several empty tables, why don't we grab one while we wait."

They chose a white Formica-topped table near the register and sat on the red-cushioned black chairs. The fact that they shared some common ancestry a few generations back was obvious. Both were big men, tall and broad-shouldered with black hair and dark complexions. Facially they didn't look much alike, Jeb's features a trifle more refined than Sloan's rough-hewn good looks, but there was a general resemblance physically and an air of toughness and purposefulness about both men. Good men to have on your side in a fight.

Sloan looked at Jeb, a funny half smile on his face. There was an expression in his eyes that made Jeb shake his head disgustedly. "She told you, didn't she?"

Sloan grinned and nodded. "Sure did. The moment she came in the door. She was spilling the beans so fast, I had to have her slow down and back up." It was Sloan's turn to shake his head. "You and Roxanne. Even in the coldest weather, the air seemed to sizzle whenever you two came in range of each other. I always thought that there might be something going on between the pair of you. Just never thought either one of you was smart enough to realize it." Sloan laughed. "Oh, man, are all the folks going to be jumping with joy when they find out about it. Mom's been terrified for years that one of these days Roxy would bring home an empty-headed pretty-boy husband. She'll be thrilled, fall on your neck when she finds out you're going to marry Roxanne. And as for the Judge. . . ."

"Whoa. Wait. Who said anything about marriage?" Jeb said hastily.

Sloan's grin slid away and a hard light came into those golden eyes that so resembled his sister's. "You don't want to marry her?" he asked carefully.

"That's not the point," Jeb muttered. "Just because you and Shelly got married, doesn't mean that marriage is for everyone. That's the problem with deliriously happy newlyweds, they think everyone else should be married, too." His face bitter, Jeb added, "I've tried marriage—*twice,* remember? I don't think I'm a good candidate to be anyone's husband, let alone Roxanne's."

Sloan sat back in his chair and stared at Jeb. "You want to elaborate on that subject just a bit more?"

Jeb shot him an unfriendly look. "Think about it, Sloan. You gotta be nuts to believe that your sister would ever be happy married to a guy like me. Twice divorced and determined to stick with a career I love in an area that doesn't offer a lot of advancement. My roots and home and career are all anchored in Oak Valley. Someday I *might* run for sheriff, but I'm never gonna be famous or rich."

"What makes you think Roxy wants someone who's rich and famous?"

"Come on, Sloan! We're talking about *Roxanne* here, the toast of New York and all that shit. Sure, right now she's happy as a bug in the rug playing in her new house, but that's not going to last. Sooner or later, she's going to get bored and go flying off to New York or Bermuda or some other place at the other end of the world and leave Oak Valley behind. You know it. She's done it before. Done it any number of times these past twenty years. What makes you think this time is different? Nothing's changed."

Sloan sat back and regarded Jeb. "You know," he said slowly, "I never thought of you as a stupid guy before, but what just came out of your mouth is one of the stupidest things I've ever heard." He bent forward. "I know my sister and she may act crazy at times, but she's not nuts."

Jeb smiled wryly. "That's a compliment I'm sure she'll be glad to hear."

Sloan shrugged. "So I guess that no wedding bells are in your future, huh? You and Roxy are just going to shack up together for a while and that'll be that."

Jeb's face tightened. "I'm not just shacking up with her." He glanced away, his jaw working. "She means the world to me, Sloan, but despite what you think, I'm not stupid. When I can think clearly about her, I realize that what I have to offer wouldn't be enough and that sooner or later she's going to grow bored with the valley and . . . me and take off for the glamorous life again. It's inevitable."

The waitress called to them, motioning that their orders were ready. Sloan stood up. "I'm not going to argue with you. She might do just that. But think about this: what if you're wrong? What if you screw around and mess up something that might have been wonderful and lasted forever? And how about giving Roxy a chance to say how she feels? You're making a decision for her—something that will really piss her off if she finds out about it." He bent forward. "I lost seventeen years with Shelly because of the interference of other people. You don't have that problem. You're running a chance of losing a good thing; probably the best damn thing that ever happened to you, because you're too damned scared to risk getting hurt. I never thought you were a coward."

His mouth grim, Jeb stood up, pushing his chair back with a violent movement. For a tense second, Sloan thought Jeb might deck him. "Think what you want to," Jeb growled. "It's my business."

"Yeah, but it's my sister you're involved with," Sloan said softly. "And I won't stand by and let you break her heart—think about that."

They paid for their food at the counter and silently accepted the brown paper bags packed with steaming hot Chinese food. An air of restraint between them, they walked out of the restaurant and to their vehicles. They didn't speak again. Just gave each other a curt nod and got in their vehicles.

Jeb sat there in the parking lot for a few minutes, staring after Sloan's disappearing Suburban. He was angry with Sloan, but he couldn't refute Sloan's words. Maybe he was a coward. Maybe he should just grab Roxanne and tell her he loved her like he'd never loved anyone before in his life and that if she was willing to take a chance with a two-time loser and a guy who aspired to nothing more exciting than being a good cop in a rural county that he wanted to marry her. His mouth twisted. Sloan was right. He was a coward. He didn't want to risk losing Roxanne and so he was hanging back and letting her make all the moves. He certainly hadn't given her any sign that his heart was in her hands and that he was terrified when she found out, she'd toss it away.

His cell phone jangling at his side distracted him. Punching it on, he said, "Yeah."

It was his mother, Karen-Catherine, called KC practically from the moment of her birth.

There were a few minutes of chitchat and then KC asked, "What are you doing on Saturday? I've already got a commitment from your brother and sister for dinner that night. I'm making pot roast, mashed potatoes, lemon broccoli, and carrot and raisin salad with rhubarb upside-down cake for dessert. Clean jeans and boots optional. You want to join us?"

Despite his bad mood, Jeb smiled. His mom must want to see him—she'd just listed several of his favorite foods. His first instinct was to say no, but then he hesitated. Sloan's words stung. "Mind if I bring a guest?" he asked before he could think about it.

"Well, sure," his mother answered, surprise in her voice. "I'd sort of thought that it might just be the family, but if you have a friend you want to bring, why not?"

His jaw set, Jeb took a deep steadying breath. "Mom, it's more than just a friend." And jumping in with both feet, he added, "It's Roxanne Ballinger."

"Oh."

There was silence for a second before Jeb asked, "Is that a problem?"

"Uh, no. I'm just stunned that you're bringing any woman home for dinner and that it's Roxy is, well, mind-boggling. You want to talk about it?"

"Nope. What time do you want us on Saturday night?"

One of the things that Jeb loved about his mother was that she didn't pry. He knew she was burning up with curiosity and he was certain that she was biting her tongue to keep from asking questions, but to her credit all she said was, "Six o'clock ought to be fine. I'm going to experiment on all of you with new hors d'oeuvres—and you know your father doesn't like to eat late."

"Want us to bring anything—wine?"

"No, just yourselves."

They hung up and Jeb looked at his cell phone. Well, he'd stuck his neck out. Sloan thought him a coward, did he? Ha. Only a brave man—a very, very brave man at that—brings home a woman to meet his mother. After Saturday night, there'd be no turning back. His relationship with Roxanne Ballinger would be out there for everyone to see. He grinned. Hell, he'd bet that at this very minute his mother was running into the Judge's study with the news that their eldest son was bringing home a woman. Jeb knew KC would be discreet; she'd keep the news within the family, but his relationship with Roxanne was no longer a secret. It felt good. Like the tightrope he'd been tottering on had become solid ground beneath his feet. He started the vehicle and nosed out into the traffic, heading north. Heading home. To Roxanne.

For those unfamiliar with the road, it could take over an hour and fifteen to twenty minutes to reach Oak Valley from Willits. Jeb had driven the narrow road nearly thirty years and he was comfortable with its many twists and turns and could usually make it to the valley in well under an hour. Today was different. Today he was preoccupied and the truck just loafed along at a leisurely speed.

The conversation with Sloan played over and over in his mind. He wanted to take heart from Sloan's comments, but he was having a difficult time believing that Roxanne was really and truly back in the valley for good. He was convinced that one of these days an offer, a plum assignment that she simply couldn't resist, would come through and Roxanne would be off to the frenetic and glittering world that was her natural setting. Once there he suspected her current enchantment with Oak Valley would vanish and that she'd settle back into the sophisticated life she'd supposedly given up. Oh, she'd show up in the valley now and then, just as she had in the past. She'd open up her house and fill it with her sophisticated, worldly friends and for a few weeks the valley would buzz with gossip and stare agog at all the famous and occasionally infamous people that Roxanne had brought with her. Then like a brilliant, warm sunny day in January, she'd be gone, leaving behind the icy winter, not to appear until the next whim to see the valley overcame her. Jeb believed this. He believed it with every bone, sinew, and fiber of his being. He didn't resent it. He accepted it. For his sake, he wished it was different, but he'd fallen headlong in love with Roxanne, knowing that someday she would once again leave the valley . . . and him behind—despite what Sloan said.

He supposed that the reason he hadn't pushed for their relationship to become public had been because he'd been hoping, rather foolishly he now thought, to protect himself. If no one knew of their affair, then no one would pity him when Roxanne left him for the neon lights of New York. He hadn't brooded over it, but he admitted that he wasn't looking forward to being viewed as a three-time loser—nor pointed out as one of Roxanne's discarded lovers. Losing her was going to be agonizing enough without having to be the object of stares and whispers in the valley. He took a deep breath. He'd handle it when the time came and in the grand scheme of things, being gossiped about would be the least of his pain when Roxanne left him.

Losing her was not going to be easy or simple. Somehow she'd entwined herself so tightly around his heart that he couldn't imagine a life without her. He'd thought he'd suffered at the failure of his two marriages, but compared to what he felt for Roxanne, the emotion his two ex-wives had engendered was a pale, weak thing. Roxanne meant *everything* to him. She was his whole world and without her, he'd be half a man, an empty shell.

That Roxanne cared for him, he didn't doubt. She might even love him a little and he was confident that he made her happy. At least for right now. But he never doubted that when she heard the siren's call of those faraway places that she'd be gone, leaving him behind. . . .

Jeb stiffened. So when she took off like a will-o'-the-wisp why in the hell didn't he follow after her? Go with her? Where was it written that he *had* to remain in Oak Valley for all of his life? Other people moved away, took jobs in other cities, why the hell couldn't he?

He realized suddenly that something fundamental had happened to him when he had fallen in love with Roxanne. Without him even being aware of it, she had become the most important thing in his life. The life he had made for himself in Oak Valley, the career he valued and took pride in, suddenly meant nothing if he couldn't have Roxanne. If he had the choice between having Roxanne and leaving his world behind or remaining in the valley without her, there was no choice to make. Roxanne won every time.

Something tight and painful shook loose in his chest. The choice was so simple. Roxanne or not. The "not" was unthinkable and when he looked at it in those simple terms all of his agony and dilemma vanished. Determined to stay in Oak Valley, resolved to bravely watch her leave when the time came, he'd imprisoned himself, not given himself any options or choices. By jettisoning his determination to remain locked to his career and the valley, everything fell into place. He loved her. And he loved her enough to follow her wherever she went.

Would he like living somewhere else? Somewhere like New York? He grimaced. Probably not. But if he had Roxanne in his arms, it wouldn't matter where they lived, as long as it was together. Other people lived in and liked New York just fine, maybe in time, he would too.

When he pulled into his usual spot in front of the house, he was grinning like an idiot. He had no doubts, no regrets. Roxanne didn't know it yet, but she was his woman. And he was her man. For all time.

Roxanne and the dogs met him at the front door. At the sight of those bags held in his arms Roxanne blinked.

"Hungry tonight, are we," she asked with a smile.

"You bet," Jeb replied, his heart pounding joyfully at the sight of her. Even without makeup and wearing blue jeans and a dirt-stained orange sweatshirt, her hair curling wildly around her head, Jeb thought she was the loveliest creature he'd ever seen. He wiggled his eyebrows. "And not just for food."

"Oh, really," she said with a dimple as she took a couple of the bags from him. "Now I wonder what that could be."

Dumping the bags on the counter in the kitchen Jeb grabbed her and buried his face in her neck. "Miss me today?" he asked huskily.

Roxanne turned around from her task of taking the various cartons out of the brown paper bags and looked at him. There was something different about him, but she couldn't put her finger on it. He'd never asked her that sort of question before; in fact, they didn't talk about their feelings for each other at all.

She met his gaze and the warm glitter in those black eyes made her heart turn right over in her chest. Flustered, she muttered, "Of course. It's very quiet when you're not around the house."

Jeb made a face. "Ah, you miss my noise. Great."

"I miss you, too," she added hastily. Shyly she said, "It *is* a bit lonesome without you."

His hands tightened on her waist and he kissed her hard on the mouth. "Good. Don't you forget it."

Dinner passed pleasantly, although Roxanne picked at her food. When Jeb noticed and commented, she said, "I think I'm coming down with that flu that's going around the valley—I've felt queasy off and on all day. I don't have a fever—at least not yet. I'm hoping it's nothing more than an upset stomach. If it is the flu, according to what my mom said, I'll be spending at least the next couple of days retching my innards out. Yuck."

Jeb looked worried. "You want me to call in and see if I can get a couple of days off?"

"Nah, I'll be fine." She wrinkled her nose at him. "I'm a big girl, remember? And I know the drill for flu: rest and plenty of fluids."

He didn't argue with her, but his mind was already made up. If she had the flu, he'd take those days off. God knew he had enough of them—Craddock had been dinging him about them only last week. He smiled to himself. Somehow he rather thought that the days of his vacation time stacking up unused were over. With Roxanne in his life, spending every available moment on the job didn't seem quite so important anymore.

"Saw Sloan tonight when I picked up dinner. He was at the restaurant doing the same thing," he said a few minutes later. "He'd been down to Santa Rosa. Shelly'd stayed home to paint."

"Probably something to do with the business. It hasn't been that long since Ross took over and I expect he still wants big brother to cast an eye over things now and then," Roxanne remarked.

"You think Sloan will ever regret giving up the

business and coming back to the valley?" Jeb asked quietly.

Roxanne laughed. "Are you crazy? It would take an atom bomb blast to get Sloan to move out of the valley. He loves it here. Unlike me, it's where he always wanted to be. When I was nineteen all I could think of was how fast I could get away, but not Sloan. He wanted to stay—he and I used to have these horrific arguments about it—for a long time I never understood why he hated living in Sonoma County, why he was always counting the days until he could come home. Nope. Sloan won't be moving back down to Santa Rosa or any other place. Especially since he's married Shelly." She smiled softly. "They're here to stay."

Jeb nodded, a crooked smile on his face. "Nice when everything works out."

When dinner was over and the dishwasher was burbling away, they wandered into the great room and settled on the couch. With groans of bliss the dogs took up their favorite positions on the floor at their feet.

"Besides seeing my handsome brother, anything exciting happen today?" Roxanne asked. "Capture an ax murderer or something like that?"

Jeb shook his head. "Nope. But I did learn something interesting about the former owner of this place."

Roxanne cocked a brow. "What?"

It wasn't a decision that he'd made lightly, but it

had dawned on him that by not telling Roxanne what he knew about Aston that he might be putting her in danger. "It's mostly street gossip," he warned her as he began his tale, "but apparently Dirk Aston skimmed off money and drugs from some big guys in Oakland."

He related everything that Gene had told him, including his own suspicion that the money and drugs might be hidden in the floor of one of the greenhouses. Reluctantly, he added, "I know you're not going to be happy about it, but I think we're going to have to get a small backhoe in and find out for ourselves if Aston did hide the money there."

Roxanne's eyes were huge; she'd hung on every word he'd uttered. "Are you kidding?" she demanded. "I can hardly wait! It's such a relief to know what was behind all the vandalism and break-ins. It'll be wonderful to finally have the mystery solved." She smiled grimly. "And as for Milo Scott . . . I want to be around to see the expression on his face when he learns about the backhoe."

Jeb slanted her a look. "I thought that Scott was a great friend of yours."

"Get real!" Roxanne said with a snort. "That lowlife? I never liked him in high school and I can't say that he's improved with age." She dropped her eyes demurely and murmured, "I only acted that way to make you jealous."

Jeb plucked her up into his arms. Settling her on his lap, he said, "Well, it worked. I'd appreciate it if you wouldn't employ those tricks in the future. Very bad for my temper."

Roxanne nestled her head against his shoulder, her fingers playing with the buttons of his shirt. He'd been jealous! Of Scott of all people. A delicious little flutter went through her. Jeb jealous. How divine.

He caught her wandering fingers and dropped a kiss on their tips. All evening, the subject of the dinner with his parents had preyed on his mind; half a dozen times he'd almost mentioned it, but he'd uncharacteristically held back. The dinner at his parents wasn't just about dinner; it was a public announcement that he and Roxanne were an item and he wasn't certain how she was going to receive that news. The other night, after Shelly had found out about them, she'd indicated that it didn't matter to her who knew about them, but the fact remained that she *had* asked Shelly to keep their relationship a secret. It occurred belatedly to him that she might not view his actions with a kind eye. In fact, she might be pissed. Very. He grimaced. Well, it wasn't a secret anymore and figuring the sooner he told his princess what he'd done, the sooner he'd know if he was going to keep his head or not, he decided to 'fess up. Feeling as if he were stepping off a cliff, he asked, "Uh, you have anything planned for this weekend?"

"Hmm? No, not that I can think of. Why?"

"I thought we'd have dinner at my folks. My mother called and invited us for Saturday night. I told her that I'd be bringing you along."

Roxanne sat up as if shot. *"What?"* she demanded, staring at him as if she'd never seen him before in her life.

Patiently he repeated, "My mother, you know, KC Delaney? She invited us to dinner on Saturday night."

Roxanne glared at him. "I know who your mother is, smart ass. You told her about us?"

Jeb scratched his ear. "Sort of."

Her thoughts were whirling. She was frightened and elated; scared and excited, hoping desperately that the peculiar limbo they'd been living in, neither fully committed to each other nor *un*committed, was finally about to end. What she didn't know and what terrified her was whether she was ready for it. Ready for the next step. Dropping her gaze from his, she asked, "What exactly did you tell her?"

Jeb looked at her averted face, the love he felt for her flooding through him. It seemed he'd waited all his life for her and he wasn't going to wait one second longer. With a lean finger, he turned her chin until she was looking straight at him. "How about," he said huskily, "we talk about what I didn't tell her? Such as I love you more than I ever thought it was possible to love someone? Such as I want to marry you and spend the rest of my life with you?"

Roxanne's heart felt as if it would burst. Oh, God, she was so happy, she didn't know whether to laugh or cry or both. Jeb loved her. He'd said those magic words she'd longed to hear. I love you. Words that she had once sneered at, but coming from Jeb, now meant the world to her. Her eyes flooded with tears, happy, joyous tears. A lump formed in her throat. She swallowed. Scrubbed her eyes like a little child and sniffed back more tears. Eyes shining like stars, she smiled brilliantly at him and said smartly, "Well, it's about damn time that you admitted it!"

Chapter
18

Jeb shouted with laughter, his arms tightening around her. Trust Roxanne. No sign of a simpering miss about her. But then what had he expected? She was a princess. His princess.

He kissed her, his mouth warm and tender. They clung together, their arms holding the other close. It was a sweet moment. A moment to remember and savor. And they did.

"So," he said, several minutes later, "isn't there something you want to say to me?"

She smiled impishly. "Gee, I don't know. Is there?"

His eyes darkened. "I love you, Roxanne. I'd like to hear that you share my feelings."

She twisted in his arms, raining soft kisses on his face. "How can you even doubt it? I've been crazy in love with you for weeks, but I was afraid that you. . . ."

"What? That I was just hanging around you for my health?" He gave her a little shake. "You've had to know that I've been off my head about you." He smiled wickedly. "Probably since we first made love on your countertop." He rubbed his jaw. "You know, now that I think about it, I should have rescued that damn thing from the rubbish pile—could have shown it to our grandkids. Great family relic."

She slanted him a reproving glance. "I don't think that sort of tale would be appropriate for family gatherings. That little episode will be our secret. Deal?"

"I dunno, I think that it would make a . . . ouch! What'd you pinch me for?" he demanded, his eyes dancing with amusement.

Roxanne laughed and hugged him tightly. "Oh, Jeb, you just can't believe how happy I am." She kissed his brow, his nose, and finally his mouth. Lifting her mouth breathless moments later, she said, "I *do* love you, you know—so much it frightens me and I can't imagine a life that doesn't have you in it." She looked tenderly into his eyes, her fingers caressing his hard cheek. "You mean everything to me—more than just simple words can convey. I want to spend the rest of my life showing you *precisely* how much I do love you." She kissed his nose. "Is that OK with you?"

A muscle jumped beneath her trailing fingers. "Better than OK," he said huskily, his heart so full of love for her, he could hardly speak. He hugged her so hard, she'd thought her ribs would break.

"I never thought I'd fall in love again," he said quietly. "And when I did, I realized that I had never really been in love before—that I'd only *thought* I'd been in love. What I feel for you doesn't compare to anything I've ever felt before in my life. You blindsided me." He shook his head and laughed ruefully. "This may come as a big shock, but I think I've probably been half in love with you for the past ten years or so. As I look back, I figure half the reason I was always chewing you out was to keep from kissing you. "

She beamed. "Good! Because I suspect the reason you irritated me so much was because I was attracted to you and didn't want to be. It seemed so old-fashioned. Girl leaves small town behind; becomes rich and famous and then gives it all up to return home to marry small-town boy."

A stillness came over Jeb. "Have you really given it all up?" he asked carefully, his gaze not meeting hers.

Roxanne's eyes narrowed. "Don't tell me you think that this is all a whim? That I'm just playing house? And that at the first chance I'll be out of here like a bullet from a gun?" She tapped him smartly on the cheek, making him look at her. "Jeb, I love you. I want what you want. I've had my moment of fame and you know what? If it all went away tomorrow I wouldn't regret it and if I had a choice of remaining *Roxanne* or becoming just plain old Mrs. Jeb Delaney—being your wife wins hands down every time." Her lips twisted. "Now how's that for an old-fashioned girl?" Jeb didn't appear to be convinced. She bent nearer, her face inches from his, her eyes locked on his. "Jeb, how can you even think for a moment that I want to go back to that life? It's sort of a 'been there, done that.' I had a great run and I wouldn't have missed it for the world, but I've moved on. I've grown up—I hope. And now I know what's real, what's lasting, and what I want." She brushed her lips against his. "I want you. I want Oak Valley. I want to have your kids and watch them grow up here in the valley."

He still looked skeptical. "You sure you won't be pining for all the attention, the glamour when you're knee-deep in diapers?"

"Come on, I'm not nuts. I'm sure there'll be moments when I'll miss being one of the hottest cover girls in the U.S. But, darling, they'll only be *moments*. Face it—being knee-deep in diapers is going to be a whole lot more . . . interesting than standing for hours on end under burning lights with some guy pointing a camera and yelling, 'Smile! Toss your head back! Eat this camera with your eyes!' Believe me, all I want is to be your wife and raise our children—that's going to be my career now." She kissed him. "My last and only career."

He wasn't entirely convinced, but she felt him relax beside her. Words alone weren't going to convince him; she'd have to prove it to him. She smiled. And she had the rest of her life in which to do it.

They nestled together on the couch, speaking in low murmurs, kissing, caressing, and exchanging those words that only lovers share. It could have been an hour or only moments, but eventually, arms entwined, they wandered off to bed.

When they made love that night, it might have been

imagination, but each touch, each caress, each kiss, seemed richer, more intense, and the sensations they shared seemed more powerful, more meaningful than previously. It was magic. It was love.

Later, lying with her head on his shoulder, their hands locked together, they spoke quietly about their love. "I almost need to pinch myself," Roxanne said at one point. "It seems like a dream."

"If you'll give me a couple more minutes," Jeb murmured, lazy amusement in his voice, "I'll show you it's no dream."

Roxanne giggled and, twisting her head slightly, blew in his ear. "Hey! Cut that out," Jeb grumbled. "No fair when I'm too weak to retaliate."

Dawg indicated that she and Boss had been polite long enough and that it was urgent they be put outside. Muttering and complaining, Jeb snapped on a light and scrambled into the nearest available clothing. Half dressed and loath to leave Roxanne, he wandered out the front door to keep an eye on the dogs while they took care of nature's calling. They didn't take long.

Back inside, Dawg rushed ahead and made a bee-line for her side of the bed, curling up against Roxanne's back. Coming into the room, Jeb eyed the dog. "I guess romance is over for tonight."

Roxanne sent him a seductive smile. "I can always push her off onto the floor."

Jeb shook his head and crawled into bed beside Roxanne. Turning to flick out the lamp near the bed, he said, "Nope, that's all right. Besides, we've still got important things to talk about."

"Oh? And what would that be?"

"Such as when and where we get married."

Roxanne yawned and snuggled closer. "Can't be soon enough for me. Reno, tomorrow would suit me just fine."

Jeb shifted, his gaze incredulous. "Are you serious?"

"Sure. Why not?" She reached up and kissed his chin. "I want to marry you. And unless it's what you want, I don't want a big, elaborate wedding. Quick and quiet is my preference." She made a face. "Very quick and very quiet—especially if we don't want the paparazzi to find out about it and hound us to death."

Jeb hadn't thought about that aspect of it. That the news media might be interested in their wedding hadn't even occurred to him. He didn't care what kind of a wedding ceremony they had—he'd been through the big wedding routine—twice. But he didn't want to deny Roxanne her moment in the sun.

"Are you sure?" he asked uncertainly. "Reno sounds great to me, but, honey, I've done the splashy wedding before—you haven't. Are you sure you don't want to get married here in the valley surrounded by our families and friends?"

Roxanne sat up, her hair falling in glorious disarray around her shoulders. "Jeb, what do you want?"

His eyes traveled over her silky skin, lingering on

the tempting thrust of her naked breasts. "You," he said thickly. "Only you."

"Then Reno it is, just as soon and as quiet as we can arrange it."

How they got through the next couple of days, they never knew. It had been decided that on Friday morning, they'd leave the valley, drive the six or seven hours to Reno, stay the night, get married, and drive back in time to attend the dinner at Jeb's parents'. The time in between was magical and passed in a blur. Jeb knew he got strange looks at work; the perpetually goofy grin on his face might have been the reason. He didn't care. He was so happy, he felt certain his feet never hit the ground.

Roxanne was little better. She giggled. Constantly. And caught herself laughing aloud for absolutely no reason at all. She was giddy with delight; drunk on happiness.

And when they were together it was even worse. They laughed. Made love. And laughed some more, before making love again. They lay in bed each night, whispering and giggling over their elopement to Reno like a pair of teenagers.

Thursday night, Jeb dropped off Dawg and Boss at his house, locking the dogs in their kennel with the promise that he wasn't deserting them forever. The looks they gave him told him they didn't believe one word of it. He'd already made arrangements with Mingo to feed and water the dogs on Friday and Saturday so he could leave them with only a slightly guilty conscience. "I'll be back, guys," he said softly, tickling their noses through the kennel fence. "And then we'll all move up to Roxanne's for good. You'll like that, won't you?"

Dawg whined and licked his fingers. Boss sniffed, turned his back on Jeb, and sauntered off to the doghouse. Clearly he was not impressed.

Roxanne and Jeb made good time on Friday, leaving Oak Valley just after daylight. The traffic and weather cooperated, no pileups or storms to slow them down. They arrived in Reno in the early afternoon. Roxanne was media shy and suggested that they wait until almost closing to purchase the wedding license. Wryly she'd said, "Less time for the news to leak." So they drove around checking out wedding chapels. They found a little ivy covered place tucked off the main drag and after talking with the couple who ran it, made an appointment for 9:00 A.M. the next morning.

Buying the license made it clear to Jeb that Roxanne had been smart to suggest a quick and quiet wedding. The clerk behind the counter recognized Roxanne's name, and despite Roxanne's halfhearted attempts at a disguise, scarf and sunglasses, she took a second look and gasped, "Oh, my! It *is* you!" Her words were heard by everyone in the vicinity and in seconds Roxanne and Jeb were the objects of an excited group of coworkers.

Roxanne was nice about it. She smiled and answered questions and autographed the slips of paper that were thrust at her. Several minutes later, she and Jeb made their escape.

"Think they'll notify the news?" Jeb asked as he started the truck.

Roxanne shrugged. "Probably, but by the time they run us down, we'll be married and headed out of town—I hope."

Wedding rings were next and they lingered over their selection. They finally decided on heavy, plain gold bands adorned with delicate filigree. Staring at the ring on her finger, Roxanne's eyes filled with tears. Jeb must have guessed her emotions, because he took her hand and kissed the trembling finger wearing the gold band. She smiled mistily at him.

The people who ran the chapel proved to be discreet and to Roxanne's relief they were not greeted that morning by a shouting horde of news media. She wasn't even sure if she had been recognized. Neither the gentleman who would marry them, nor his wife and secretary who would act as witnesses, gave any sign that she and Jeb were anything other than just another couple getting married.

The chapel was tiny; three golden oak pews on either side of the room provided seating for guests. The walls were white, broken only by two stained glass windows on either side of the chapel, and the thick carpet was a tasteful swirl of rose and cream. On each side of the tiny altar, bouquets of pink and white gladiolus, baby's breath, and ferns stood in tall pale green vases. The man who would marry them, wearing a dark blue suit, was standing there waiting for them, his wife and secretary smiling as they waited just off to the side. Jeb gave Roxanne a quick kiss and then hurried down the short aisle to await his bride. A second later the sounds of the wedding march filled the room from speakers on each side of the room.

Roxanne had chosen to be married in a pale peach silk pantsuit with a matching broad-brimmed hat that framed her face. Jeb had surprised her that morning by arranging for a charming bridal bouquet of deep apricot-hued baby roses and white carnations to be delivered to the suite at the hotel where they had stayed. She'd teared up when he'd handed them to her.

"Oh, damn," she half laughed, half cried. "You're ruining my makeup."

"And I'll ruin it a lot more later on," Jeb murmured, wiggling his brows.

As Roxanne walked down the aisle, she was aware of nothing but Jeb standing there, tall and handsome in a dark gray suit. Until this morning when he'd put it on, she'd never seen him in a suit and he'd taken her breath away. He still did, she thought, as she drew nearer. He always would.

It was a simple ceremony, but meant so much to the pair of them. And when they had promised to love, honor, and obey and exchanged their first kiss as man and wife, Roxanne thought she'd melt right there in a puddle of love at Jeb's feet. Smiling into her face, Jeb said, "Hi, Mrs. Delaney."

Roxanne's eyes filled with tears again, but she managed to say, "Hi there, husband."

Afraid the paparazzi might still run them down in Reno, as soon as the paperwork was finished, they turned the truck west and lit out like bandits for home. The long drive to Oak Valley seemed to pass in minutes. They were so busy making plans for the future, speculating on how the news of their sudden and unexpected marriage was going to take the valley.

"Are your parents going to be unhappy that they didn't get to see you married?" Jeb asked as they left I-5 and turned onto Highway 20.

Roxanne shook her head. "They'll be taken aback, but then I'm always surprising them, so no, I don't think they'll be disappointed. Don't forget when Samantha was married they got to put on a huge affair. I remember Mom saying afterward, only half teasing I think, that one big fancy wedding was enough for any parent to suffer through. And they were there to see Shelly and Sloan married." Roxanne looked thoughtful. "Of course they did miss Ilka's wedding . . ." She made a face. "I guess the less said about that the better."

"I agree."

"What about your folks? Think they'll be upset that we eloped?"

"Nope. I think they'll be so glad that I'm not wasting away into a bitter old bachelor that they'll probably fall on your neck with gratitude." He slanted her a smiling glance. "Think you can handle it."

"With you at my side," she said softly, "I can handle anything."

Jeb reached for her hand lying on the seat beside him and lifting it to his mouth, kissed it. Holding hands, their drive continued.

It was after five o'clock when they finally reached home and they dashed from the truck to the house. Mindful of the six o'clock dinner, they quickly showered and dressed and less than forty-five minutes later they were out the door driving to Jeb's parents' house.

Roxanne and Mingo had been classmates all through school and she'd spent some happy times at the Delaney home either planning rallies or school dances or attending parties, so the long, low log style home was familiar to her. It was an old comfortable house built by Jeb's grandfather; the logs had been felled on Delaney land around the turn of the century. The house had covered porches on three sides and in the spring and summer was covered with wildly blooming wisteria and white roses. Roxanne remembered the sweet scent of the roses that had perfumed the air. If she was familiar with the house, she was also very familiar with the Judge and KC and had always liked them, but as she and Jeb pulled up in front of the rambling ranch house, a knot formed in her belly. It was one thing to enter the house as a classmate of Mingo's and another as the wife of their eldest son.

She bit her lip, looking uneasily at the house, watching the smoke rise from the stone chimney in the middle of the dark shake roof. "Are you sure your parents are going to be happy about this? What if they hate me? I mean they don't know me as an adult." She swallowed, twisting her gold wedding band around and around her finger. "There's been a lot written about me that wouldn't make me every parents' dream bride for their son."

Jeb glanced at her, surprised. It never occurred to him that Roxanne might be nervous about meeting his folks as his bride. "Princess, I can't guarantee how they'll react, but I doubt they'll eat you alive. And remember I'm a big boy—I don't need their permission to get married." He smiled and added slyly, "Surely you're not afraid of them?"

Roxanne's chin lifted, as he'd known it would, and she gave a toss of her head. "Of course not! Let's go and get it over with."

Smiling to himself, Jeb got out of the truck and walked around to open the door for her. Holding her in his arms he waved his hand in front of her eyes, the fading sunlight glinting on the gold band. "We're married, honey, and nothing is going to change that. Nothing." Huskily he added, "You only have to remember one thing: I love you."

"Oh, and I love you, too," she breathed, stars peeping into her eyes.

KC and the Judge met them at the door. They were a striking couple. The Judge would turn seventy years old in July, but he still stood as tall and ramrod straight as he had in his youth. It was easy for Roxanne to see how Jeb might look in another twenty-five years or so when she looked at his father. The Judge's thick hair was silver and he continued to sport the Clark Gable mustache he had all his adult life even though these days there were more silver hairs in it than black. Jeb had inherited his height, build, and black eyes from his father, but it was obvious that his stubborn jawline and mouth had come from KC.

KC was a tall woman, and approaching sixty-five, her hair was steel gray. She wore it short and straight in a no-nonsense cut with only the hint of wave over her brow. Even in her youth, KC would have been labeled "handsome" rather than pretty; with age those strong features had only grown more handsome. She was outspoken, quite able to put even the Judge in his place when necessary.

There were the usual exchange of greetings and Roxanne was welcomed into the house, receiving a thorough look over and a warm hug from the Judge and a big smile and a kiss on the cheek from KC. As she entered the house and was shown into the spacious living room, she was aware that Jeb's mother was discreetly sizing her up; she could almost feel the curiosity radiating from KC's body. KC hadn't noticed the wedding bands yet, but to Roxanne it felt as if her wedding ring was the size of an elephant, sitting right there on her finger in plain sight for everyone to see.

The first person Roxanne spied as she walked into the living room was Mingo. Wearing blue jeans and a navy-blue patterned western-cut, long-sleeved shirt, he was sprawled on a dark green leather couch, a bottle of beer resting on the low oak coffee table in front of him. Curled up in a chair on the other side of the room, near the stone fireplace, was Cheyenne, Jeb and Mingo's sister—and the only one of the three children who had followed in their father's footsteps. She had graduated from Yale Law School at the top of her class and had almost immediately started working in the Mendocino County District Attorney's Office. Cheyenne had been born late in the lives of the Judge and KC and she had only been about seven years old when Roxanne had left the valley.

Cheyenne was living proof that genetics is a crap-shoot. To her chagrin, coming from a family known for its tallness and striking good looks, she only stood five feet two in her bare feet. Worse, she had a pug nose, a wide mouth, and ginger-colored hair and looked, she claimed, like a marginally intelligent monkey. Cheyenne was too hard on herself. She was very intelligent and if she would never be called a beauty, she had a gamine attractiveness and a smile that lit up the darkest day.

Meeting Roxanne's eyes, Cheyenne flashed that smile and stood up. "I remember you from a kid, but I don't think we've ever officially met. I'm Cheyenne."

The two women shook hands, both of them liking what they saw.

Cheyenne glanced at Jeb standing right behind Roxanne. The smile became a wicked grin. "Oh, man, are you ever brave to bring a woman home," she said to her elder brother. "Mom's been all atwitter since you told her."

"You've got that right," Mingo chimed in. "You'd have thought the Queen of England was coming for dinner. She's been cleaning and cooking and warning us all to be on our best behavior." He grinned at Roxanne. "It's been years since Jeb brought a woman home, Mom doesn't want us to frighten you off."

KC lifted a brow and tried to look haughty. "I don't know how it is that I have such gabby children. I have not been 'atwitter,'" she said grandly, her blue eyes dancing. "I've been *thrilled!*" She beamed at Roxanne. "I always thought you were a nice young woman—despite the tabloids—and I'm delighted that Jeb's had the good sense to realize it, too."

"Now, now," said the Judge from across the big room where he stood at a bamboo and brass bar lining up several glasses on the polished top. "Don't scare the poor girl off." He glanced back at Roxanne. "May I interest you in a drink?" A small smile played at the corner of his mouth, and those shrewd black eyes dropped to Roxanne's hand where it hung at her side. "Perhaps champagne? Because unless I'm mistaken, this is going to turn into a very special event."

KC, Mingo, and Cheyenne looked puzzled. Roxanne gasped, her eyes widening, and Jeb laughed and shook his head.

"Spotted them right off, did you?" he asked his father, one hand resting comfortingly on Roxanne's shoulder, his gold band obvious against his dark skin.

"Indeed. I was, you may remember, a judge for many years. Had to size up people in an instant. Figure out who was lying and who was telling the truth." He tapped the corner of his eye. "Nothing escapes these eagle eyes."

KC was staring transfixed at Jeb's hand lying on Roxanne's shoulder. Her mouth formed a big O. Her gaze dropped to Roxanne's hand, honing in on the gold band. She let out a loud shriek and a smile as big as Texas covered her face. "My prayers have been answered," she cried. "Oh, yes, I do think that champagne is definitely in order." She grabbed Roxanne and hugged her tight. "You naughty, naughty children—I may not speak to you for thirty seconds. When?"

"This morning at nine o'clock in Reno," Jeb said proudly. "You're the first to know."

It was bedlam for a few minutes, congratulations and questions flying around the room. Once things had settled down, KC said briskly, "Well, I'm not starting out at odds with my new in-laws." She looked at Roxanne. "Go call your parents and tell them the news and tell them to get over here for dinner. No excuses. We have a wedding to celebrate."

It was a celebration. Roxanne's parents were as surprised as Jeb's, but they took the news of the sudden wedding in stride. They arrived at the Delaneys' less than twenty minutes later.

In the Delaney living room beaming from ear to ear, Mark swept Roxanne into a bear hug. "That's my girl!

I always knew you'd have enough sense to choose a valley man."

He pumped Jeb's hand up and down enthusiastically. "Welcome to the family, Jeb. I sure hope you're going to be better at controlling her than I ever was."

"Hey, come on," Roxanne said. "I wasn't that bad. And besides, I don't need anyone to control me."

"Absolutely," KC agreed. "If anything, it'll be Roxy controlling Jeb, not the other way around."

Helen looked from Roxanne's face to Jeb's. Her eyes were soft, her expression misty and tender. "Oh, I don't know. I think they'll control each other." She flung her arms around Roxanne's neck. "Oh, sweetie, I'm so happy for you. And pleased." She glanced at Jeb. "I always had a soft spot for your new husband and I'm delighted to welcome him to our family." She turned back to Roxanne and kissed her on the cheek. "Be happy. You deserve it."

The meal that followed was full of excited chatter and laughter and Roxanne decided that if she had planned it, she couldn't have thought of a better way to celebrate her marriage to Jeb. KC and Helen were busy with plans for a reception to be held in two weeks at the community center and while Roxanne thought it unnecessary, she realized that it was important to the two older women. They were in their element and she would have had to have a harder heart than she did to deny them the pleasure they took from all their schemes.

It was late when Jeb and Roxanne finally drove

away from his parents' house, but not too late for them to swing by and load up Dawg and Boss. Dawg was ecstatic to see them, jumping up and sharing slobbery kisses with them and Boss even seemed to have missed them, deigning to give both Roxanne and Jeb a damp lick on the cheek before settling down.

In bed that night, Dawg nestled in her habitual spot at Roxanne's back and Boss keeping guard at the foot of the bed, Jeb pulled Roxanne next to him. "Happy?" he asked.

Roxanne smiled dreamily. "More than I ever thought possible." She turned her head slightly to look at him in the darkness. "You?"

He kissed her. "You bet." He hesitated. "What sort of a honeymoon do you want?"

"Well, unless you want to travel, I'd just as soon stay home," Roxanne answered truthfully. "Although I suppose we could go away for a weekend to the Napa Valley or something."

They looked at each other, grinned and said simultaneously, "Nah."

"How did I get so lucky?" Jeb asked. "A Reno marriage and no honeymoon—what more could a guy ask for?"

"Don't push your luck," Roxanne warned with a smile. "I'm sure I'll think of some way to make up for it in the future."

Roxanne woke up early Sunday morning with the flu. Staggering back to bed after her third trip to the bathroom in minutes, she lay back down and groaned, "Fine way to start out our married life together."

"Hey, we swore in sickness and in health, remember?"

"Yeah, but I thought the sickness was way in the future, when we were old and gray and doddering around."

"Want me to fix you some chicken noodle soup or something?"

Roxanne's stomach roiled and as she raced for the bathroom, she cried, "No!"

By afternoon the worst of the virus seemed to have passed and they spent the day, in between the constant jangle of the phone—the news of their marriage had spread fast—just puttering around, making plans, making love, and laughing. Jeb had made arrangements to take the following week off and they were both looking forward to it.

Roxanne still felt kind of punky Monday so they spent another quiet day. The phone had ceased ringing every five minutes and they figured the worst of the storm was over. Jeb even risked a brief trip to town for milk and 7-UP and reported back that he was only mobbed half a dozen times. Smiling as he put away the milk and fixed Roxanne a glass of 7-UP with ice, he said, "I ran the first gauntlet—next time it's your turn."

"Hopefully by then we'll be old news."

"Hopefully." Handing her the glass, he said, "By the way, I bumped into Don Bean and after thumping me on the back with that ham-size fist of his, he mentioned that since we're having a dry spell, he'd like to get started on the well house. I told him I'd discuss it with you and that one of us would get back to him."

It was decided between them that now was as good a time as any to tear down the old well house and get started on constructing the new one. They also talked about the barn that Don would be building once the rainy season was over.

Sipping her 7-UP Roxanne said, "Why don't you talk to Don about the barn? You'll know more than I will about what we'll need. All I ask is that it not be painted red and that it's not just a big square box. Oh, and that it doesn't block any views."

"OK."

Jeb called Don Bean and they made plans for Wednesday.

Don Bean accompanied by Profane Deegan arrived bright and early Wednesday morning. Still not up to par, despite Jeb's objections, Roxanne insisted on dressing and hobbling into the kitchen and fixing coffee for them.

Seated at the kitchen table both men congratulated her on the marriage and several minutes were spent relating how surprised everyone was in the valley about it. Roxanne listened, nodded, and smiled wanly. "Sorry, fellas," she said after a bit, "but I'm going to have to go back to bed." She waved a hand in Jeb's direction. "He can supervise."

Reaching the bedroom, heedless of her clothes,

Roxanne crawled back into bed, only to rise five minutes later and race to the bathroom. She was not enjoying the flu at all.

Jeb got the men started. It was decided that before tearing down the old well house that they'd go ahead and use the backhoe Don had brought and dig out for the new foundation. They could get it dug and poured today and worry about demolition of the old well house while the new foundation was setting up. Jeb watched them for a while, hoping the sound of the big equipment wouldn't bother Roxanne. Concerned about her, after a minute or two, Jeb left the two men at it and walked back inside. Finding her lying limply on the bed, he sank down beside her and felt her forehead with his hand.

"It's not my forehead," she said grumpily, "that's sick. It's my stomach."

"That's why it's called stomach flu," Jeb teased, brushing her hair back from her brow. "Feel pretty bad?"

She made a face. "Awful, but I feel even worse that I'm making your time off miserable."

"Better or worse, remember?" he said softly, his eyes full of love.

She smiled and kissed his hand. "Better or worse."

They both heard the sound of an approaching vehicle. "Expecting company?" Jeb asked.

"Not me."

He got up and walked into the bathroom to look out

the window that faced the front. His face grim, he came back into the bedroom. "Milo Scott," he said.

Roxanne grimaced. "At least we know why he's so interested in what we're doing."

"Yeah, but I think it's time I run him off for good and let him know that his company isn't welcome here anymore." He cocked his brow at her. "You mind?"

"Be my guest."

Chapter

19

The more Roxanne considered it the more she didn't like the idea of Jeb confronting Milo. She wasn't afraid anything would happen, but she decided that she'd feel better about it if she were there to make certain that Milo didn't start trouble. Not, she reminded herself as she levered up out of bed, that Jeb couldn't handle the situation just fine. He could. But Milo might need to know that Jeb wasn't acting solely on his own. That she concurred with his actions. She wouldn't put it past the little weasel to come back and try to inveigle his way into her good graces. Better he find out right now that she and Jeb were in this together.

She staggered to the bathroom, stuck her tongue out at her pale features, and threw cold water in her face. She dragged a comb through her hair, pinched her cheeks, and straightened her clothes. God! She felt like death warmed over.

Hoping she wouldn't embarrass herself by falling in

a faint at Jeb's feet, she wandered outside. Milo's truck was parked next to the truck and trailer that Don Bean had hauled the backhoe on. Milo was standing near the well house, Jeb right beside him. So far, it looked to Roxanne as if the conversation had been amiable.

Jeb spotted her and frowned. He stalked over to her and demanded, "What are you doing out here? You're sick."

"I thought maybe you could use a little moral support," she muttered. "Milo can be awfully hard to convince sometimes—especially if he doesn't want to be." She smiled at him. "United front and all that. I think he needs to see that I'm 100% behind you in this—that it isn't just your idea."

Jeb nodded. "OK. I'll accept that."

She looked in Milo's direction. "He give any reason for being here?"

Jeb smiled grimly. "Oh, yeah, said he heard in town that Don was working here and drove out to see if he needed any help. Real Samaritan our Scott."

They joined the others. Don Bean was operating the backhoe, Profane standing nearby with a shovel to clean out any dirt left behind by the big shovel. Milo Scott was off to the side watching.

It was amazing the amount of work machinery can accomplish. The original well house had been about three-by-four. It was adequate, but left very little room to work on the pump should the need arrive. Don had suggested that the new building be expanded to six-by-eight and Roxanne had agreed. The backhoe was making short work of digging the foundation trenches and Roxanne stared at wide swathes the shovel had already made around the building. There were only a couple of feet more of shaley clay soil to be dug out on the south side of the small building before the trenches were done.

It would have been hard for Jeb to have any sort of a conversation, friendly or otherwise, with Milo over the noise of the backhoe and so he bided his time.

After nodding curtly to Milo, Roxanne walked around to stand in front of the backhoe, near one of the small piles of dirt scattered around the perimeter. The ease with which the machinery accomplished a job that would ordinarily have taken a man with a shovel several hours of hard backbreaking work fascinated her. She watched mesmerized as the big shovel bit down into the earth right on top of a wispy little pine tree and scooped up the pine along with a wheelbarrow or more of dirt and then dropped it on the nearby pile. Amazing, she thought. Just amazing.

She was so riveted by the action of the backhoe that when the metal box fell out of the shovel and onto the pile of dirt she didn't realize what it was. She stared at the rectangular shape and then it hit her.

She yelled and scrambled over to the pile of dirt. "Jeb! We found it! We found it!"

Scrabbling around in the dirt, she pulled out the rusty metal box. "It was the pine tree," she said excitedly. "He buried it near the well house and then had to have planted that little pine tree to mark the exact spot."

Everyone heard her shout. Don Bean stopped the backhoe and climbed down. Profane, shovel still in hand, ambled over. Jeb was at Roxanne's side in two swift strides. Only Milo hung back.

Jeb took the box from Roxanne. "Well, well, well," he said, "I wonder what we have here." He cut his eyes over to where Milo stood stiffly. "You got any ideas?"

"Hey, don't look at me," Milo said, raising up his hands defensively. "Your wife found it. Maybe she knows."

"You think maybe it's what you were looking for in the greenhouses?" Don asked with a frown.

"I wouldn't be surprised," Jeb replied, examining the box. It was small, but not so small that it couldn't comfortably hold the amount of drugs and money Dirk was reputed to have stolen. A cheap lock hung from the clasp.

Taking his cell phone from his belt, his gaze on Milo Scott, he called the office. It only took him a couple of minutes to explain the purpose of the call.

His call finished, he put away the phone and glanced over at Milo. "If this holds what I think it does, our mystery is solved. Guess there won't be any reason for you to keep hanging around anymore, will there?"

Milo's face was hard. "Don't know what you're talking about. I only came out here as a friend of Roxanne's."

"Wrong," said Roxanne. "I warned you right from the get-go that we weren't that good of friends. I think you ought to get in your truck and mosey on down the road."

"And don't come back," Jeb growled, a threat in his voice.

Milo hesitated and Roxanne said firmly, "That goes double for me, Milo."

As if to emphasize Roxanne's words, Don Bean formed a fist in one big hand and rubbed it in the other. Profane stepped up beside him, the shovel held at an unfriendly angle. Milo looked at the four of them lined up against him and calculated his odds. Not good.

Jeb could see Milo turning over the situation in his mind. It must be killing him to know that Dirk's stash had indeed been hidden on the property and that he had missed it. The property and buildings had been searched and re-searched and even Jeb had decided that Dirk must have hidden the money and drugs somewhere else. But he hadn't. Dirk had buried it right here. The spot marked as Roxanne said by the well house and that straggling little pine tree.

Knowing he didn't have a chance in hell of getting his hands on the drugs and money, Milo shrugged. "OK. Fine. I know when I'm not wanted." He swung around and headed for his truck.

"Make sure you tell the people you work for that there's no reason to keep looking. You can tell them from me that everything is safely in the hands of the law," Jeb called out.

Don Bean burst out in a loud laugh. "Yeah, and I'm a witness."

"Goddamn right," added Profane. "We're all goddamn witnesses."

"Think I'll go put on another pot of coffee," Roxanne said. "Anyone else ready for a cup?"

The three men followed her into the house and soon they were gathered around the kitchen table, drinking coffee.

Profane eyed the metal box. "You gonna open the goddamn thing? Let us see what the fuck we dug up. It's only fair."

It was against procedure but Jeb decided that Profane had a point. He made short work of the lock, flipped open the lid. In silence they all stared inside the box . . . the *empty* box.

It was Profane who said it all. "Goddammit! The damn thing is empty! We've been tricked. Who in the hell would take the time to hide and bury a goddamn *empty* box? Why the fuck was Milo so damned interested in it?"

Jeb rubbed his chin. "I think that old Dirk fooled all of us—including Milo Scott."

Profane muttered something exceedingly profane under his breath.

"Maybe it's the wrong box," Roxanne said slowly. "Maybe he had more than one hiding place."

"He could have, but I doubt it. He obviously hid this box for some reason."

"What's supposed to have been in the box?" Don Bean asked, his pale blue eyes fixed on Jeb's face.

Jeb grimaced. He should just tell Don that this was an official inquiry and he wasn't at liberty to comment, but an idea was taking shape in his brain. Milo believed that they'd found the money and drugs. Milo was probably even now letting the drug lords in Oakland know that fact. If there was ever a hint that Dirk's stash *hadn't* been found, Roxanne's place would again become the focus of some not-very-nice people. So why disillusion them?

He glanced across from Don and Profane and made a decision. "How," he asked lightly, "would you two like to be part of a scam? But you have to swear never to mention to a soul what we did."

Don leaned back in his chair, his eyes dancing. "Something to do with Milo Scott thinking that we found more than an empty box?"

Jeb nodded.

"Sure, why not?" Don replied, a grin spreading across his big face. "What did you have in mind?"

"Me, too," exclaimed Profane. "Won't say a word to nobody."

"Milo Scott thinks that we've just found money and drugs, hidden by Dirk before he was shot in Oakland," Jeb began. "So why not make that a fact?"

Roxanne frowned. "But it was a lot of drugs and money. I'd be willing to throw in a little cash, but not thousands. And where would we get any drugs?"

Profane blushed and coughed. "Uh, I might have a

little weed in the truck." He shot Jeb a nervous look. "Um, I just use it for medicinal purposes, you know."

Jeb shook his head and put up his hand. "Don't tell me any more. Just go get it."

As Profane disappeared out the door, Jeb said to the other two, "We don't need to bankrupt ourselves—a couple of hundred dollars should do it."

Roxanne ran to get her purse and riffling through her cash counted out about a hundred dollars in small bills. When she came back to the kitchen, Profane was handing Jeb a little plastic bag with loose marijuana in it. Jeb gently placed it in the empty box.

Roxanne gave Jeb the cash. He checked his wallet and added another hundred. Looked across at Don. "You with us?"

Good-naturedly Don counted out about seventy-five dollars. "Getting to be an expensive scam," he commented mildly.

"But it ought to do the trick," Jeb answered with a grin. "The box you dug up and Scott saw now holds money and drugs—which is all we care about Scott knowing." He glanced at Don and Profane. "Of course, it might help if you two started the valley gossip going about how much money and drugs were found in the box."

Profane and Don grinned. "Be our pleasure," Don said, chuckling. "A real pleasure."

"So what do we do now?" Roxanne asked.

Jeb smiled. "We wait for the nice officer on duty to come and pick it up from me."

The men returned to their work and Roxanne did a few housewifely things, her thoughts on their "find." What had happened to Dirk's real stash? she wondered as she put the cups in the dishwasher. Had he spent it all before he'd been murdered? Or was it still buried somewhere on her property? She didn't really care—it was now something she no longer had to worry about—or continued "visits" by Milo Scott.

Don and Profane were thrilled and excited about their part in the scam and Roxanne knew that by this evening the news of the "find" would be all over the valley. Not such a bad thing, she thought, as she watched the two men leave to continue work. With Milo thinking that the drugs and money had been found and Don and Profane confirming it for all and sundry they shouldn't have any more break-ins.

Jeb came up and kissed the back of her neck. "You OK?" he asked.

She smiled and nodded. "A little woozy but I think I'll live—barely." She glanced back at him. "What do you think happened to Dirk's real stash?"

Jeb shrugged. "A couple of things occurred to me. I don't think that the people who were after Dirk underestimated by much the value of what he pilfered. If we go with that idea, it means that Dirk either disposed of it all before he was killed or that the money and drugs are still out there buried or hidden somewhere that we haven't discovered yet." He grimaced. "We can't even be sure that he ever hid the stuff on the property. Hell, for all we know, he had a safety deposit box that no one here knows about." He rubbed his chin and looked thoughtful. "Or, and this isn't out of the realm of possibilities, someone else knew about the stash and where Dirk had hidden it and came back and dug it up and left the empty box for someone else to find—leaving the impression that Dirk had spent it all before he died."

"Well, I vote for the theory that he spent it all before he was killed," Roxanne said. She frowned. "But then why would he bury an empty box?"

"Your guess is as good as mine. Maybe he used the box and that place to hide lots of things and when he emptied it, he just put it back where it was. Unless the real stash turns up, we'll probably never know the truth."

"I can live with that," Roxanne muttered, looking wan.

"Go back to bed," Jeb said, dropping a kiss on her cheek. "There's nothing that needs doing that I can't take care of or that can't wait until you're feeling better."

She followed his advice, crawling gratefully back into bed.

Of course the news of the finding of Dirk's buried stash brought another round of telephone calls from family and friends. Roxanne had to laugh as the story was passed from lip to lip and grew out of recognition.

Shelly called her on Friday and demanded, "What's this I hear that a million dollars in drugs and jewels and gold was found on your place?"

Roxanne made a mild comment about valley gossip and Shelly remarked, "Well, I knew it couldn't be entirely true. The Oak Valley rumor mill absolutely amazes me sometimes." She paused. "How are you feeling? When I bumped into Jeb at McGuire's last night he said you were down with the flu. Feeling any better?"

"Some."

"Feel like a little company tomorrow night? I'm making up a big pot of vegetable-beef soup and if you'll supply the French bread we can make a meal of it." When Roxanne hesitated, she added, "I'll bet I can even pilfer one of Maria's apple pies from the freezer."

"Deal," Roxanne said with a laugh. "Provided you don't expect me to do much more than lay around and look pale and interesting—or Jeb hasn't made other plans."

"Deal!"

She hung up the phone and went looking for Jeb. She found him outside, measuring off a portion of land with a steel tape. Several steel fence posts tagged with yellow plastic tags had already been driven into the ground.

"What are you doing?" she asked as she strolled up.

He glanced back at her and grinned. "Laying out corrals and a possible site for the barn. Don't forget I've got those two mares and that one of them is due to foal in May. We need to get them over here as soon as possible."

"Oh, right."

She walked up to him and put her arm through his and laid her head on his shoulder. Together they glanced down at the valley below them.

Spring wasn't far off and though March could bring storms and endless days of rain, right now the scent of spring was in the air. More and more fields below them were turning green, more and more trees were sprouting fat buds, and there was a feeling that one morning you'd wake up and the winter would be behind and nothing but sunshine and flowers lay ahead. That's how Roxanne felt today. Actually she felt as if for her spring had already arrived.

"So you feeling a little better than you did this morning?" Jeb asked, pulling her a little closer to him and brushing a kiss on the top of her head.

Roxanne nodded and said, "So much so that when Shelly called and offered to bring along a pot of soup for dinner tomorrow night I didn't say no." She grinned at Jeb. "But it was her promise to bring one of Maria's apple pies that sealed the deal. You have any objections?"

"Are you kidding? Forgo a piece of one of Maria's apple pies?" A thought occurred to him. "Acey won't be coming along, will he?"

Roxanne laughed. "No, Acey won't even know about the pie."

"Just as well—he takes a rather proprietary interest in Maria's baking," Jeb said, smiling—and only half teasing.

Dinner Saturday night was most enjoyable. It was a

relaxing evening. Shelly's soup was excellent, full of almost crisp vegetables and chunks of tender beef in a tomato/beef broth seasoned with garlic, onions, rosemary, bay leaf, and even a little cilantro to give it a faint taste of Mexico. Coupled with warm French bread and butter it made a wonderfully simple but filling meal. Followed by Maria's pie they decided it was a perfect end to a perfect meal.

Afterward they scattered around the great room, sipping coffee and talking and laughing about nothing in particular as friends do. The finding of Dirk Aston's stash was naturally discussed, as were the plans for the new barn that Jeb and Roxanne were having built and the new house that Sloan and Shelly had under construction. And of course, the sudden marriage.

"I still can't believe that the pair of you just picked up and ran away to Reno," Shelly said for perhaps the tenth time. "Sloan and I considered it, but in the end we gave in to pressure."

"It was different for you guys," said Roxanne, setting down her cup of coffee on an end table. "Too many people knew about the pair of you—no one had a clue that Jeb and I weren't still sniping at each other every time we saw each other."

"I beg your pardon," Jeb said from where he sat in the big black recliner brought over from his house. "That was love play—you just didn't recognize it."

Roxanne smiled at him, the love between them almost palpable.

Sprawled in the other chair near the end of the

couch, Sloan cast a mocking look at Jeb. "I did. I always thought that the two of you disliked each other *too* much. Had to be some reason you both kept pecking at each other." He grinned. "I, for one, am delighted that you discovered the reason in such a timely fashion. Congratulations!"

The conversation wandered onto Sloan's breeding program for spotted cutting horses. They touched briefly on Jeb's mare that had been bred to Sloan's prize black and white paint horse the previous summer.

"What are you hoping for?" Sloan said.

"Healthy," Jeb replied instantly. "But after that, I think I'd like a colt—spotted or not. Something that would make a nice gelding when he grows up."

Leaving the two men talking horses, Roxanne and Shelly gathered up the cups and walked back to the kitchen. As she poured fresh coffee for everyone Roxanne asked, "So everything is OK with the pair of you?"

Shelly smiled. "Couldn't be better. I had that talk with Sloan that you suggested and I think we both feel as if a weight has been lifted. We agree we both want children—probably desperately, but if it doesn't happen it'll be a blow, a huge disappointment, but it won't be the end of the world. As long as we have each other we'll be more than satisfied with life. I don't feel quite so guilty now about not conceiving." Shelly made a face. "Just as well—my period started on Thursday. It's gotten so I dread the sight of it." She sighed, her expression pensive. "I know Sloan and I discussed the subject thoroughly and I can't stop thinking about it. Getting pregnant is still at the front of my mind." She laughed wryly. "And worse, despite my best intentions, I carry around one of those quick pregnancy tests you can buy at the grocery store. I haven't gotten so bad that every time we make love I run and pee on the stick, but almost. I guess having one always at hand means that someday when I least expect it, I'll take the test and the damn thing will finally turn blue."

Roxanne smiled at her and handed her a cup of coffee. Taking a sip, she said, "Well, here's to blue. My fingers are crossed for you."

"What about you and Jeb? Babies on the agenda?"

"It's been mentioned," Roxanne said, "but I don't know that we're in any hurry." She grimaced. "We probably should be since we're both older than you but we'll see what happens."

"I wish I could take that attitude," Shelly said, picking up Sloan's cup. When the two women entered the great room, Sloan and Jeb were still talking horses.

"You know," Sloan was saying, "you really ought to think about starting a small horse operation of your own. If you keep it small this place would be ideal. You've got, what, twenty-thirty acres of fairly level ground? You could easily breed three or four mares a year. There's a lot of rough ground, but some of the hillside isn't so steep that you couldn't fence it and put it to use, too. Many old ranchers used to turn their yearlings and two-year-olds out in the hills for the winter to get them used to uneven terrain and creeks and things like that. You could take a page out of their books."

Jeb rubbed his chin. "Something to think about." He looked up and grinned at Roxanne. "But I've got my hands full right now, thank you very much. My brand-new wife is going to demand a lot of my attention."

"I should hope so," Roxanne replied tartly.

"Can you believe this?" Shelly asked. "The four of us married. This time last year Roxanne was still in New York, I was still in New Orleans . . ." She swallowed hard. "Josh had just committed suicide and my life was in a turmoil. Now Granger Cattle Company is on the road, I've discovered Nick is my brother, and we're all married. Incredible, isn't it?"

"Incredible," Jeb agreed, a teasing glint in his dark eyes. "The bachelors of Oak Valley are falling like flies right into the traps of wily females. This time next year I wonder how many will be left?"

Sloan nodded. "Yeah, if this trend keeps up, a bachelor in the valley is going to be a vanishing species in no time at all. They'll be snatched up by some wide-eyed innocent-looking woman and herded down the aisle and led around by their noses for the rest of their lives before they even know what happened. Sad, sad fact of life."

"Oh, gimme a break," Roxanne groaned. "Nothing less than an atomic bomb would have stopped you from marrying Shelly and—" She slanted her eyes at

Jeb. "I don't remember anyone holding a gun to your head."

"Guilty as charged," Jeb said, grinning. "You just gotta let us complain about it a little—let the world know that we put up a good fight before being overcome by an irresistible force."

"I like that, an irresistible force, don't you?" Shelly said smiling, glancing at Roxanne.

Roxanne made a face and put down her cup of coffee. "Sorry, right now the only irresistible force I'm thinking about is dinner." She jumped up to her feet and muttered, "I think it's about to make another appearance."

She took off at a good clip toward the bathroom.

Jeb jumped up, but Shelly rose to her feet and said, "Stay here. No woman, especially a bride, wants a man around while she's being sick."

Jeb rubbed the back of his neck. "You're right. But I'm really worried about her. She won't go to the doctor, tells me it's only the flu, but I think she should be getting better by now, but she's not."

"Don't worry about it," Shelly said. "I'll check on her. She's going to be fine, Jeb. It's only the flu."

Finding her way into Jeb and Roxanne's bedroom, Shelly found Roxanne bent over the bathroom sink, throwing water in her face and rinsing her mouth with Listerine.

"Feeling better?" Shelly asked as she walked up to the doorway.

"For the moment," Roxanne replied. Wiping her

hands and face, she hung up the towel and walked over to her bed. Sinking down onto it, she said, "My mom said that it was bad—I just didn't think it would be this bad. I feel pretty good most of the time, but it's the nausea and vomiting that are getting me down. Seems like everything is fine and then all of a sudden, boom, I'm racing for the bathroom—especially in the morning or at the sight or smell of food."

"Just as a matter of interest," Shelly said, "you and Jeb *are* practicing birth control, right?"

Roxanne flashed her a wan smile. "You have babies on the brain, Shelly. We've always been very careful about that sort of thing, except for. . . ." Roxanne paled. "But I couldn't be pregnant," she said dazedly. "I had several periods after the first time. And after New Year's . . ." She looked up at Shelly, her eyes getting very big and very round.

"And after the second time?" Shelly prodded.

Roxanne swallowed. "A-a-after that, I don't th-th-think I've had a period. It was New Year's Day. After your party."

Shelly giggled, her eyes dancing. "I'll bet dollars to doughnuts that you don't have the flu at all."

Roxanne clutched her arm. "Didn't you say you carry one of the test things around with you?"

Shelly nodded and dashed out of the room. A couple of minutes later she came rushing back in, her purse in her hand. "I told the guys that I had some Maalox tablets in my purse—that you were going to try them to settle your stomach."

Roxanne grabbed the package Shelly handed her and disappeared into the bathroom. She was in there for what seemed like a very long time to Shelly. When Roxanne finally opened the door, she pounced on her. "Well? Are you?"

Roxanne seemed stunned. She looked at Shelly, but Shelly had the impression she didn't even see her. Slowly Roxanne nodded her head. "Yes. I'm pregnant."

Saying the news aloud seemed to make it real. She laughed and clutched Shelly's arms and they danced crazily around the room. "I'm pregnant," Roxanne crowed. "I'm pregnant. I'm *pregnant!*"

Shelly hugged her tight when they finally slowed down. "Oh, Roxy, I'm so happy for you. This is great! Jeb is going to be blown away. And Helen and Mark are going to be ecstatic. A grandchild. How wonderful."

Roxanne's bubble burst. She looked at Shelly and saw behind the joyful facade the pain, the deep longing. "Oh, Shelly! I feel terrible. You're the one who should be pregnant."

Shelly sniffed back a tear. "Nope. This is your time." She shook a finger at her. "You be happy for you and Jeb. Don't you worry about me." She put her arm through Roxanne's and wearing a gallant smile said, "So? We gonna go tell the guys?"

When the two women entered the great room, Jeb stood up and hurried over to Roxanne. "How are you feeling, Princess? Did the Maalox help?"

Shelly and Roxanne looked at each other and burst out laughing. Shelly left Roxanne and walked over and sat down in Sloan's lap. Grinning from ear to ear she waited for Roxanne's announcement.

"No, I'm afraid that Maalox didn't help. Shelly made a diagnosis and we're afraid that nothing will help me. It'll be a lifelong situation and I'm afraid there's no cure."

As Jeb stared blankly at her she broke out in the biggest, most beautiful smile he'd ever seen. She hugged him; rained kisses on his cheek and mouth. "I'm preggers," she cried joyfully. "We're going to have a baby."

"Jesus Christ!" Jeb shouted, only half aware of what she'd said. "You scared me to death. I thought something was really wrong with you." Then the import sank in. "Pregnant?" he gasped, his eyes widening. "As in a baby?"

"Yes sir. If calculations are right in about seven months or so, you should be bouncing your first offspring on your knee . . . Daddy."

With a whoop, Jeb caught her up and swung her around. Their joyful laughter filled the house.

Lost in their own world, they weren't aware of Sloan and Shelly watching them from across the room. Sloan reached for Shelly's hand and kissed it warmly. "You OK?" he asked softly. Shelly nodded. She smiled mistily at him. "Like I told Roxanne, our turn will come." She kissed him. "When it's time we'll be the ones dancing around the room."

He stared at her, his expression neutral. "And if it never comes?"

Shelly ran a gentle finger over his lips. "As long as I have you—that's what matters most to me. You. Only you."

Heedless of the location, not that Roxanne and Jeb were paying them any mind, Sloan kissed Shelly. Hard. "God," he said, "I love you."

"And I love you," Shelly said and kissed him with all the love and tenderness within her.

Roxanne and Jeb came back to earth and caught sight of the other two kissing in the big chair. "Hey, hey, none of that," Jeb called out, teasing. "You guys want to neck, you've got a place of your own."

"Good advice," Sloan said, sliding Shelly out of his lap and standing up. "I think we'd better be going." He winked at his sister. "Expectant mothers need their rest."

Walking over to where Roxanne and Jeb stood, Sloan took Roxanne into his arms. "Congratulations, Sis! I'm happy for you."

She gazed into his eyes and saw only affection and delight in their depths. She knew that, like Shelly, he must be hurting inside, but there was no envy in those golden eyes staring back at her, only love. Wordlessly, she squeezed his arm, too full of emotion to speak.

Roxanne and Jeb accompanied them out to the Suburban. They exchanged good-byes, Shelly yelling out as the big vehicle pulled away, "Was this a *great* night or what?"

Silently Jeb and Roxanne walked back into the house. They picked up cups and straightened cushions, their bodies touching lightly as they moved about, bemused smiles on both their mouths. Snapping out the kitchen light a few minutes later, the last of the cleanup done, they wandered out to the back terrace and stood staring down at the winking lights of town below them.

Jeb pulled Roxanne next to him, his head resting on the top of hers, her cheek resting against his chest.

"Happy?" he asked.

"Hmm, can't remember a time when I was happier." She looked up at him. "We're so lucky, aren't we? We found each other and now a baby." Her face clouded. "I feel bad about Sloan and Shelly. I'm thrilled for us, but I can't help thinking about how much they want a baby." She blinked back a tear. "Shelly said that their time would come. That this was our time."

Jeb nodded slowly. One of his hands drifted down to her stomach, to the place where their child grew. His heart swelled with love for the unborn baby, for the woman that carried it, his wife, Roxanne. "She was right," he said huskily. "This is our time." And just before his lips found hers, he murmured, "Our time . . . *forever.*"

WARNER BOOKS EDITION

Copyright © 2003 by Shirlee Busbee
All rights reserved. No part of this book may be reproduced in any form or by any electronic or mechanical means, including information storage and retrieval systems, without permission in writing from the publisher, except by a reviewer who may quote brief passages in a review.

Cover design by Diane Luger
Cover illustration by Ben Perini
Book design by Giorgetta Bell McRee

Warner Books, Inc.
1271 Avenue of the Americas
New York, NY 10020

Visit our Web site at www.twbookmark.com

An AOL Time Warner Company

Printed in the United States of America

First Printing: September 2003

10 9 8 7 6 5 4 3 2 1

Coming Home

SHIRLEE BUSBEE

WARNER BOOKS

An AOL Time Warner Company

SHE WANTED TO FIGHT WITH HIM, AND SHE FOUGHT TO RESIST THAT GRIN OF HIS...

"I've already admitted that there's something between us," she finally replied. "What more do you want?"

"Loaded question, princess."

"You know what I mean."

To her absolute terror, he scooted to her end of the couch. Too close, she thought hysterically. He's too close. Don't touch me. Oh, please don't touch me.

But he did. And it was like flame to gasoline. The instant his hands reached out for her, Roxanne swore she heard an explosive whoosh. And that was her last coherent thought for a long, long time.

❧

"I've always loved her novels... intricately woven, deeply romantic, and spellbinding."
—Rosemary Rogers

"Busbee delivers what you read a romance for."
—*West Coast Review of Books*

"Sweet and fiery."
—*Heartstrings* on *Return to Oak Valley*

"An exciting romantic suspense tale."
—*Midwest Book Review* on *Return to Oak Valley*

ALSO BY SHIRLEE BUSBEE

Lovers Forever
A Heart for the Taking
Love Be Mine
For Love Alone
At Long Last
Swear by the Moon
Return to Oak Valley